For Paddy

Of what use was it to be loved and lose one's beauty and become Real if it all ended like this?'

Margery Williams, *The Velveteen Rabbit*

' . . . our reality arguably consists of the stories we tell about ourselves.'

Jonathan Franzen, 'Mr Difficult'

ACT I

The Present. London and King's Lynn.

1

The card lay face up on the table between them, solemn as a writ, pregnant with symbolism.

'Well, let's see now. Ooh. You're an actress.'

This is how it was offered over the first card: a declaration. But the woman in the hemp smock was not looking at Sally; she was looking down at the cards still, and there was just the smallest rising inflection at the end of the sentence, a hint of an upward cadence, enough to admit the possibility of doubt. She seemed to be requesting confirmation.

Sally McGinley shifted position – the swivel chair, its nylon upholstery pilling, came from an office discount store, evidently, which contributed to the sense of being at an interview for a job she didn't really want – and looked out briefly at the slab of April sky through the window. What to say? She was not an actress, of course, and yet the woman could have been so much further off the mark.

This woman – Sally thought of her as Claire, because of the sign outside saying 'Clairvoyant and Tarot' – had wiry grey hair that was parted decisively down the middle and had the look of not having been cut since the Vietnam protests. She was American, which Sally found in some indefinable way a let-down, as if her voice confirmed the kooky West Coast whimsy of the whole business.

She felt she ought to say something.

'No, I'm not. Sorry.'

'But you wanted to be, Sally. When you were younger. Then you lost your confidence and you gave up your dream.'

Sally stiffened, because this was true. How could she have known that? On the night of her fifth birthday, Sally's father had taken her to *Cinderella* at the Old Vic where, in pantomime tradition, the event of the birthday had afforded such temporary status that she and the other birthday children were invited on to the stage to receive a bag of sweets from the Ugly Sisters and, as a quid pro quo, required to sing a verse of 'Ten Green Bottles' for the indulgent amusement of the parents. But the other birthday children, rabbit-eyed, had barely squeaked, so Sally had cheerfully belted through the lot on her own with gusto and without pausing; she was rewarded with keen applause, and instantly infected with a craving for the adoration of a theatre audience. It had looked promising all the way through school and amateur productions, until the moment in the sixth form when her voice had cracked and frozen unaccountably on the first night of the end-of-year production of *Cabaret* in which she was playing the lead, and she was stranded in a basque and a bowler hat in front of three hundred people, unable to produce a note, a memory that still prompted the beginnings of a panic attack. And that had been the end of it, on that side of the curtain, anyway.

'No, I'm not an actress.'

The woman tapped the card with a blunt nail.

'The Magician. In the first position of the spread. Such a powerful card, see? It's clear that you are a creative person, Sally, full of originality and imagination.'

The chink of belief briefly permitted by the apparent insight into her abortive dreams irritated Sally, and her earlier cynicism reasserted itself. Every girl has dreamed of being an actress at some point, she thought; any variety-show spiritualist could guess at that. And Sally was obviously of working age and sound mind, but instead of working she was sitting here with her shoes off listening to this hokum on a Wednesday afternoon, so it hardly needed guidance from beyond to suggest that she was not bound to a desk. And she had unbelievably paid twenty quid for this in the name of research, which, if she was lucky, she might at least claim against tax.

In order to witness at first hand the workings of the Celtic Cross, she had approached the door of an indifferent Georgian house tucked away in a Camden crescent after finding the details in the back of a high-fashion magazine, among four pages of similar advertisements that followed the catalogue of surgeons touting gravity-defying miracles and the painful erasure of imperfections. Sally had felt both pleased and astonished on discovering these pages; astonished that there could be such a market for Tarot, palmistry, stichomancy, astrology, cabbala, I Ching, scrying, runes and assorted divinatory arts among the demographic usually associated with such a magazine, and pleased because it confirmed the potential audience appeal of having a Tarot-reading scene in the play. She'd liked the idea of it as a device, but the magazine had persuaded her that if the well-groomed classes were now turning to the cards in such numbers as the rash of advertisements implied, then she should spend some time on authentic detail.

When she booked the reading, Sally had cherished what she knew to be an unlikely image of a cryptal room, where she would chink a few coins into the filthy palm of a beshawled crone and watch, rapt, as she dealt the cards with crooked fingers, shaking her head as they dropped: 'I see The Hanged Man,' she'd say, in a voice to crack ice. 'Beware The Hanged Man!' Sally didn't know a great deal about the symbolism of The Hanged Man, but the assonance was pleasingly chilling.

Instead, at the top of the stairway, she'd found a glass door with an intercom, and through it a neat vestibule with a hatstand and a print of a Lichtenstein, then another room that smelled of new carpet and peppermint tea where she'd had to take off her boots, apparently to help the conduit of energies, but rather more, she suspected, because outside it was raining and the carpet was beige.

'What is your question?' the large woman in the fibrous smock had asked, with a mystical tilt of the eyebrow.

'What question?'

'You've come to seek an answer of the cards today. So you must bring to them a special question. What answers do you seek?'

The woman seemed kindly, if slightly fake. Perhaps that was just the jargon. In fact, Sally had thought, it was she who was the fake, since the only real question she had in mind was: what exactly goes on in a modern Tarot session because I've decided to put one in my play.

'I'm not really all that – anything, really, you know. About the future?'

'No, Sally. The cards need something more specific that you can focus on. I sense that you're concerned about your future?'

No shit, Sally had wanted to say. Then she remembered that she had promised herself not to be snide. She was allowed to be analytical and a little bit superior, because she was a writer and the wise woman was by definition a fruitcake but, still, there was no need to be sarcastic. And then it had just blurted out:

'Will I find love in the next year?'

The indulgent smile that had greeted the question said it all. Sally was distracted from the turning of the next cards, surprised at herself and embarrassed that she had just confirmed precisely why fortune-tellers were prepared to spend whatever it must cost these days to advertise in magazines read by single women with disposable income. And why *in the next year*? Where had that come from – as if it might feel more like a controlled experiment if she imposed a time limit? As if with scientific parameters she could definitely test it one way or the other?

'The interpretation of all these cards depends on their position in the spread, Sally. For example, here in the fourth position is the Three of Swords, signifying the influences on your past that are receding away from you, opening you up to new opportunities. Your time of disappointment and sorrow is coming to an end.'

The woman had the kind of crapy cleavage that told of a youth spent sunbathing without due caution, and around her neck dangled a dull silver pendant with tiny bells that caught in the folds of skin. Sally fixed her eyes on it and didn't look up, because she sensed that every pronouncement now was largely guesswork, and to give any kind of indication to the woman of her accuracy or otherwise would be to condone her cheating, when what Sally secretly wanted was for her to produce one hard fact that would show her knowledge to be authentically imparted from elsewhere. This, Sally knew, was the diametric opposite of faith and therefore self-defeating. In truth, she didn't recall having been through a time of disappointment and sorrow, excepting the general mist of disappointment that had hung over her life since college: that she was not richer, that she was being left behind by events (more specifically by Rhys and Lola and especially Freddie), that nothing she had written so far had ever been adapted for television.

'Ah – now,' the woman said, turning another card. 'This is highly significant. Here's The Emperor, in the fifth position. The fifth card shows a possible influence on your future, Sally, and tells us about your defining attitudes. The Emperor is a patriarchal figure.'

Sally nodded and smothered a yawn.

'A father, or someone in the role of a father.'

'Yes, I understood patriarchal.'

'Are fathers significant to you, Sally?'

'Fathers in general?'

'Well, your own, say.'

'Is my father *significant*?'

Sally's father lived in Dublin now, and she had not spoken to him for sixteen years. There was a very good reason for this, but she had paid to see a psychic, not a shrink, and she had no intention of talking about it. Let the woman divine it for herself, if she was so gifted. She was also becoming irked by the woman's excessive deployment of her name, something she must have learned on a course in the belief that it would make her clients feel individually cherished.

'What's *your* name?' she said, to avert the father question.

The woman straightened and looked surprised.

'My name is Arielle.'

'Like the Israeli Prime Minister?'

Her forehead creased into a sharp V, a child's drawing of a seagull.

'Like the spiritual character in Shakespeare's *Midsummer Night's Dream*.' She frowned slightly. 'Only with an extra "le"'.

'Is that your real name?'

'It's my spiritual name.'

'What's your real name?'

Arielle hesitated.

'Pam. But we're not here to talk about me, Sally. Let's move on. The sixth card is all about your future, so this is really a very important moment. I think we should take a little time to focus on our inner guide. Close your eyes with me, please, Sally.'

In a spirit of rebellion, Sally only squinted. Arielle pinged a tuning fork against a crystal and a sweet high note vibrated and gradually melted away to silence.

'Are you concentrating on your question, Sally?'

Sally nodded. Will I find love? *In the next year?* For goodness' sake. She opened her eyes. Arielle breathed in through her nose and allowed her hand to hover meaningfully over the deck before turning the sixth card, and Sally wondered idly how many levels of irony were at work in the room. Was she one step ahead of Arielle because she regarded her as a ludicrous charlatan and was here only for academic reasons and was inwardly mocking her faith in the arcane mysteries of the universe? Or was Arielle laughing at her because *she* knew very well that she was a ludicrous charlatan, but she had just made twenty quid out of Sally, and if she did one credulous fool

7

every half-hour she could look forward to at least another eight lots of twenty quid by the end of her working day, which multiplied over a year was a good deal more than Sally would be making out of writing snidely about it? Or – and this really *would* be ironic, Sally thought – was she actually, reluctantly, one of the credulous fools? Could Arielle have discerned that, in spite of her detachment and her occasional mordant remarks, part of Sally really wanted to hear her say 'yes' to the ridiculous question, and to believe it?

The card was turned to the table with a satisfying clip, and they leaned forward to examine it. Sally briefly took in the couple in Flemish dress clasping hands, but her eyes were drawn to the caption and in spite of herself, her heart gave a little kick.

Arielle looked from the card to Sally and back, wordless with excitement and appearing as if she might climax right then and there.

'Well, Sally.' She laid a plump hand over each of Sally's and fastened her with motherly eye contact. 'Well. I simply don't know what to say. It's quite extraordinary.' She shook her head again to emphasize her amazement.

She's overdoing it, Sally thought immediately, it must be a set-up. How could it not be?

'The Lovers is a very powerful card, Sally. To get any of the major arcana in a spread indicates very powerful influences on your life, but to have The Lovers as your future card, with a question like yours . . .'

'So what does it mean?'

Arielle released Sally's hands and looked serious.

'Well, you already have a lover, don't you, Sally?'

Again Sally jumped, as if she'd been poked, and thought of James, who even now would be seated blithely at his desk at the magazine, beneath his original poster of *The Italian Job*, with no notion that she was at that moment eagerly hoping for an overweight hippy to tell her that he would soon be replaced.

'But you're unhappy. Your relationship is stale and tired and there's no passion.'

On the other hand, Sally thought, it was a fair assumption that someone of her age would probably have a lover of some description in the picture, and in the light of her question to the cards it would also be a fair assumption that she was hoping to upgrade.

'Your problem is that he doesn't make you feel like a woman.'

Sally jerked her head up and was caught by the blue stare and half-smile that wanted to seem prophetic, but those words had shocked the sarcasm out of her and in that moment she did, for a second, believe that this woman knew her. Just those exact words, because in all her griping to her friends and in her endless circular arguments with James about the cul-de-sac of their relationship, she had never said it quite so bluntly and hadn't even realized, until that moment, that there was no better way to sum up its failure. He didn't make her feel like a woman. How could Arielle, with an extra 'le', have known that, and got it so right?

'What The Lovers is showing us, Sally, is that the time is ripe for you to meet someone who does bring you passion and fulfilment in your life. And we must always see each card in the context of the whole spread, but I believe that man is coming into your life, Sally, the man who will make a dramatic change in your fortunes.'

At this point, Sally more or less stopped listening to the other cards. How did she *know*? she kept wondering, over the suppressed thrill of the idea that her lover was, if not on the horizon, at least now appearing on the signposts. The previous year Lola, usually so sensible, had been through a wintry period in terms of dates, and a corresponding phase of reliance on the advice of horoscopes, and for a few months had spent a great deal of money on private readings from a well-known astrologer who wrote for a celebrity magazine. Sally's sense of the supremacy of the individual and the sheer chaotic chance of the universe had been offended, as she had tried to point out to Lola.

'You make the choice of whether or not to stop for coffee on the way to the Tube, one little thing, and it could alter the path of your whole life. Getting the coffee means you get on the train that blows up instead of the earlier one that doesn't, not getting the coffee means you get a different train and on it you meet your future husband, but *you* don't even know if you want the coffee until you're going past the door and you make a choice on the spur of the moment, so how can you tell me that any of that was written in the sky,' Sally had said, and Lola had considered this for a moment, then said, 'Oh, I don't think I'm going to meet my husband on the *Tube*. I like to think he'll have a car', and Sally had concluded that you couldn't debate free will and predestination with a romantic literalist. Sally herself was more of an existentialist, if anyone asked. There was blind stupid chance, and us.

9

Absently, she watched the turning of the subsequent cards, super-ficially aware that while there might be every chance that in the course of the next twelve months she would meet someone who excited her more than James did (and in recent months she had found most evenings that reading a biography of Christopher Isherwood excited her more than James did), there was no guarantee that Arielle had actually received confirmation of this occurrence from the cards, nor that they had any specific date or person in mind, which was pre-cisely the information Sally was keen to possess, since it would take just this element of blind stupid chance out of the situation. What surprised her most, however, was that this awareness did nothing to quell the budding sense of anticipation born of a stubborn desire to believe.

Only the placing of the final card brought her back to the present moment.

'You remember, don't you, Sally, the significance of the tenth card in our reading?'

Sally nodded, sucking in her bottom lip in such a way as to imply understanding.

'The tenth card shows us the overall outcome of your reading, Sally, it reveals to us the forces that are at work over your life and which will influence your progress towards an answer to your ques-tion. You understand that, right?'

Again, Sally nodded.

'Tell me what you see.'

Sally looked at the card and took in the figure of a woman in a pur-ple braided dress, approximately medieval, seated in a Savonarola chair with her chin held wistfully in her hands, while around her head antique goblets, aureate and intricately carved, floated, spilling their contents. Sally had warmed to the Tarot over the other clairvoy-ant practices because in her mind it at least pretended to some liter-ary significance; its major figures corresponded in many ways to Jung's Archetypes of the Unconscious, those figures who reappear in folk tale and myth from the earliest recorded stories and who articu-late the deepest human need for pattern and symbol. This she had appreciated, this resolutely non-scientific urge towards the human universal; it was how she attempted to define the world in her drama. The card before her didn't resonate with any of her Jungian models, however; its interpretation seemed instead like a difficult exam question on which her future depended and which she was bound to get wrong.

'Seven of Cups,' she said, as if playing knockout whist.

'Exactly, Sally. Do you know what The Seven of Cups represents?'

Sally acknowledged that she did not.

'Fantasy. The Imagination. We already know that you have a strong imagination, Sally, because you're gifted creatively *as a person*. But the Seven of Cups also represents the dangers of the imagination. You have a tendency to live in a fantasy world, Sally, you want the world to be a little less real, a little more how you dream it should be. You're a romantic.'

She put her head on one side sympathetically.

'I'm not, though,' Sally said. 'I'm a terrible cynic. Honestly.'

'Well, OK, Sally, but perhaps you don't know yourself very well. Maybe, huh? This card in the tenth position suggests your dreams can have a little too much of an influence in your life if you don't make sure you're keeping one foot in the real world, Sally. Daydreams can't give you everything you need.' Arielle nodded a twinkling punctuation. 'Not if you want to find love. You have the power to make your dreams real, but you can't make reality into your dreams.'

This rang of having been said before, by no one of note.

'Right. What does that actually mean?'

'Sally, you must ask your inner guide to show you what it means.'

Tempted to respond with a real expression of contempt, Sally instead took her leave, tugged on her boots at the top of the stairs and concluded irritably that the afternoon had not lent itself usefully to finishing the play, unless she should somehow decide to add in the character of a large earth mother throwing out worthless aphorisms. While descending the stairs, she also checked the date on her watch, just in case. It was April 18th. She would give him a year, then, who-ever he was.

' . . . and Sophie got hers from this shop in Norwich called Bangles and they cost twenty-nine ninety-nine but these ones in here are only twenty-four ninety-nine so really if I got these ones instead of getting the exact same ones as Sophie I'd be saving five pounds anyway – Dad are you *listening* – and they're nearly the same as Sophie's only hers are more purple but I don't mind about that because I'll be saving five pounds and I'd rather have these ones because Kayley's going to get the purple ones that are exactly the same as Sophie's so I'm going to get the pink ones because it's better if we're not all the same, isn't it, Dad, but only if you say I can –'

Daisy Burns allowed a pause, not quite enough to admit a response, and resumed her petition: 'So can I, Dad? *Pleeeeeeease?* I'd be saving five pounds if I get them from the catalogue and Mum says she doesn't mind only you have to say if they're *appropriate.*' Her over-enunciation of the final word conveyed her opinion of it as a concept.

Greg looked up from his script and his gaze was immediately snagged by the flickering of the muted television beyond the flapping figure of his daughter. He capped his green highlighter and laid it carefully on the table in front of him in order to give Daisy the impression that she had his undivided attention. Three lithe young girls, none of them out of her teens, one blonde, one black, one some variety of Oriental – very democratic, he thought, something for everyone – were gyrating in formation on a beach, taut little stomachs glistening with body oil, mouthing the lyrics to one or other of the bleakly tinny Europop jingles that Daisy and her friends had the front to describe as 'R & B'. They must have to shave it all off to get into those shorts, Greg thought, conjuring without conscious intent images of shaved teenage pussy pressed damply against tight satin hotpants. He watched more attentively, through a slight glaze of arousal. The blonde one was best – no offence, he would of course do the other two willingly, but he was a traditionalist in many ways – and she had the sort of sharp, slutty face that suggested she'd be dirty if you wanted, even if her tits were clearly not real. Probably not, anyway; he found it hard to tell but Caroline, in her slightly embittered way, had taught him to doubt the authenticity of any breasts on television. Mesmerized by movements he could not remember seeing in the flesh within living memory, he felt his cock stir hopefully, as if in defiance.

'. . . because I've still got ten pounds left of my birthday money and Mum said she would lend me the extra fifteen pounds and I can pay it back out of my pocket money if I pay two pounds a week for the next eight weeks, that's sixteen pounds if you add it up but that includes the pound for the post and packing and Mum says she'll ring up and order them tomorrow and then they might come by next weekend because that's when Kayley's getting hers and if Kayley and Sophie have both got them and I haven't, well, it'll be –' Daisy looked at the floor and fell silent momentarily. 'You know. So, any*way*, I have to show them to you first Mum says in case you think they're too old for me and you don't think I should have them.'

Distracted as he was, Greg could not miss the heavy-handedness of the implied reproach in the last sentence, pre-emptively accusing him of ruining her life, learned with admirable accuracy from her mother. With some effort he wrenched his attention away from the synchronized thrusting on the screen, aware that he now had a semi-erection from his daughter's pop video and feeling a consequent anger towards the knowing marketing men whose sole aim in dressing barely pubescent little tarts in shorts slung so low over their bony hips you could practically see their clits popping over the top was to trick him into just such thoughts, and thereby immediately spike him with guilt and reveal him to himself as the pathetic under-sexed middle-aged pervert he undoubtedly was; an anger which he directed by extension towards Caroline for having bought the video in the first place and for not looking or moving like any of the girls in it, and towards Daisy for being so ignorant and undiscerning as to believe that such computerized bleating in any sense constituted music.

'Are you watching that?'

Daisy stood on one leg like a stork, the right foot crooked against the left knee, hopping urgently as if she needed the toilet and holding out a magazine. She turned to the television, as if surprised by it.

'Not really. There's not much point with the sound off, but Mum said you were working.'

Again, the implied criticism. Greg felt his skin prickle with the effort to remain calm.

'I *am* working. Turn it off if no one's watching it, it's a waste of electricity.' He couldn't quite believe he'd just said that. Terrifying, it was, how quickly he was turning into his father. His father, who had been given a mobile phone in case of emergencies but never switched it on for fear of using up the battery.

Daisy sought out the remote control, eager to show a total willingness to obey during this crucial stage of negotiations.

'What was that song called, Daisy?'

'"You Get Me High".'

Greg rubbed his forehead for a moment. Somehow the world seemed to be speeding up around him while he struggled just to keep going forwards. How could they be selling this to ten-year-old kids? What else was she listening to?

'Do you know what that means, getting high?'

'Yeah, it's like, when you're flying. It makes me think of a hot-air balloon.' Daisy shifted her weight to the other leg and giggled.

Greg looked at her and felt again the irrational anger; how could she be, at ten, simultaneously so worldly and so stupid?

'It's to do with taking drugs. Do you know what that is?'

'Oh, duh! *Earth to Dad!* Stew off of *Saturday Morning Club* got sacked because he took some drugs and he wasn't allowed to be a presenter any more, because it's really bad for you.' She paused and added meaningfully, 'Like smoking.'

'It's much, *much* worse for you than smoking, and it's also illegal, which smoking isn't when you're a grown-up.' Justifying the unjustifiable to a ten-year-old did nothing to make him less pathetic in his own eyes, he noted. I smoke because it's one of the few means I have of still feeling like me, he might have said, if she'd been another forty-four-year-old who could understand. And because I like it, and Caroline disapproves.

'Mrs Penny says it isn't. She says smoking is a drug too and her brother died from smoking.'

Greg ran a hand wearily through his hair.

'Well, she's right in a way, smoking is a kind of drug and, yes, it

14

isn't good for you, but it's nowhere near as bad as real drugs that get you high like Stew off whatever takes, so I don't want you listening to that song any more, OK?'

Daisy stared incredulously at her father for a moment and teetered on the brink of a protest, but, determined to indulge the eccentricities of the man whose yea or nay could affect her whole future, she swallowed it and instead pushed a creased catalogue supplement across the pages of script in front of him.

'OK, Dad, whatever, it's not even in the charts now and they don't even sing their own songs, you know, they just mime, Sophie says, so I don't really like them any more. Now can you look at these boots and see if you think they're too old for me because Sophie's got them and her mum bought them for her and her birthday is four months after mine so she's not even ten yet, and Kayley's getting hers next weekend so if you say yes Mum can ring up for them first thing tomorrow and they might come by the beginning of next week –'

'What might?'

'*Those*,' Daisy said, jabbing a small finger at the open page on a photograph of hot-pink suede ankle boots, vicious winklepickers revived from the worst atrocities of the 1980s, with a two-inch silver stiletto heel. Greg looked up blankly at his daughter's expectant little face, contorted with silent pleading, and felt baffled into silence by the glaring absurdity of the request. It was as if she'd asked him to buy her a packet of condoms.

'You're not seriously asking for a pair of those?'

Apparently not the response she'd been hoping for. Daisy's gurning intensified and her hopping became more anguished.

'*Da–a–ad!*' She endowed the word with about nine syllables and clenched her teeth, still clearly praying to find that he was only kidding her.

Greg glanced at his daughter's feet, elongated by the Barbie socks half hanging off them – soft little perfect children's feet – and felt a sudden fury at the evil of people who would force a child's feet into shoes like that, the same people who want kids singing about getting high, who want to turn ten-year-olds into eighteen-year-olds and sell eighteen-year-olds to ten-year-olds by dressing them up in porn gear to dance on beaches – Jesus, what kind of a world is this –

I *am* becoming my father, Greg thought, with despair.

'Don't be ridiculous, Daisy. You're ten years old. Did Mum really say you could have these?'

'If you said they were *appropriate*.' Daisy's voice was miserably choking up with tears.

'They're absolutely not appropriate. I can't think of anything less appropriate.' He closed the catalogue decisively.

Daisy emitted a great gulping astonished sob, and unleashed her final salvo: 'But Sophie's got them!'

Greg had the impression, as he often did with his daughter, that he was arguing in the wrong key; he could never quite comprehend her child's logic and if he tried to parry it with what he considered to be a reasonable answer, he usually provoked unimagined hurricanes of grief and outrage. Why, for example, should she imagine that Sophie, whom he remembered as a bonsai, nine-year-old version of the knowing, slutty girl in the video, would sway him in any direction?

'Well, I don't care. Perhaps Sophie's dad doesn't mind if she looks like a little tart, but I'm not having you –'

He stopped; it was happening again. Daisy halted mid-sob, blanched and then drew in a huge dramatic breath through her nose as the clouds began to gather in her cheeks; Greg braced himself as she balled both hands into fists, half crouched in a gesture worryingly reminiscent of Caroline in similar moods and screamed at him with all the forces mustered in her small lungs, properly screamed –

'*She hasn't got a dad!* And she's not a tart, she's my *best friend*! But she won't be now if I can't have them, she'll be Kayley's best friend and it's all your fault! *You don't understand anything!*' – then belted out of the door and up the stairs, howling.

'Don't trip over your socks,' Greg said automatically to her disappearing back.

An accusing silence swelled in the living room; dimly, from the floor above, he could hear the muffled hiccuping of Daisy's cries and the click of another door opening – undoubtedly the prosecutor on her gleeful way to record the evidence of his latest crime. He looked down at the catalogue, still covering the script he had less than a week to learn, and was suddenly very tired. He'd been led to expect this sort of scene when she was fourteen or fifteen, had been treated to doomy prophecies from those who had walked that path before him more or less since she was out of nappies, but to have his ten-year-old mutate without warning into a full-blown teenager exploding with hackneyed rebukes – that was simply unfair. He had the same sense of being cheated that comes from waking an hour or so before the alarm clock and finding there is not quite enough time to recover your deep sleep. Surely he should have been allowed to keep her as a little girl for a couple more years?

Depressed, he hunched on his denim jacket, took out the cigarette packet and propped one, unlit, in the corner of his mouth, the better to enjoy the anticipation as he wandered through the kitchen to the patio doors.

Outside in the yard the night air was cold and clean, busy with the hushed noises of scavengers; a fox or a cat scratching through bushes at the end of the garden, seagulls with their unmistakable coastal yelp. Greg flared a match to the tip of his cigarette and stretched back as far as he could to look up at the stars, sharp as Christmas lights in the uninterrupted dark. When the house and all that it implied became claustrophobic, out here the night sky calmed him with its vast space; he was comforted by the idea that he could fill his lungs with air and shout and shout and his voice would carry into infinity and never echo back to him, so huge and empty was the sky and the sea beneath it. He never did, of course; Caroline would use it as proof that he was insane and since she daily discovered new reasons to find fault with him it was as well not to provide any further ammunition himself if he could possibly help it.

September had been mild, the leaves only just beginning to darken and curl, as if by way of compensation for the bleary summer, but the air had gained the hard edge of autumn over the past couple of weeks, Greg noticed; there on the northern coast of East Anglia, where the sheltered waters of the Wash bled out into the North Sea, the winds often came knifing in from the Urals and winter arrived earlier and left later than when they'd lived in London, before Daisy.

It would be warm in London now, he thought, slowly leaking trails of violet smoke through his lips, and pictured the phantasmagoric lights and sounds of Soho, a pop video of music and colour, the dance of the crowds, the women all dressed up for expensive bars, eyes and cheeks bright with night air and the anticipation of sex. London was the Unreal City of his fantasies that became, paradoxically, more real to him the more he felt pushed to the margins of his home life. Then it lurched in his chest again: the old longing for something nameless he couldn't remember, a homesickness for a place that had never truly been his home, mingling with a stifling fear that he was somehow being left behind here, in King's Lynn, in the repetition of his life slowly passing, where he would surely be worn down before too long by boredom and routine and relentless niggling criticism, and at his funeral passers-by would eye his cortège and nudge one another and say, 'Wasn't that the bloke who used to be in that vet thing?'

Greg inhaled and in vain tried not to conjure the infinite possibilities suggested by the script lying on the living-room table, with its stripes of lime-green highlighter. Idly he wondered, not for the first time, if he might have been better equipped to communicate with a son. During her pregnancy, Caroline had been acknowledged by midwives and well-meaning female relations to conform so exactly to the received wisdom regarding carrying boys (up high and out front, no extra weight on the hips and a healthy profusion of leg hair), and in the rare moments when he managed the leap of imagination required to picture himself as a father, he found it easier to picture himself as the father of a son (perhaps a vestige of his father's gruff northern machismo), and it would have been such a cruel joke of Fate to force Caroline – who was Shakespearean in her jealousy of every woman with whom he came into contact – to have to share his affection with another female for the rest of their lives, that they hadn't even considered the possibility that the baby might be a girl. So that when she slithered out like a little Fury, and the doctor routinely flipped her over and declared her so to be, Greg's only coherent thought was of all the tiny boy's clothes, all wrong, freshly washed and folded in the baby's new (blue) room, and his involuntary response had been simply: 'Oops-a-daisy.' So there she was, Daisy, and she had remained a stranger to him more or less from that day forward. As, in many important ways, had her mother.

'Well, you handled that with your usual sensitivity, Greg, well done.'

He turned to see Caroline in her painting overalls leaning against the doorframe, shadowed against the rhombus of yellow light from the kitchen. Moths flitted erratically across her silhouette.

'You're letting insects in.' He pointed.

She closed the patio doors behind her.

'Do you care at all that your daughter is in floods of tears up there?'

Greg dropped his cigarette and gave his full attention to grinding it beneath his heel, then picked up the flattened stub and dropped it neatly into the wheelie-bin that stood against the far fence. Why did she feel this need to be so confrontational, always – why? What did she expect him to say to that – *no, not really*? Could she not, for once, ask a question that wasn't intended to provoke another flare-up?

She stood with her arms folded, expectantly.

He shrugged, knowing the effect this would have.

'She's got to learn to accept when I say no without a tantrum.'

Caroline knotted her arms tighter around her chest.

'And you didn't think to even try discussing the issue with her?'

'What *issue*? There is no issue. I'm not buying her shoes like that, end of story.'

'She was going to buy them herself, didn't you listen to a word she said?'

'Caro, why did you send her to ask me if you'd already said she could have them?'

'I said she could have them if you agreed. I like to at least try for her sake to keep up the impression that we still make decisions together.'

'Then you should have talked to me first and we could have told her together that we both disapproved, instead of pulling this good-cop/bad-cop trick where you make her hate me and then side with her about how unfair I am.'

Caroline mimicked his dismissive shrug.

'The fact is, I don't disapprove.'

'Oh – OK, what – you think those are *good* shoes for a ten-year-old to wear?'

'I think, Greg, that there are more important things going on here than the shoes. You know she's been having a hard time at school.'

Greg gave a small, impatient shake of the head; again he felt foxed by feminine unreason.

'What, and I have to make it easier by letting her dress like a hooker? What's that got to do with anything?'

'God, Greg, you really have no idea what goes on in her life, do you?'

Or mine, was the unspoken suffix, as loud as if it had been sung from the roof by a full Greek chorus. Or mine.

Greg turned to look down the shadowy garden towards the sea, and took out another cigarette.

'Perhaps you've been very preoccupied with your audition.'

She had barely opened her teeth to let the words through, her voice thick with coiled-up accusation. He waited.

'It seems as if it must be very important to you, this play.'

And there it was – the match poised above the kindling. This was what lay behind the coldness and sniping of the past couple of weeks, the deliberate and eloquently hostile shape of her back when they went to bed, even more so than usual, and he had known it very well, had expected it ever since Patrick's first phone call to let him know about the audition. The play was indeed the thing.

He felt inclined to take refuge in Daisy's favourite mode of industrial-strength sarcasm, to say, 'Oh, duh! *Earth to Caroline!* It's Freddie Zamora! Freddie Fucking Zamora, hel-*lo*?' but there seemed so little point in precipitating a full-blown onslaught when he hadn't even auditioned for the play yet, when the word on the street according to Patrick, his agent, was that Richard E. Grant had shown some interest in the part of Allan which dismal news, if true, made an utter mockery of Patrick's even bothering to submit his name, so instead he said quietly, 'It's directed by Freddie Zamora.'

Since this produced no surface reaction, he added, 'Patrick says there's some talk that Barbara Bathurst might be the female lead.' Perhaps that would reassure her. Dame Barbara Bathurst was in her sixties. Again, nothing. Greg hesitated.

'He got the Bafta for Best Director last year for –'

'Jesus, Greg, I know, we saw it together, I know who Freddie Zamora is. Don't get patronizing.'

'Well, then – why are you asking if this is important to me?'

She didn't answer. After a bitter pause, she said, 'And where will you live?'

Christ. Greg ran a hand through his hair and effortfully simulated patience.

'Let's wait and see how I get on first, shall we?'

'Because you'll be commuting to London and back every night, won't you, that would be practical.'

'I would imagine that *if*, assuming I were to beat Richard E. Grant to this part, *if* I did the play then, yes, I would probably have to arrange some accommodation in London during the run, if that's what you're asking.'

Caroline appeared triumphant, as if she had wrested a full confession. 'And I would *imagine* that that would make you very happy, wouldn't it, a few months away to do what you like?'

As if following stage directions, Greg walked a few paces away and sat down heavily on the picnic bench with his back to her. Immediately he wished he hadn't; its surface was slick with dew which seeped coldly through his jeans and underwear.

'I'm not even going to have this conversation, Caroline.'

He heard the click of the kitchen door opening, followed by her nasal laugh.

'You're right. It's not as if you'll get it.'

'Thanks for your support.'

'Just trying to keep you in touch with reality, darling. I'm sorry if it bruises your fragile ego, but can you really see yourself on stage with Barbara Bathurst?'

The door closed behind her. Greg stubbed out his second cigarette on a paving slab and let it lie there while he craned his neck up at the constellations, until he was forced by the deadness of his buttocks to retreat to the warmth and froideur of the house.

3

Under such a sky – a high planetarium of undamaged blue – London seemed visionary, Sally had thought that morning, crossing Southwark Bridge on her motorbike with the sun shearing through her hangover. Glazed in its soft sheen, the Embankment to either side was illuminated like the Heavenly City, white stone and windows refracting the sky, water beading back light in scattering patterns. It was early October. This riverscape on a bright autumn day was one of the few sights that could move Sally close to epiphany, a sentimental swelling of civic pride that convinced her, even momentarily, that she was where she was supposed to be. London glowed autumnally, a retouched postcard of itself.

On such a day, under such a sky, Sally's ideal self would have been drinking red wine and smoking Continental cigarettes at a table outside one of the fashionable pubs in Primrose Hill, most likely wearing a suede coat and expensive sunglasses. Such a day was designed for such a girl, and Sally never quite gave up hope that, given the right economic conditions, she might one day transform herself into someone who didn't have chain oil on her hands and carried a tiny, monogrammed handbag instead of an old rucksack full of playscripts and neglected correspondence with utilities companies. Her real self, by contrast, was hovering at the shoulder of Rhys Richards in the Southwark office of Avocet Productions, while he made a one-man show out of contemplating the newly delivered proof of the playbill.

Turning his head first to one side, then to the other, Rhys folded his left arm across his body and clasped his right elbow, cupping his chin contemplatively in his right hand. He shook his head. Then he shifted his weight elegantly and rearranged the hand–chin–elbow configuration to its mirror image. Then he opened his mouth, raised a finger, hesitated as if to give the poster one final opportunity to redeem itself, then minutely twitched his head again and said, 'I'm sorry, angel, it's *got* to go.'

The poster – plain red sans serif against a sepia panorama of rooftops – said:

> ### The Oak Grove
> A new play by Sally McGinley
> Directed by Freddie Zamora, Bafta-winning Director of *Hoxton Fox*, starring Barbara Bathurst, with XXX and XXX.

The last sentence loomed in 48 point. Unwittingly, Sally ground her teeth.

'What's wrong with it now?'

'*Angel.*' Rhys folded his arms. 'You're in a proper theatre now. Learn the art of collaboration.'

'Rhys, you promised –'

Rhys held up a forbidding hand. 'Sal, if you're going to be wedded to authorial purity, by all means go back to your pissy little arts centres and I guarantee no one will change a word you've written. Or you can be flexible. Up to you. But *The Oak Grove* is just not selling it to me, angel, not now I see it in print. It's not telling me anything.'

'It's the Irish for Derry. Where they live. I've explained that.'

'Is your average punter going to pick up that nuance? Or indeed care?'

'Would you prefer me to call it *Shopping and Fucking*?'

'Well, frankly, if it wasn't already taken, I'd say yes. At least *Shopping and Fucking* whets the appetite a little. People go and see a play called *Shopping and Fucking*. I'm not so sure I'd rush to one called *The Oak Grove*. It suggests *hobbits.*'

Rhys executed an elaborate frisson.

'Let's just call it *Fucking* to avoid ambiguity.'

'Now you're being silly.'

Avocet Productions had acquired its office space, the top floor of a converted warehouse edging the river next to Southwark Cathedral, for an enviably low rent three years earlier, partly through the intervention of a friend of Lola's father and partly because it had an almost intolerable micro-climate; impossible either to heat or cool effectively according to the season. The room was long and narrow, with a wide semi-circular window reaching almost from floor to ceiling at either end, contributing, along with the cold and the floor polish, to an ecclesiastical air. At the end that overlooked the river and let in all the light, an arrangement of ageing invertebrate sofas surrounded a low table piled with copies of the *Stage* and dated *Spotlights*, and against one wall a bookcase strained to support Rhys's manuals of stagecraft, together with a retired coffee percolater and a browning spider plant. The opposite end efficiently housed three desks with computer terminals, each paired with an orthopaedically correct chair, on one of which was now perched Lola Czajkowski, occupied with matters of finance, her Pre-Raphaelite hair fixed with two combs so that it hung on each side like spaniel ears. On the walls, below the naked entrails of the heating system, the whitewashed breezeblocks displayed posters of Avocet's previous productions in cheap clip-frames while, opposite the door, the first artefact to present itself to visitors was a lavishly mounted photo of Freddie Zamora receiving his Bafta from Jeremy Irons.

Sally sighed.

'What do you want it called, then?'

'Well – you may laugh –'

'I doubt it.'

'Freddie thought *Real*.'

'Why?'

Rhys made dismissive arm movements and gestured to Freddie Zamora, who was deep in the plump embrace of the sofa, washed in sunlight beneath a mezzanine floor of cigarette smoke as he riffled through papers from a foolscap wallet. He looked up and smiled.

'Here, Sal. Come and look at these.'

Sally couldn't help but marvel at the sheer *normality* of Freddie Zamora. The smallness, the everydayness of him. Anyone else would have changed, she thought, even a bit, even just in the clothes they bought. But Freddie remained the still centre of wherever he happened to be, managing to look infinitely younger and sound infinitely older than twenty-eight, radiating the kind of reassuring calm that Sally imagined to be born of true self-confidence, though she had never experienced this subjectively. He was the only person she knew who appeared convincingly happy being who he was, even before *Hoxton Fox* and its accompanying tsunami of international celebrity. Freddie didn't have an ideal self; at least, he had mastered whatever Zen trickery was required to square his ideal self so precisely with its actual counterpart that there was no margin for disappointment or reproach. Sally wondered, perching on the arm rest beside him and examining his shiny hair, what it would be like to have that level of faith in your own talent, the faith – or perhaps it was a genuine quest for integrity, perhaps that really did exist – that gave you the confidence to wave aside the Hollywood suitors and their multi-zero contracts and to decide that, considering all the limitless vistas presented by a Best Director Bafta, what you most wanted to do next was to return to your college friends and direct a new stage play by a writer whose work had never been performed to more than sixty people at a time. In his place, Sally would have been so afraid of missing her chance that she probably would have grabbed at the wrong one. This had been true of most areas of her life so far. Insecurity and impatience equipped her poorly for taking the long view.

'*Real?*'

'Mm. Because, you know, what is reality? Do the characters even know? How much of what happened to them is real and how much is in their minds? Does that make it any less real? Is it real, in the sense of authentic, or is it really –'

'Yes, I see the theme.'

'It works on multiple levels.'

'So did *The Oak Grove.*'

'No,' Rhys said, 'that worked on two levels, one of which was only available to you.'

'Trust me.' Freddie smiled encouragement. 'We've talked it over.'

'Not with me, you haven't.' She sighed. 'I want the city to be present as a backdrop right from the start, even in –'

'Ah,' said Rhys, diplomatically.

'Tell her,' said Lola from behind her monitor.

'It's not set in Derry any more.'

'What?' Sally twisted to face Rhys, who was still standing with folded arms.

'Freddie's thinking, it's a bit inflammatory. Political resonances.'

'It's not political at all. It's about a family – but it needs a context –'

'Well, exactly,' said Rhys. 'It's three people talking in a room, so it doesn't matter where it's set, does it?'

'Barbara can't do the accent,' Freddie said, in a quiet aside to the window.

Rhys pouted. 'And Barbara can't do the accent. She doesn't feel she can, anyway, not for the whole play. It's not one of her stronger ones and the last thing I want is her throwing a hissy at this stage.'

'I've tinkered with the latest draft,' Freddie said, gently. 'It'll be fine. But I think it needs a metropolitan feel.'

'That's exactly what it doesn't need. It's about tensions in a small town that already has its own tensions.'

'You've only set it in Derry because that's where your father was born, but you keep insisting that it's not about your father, so it ought to simplify things if we set it in London,' Rhys said.

'We'd like to keep an open mind about the ethnicity of the characters,' said Freddie.

'Oh, I get it.'

Sally ground her teeth quietly. None of this mattered, really, except that if she gave ground now, she might come in tomorrow and find they'd decided to make all the characters pre-op. transsexuals, if Rhys thought it would better appeal to some perceived missing demographic.

'This was a commission, angel,' Rhys reminded her. 'You *are* being paid.'

With some reluctance, Sally acknowledged that they were right; they had given her this opportunity over a number of more established writers, with the result that her name would be appearing on a playbill with Freddie's and with Dame Barbara Bathurst, double Oscar nominee. Who, even with an accent handicap, was undeniably a step up from the actors in Sally's previous stage plays, many of whom spent their working week on stilts in Covent Garden Market, painted silver.

'London contains the world.' Freddie opened his hands to illustrate this self-evident truth.

'All right. Not Hoxton, though. I don't want you becoming a parody of yourself.'

Freddie grinned and remembered his cigarette, combusting unattended in the ashtray. He leaned forward and stubbed it. 'I knew you'd come round. Didn't I say, Rhys? I said I didn't think you'd try to be all *auteur*-ish. Let's get some coffee before we start on these.' He flicked the sheaf of CVs with their paperclipped photos in his lap. 'Look, these are the three we're seeing this afternoon. I want to witness your first impressions. Who's your ideal Allan? Ah-ah' – he jerked the pages away as Sally reached for them. 'Run and get some coffee first, there's a good lass.'

On her trip down the five flights of stairs and through the court-yard behind the Cathedral to the coffee chain whose clean-angled, homogenous frontage had recently replaced the boarded-up windows of the George on the corner of Borough Market, doing its bit to bring a little touch of the universal to their patch of time and geography, Sally had the opportunity to be impressed once more by Freddie's ability to read people. This afternoon's casting, for instance. It had been Freddie who had insisted on her presence; Rhys was dogmatic in his belief that a writer should deliver the script and disappear, which was why he preferred to work with playwrights who were incapable of interfering by virtue of being dead. Nor would he have noticed, as Freddie did, how much she had invested in the character of Allan, who was, in all his salient characteristics and personal history, a portrait of her father. Only Freddie could see how much she cared that Allan should be played by the right person, and she was grateful to him. In spite of her gratitude, though, she thought, as she balanced four super-grande lattes and a pack of biscotti in a recycled paper bag that didn't look up to the job, she had never quite shaken her reservations about Freddie. Even at university she had felt that his warmth, without ever being insincere, was underpinned by a steely shrewdness engineered to ensure that he always got his own way.

Since the supernova of *Hoxton Fox*, Freddie was widely described as a genius. 'The most we can hope for', Rhys had declaimed, raising a glass as they gathered in an awed huddle at the Bafta party, 'is that, if we are remembered at all by future generations, it will be in footnotes to biographies of Freddie Zamora.' Sally had snorted into her champagne, which some present had taken for the sound of envy. Freddie was above-averagely talented – just – but he was also, in Sally's opinion, above-averagely lucky, and this was not reason enough to genuflect in his presence.

For example: who could have predicted that two and a half years ago, at the launch of a small arts magazine panting to confer on itself cult status, he would find himself seated next to a celebrated young comic novelist and happen to mention how he'd love to make a tongue-in-cheek film about cultural entrepreneurs and web designers and the bursting of the dot.com bubble set in the self-congratulating salons of Shoreditch, or that the young comic novelist would thereupon exclaim that it was the most incredible coincidence, but she'd been thinking of writing something on that exact same subject, or that the resulting collaboration would attract the attention of a celebrated and marketable young actor friendly with the celebrated young novelist, who immediately offered his services for a fraction of his usual fee, thus making it possible for Avocet to attract enough funding to film the thing independently and find a distributor in only a few months? Sally, who considered *Hoxton Fox* to be mildly funny, no more, no less, had found herself inwardly paralysed by indignation – partly because she wished Freddie had asked her to co-write the screenplay – she had known him for ten years – but mostly at the injustice of the outrageously snowballing hype. No one – not even Freddie – could have predicted the extent to which a low-budget black comedy would come to define a picaresque and evanescent moment of modernity, or find itself hailed on both sides of the Atlantic as a near-perfect satirical snapshot of its age. No one could have predicted it, but Freddie seemed happy to take the credit for such foresight while modestly shrugging it off as lucky timing. It would be fair to say that, in common with most people, Sally's resentment of her friend was in direct proportion to the measure of his success.

'Ah, cheers, you're a star,' Freddie said, opening the door to her and exchanging a cardboard cup for his folder.

Sally arranged the bag on the table and began to sift the photographs. 'No Richard E. Grant, then? Talking of stars.'

'I don't know where that rumour came from. Not at all. I'm not interested in stars for this, I told you.'

'Except Barbara,' said Rhys.

'Barbara's not a star. She's a genius.'

'Who can't do accents,' Sally said, discarding the first photograph at once because the actor was too fat and inwardly apologizing for doing so. She wasn't sure exactly how she pictured Allan physically, but she knew that there were two basic requirements: first, that he should not look at all like her father and, second, that he should not look so *un*like her father as to seem that she was deliberately trying to make him a figure of ridicule. Not fat, not bald, certainly not bearded, not badly dressed.

'All genius has a flaw, Sal.'

'What's yours then?'

Freddie crossed his ankles on the coffee table and sighed. 'I can't wear green.'

The face in the second photograph was familiar. It was a curious face, in that all the individual ingredients for good looks were present, and yet the asymmetry of the assembly meant that the whole somehow added up to less than the sum of its parts. His expression was quirky, as if hinting at a roguishness that he wanted you to believe in. Sally turned the picture and read the printed label.

'Why do I know him? Patrick Williams Management?'

'That's the agent. He's called Greg Burns. He used to be in that vet thing.'

'Oh yeah.' A vague recollection stirred, of a Land-Rover on a winding road under credits. 'What was it?'

'*Valley Vets*. Huge ratings it got, in spite of being unremitting shit. He was the housewives' pin-up at one time, you know.'

'Set in Wales?'

'That's the one.'

'I remember. He wasn't so bad, was he?'

Rhys sniffed. 'Tolerable, for Sunday tea-time viewers. I'm not sure he's quite West End, though.'

'You fancy him, then, it seems?' Freddie said, looking at Sally.

'*Fancy* him?'

'For Allan.'

Sally met the stare of the man in the photograph again, liking the boyishness of his lop-sided smile that argued with the lines around his eyes.

'Potentially. But I need to see him in action.'

'There'll be no action in here, girlfriend,' Rhys said, through a moustache of milk froth. 'I'm running a tight ship. No fraternizing with the talent. Try and raise your mind above your quim for the duration, angel.'

Sally saluted this with a finger and plunged backwards into the sofa to read the potted biography of Greg Burns, formerly Doctor Jeremy Glendower, Valley Vet.

4

Greg Burns, in common with a number of family men of similar age, was the owner of a modest collection of pornography which he kept in the bottom drawer of a filing cabinet in the room he used as an office, beneath a ring binder labelled 'Tax Assessment: Receipts', and which he had not declared to his common-law wife. It was modest both in quantity and scope – nothing remotely bordering on the imported, nothing any blushing and stammering schoolboy couldn't hoik off the top shelf – and his use of it these days was desultory at best; nevertheless, it occurred to him during his frantic last-minute steeplechase around the room in search of his keys that Caroline, faced with all the empty hours afforded her by the overnight absence of someone with whom to have a needless argument, might take it upon herself to riffle through his papers in search of incriminating items, and that a half-dozen dated *Playboys* and *Razzles* would certainly be enough to convict him as an irredeemable pervert and probable rapist and child-killer in her absolute system of values. So he scooped them up and folded them haphazardly into his leather case on top of his clean shirt and his pages of script to read on the train, and felt more than usually guilty and furtive as she drove him wordlessly to the station and Daisy in the back seat strafed him with streams of consciousness, of which he caught about one word in ten.

Opposite him on the train to London sat a woman of mid-middle age, who was simultaneously reading a library book and staring at him. Greg caught her eye and looked quickly away, embarrassed. She continued to stare, and it continued to irritate him, thereby allowing him to offload the blame for his distraction on to her. He had intended to read the script for a final check during the journey, but the old familiar clenching in the gut, the quickening of the blood, was upon him now every time he tried to focus on the page, making the words dance and scramble. God, he wanted this! And not just because it was

Barbara Bathurst and Freddie Zamora and a West End theatre and all that that might mean for the future, but also because on the basis of one scene and a synopsis he already felt a profound and sympathetic concern for Allan Duddy and his fate. He knew where Allan was coming from; grudgingly he recognized that fermenting urge to put a bomb under the life you've spent years carefully building – though Allan's difficulties all appeared to stem from his being an incurable altruist, and the most selfless gesture Greg had ever made was allowing Daisy to make a telephone donation of twenty pounds to *Children in Need* with his credit card because her favourite boy band had been featured earnestly cataloguing the miseries of homelessness – still, Greg felt he understood Allan, and he knew beyond any doubt that no one must play Allan but him. He also knew that this intensity of desire was fatal; the only way to relax into an audition was to convince yourself that you didn't care. This ancient advice was beaten into his very soul by years of bitter experience, but he knew it was redundant. You can't persuade yourself not to care. Nor to care about something more than you really do, he thought, visualizing Caroline's wintry profile as she strained up slightly to see over the steering wheel of the Toyota Land Cruiser. All you can do is act.

Inadvertently he glanced up again and this time the woman caught his eye and smiled nervously. Greg was familiar with the type – home-dyed hair with the greys cresting through, a scent of handcream that reached him across the space between them, the wistful expression of the unenjoyed – and knew that the nervous smile was only one or two steps away from greeting him as Doctor Jeremy. He returned it politely and unconvincingly with a half-nod, as if they'd met once at a wedding and couldn't place each other, and affected extreme concentration on his page. He couldn't remember the last time he'd seen a library book. Didn't everyone just *buy* books these days, off the Internet, when they wanted them? Apparently not everyone; and the image of this woman making her special weekly trip to the library to choose her next book in its forlorn plastic sheath (he checked the cover; yes, a historical romance involving spitfire pilots) seemed so terribly sad suddenly, the loneliness of it, for a moment he felt he wanted to cry. He turned; fields repeated at speed beyond the window, sunlight strobing through the glass, and as quickly Greg thwarted his own sentimentality and reassured himself that she was probably perfectly happy. Probably happier than him, for a start.

'Pardon me –'

'Hm?'

'I feel ever so silly asking, but – it *is* Doctor Jeremy, isn't it?'

Greg dipped his head in practised modest assent and laid his hands flat on the page to meet her eyes.

'Oh.' She giggled, embarrassed. 'Fancy seeing you on a *train*!'

'Mm. Yes.' He smiled. She probably imagines everyone on television has their own driver, he thought indulgently, and then realized with gloom that she would be referring to his Land-Rover, because on some level she believed that Jeremy Glendower MRCVS. was real.

There was a short silence, interrupted by the double bleep of a text message landing somewhere proximate. The woman started, placed a careful thumb in her current page and with the other hand sought in her bag a phone the size of a corn cob, which she laboriously checked and replaced.

'Ooh. Not me this time.' She looked at him expectantly.

Greg felt irked. Even she – even this evident spinster – was in a position to receive texts. She had people in her life who might at any time want to send her a text. Who? A lover? He made no move to find his own phone; without looking he knew there was no need. No one ever sent him texts. The medium existed wholly for flirting, and Caroline's stringent observation made it too high risk for him ever to hand over his number to anyone with whom he might like to flirt. At intervals, he suspected, though she always denied it, she invaded his phone's memory for calls made and received in her absence, and verified any unfamiliar numbers.

The woman smiled some more; Greg suspected her of formulating a means of prolonging the conversation.

'It's terrible, that, isn't it?' she said eventually, nodding to the tabloid paper he had discarded on the adjacent seat.

'Terrible,' Greg agreed, with hesitation.

In fact he had read all nine pages of the latest revelations about the unfortunate (or highly fortunate, depending on your point of view) chat-show host whose seventeen-year-old lovers had kissed and told, and it reminded him of Daisy's Magic Eye books, of how he used to peer and peer at the picture for hours and still fail to see what everyone else claimed to see clearly. He simply could not understand what the presenter had done that was so wrong. So he had sex with girls – but why had it triggered this mass retreat to the moral high ground, this utterly disproportionate censoriousness and stone-casting, and – most baffling of all – largely from other men? He could understand why women columnists might readily find fault. The presenter was married to a beautiful and intelligent actress who, despite her beauty and intelligence, was not and never again would be a pliable seventeen-year-old, and women would understand – indeed, could not avoid – the incontrovertible lesson therein: that this is how men are, given the opportunity, this is the shadow all women must live under, even the celebrated and beautiful and intelligent, so what hope is there for the rest of you? The presenter is Everyman; he is man in his default setting – responding to a set of pushed buttons, not cut out for monogamy by evolutionary design. He is no more or less principled than other men – it's just that he gets the chances. But for other *men* to take arms against him for it – that was the kind of small-minded *schadenfreude* that Greg despised, for it was a betrayal of solidarity, of brotherhood. The *I wish I were doing it but since I'm not I don't see why he should get away with it* mentality reserved for sexual misdemeanours and tax evasion.

As Greg increasingly saw it, or liked to think he did, they were all engaged in a relentless battle with women and their constricting morals, who were trying to force them into a role for which nature had never intended them, and society was colluding. The presenter was a freedom-fighter, for goodness' sake. He had apparently slept with a lot of women. He had sometimes slept with a lot of women *at the same time*, to Greg's particular admiration and envy, and he was not an attractive man, but he was funny and he was famous; had he been a civil servant or a dentist, his only chance of snorting cocaine from the buoyant breasts of teenage models would have been to pay for it. But certain professions by definition ensure that you get it served up on a plate, and any man with a conscience would acknowledge that this must be one of the prime reasons for choosing those professions in the first place. It was certainly one of the reasons why Greg had wanted to be an actor, but it hadn't entirely worked out. Women do want to sleep with actors, but not the kind who scrape a living in rep and mainly work as hospital porters; they want to sleep with well-known actors who are on television, and by the time he had become one of these, he had also shackled himself to Caroline, produced Daisy and moved away from London. The tiny window of opportunity opened by *Valley Vets* slowly shrank and shrank until it

33

was no more than a chink, and finally it closed altogether with the series, though Caroline plainly did not believe this to be true, or behaved as if she did not.

Women still wrote fan letters sometimes, or emailed Patrick's company website with flattering comments about him, but they were women like this one opposite, who nurtured chaste fantasies of marrying Doctor Jeremy and lending a feminine touch to his endearingly messy little cottage, rather than keen, uninhibited girls who wouldn't mind blowing Greg Burns in a hotel room while their friend sat on his face and played with her tits, which was what he'd ideally like in a groupie.

'And him with young children,' the woman opposite said, interrupting his thoughts with the unspoilt faith of the childless, that parenthood should somehow make you a better person. Greg found the reverse to be true; at least in his single days he had never had very high expectations of his own character, so he was spared the disappointment of letting himself down. Parenthood had served only to make him dismally aware of his own shortcomings, and increasingly sorry for Daisy that she had been put at such a disadvantage, father-wise.

He returned to his audition scene; excluded, the woman settled back into her seat and wrapped her cardigan tighter across her chest. It was only when they pulled into King's Cross and Greg stood to retrieve his case from the overhead luggage rack that he discovered the faulty zip; as he tilted it vertically he heard the stitching give way and was powerless to stop the magazines slewing over the floor of the carriage at his fellow traveller's feet. In spite of his flustered apologies and protestations, she knelt eagerly to help him collect them and then rose again in slow motion, her expression fixed in a rigor mortis of disbelief as she looked from his scarlet face to the buffed and hairless undercarriage of the Playmate of the Month, May 1996, and back again.

'Oh, Doctor *Jeremy*,' she said, with infinite sorrow.

The label by the buzzer read 'Avocet' in old-fashioned courier script and was unevenly angled, as if someone had typed the name and cut it out in a hurry to insert behind the plastic. The understatedness of it pleased Greg, the air of urban bohemia, like the wharf itself, narrow and cobbled between its high-walled buildings, all chichi photographic studios in a Dickensian film set. Opposite the red door to the converted warehouse was an incongruous nugget of medieval masonry, the last surviving lump of Westminster Palace, with an orange-brick office building grafted unconvincingly on to one end like a prosthetic limb. Next to the building, at the end of Pickfords Wharf, was the *Golden Hind* – the real one, apparently, as if this corner of London were a bric-a-brac yard of historical trophies.

He had dumped the magazines in a recyling bin outside Blackfriars Tube with a twinge of nostalgia and, because he had arrived too early, anticipating delays with the trains, decided to walk the remaining distance over the bridge and along the South Bank. The sun was unexpectedly warm; after a short distance he flipped his jacket over one shoulder and snapped on sunglasses, as if he belonged with the drifts of unhurried, unworking people who leaned on the balustrade watching the river, or tangled their arms and breath together, laughing, with their primary-coloured rucksacks, asking strangers to take their photograph in front of the Globe or the thuggish slab of Tate Modern's façade. On the facing bank, they were piecing together the glass carapace of a tall building in the shape of a fir cone, a shiny fir cone patterned in diamond light. He ought to bring Daisy for a day out, he thought; they hadn't had a trip together for ages and she'd enjoy the wheel and the wobbly bridge. She'd ask if people lived in the shiny fir cone.

The river, even in this glassy light, took on the tones of industry without the substance, save for one or two flat landfill barges, low in the water, shabby and apologetic, heads down among the lambent pleasure boats. He felt briefly full of optimism and was moved to direct a smile at passers-by who, on the whole, returned it with uncharacteristic heartiness for Londoners, in the manner of wartime, as if they recognized their luck in having cameos in his film. Odd, what a bit of unseasonal sunshine could do. Although, he reflected, they were probably not Londoners, these smiling people. The pallid misanthropic natives would be clenched at their desks, not strolling by the river, and definitely not smiling.

On the corner of Clink Street he had passed a bar inhabited by smooth-skinned people, silent behind the plate glass and watching the world, sipping espressos as if the notion of work had never threatened their charmed lives. None of them was over thirty. They all looked like actors, film-makers, writers, composers. European-looking. Greg too was European now, in passport if not sartorially, and he could picture himself living here, a little flat with river views and wooden floors, a morning trip to the bar where he would sit and smoke and browse the papers with Continental ease, while the girls behind the counter pointed him out to their other customers. That's Greg Burns, the actor, they would say. Already he had warmed to the kind of people who would choose to work in an area like this, and it worried him; the more appealing Avocet and all its trappings became, the more he began to feel that his life would certainly be drained of all hope and purpose if he was not cast as Allan. Should he take off his sunglasses, or leave them on – or would that appear to be trying too hard?

'Hi there, Lola Czajkowski, we spoke on the phone. Come on in.'

The door on the fifth floor was opened to him by a smiling girl with voluminous hair and cleavage. He knew who she was already; her father was Anthony Czajkowski, whose adaptations of classic novels for the BBC hauled in endless gongs and headlines insisting that costume drama was the new something – rock and roll, probably – and Greg had read in a recent interview a propos his *Two on a Tower* that he was very close to his daughter and saw all her productions several times over with a proud but critical eye, which meant another good reason to get himself inside the Avocet fold. He would sell his own mother, had she not already passed on, to be in a costume drama. Lola wore platform boots and a translucent dress with floaty sleeves, and gestured for him to come inside. Past her hair, he could see a photograph on the wall of Freddie Zamora receiving his Bafta, and the swarm in his stomach lurched into life once more.

'You can leave your coat down there. This is Rhys Richards, my business partner. I'm sending him out for coffees, do you want something?'

'Oh.' Greg looked around as if for someone more appropriate to take his order, feeling somehow that he should not be waited on by the producers themselves, despite their alarming youth. 'Thanks – I'll have a decaf, please.'

'You will not,' said the slim young man with the dyed black hair. 'While you're under our roof you'll have everything with all the fat, tar and caffeine that nature intended. We have no truck with Apollonian restraint. Unless of course you have a medical condition. Do you?'

'No.'

'I'm pleased to hear it.' He winked over the top of his tinted glasses. 'Now – I need money. No, no – not you,' he added, as Greg moved for his pocket. 'Goes on entertainment expenses, for the Revenue. You understand.'

Greg stood holding his coat while Lola reached into her desk for a cash box and withdrew a note.

'Don't believe it. I only went to the bank yesterday.'

Rhys shook his head.

'We could have bought *Brazil* by now with the money we spend in there. You have *no* idea.' He looked at Greg. 'Single-handedly we're bankrolling their rape of the developing world because we do not have between us a useful skill that would lead to the fixing of the coffee machine. You seem like a man who would know how to mend a coffee machine, though, Mr Burns.'

Greg, unsure if he was being flirted with, said, 'Probably the element's gone', and then wished he hadn't.

Lola propelled Rhys towards the door and took Greg by the elbow. 'Come and meet the team.'

Rubensesque, his mother would have called her, Greg thought as he followed the movement of Lola's hips through the room. Caroline would have been less kind, but Caroline, with her small, wiry, adolescent body (and the thought had disturbingly occurred to Greg more than once in the early days of their relationship) had always been envious of obviously womanly women. Lola had the kind of creamy skin that made him curious to stroke her face almost as a reflex, and it crossed his mind that if he got the part he might well see if he could sleep with her, though he would need to weigh up the extent to which this might help or hinder his equal if not greater interest in meeting Anthony Czajkowski.

Greg often entertained such thoughts about the women he met, but he also knew (and this distinction would have been difficult to communicate to Caroline) that he both did and didn't mean it. The possibility that there might be other women who would be prepared to sleep with him; that the path of his life was not unalterably mapped and was within his power to change; even his highly developed theory that monogamy was a form of repressive social engineering developed by the Church and perpetuated now by women – all of this was good enough for Greg on an abstract plane. He imagined other women – younger, sunnier, less burdened women – and the adventure they promised all the time, but these fantasies almost never translated into reality, through self-interest as much as conscience. He had a comfortable home and a child whose preservation and contentment was the only real point of his otherwise self-indulgent life, and every man needed somewhere to come back to; only a fool would put that in jeopardy, unless for something of cosmic significance. At the same time, the thought that he would never again have extraordinary – or even moderately enthusiastic – sex was too depressing even to contemplate. The absence of it was not solely Caroline's fault, either; merely the product of twelve years of shared life and its necessary tarnish. He was aware that he would never again have that kind of sex with Caroline, not with all the counselling in the world; that was lost to them. And yet if Caroline had been the kind of woman who allowed him the extra-curricular freedoms he believed he wanted (and there *were* apparently such women, he had read about them) with her blessing, she would not have been Caroline, and he would have loved her less. There was no obvious solution, except to have two lives.

'And this is the famous Freddie Zamora!' Lola said, with a flourish.

At the far end of the room, late afternoon light fanned through the glass spotlighting a series of couches. Greg held out his hand to a boy who looked about seventeen and was unexpectedly short.

'Hi, Greg.' He clasped Greg's hand with both of his. 'Good to meet you. How was your journey?'

'Fine. Thank you.'

Greg felt the young director's eyes travel unmistakably up and down him and his insides clamped again; he knew he was being sized up for the part already, and if he didn't look right there was nothing he could do to change their minds. He squeezed his shoulder blades back and tried to look as Allan Duddy might have looked.

'I saw your *Becket* at the Young Vic,' he said, pointing to the poster above the bookcase as if Freddie might have forgotten his directorial debut of the Anouilh classic, back in the days before *Hoxton Fox*, and immediately felt that only a dullard would have said so.

Freddie smiled in the fashion of an ambassador at a function.

'God. That was, what, four years ago? You liked it?'

'Oh yes.' Greg nodded hard, to emphasize that this was beyond doubt. 'Very – um – very much.'

'Great.' Freddie smiled with even more sincerity.

'Oh – listen,' said Lola, waving a hand, 'feel free to smoke, Greg, if you do. We're very informal here.'

He turned to her with surprised gratitude. Such a small thing, such a little personal freedom, the freedom to kipper himself in the warm, in a comfortable chair with a lovely and presumably killingly expensive view, if that was his choice, but the fact that they granted him that freedom spoke volumes to Greg about the spirit of these kids. They were not kids, of course – he guessed them to be thirtyish – but they seemed like students, with the same carelessness and self-belief that he dimly remembered having once possessed. They looked like people who enjoyed their days, which Greg could not honestly have said of himself for some time, and they held in their hands the power to make his future something worth looking forward to. Or not.

'Have a seat,' said Freddie. 'We'll start when Rhys gets back. I wanted to chat to you a bit about the part. Would you excuse me for just a second? This is Sally McGinley, the writer.'

The girl on the opposite couch raised her head from the papers she was reading and looked directly at Greg. Something caught.

He thought at first that he recognized her, which seemed unlikely. Then he understood; it was the look he recognized. Long ago, at drama school, there had been a girl who had looked at him like that, across a bar. She had been exhilarating and manic – to a degree that required medication, it had turned out – but also compelling, and for a while she had obsessed him. In appearance she was nothing like the blonde girl who now sat with her legs tucked under her and continued to watch him without smiling, but the sudden intensity of her stare disturbed a memory twenty-five years hidden, and he was unsettled.

'Hello.'

'You didn't really like his *Becket*?'

'Oh yes. No, I did. I like Anouilh.'

'Yeah, the audience was overcome with ennui.'

Greg looked blank.

'That was a pun. So, look,' – she dropped her eyes to consult a sheet on her lap – 'Greg. How do you understand Allan?' She leaned suddenly forward.

'Well,' he sat back, disconcerted, 'I've only got the one scene –'

'It's a pivotal scene. You've read the synopsis. How do you understand him? What kind of man is he? In *your* opinion.' She added these last words as if the very idea were laughable.

'He –' Greg wanted to light a cigarette as ballast against his nerves, but found he had left the packet in his coat. To contrive the answer he thought she might want to hear was bound to trip him up, so he said, simply, 'He's a disappointed idealist.'

She gave no indication of whether this might be the right or wrong answer.

'In what way?'

She was dishevelled, as if she might have been out all night, and looked pale and underfed, but in an attractive, enviable way, as only young good-looking people can manage. If Greg stayed out late these days he tended to look frayed and leathery. He wondered briefly if he might try to sleep with her instead, or as well, but sensed a razorwire defence that would not tolerate clumsy or half-hearted attempts, and could prove more demanding than he was prepared to take on.

'He's – well, he's given the best years of his life to something he used to think mattered. Then he gets to his forties and looks around and wonders why he's always the one doing the giving and no one seems to give anything back to him. And he sees,' – Greg wondered whether to go on, but she was still staring unreadably at him so he felt obliged – 'you know, he can see his future and there's nothing to look forward to except the same old thing, and it's fear, really, that makes him take off. Fear of losing his self.' He felt that this sounded gauche. 'His sense of self, I mean.'

'OK, but how do you judge him?'

'Pardon?'

'How do you judge him.' She mouthed the words slowly, as if he had learning difficulties. 'It will make a difference to the way you play him. Whether or not you're on his side. Whether you think what he does is understandable or unforgivable.'

'It's both.'

Her eyes narrowed and after a pause she inclined her head in what might have been a nod, then brusquely switched her attention to the script on her knee, as if she did not expect to hear anything else of interest from him. Greg had the impression that she had taken against him, but couldn't imagine why. Unless . . . If he'd been more intuitive, he thought, and less nervous, he might have picked up on the weight in her voice when she asked that question. Now that he thought about it, perhaps, it looked as if she personally considered Allan's behaviour to be unforgivable, despite having herself created him as a sympathetic character. Her youth rattled him, too; how, at her age, could she have shaped Allan's middle-aged frustrations and self-justifications with such acuity? Where did such knowledge come from? He was about to qualify his answer in the hope of opening the discussion once more and turning it in his favour, when Rhys returned with his arms full of steaming cups and a neglected phone bleating through his clothes with the rhythmic insistence of a colicky infant.

'Take these off me, someone. Forgot what you all wanted so they're all the same, hope you don't have a dairy allergy, if you do you're fucked. Excuse me.' He flipped the phone out of his jacket, observed the screen, said 'Huh,' pressed a button and stuck a finger in his left ear.

'I thought you were tanning your arse in Indonesia [. . .] Oh, did you? [. . .] Very wise, nowhere's safe any more, is it? [. . .] No, not since Costa Rica, angel, and I won't get one now till after this bloody thing and frankly you wouldn't get me on a plane these days. [. . .] No, still auditioning. [. . .] Oh, Barbara, yes. I *know*! She's *marvellous*, you wouldn't believe. She's an *icon*. [. . .] Wait a tick, I'll enquire.' He lowered the phone. 'Kris Ackland's asking if we want to be on the guest list tonight at the Albert Hall for this Iraq benefit.' He made a face. 'All proceeds to the homeless and amputees. Takers?'

'I'll come,' said Lola, who was busy at the other end of the office diverting all potentially noisy communications equipment in preparation for Greg's audition piece. 'Those poor people.'

Sally didn't look up. 'Does it promise to be an evening of plangent and badly rhymed protest songs?'

'Almost certainly. Coldplay will be there.'

'Go on then, count me in. There's a late bar, isn't there? That should get us through.'

'I admire your spirit of charity. Freddie Zed?'

Freddie had been watching Greg quietly and unobtrusively from his corner of the sofa, and Greg had been trying not to look at him doing it. Now Freddie offered his wrists as if bound.

'I've already told Kris I can't. I've got some government arts funding committee presentation thing.'

'Get you. At Number Ten, is it?' Sally asked.

'As a matter of fact, it is,' said Freddie, pleasantly. There was a silence.

'OK, Kris, so it's me plus two. [. . .] Freddie's not, no. [. . .] Well, *I'll* be the judge of that. [. . .] *Bon, à tout à l'heure*, then.'

Greg experienced an absurd rush of disappointment, like a drop in altitude, and an accompanying scorn, directed at himself. These kids were not his friends. They were not even yet – and might never be – his colleagues; they were young and spontaneous and untethered and brimming with possibility, and many other things that he was not; there was no earthly reason why he should have imagined that they would include him in their plans, but his new urge to belong in some small way to their desirable lives had encouraged him to half believe that they might just glance over and say, 'What about you, Greg, do you want to come?' The sting of being so irrelevant, so undisguisedly glossed over, was, he discovered, no less mortifying at forty-four than it had been as a teenager. He was only relieved that he hadn't said anything out loud.

'Right,' said Rhys, folding his arms and nodding towards the empty floorspace before the sofas. 'Lo, you're reading Barbara's part. Come on then, Mr Burns. *Etonnez-moi.*'

5

Five days after Greg's audition, Caroline burst open the door of his office where he had rooted himself, staring fruitlessly at his inbox as he listened to the test match, as if by this vigil he might draw the reluctant email down from its ethereal flight through the sheer force of his desire. For five days the telephone had been off limits as he watched his screen and waited for the electronic triad that would herald the arrival of news, except for isolated incidents when Caroline or Daisy, pushed to exasperation, had forced him to sign off so that they could make contact with the outside world, none of which had ameliorated Caroline's feelings towards the play. The limbo of waiting, with the phone rendered impotent and Greg in this suspended state of neurosis, was straining the already taut appearance of family life. He felt as if the air in the house might be in danger of running out; it seemed that as the days passed their collective breathing became increasingly shallow and forced, using it up. The call, when finally it came, would bring only a qualified relief, since its news could only make one of them happy at the other's expense.

For the first day he had felt pleased with his performance at the audition, hopeful that they had liked him, patient and only slightly nervy, because no one really expected to hear so soon; they must have been seeing other people. A colleague of Caroline's had come to dinner with her husband and Greg's only sign of obsessive behaviour had been to keep his phone, usually such a mute companion, on the table beside him, just in case. On the second day, he had telephoned Patrick's office to see if there had been any news overnight, though he knew there wouldn't have been; Patrick had been in meetings all day so he had called Patrick's assistant at half-hourly intervals to check that Patrick was getting his messages, until Patrick returned his call in the late afternoon and gently asked him to remember the protocol and to please stop swearing at the poor girl who was only doing her job. On the morning of the third day he banned any non-emergency telephone operation from any member of the household, and judged – wrongly – that this might be an excellent time to reopen the debate about Broadband, to which Caroline had responded with unreasonable acidity that she wasn't going to say it again, but there was no way he was paying twice as much every month just so that he could sit there and download God knew what all day, in a tone that implied she had a keen idea of exactly what.

By the evening of the third day Patrick had neither called nor emailed, and Greg had convinced himself that his audition piece had been abysmal, that he was too old and washed up, that his talent had never been recognized while it briefly existed and now it had all evaporated and he would not only never play Hamlet but would certainly now end his days in suburban panto or taking on a milk round, and on the fourth day he drank a bottle and a half of Pinot noir in front of the television while Caroline was at Pilates, remonstrating with every actor in every programme for their sub-standard performance which he could easily better with all his limbs missing, if only he had the chance, and smoked half a packet out of the sitting-room window in a gesture not of rebellion but of resignation; even Caroline's sanctions couldn't touch him now. Later, when he sniffled plaintively in the dark, twisting his limbs in ever changing arrangements around the duvet and huffing in insomniac despair, she had sent him to the spare room.

'Well?'

Greg peered through hooded eyes and saw that she was holding up a woman's black vest top by its lacy straps, and that her face was quivering with the pent energy of whatever it was she was not saying. He saw also that this was one of those tricksy things women do, where they make you guess the question you are expected to answer before you can begin to do so, and to guess either the question or the answer incorrectly would instantly confirm whatever it was that they were trying to catch you out in. Or perhaps not women, perhaps just Caroline.

'Greg?'

She held the straps forensically between finger and thumb, as if afraid of contaminating them, or possibly the other way around.

'Uh – it looks very nice.'

'I'm sure it did!'

She balled the item in a fist and threw it at him with furious force but insufficient trajectory, so that it landed softly on the floor between them. Neither of them moved. 'Maybe you'd like to give it back to her.'

Greg was entirely perplexed.

'Who?'

'Oh, what – you can't remember her name?'

'I don't know what you're talking about.'

'One night, Greg. You go away for one night and there's *this*. What am I supposed to think? And then you tell me I'm not being support-ive about the play? What's going to happen if you go away for three months, how many women's clothes do you plan to collect then?'

'What?' Greg leaned to switch off the radio; he felt it was the least he could do. It was not as if the cricket were in any way uplifting, and his headache could not filter anything polyphonic. 'I don't know what that is and I honestly don't know what you're talking about.'

She made a small movement of concession with her shoulders.

'Where did you go on Monday night, then? After the audition?'

Greg rubbed his eyebrows. Monday night had been disappointing, in truth; buoyed up from the audition, he had been looking forward to a long night out in London, but for Patrick it had been just anoth-er Monday, with early meetings looming. They had been home by eleven; Pat had gone up to bed and left him watching a film in Mandarin with a bottle of Famous Grouse.

'I was at Pat and Ashana's. You know I was.'

'Do I?'

'Where else would I have been? What's this about?'

'Well, forgive me for sounding suspicious, Greg, but I was taking your dirty washing out of your case, since you weren't going to both-er doing it yourself, and I was wondering how *that* came to be in there.'

Greg experienced a sudden rising panic, an instinctive guilt thrown into relief by the absolute knowledge on this occasion of his own innocence. In his *case*? How could that be – was it a double bluff on her part, to see how he reacted? He rummaged urgently through late images of events. In Patrick's bathroom, the next morning; chil-dren's dirty washing by the laundry basket, little socks knotted up on a heap of towels. On his way to shower, he had bowled his shirt and underpants automatically on to the pile, before remembering, as he yawed under the hot spray that solidified his hangover, that he was not in his own house and that he would therefore have to retrieve them. One of Ashana's tops, then, it must be; he would have scooped it up with his own clothes, also black, and not noticed. There was no other explanation; much as he would have liked to have relieved a woman of her vest and kept it as a trophy, Patrick shepherded him quite well on these occasions.

'It must be Ashana's. I probably picked it up by mistake.'

'Ashana's. Is that what you probably did.'

The focus of her anger was shifting, Greg saw; now she was angry with him for making her admit she had been wrong.

'What – do you want to call her and ask?' He held out his obdurate phone and she stepped back.

'No, I don't want to call her and ask, because I don't want to advertise the fact that I have to check up on my own husband.'

Technically he was not her husband, not in the eyes of the Lord or the Inland Revenue. There was a time when this had been an issue, though one that was rarely discussed because they were at an impasse. Twelve years ago, in the early days of their relationship, they been obliged to attend as a couple a spate of weddings, an expensive phenomenon that usually occurs at the end of the twenties, a few years before the consequent run of babies and then divorces, and each time Caroline had watched one of her friends stride triumphally down the aisle with her catch bagged, she would squeeze Greg's arm and smile up with eloquent, brimming eyes, and he would reply jokingly that God would now strike down the nuptial pair for their hypocrisy and self-deception, and could never understand why this always made her refuse to have sex with him later.

If Greg's objection to marriage had been political instead of personal, if he had been eschewing the institutionalization of love or asserting that he and Caroline needed no forms, no ceremony, no official stamp for their commitment, she would – outwardly, at least – have accepted his stance more gracefully and perhaps even admired it. But Greg's objection was merely an unusual display of honesty. It came from a belief to which he still subscribed, although academically now, that marriage is an act of gross hypocrisy because no one, except perhaps the sincerely religious, really aspires to monogamy or considers it a viable way of life. At the time when it seemed to matter to Caroline, if only because she was nearing thirty and craved a ring

46

and a big day and was afraid of losing him, Greg had certainly had no intention of confining his adventures to her for the rest of his life; he would not have dreamed of making such a rash and impossible promise in private, never mind in front of her entire family and the Lord of Hosts who, whatever you thought of him, would have to be present in the trappings and would not, if he existed, care to be mocked with such deliberate insincerity. He experienced the same incredulity at every wedding he observed, always had. Did they really believe they meant what they were saying? Had they even read the words properly? Look how young they were! Did the bridegroom really believe that in five, ten, fifteen, maybe two years, she will be the only woman he ever wants to be in? For the rest of his *life*? When the novelty and the chemistry have faded, when they're constantly tired and preoccupied and find themselves arguing over who gets to lie down this time, when she's only prepared to entertain two positions, three if she's really drunk or pregnant, and she hasn't gone down on him for years and the thrill of the chase, which is at least half of it, is so long forgotten it seems like someone else's life, does he really believe then that he'll stick to his promise to keep himself only unto her? Because if he does, he's a naive idiot, and if he doesn't and promises it anyway, he's a liar. However much he loves her.

Greg would not have described himself as an honourable man; he did possess at least that much self-awareness. He knew that he was not the sort of man who would hand in a wallet full of notes found in the street; he would not, in the event of a transport disaster, pause to save a stranger before himself; he had never been sufficiently moved by any cause to take the kind of action that required effort, though he sometimes signed petitions against the closure of various wards of the local hospital if the woman brought them to the door and didn't expect him to find his own pen. He would never be remembered as a man of principle, and he was OK with that, on the whole. But he did feel that there was something distinctly unadmirable about making promises you were fairly sure you'd never be able to keep, and he did try to avoid it with the people he cared about. Marriage was too final, too end-stopped; it was too frightening to look down the years and see all those branch lines barriered off for good. Caroline, who had a working knowledge of basic psychology, after a time had given the appearance of accepting his reservations and stopped hinting. It worked. Twelve years on, there was no ring, and he was still there.

'For Christ's sake.' He shut down his Internet connection, dialled Patrick's office on the landline and with a look of defiance clicked it to speakerphone. 'Heather? It's Greg, is Pat there?'

'He's in a meeting. And he hasn't heard anything.' Patrick's assistant audibly flinched.

'No, I appreciate that, it's about something else.'

She hesitated, doubtful. There was nothing else.

'I'll see if he's finished.'

'Cheers, love.'

Caroline made a face and folded her arms across her chest, but she didn't move. He picked up the incriminating garment and examined the label.

'I haven't heard, Greg,' said Patrick's voice, with the cricket clearly audible behind it. 'I'll call the minute I do, I've told you, you've got to relax until then. And send Heather some flowers or something, for God's sake, you made her cry on Tuesday.'

'Sorry. I think I've got some of your wife's underwear.'

'If one more person tells me that today. Did you actually want something?'

'Yes. I'm serious, I really did find – rather, *Caroline* found' – he fixed his eyes on her – 'this kind of black top thing with lace . . . bits, in my suitcase, I must have picked it up by mistake. Is it Ashana's?'

'I'm not au fait with the full inventory of her wardrobe off the top of my head. It's plausible. She has a lot of black things.'

'Off your laundry pile. Made by a Donna Karan of New York, apparently.'

'I'll check. Was there anything else?'

'No, I just thought I should tell you I took your wife's underwear home by mistake, and it *was* a mistake so please pass on my apologies, next time I'll ask. I was just hoping you'd confirm because Caroline seems to think it belongs to a hooker or something.'

'Ash will be pleased to think that her underwear looks like it might belong to a hooker. Sorry, I've got to go, Greg, my other line's going.'

'Score?'

'Three hundred and eighty for three.'

'Makes you sick.'

'Doesn't it. I'll call you when I hear. Cheers now.'

The dial tone flatly droned like a heart monitor. Greg allowed himself a small smile, then turned to Caroline and held out the top, all pleasantness.

'Might be a nice gesture if you washed that for Ashana before we give it back to her, to thank them for their hospitality.'

He put the radio back on; Caroline moved to turn it off, snatched the top from his hand and flung it down again.

'Did you enjoy that?'

'You do it to yourself.'

'It's not as if I don't have good reason.'

Greg stopped, pre-empted. There was the endgame. There was no comeback to that; it meant that all such arguments were already determined, and he had lost. She didn't even have to mention the specifics any more, it was so well rehearsed, so much a part of the fabric of any conflict between them that he would capitulate before she could say 'Paula', as if preventing her from speaking the word might compress the blame, stop it escaping.

In practice, his resistance to the actual moment of marriage had availed him little; he had realized, over the years, that he was expected to conform to the same standards as any legally defined husband and was subject to the same laws and judgments despite his marked refusal to parrot them for a priest. He even referred to her as 'my wife', because he was too old to say 'girlfriend', and he'd tried 'partner' on occasion but had felt compelled to clarify immediately that his partner was a woman (it was potentially ambiguous), so effectively he'd been cornered. But he had never officially promised to be sexually continent, that was simply her assumption about how things should be. About the nature of their roles. Fulfilling your role correctly; that was important to Caroline. In twelve years he had been unfaithful to her on six discrete occasions, five of which were one-off incidents and were the ones she didn't know about.

The one she had uncovered, to which she referred scathingly as his 'affair', had occurred five years ago, after the final series of *Valley Vets*, during a three-month touring production of *The Crucible*, with a twenty-five-year-old called Paula Jackman who understudied Mary Warren to his John Proctor. Paula Jackman – Jack*son*, was it? – he couldn't remember, if he had ever known – was a moderately attractive girl who had no confidence at all in her looks and an entirely misplaced confidence in her acting talent, and plaintively blamed her failure to get better parts on this unjust distribution of gifts by nature, when the most cursory self-examination should, Greg felt, have con-

49

vinced her to reverse the equation. He had not set out to seduce her – outside the act itself, and sometimes even during it, he found her company chafing – but she opened up so eagerly to a patient ear and a flattering word, and they had been daily thrown into each other's company for those months, during which he drank determinedly and saw Caroline once a week, if that, that it had been a much needed fillip to his confidence, bruised and tender as a discarded fruit after the BBC's remorseless axing of Doctor Jeremy and his colleagues.

But he would never have called it an affair. Paula at least gave the appearance of being attracted to him, and responded to him in bed as Caroline had not for years, but at no point was she ever a threat to Caroline, and this was the aspect that had proved difficult to explain convincingly, both in the immediate aftermath, when Paula failed to get the message and repeatedly phoned the house for weeks, so that eventually they had had to have the number changed, and thereafter. He had not had one conversation with Paula that had not been about the play and hadn't featured her whining about the rest of the cast while he nodded in sympathetic boredom. He had hurried away from any chance to spend time with her clothed; he had not given her a second thought when she was not immediately in front of or underneath him. He had felt nothing for her beyond pity and a slight disdain. His affection for Caroline had not flickered – if anything, the experience had imparted a greater tenderness towards her for being, by contrast, so sane and manageable. Paula was a brief sexual diversion whose indulgence had not been worth the recrimination that piled up afterwards, but such Ciceronian arguments had not worked in his favour, and Caroline still considered herself in credit.

They had not always been like this. Caroline at twenty-eight, when they first met, had struck him as exciting and compelling; electric-thin, a whir of restless energy and plans, with her strange nocturnal life and cross-section of friends from the most unlikely strata of society – the Jamaican blues band from Dalston, the trippy performance poets from Stoke Newington, the silky auction-house PRs from the King's Road. She had taken him on tours of a London he would never have uncovered on his own and he had been happy to follow, barely able to chisel a word in at the edges of her monologues. Then, she had been teaching art as charity to disadvantaged kids at a Streatham community centre, and on alternate days threading her way up the black cable of the Northern Line to the Edgware studio she shared with other members of her unspecific commune of painters and drifters, where she worked through the night on her six-by-eight canvases of lurid gardens, some of which had been exhibited in a friend's workshop to a small amount of interest. Someone from a printing company with offices in the Euston Road had talked about commissioning one for their foyer, but in the end nothing had come of it. They had never really been his thing, her paintings, though he wouldn't have said so and had gratefully accepted one to mark their first Christmas together, but he was not sorry when her faith in her own work began to ebb and she no longer wanted them up around the house, reminders of unfulfilled promise.

He had not intended to make his life with her, but neither had he especially fought it. His mother had at first disliked her, finding her too pushy, with too much of the small person's compulsion to make their presence seem bigger, but somehow Greg had continued and at each point where he thought he might reasonably express a reservation or announce an intention of moving on, it had always seemed inopportune; an unconnected event had upset her that he couldn't add to, or he simply didn't have the energy, until eventually he found he had become used to the arrangement, because after a while the thing becomes self-defining. What you have in common is each other and the structure you create, the albums of holiday photos you accumulate along the way, gathering dust.

Two years later, there was Daisy, who was not unplanned, he believed, although despite Caroline's insistence on her version of history he could not to this day remember ever having had any conversation leading to an unequivocal decision to have a child. But that had seemed to settle it. She didn't return to the community project after the birth – it was too tiring – and seemed relieved to have a valid excuse to give up her own painting, though Greg had tried to convince her otherwise because he thought he ought to. Instead she regrouped her energies and hurled them at the creation of a flawless home for him and Daisy, just as the first series of *Valley Vets* was cast and he was sent to Wales for six weeks of filming, which was where he had committed the first of his six infidelities.

Daisy had entirely usurped London in Caroline's affections. The sprawling colourful mass of history and architecture and mayhem that had been the backdrop of her life and her art through her twenties and whose febrile energy was second only to her own, suddenly appeared to her in riveting and horrifying close-up; she saw smoke, traffic, dogshit, muggers, litter, rats, shattered glass, needles, the IRA, black puddles with a diesel skin, shuttered shopfronts with explicit graffiti and old people shoved aside by youths in a hurry. She passed the local primary school at the end of their road in Kennington each day when she walked Daisy to the park, and stopped to watch the children scattering in their concrete yard behind high chicken-wire fencing. She thought they looked sad, these London children, straggly and diminished somehow. They reminded her of the animals at the Vauxhall City Farm; soiled, stoop-shouldered animals, bowed by an environment that nature had never meant them for and the filth it blew in. She feared for her pristine child.

They had moved to King's Lynn when Daisy was two and Caroline's mother was taken into the home outside Norwich. Greg had been passive throughout; his unvoiced reluctance to leave London for a remote and stolid market town where he knew no one except Caroline's sister Andrea and her oh-so-Liberal-Democrat husband Philip was counterbalanced by the gathering success of *Valley Vets* and the knowledge that he could contrive to be away for significant stretches of days and weeks if he wanted. London was still there. She had enlisted Andrea to look at houses with her and, when the appropriate one was chosen, he had been summoned to view it and had pronounced it to be very nice, which was all he was ever expected to say. His approval was not required.

The house had five bedrooms, a big tiled kitchen and a sloping garden bordered with conifers from which you could hear the sea and the echoes of gulls. It was meant to allow them plenty of room for Daisy and the other child, the unfinished child, who, as it turned out, hadn't needed the extra room. The little bedroom next to Daisy's which, over the years, had incrementally and without being discussed turned into a store room, full of boxes and old photo albums and toys Daisy had grown out of but which Caroline couldn't bear to give to Oxfam, yet which remained somehow hallowed ground, a memorial to a life that never happened.

Something had splintered between them in the aftermath. They had become separate people, a gulf of understanding away from one another. No matter how he tried – and he *had* tried, with a measure of desperation not experienced before – he could not grieve for this child as she wanted him to, in a way that made it seem real. This child, lost at eleven weeks, who had not even survived for long enough to be immortalized in the deep-space blues and blacks of a sonographer's still, had never really had form or substance for him; he grieved the idea as he had celebrated it – in the abstract. But she grieved for it as a mother, cramped and bleeding in a hospital gown, zipping herself inside her pain with her back to him. He had cried too, but partly – and he despised himself for this – because he wasn't an altogether untalented actor and he knew he should, and it reminded him at the time of coerced apologies as a small boy, when his mother would insist that he say sorry *as if you mean it*, which, looking back, was an extraordinary thing to encourage in a child. Caroline had not been convinced that he did mean it.

She was different afterwards; smaller in stature. Less defiant, less determined to make the world take notice of her. They could have tried again but she shied away from talking about it, as if it could no longer be a possibility. For over a year they didn't have sex, and Greg felt she was blaming him, as if some deficiency of his, some corruption in his body, had condemned the child. He would attempt the odd tentative sortie across the acres of mattress between them and each time would be impatiently shrugged away, not with lack of interest but with active revulsion. As a sublimatory activity Greg took up sailing, and over the next couple of years accomplished the second, third and fourth of his one-night stands. When Daisy started school, Caroline took a part-time job teaching art at the college of further education and they talked half-heartedly about a trial separation, although they both knew they didn't mean it. Greg had suggested attending a relationship therapist or even a doctor to deal with her hang-ups and had gone so far as to compile a list of useful numbers, knowing she would endure almost any shame rather than discuss her sex life with a medic; predictably she had endeavoured to make an effort, so that they now had sex on average once every couple of months, perhaps a little more if he was lucky. During those occasions he was almost always on top, because that didn't require her to make any show of active involvement; he would feel her gritted against him, face turned to the side, mentally pushing him away, her mouth pressed white and eyes closed not in transport but in endurance. Sometimes she even said things like 'hurry up' or 'have you finished?' aloud. At first it had hurt him, such undisguised aversion, but over the years the rejection had warped, as these things do, into a kind of perverse pleasure in her reluctance, her total absence of enjoyment. He never used force, but he often fantasized that he did; it was the only way to redeem it.

A lot of men would have left long before, he often told himself. Privately he thought himself almost heroically patient. But it was the anti-logic of her inverse equation that he found so difficult; the less interest she had in him physically, the more fearful she seemed to become that he would find someone else for that purpose. In every way he was the loser; he had a wife – non-wife, even, same difference – who chose not to enjoy sex with him but still demanded unswerving fidelity. In whose world could that possibly be fair? He still loved her, of course, in an almost mandatory way, and he conceded that there was a comfort in feeling that he was known, if not understood. In truth, though, Caroline probably did understand him as well as anyone ever would; he was not the bottomless enigma of unplumbed depths that he liked to imagine. She was no longer interested in him, except in so far as he fulfilled the roles that enabled her to fulfil hers: partner, father, all defined by their proximity to one another. But she was no longer interested in *him*. There were moments, afternoons usually, as he was trying to work on the comedy drama series he was writing, and therefore casting his mind instead over everything except that, when he would catch himself idly wondering what would happen to him if he lost her; to a reckless driver, perhaps, or a subversive undetected lump, such as had happened to the wife of Dick Carey, the writer of *Valley Vets*, who was now bringing up his two sons alone. Greg didn't really have the will to stretch his imagination that far, except that he did notice how he always framed the thought to himself: what would happen to *him*? But he would have liked her to want him again; it might have given him some hope.

'It's just – you know what life is like when you're doing a play, Greg. Everything's upended – you become a different person. You know you do. You start acting like you're eighteen or something. The way you drink, for a start. It's hard for Daisy when she doesn't know what kind of mood you'll be in.'

'I won't be drinking in front of Daisy.'

'That's right, you'll be in some bar in London every night.'

'Caro.' Greg knew how to defuse these outbursts, but it tired him to have to do it so frequently. He took her by the shoulders, bending to rest his chin on the top of her head, and felt a minute relaxing of the sinews at the side of her neck. 'Come on. I'm an actor. This isn't a new thing. You're the one who wants me to be something different.'

'No, I don't. It's just that it always has to be so far away.'

'Well, for some reason Freddie Zamora can't see the commercial potential in putting his play on at the King's Lynn Corn Exchange. Don't expect me to aim low just because –'

'Because what?'

'Nothing.'

'I don't know why Patrick doesn't try to get you more television work. Then you wouldn't have to be away for so long.'

'Because it doesn't just happen like that. And we're talking about a play in the *West End*! With Barbara *Bathurst*! It's the best chance I've had in, what, three years, and you can't even let me get excited about it. But that's not the point, is it? If I do or I don't get this part we'll have the same arguments about the next one until I settle for some mediocre old crap that's right on the doorstep. You can't have everything, Caro. You can't have my whole life in your pocket. If you wanted a bloke who comes home at five every night you should have married someone else –'

Her face narrowed; he drew breath to say sorry, but she closed the door.

It was his fault. All she wanted was a self-contained life built around her family in her undisturbed town; she was forty and she wanted quietness, she wanted someone who wanted the same things she wanted. And what she wanted, he felt, was to live like Ken and Barbie, in a world of objects with both of them vacuum-moulded smooth and featureless below the waist, a world from which desires – specifically his desires – had been expunged, excepting the desire to continue the status quo. At the root of all the discord, the small irritations, the criticisms that began with him never hanging up wet towels or putting the lid back on the Marmite and led to him never saying or doing anything the way she would have liked him to without being reminded, was her fear that his desires and hers no longer matched, and that his might eventually lead him away. She sensed that he was still on occasion looking past her, optimistically over her shoulder at a brighter prospect.

Caroline was right; he did become someone else when he was working, an approximation of the person he had been when they met, whom she had once liked but had grown out of, and who had been buried somewhere along the way beneath layers of domestic expectation, though he was no longer sure if this alternative self was real and just submerged, or a nostalgic illusion that he still strained after. He no longer really expected anything much to happen in his life, and the more entrenched this belief became, the more restless he felt, the greater the desperation to seek out some new adventure, something unexpected, even if he had to manufacture it. When he dared look ahead, he saw himself growing older with Caroline through the repeating days as his daughter moved away to a university town that was brighter and unfamiliar, to weekend visits and backpacking and friends he didn't like, and he and Caroline would be left without the one thing they still had in common, left with only each other to look at. He saw too that there were worse futures than this, but the day he accepted it would be the day he began to fade towards the end of everything, not in rosy twilit affection but with bitterness and cursing and so very many things left undone.

He was an actor. He needed to be someone else from time to time; without that, he was not sure what would be left of him.

Five days after Greg's audition, at 6.30 in the evening, Sally McGinley squeezed into the window table at BarCelona! on the corner of Cathedral Street, lit a cigarette and examined the outline of her face against the black window while she waited for Lola to return with the drinks. In this backlit half-reflection she was all angles and shadows, suggestions of edges out of the darkness like a Julia Margaret Cameron portrait, and she wished someone were there to take her photograph like that. She looked unusually photogenic, she thought. Inevitably, when the photographer came to take their portraits for the programme, the light would be morning-flat and her face would be full of dark shadows, but this time from drink and insomnia; that was the way these things worked. The table was made of metal, a kind of bruised-steel effect, set with oversize rivets along its edge, and was cold under her forearms when she leaned forward.

Sally disliked BarCelona!, with its tapas and the forced hilarity of its needless exclamation point. BarCelona! was a default choice, the only immediate alternative to the strip of riverfront tourist pubs refurbished with 'Olde' in their names to catch the coachloads of globetrotters. The closure of the George the year before had affected them like the end of a relationship; one that was stale and tired and unsatisfying on both sides, but in which you take for granted the extent to which you are accommodated and miss only when you are obliged to learn these patterns again somewhere new. The George could uncontroversially be described as terrible in almost every criterion that mattered to a pub: hygiene, decor, atmosphere, clientele, toilets, drink, food (especially the food). But it had grown into a kind of home; not merely the set, where the bloodstain and missing chunk of plaster behind the hatstand told stories now passed into legend, but the extras too, the straggle of day drinkers without gainful employment hunched around the gouged pool table, watching the shifting constellations of the balls and offering advice to those flush enough to have their twenty pees stacked along the table edge, cigarettes burning down in their mouth as they played for honour and the right to stay on. Sally could beat most of the stubbled regulars, a triumph of which she was not especially proud; inexplicably, her co-ordination improved with drink.

No one had cared to preserve the George; it had outstayed its welcome in an area rising in inverse proportion to the pub's stagnation, until its regulars were no longer its locals, and its transient locals demanded international coffee chains with logos they recognized and pubs serving authentic Elizabethan fries and pressurized beer, so that when the Food Standards Agency finally closed it down (so the rumour went) and the landlord sold up for the sake of his health (and, by extension, that of his customers), no one had really been sorry except the handful of elderly characters to whom it had been a community, of sorts, who would never be admitted to any of the borough's cleaner establishments, and would therefore have to choose between death's ante-chamber, the Community Centre Senior's Club (sic), or plastic cider bottles on a bench by the river. These, and the founders of Avocet Productions and their several hangers-on, who had done some of their best thinking around the George's fibreglass log fire.

Lola set down two large glasses of red wine and tugged at her top. 'They should introduce a congestion charge in this bar.'

Sally frowned. 'Bottle?'

'Can't stay. I'm having dinner with one of the backers.'

'Something wrong?'

It was not impossible, even at this late stage, that the promised funding would fail to materialize and the play would have to be pulled. It was Lola's role to anticipate this and take pre-emptive measures; Sally preferred not to contemplate potential disaster and instead pretend everything was and always would be going swimmingly.

'Not as far as I know. But you have to keep them sweet, you know. Especially in the current climate, everyone's nervous about the takings.'

'Hence the top.'

'Hence the top.'

Lola peered at her reflection and worried at the material across her shoulders.

'Too tight, isn't it? I look fat.'

'You look lovely. Is it Lars?'

Lola nodded.

Sally began humming 'Tomorrow Belongs to Me' from *Cabaret*; Lola smiled without depth, in a way that suggested she was tolerating a joke long past its usefulness.

Lars Faldbakken was the eccentric heir to a Norwegian art fortune, possibly in his sixties but equally possibly considerably older, with a great deal of money to scatter on capricious projects and a devotion bordering on obsessive-compulsive to acquiring memorabilia pertaining to the Norwegian National Socialists and the writer Knut Hamsun; he had recently outbid the University of Arizona for a recently discovered cache of letters and notebooks, and had decided, whimsically, to give Lola fifty thousand towards putting on the play because she had told him in her most coquettish manner that she thought Hamsun had been misunderstood by history.

'He was a fucking Nazi!' Sally had said, when Lola related this.

'He wasn't literally a Nazi.'

'What's *literally*, in your book? The Norwegian National Socialists, do they not count? Is that what you meant by *misunderstood*? What, you think he just liked the funny walk?'

'Sal, he's giving us fifty grand.'

'Well, because you told him you don't believe his idol was a Nazi. You're taking blood money from the sympathizer of a sympathizer.'

'He just likes Hamsun's writing, OK? You've read Nietzsche.

Allegedly.'

'Totally different.'

'He's not demanding we put swastikas on the programmes. It's nearly a quarter of our budget.'

'You're *Jewish*! What would your father say?'

'He's not observant. Neither am I. It's irrelevant.'

'Ah, but history is history.'

It was a measure of Lola's open nature, her willingness to see people as they chose to present themselves, that she could never really tell when Sally was joking; thereafter she had gone out of her way to reassure everyone that Lars gave a considerable percentage of his income to charities and was in all important ways an admirable human being. Whenever a potential difficulty with the finances occurred, Sally would slip in a comment about having to look for a final solution, while Lola frowned and fretted that Sally might be overcome with sudden political righteousness and withdraw her support in a grand gesture or, worse, offend Lars Faldbakken to the point that he did.

'So,' said Lola, propping her chin on her clasped hands, 'are you pleased, then?'

'That you're spending the evening with Lars? I'm pleased I don't have to.'

'Pleased with the decision. About Greg.'

Sally jutted her shoulders.

'Course. I told you, I think it was the right choice. But it's not really of any consequence what I think. In the end, Freddie has to work with them. Why do you keep asking?'

'Oh, nothing.'

'*What?*'

'Thought there was a bit of chemistry, that's all.'

Sally rotated the glass with both hands.

'Well, chemistry's important in a play.'

'Between the actors, generally, though.'

'Has he met Barbara?'

'Not yet. They'll be good together. She can create chemistry with anyone. Don't dodge the question.'

There was a smoky pause. After-work people passed the window, upright and hurried as if speeded up, on their way to London Bridge station.

'Why do you say there was chemistry?'

'You were rude to him. That's how I always know.'

'Come on. I'm rude to everyone. It's pathological. Because I have no patience. I'm the rudest person I know. I'm rude to you, I'm rude to Rhys –'

'Yes, but – we give you reason. This was just – you trying to hide the chemistry. I was afraid you might get some weird thing about him because he's playing your dad.'

Sally laid her hands flat on the table as if pressing down a rising impatience.

'How many times – Allan is not my dad. He's a character who is based on some aspects of an actual person but doctored by fiction. That's what drama is, Lo. Credit other people with some imagination.'

'If you say so. But would you want your dad to see it?'

'That question's academic, as you know.'

'OK. Anyway, he's married. Greg Burns. Doctor Jeremy.'

'Is he?'

'Well, not *actually* married. But he's got a kid.'

'So we know everything works.'

'I'm just letting you know. Though it's never stopped you before.'

'That sounded very judgemental.'

'It was meant to be a joke. Although it's the truth.'

'You need to flag your jokes up a bit more. I can't tell them apart from your moralizing. Do a funny face with them or something.'

If Sally had been asked to articulate the truth of her own sexual morals she might have agreed with Knut Hamsun, who in 1889 wrote, 'Truth is neither objectivity nor the balanced view; truth is a selfless subjectivity.' Except that she would not have used the word 'selfless'; that, given the impossibility of the concept, she would have put down to the former Nazi sympathizer's trying to be clever. But she would have concurred that there are no absolutes in human relationships, which is simply another way of saying *all's fair*.

She had had brief interludes with married men in the past, which might lead more objective-minded people to conclude that she was without conscience on the matter, but Sally would counter that *she* had never in her life cheated on anyone who trusted her, nor had she ever had an affair in which she was the one doing the deceiving. That, in her view, made all the difference. She did not like lying to people; it was serpentine and, more importantly, she was not good at it. Her philosophy was this: if you love someone, stay with them and be faithful; when you stop loving them, leave before you need to start lying. In that regard, things were drawn in black and white. She was still young enough to believe that love was all or nothing, that it should always seem like an adventure, otherwise what was the point, and fortunate enough in her job and her circle of friends regularly to meet people who were both attractive and interesting, on top of which she was a writer and so in many ways more at home in her own company, so that she had never, in twenty-nine years, felt obliged artificially to prolong the life of any relationship that had slipped into a persistent vegetative state. She didn't really comprehend the function of affairs, because she didn't understand the related ideologies of commitment and compromise.

'I suppose he's quite cute.' Lola put down her empty glass.

'He's OK. Eyes too close together.'

'All his own hair, though.'

'He's only forty-four.'

'Hey, maybe he's the one in the cards.'

Sally made a face.

'My little faith in the workings of the cards is falling into negative equity. Still got another six months, though, before I can get my refund.'

'It would be a disaster, though,' Lola said, as if, joking aside, she was now giving it serious consideration. 'You and him.'

'Why?'

'Your job is making up conversations between imaginary people and his is pretending to be someone else. Neither of you have the first idea about the real world.'

Sally nodded slowly.

'Right. Must be a great relief to you that your job makes you so grounded. All that hand-carved furniture you make. When you're not strapping your horses to the plough –'

'You may take the piss, but you don't know what I do. I spend hours of every day in meetings with money people while you sit in cafés smoking yourself blind and Freddie loafs around watching European films for "research"' – here she did the rabbit ears of irony in the air – 'and the reason we can just about afford to bring those elements together and put them on a stage is because I've had to devote many evenings like this one to having the arse bored off me by some old lech with a fat wallet, so don't waste your sarcasm on me. It doesn't get more real than money.'

Sally conceded the truth of this, and emptied her glass. If she was ever asked by those same moral fundamentalists whether she didn't stop to feel bad about the cuckolded wife, about her feelings or dignity, Sally would reply, simply, *no*, with genuine surprise that it had ever been presumed that she would or should. The key was this: betrayal was bad, unquestionably, but you couldn't betray someone to whom you had no responsibility. Besides, no one owns anyone. People lend themselves to you for as long as they choose, but surely no one really believes that a person can be stolen. Nothing is permanent. That was her father's legacy to her, anyway.

'You're right. I couldn't whore myself for art like you do.'

'Truthfully, Sal, you really couldn't. You couldn't charm fifty pee out of Bono to pay your debts. You don't know how to fake interest in someone. Anyway,' – she patted her hair in a show of winsomeness – 'I'm more of a geisha than a whore. My job is to listen and laugh at their jokes and make them feel appreciated. Do you think I wouldn't rather sit here and get pissed with you? Well, not here, maybe. But instead I've got to go and be excessively nice to a –'

'Quisling. You can say it.'

'To a lonely old man who knows that people only pretend to want his company because he's rich. Because I care about your crappy play. So piss off and get me another drink.'

'Does he try it on?'

'Lars? He's been impotent for twenty years, apparently.'

'That's what he told you.'

'He seems quite proud of it.'

'If he asked you to put on an SS uniform, would you do it for my play?'

'Don't push it.'

Sally scraped her chair back, unhooked the threads of her jumper from a rivet and picked her way to the bar. When she came back, Lola said, 'Do you ever think about that Tarot woman you saw?'

'It's not a big part of my life.'

'But when you meet people. You must have it in the back of your mind, I know I would.'

'I treat it with the indulgent amusement it deserves.'

'I bet you don't.'

'Why are you asking me this?'

'I ran into James the other day. He still doesn't really understand why you dumped him.'

'Because I was bored.'

'But you're not prepared to stick at anything. That's why I wish you'd never gone to a fortune-teller with a question like that. It's not going to help you.'

'Why not?'

'Because you already go into everything with one eye on the door anyway. And now you believe this fictional soulmate is out there, on his way – and don't tell me you don't believe it, because you make yourself out to be such a sceptic but you'd secretly really like to think there's some kind of plan at work – so now you have an excuse to run away the minute you're bored. And what you haven't grasped is that it's never going to just happen like that. Sometimes you have to compromise. You have to make a choice that it's this rather than something else.'

Lola nodded a full stop, implied there was more to follow, then drained her glass instead.

'I'm no good at compromise. It's got to be all or nothing.'

'Then you're never going to be happy. You're just going to keep chasing after some kind of, what do you call it –'

'Chimera.'

'Thank you, yes. Because with you it really is the travelling rather than the arriving, isn't it?'

'Now you're my shrink?'

'You're always complaining that things don't work out for you. I'm just trying to show you why.'

Sally shook her head.

'You may consider this anti-realist, but you have to keep looking for that indefinable – you know. The spark. Without it, I may as well go out with Rhys.'

'The spark is an illusion.'

'Don't tell me that, I'll never have the motivation to get out of bed. Or into bed.'

'Listen for once. If you ever really met your mythical soulmate you'd be horrified, because it would mean you then had to go through the rest of life without the *possibility* of meeting him, and it's the possibility that's your buzz. Imagine if you had to go up to Edinburgh in the summer without any chance of some adventure.'

Sally bristled at the unarguable accuracy of this. Since leaving college she had worked sporadically writing plays for Deus Ex Machina, a small fringe theatre company based at the Battersea Arts Centre and run by two earnest lesbians from the Low Countries. Mostly they produced, with a minimum of Arts Council funding, what Sally cringed to call 'performance art'; their most widely noticed piece (in the sense that it had two press reviews and an audience of more than seven) had been *She!*, a show that involved three female performers undressing, stepping into a functioning shower cubicle while apparently menstruating, towelling down and dressing again in a perpetual rotational sequence (there had been some dialogue, but no one could remember much about it). Nicholas de Jongh in the *Evening Standard* had described it as 'absurd'; Sally did not think he meant in the Ionesco sense. Hearing that Sally sometimes worked with Deus, people occasionally put two and two together and assumed that she had written *She!*, whereupon she would be compelled to make quite clear that if she were ever to dream up anything even vaguely in the same league as *She!* it would only be as a suicide note.

Every summer, presumably for the novelty value, she was commissioned to write a one-hour, more traditional play for the whole group which they took to a moderate-sized venue at the Edinburgh Fringe, in return for which she received a nominal fee and her board and lodging for the month of the Festival. What she wrote for Deus usually began life in her usual style, as straightforward black comedies, and in the directors' hands would end up with enough inexcusable gimmickry (mime, nudity, animals) to affect avant-garde where there was none, but the members of Deus were all whole-hearted enthusiasts and for Sally it meant a subsidized month of licensed chaos – even if Rhys now referred to all their work as 'period drama'.

In a sense, Sally's year drifted in a melancholy state of limbo from the end of one August to the beginning of the next, and had done since she first visited the Festival as a student. Each year she was mesmerized, enraptured, transported by it; the carnivalesque colours, the music, people, noise, fireworks and visceral celebration that overturned the city. It was a month-long coup by the Lord of Misrule, exemplified by the havoc played with the licensing laws. A tear occurred in the painted backcloth that separates the real world from whatever lies behind it, and fantastical, magical creatures came spilling out into the city's granite streets. You could walk up the Royal Mile in blank daylight and find yourself accosted by clowns, dragons, dwarfs, mummers, jesters in full tinkling motley, jugglers and fire-eaters, drag queens, ballerinas and harlequins, Hamlets and Othellos and Duchesses of Malfi, children with painted tiger faces, witches and wheelchair *a cappella* groups, all thrusting leaflets at you, all inviting you into their shimmering worlds. Best of all, Sally felt, night and day became indistinct; you could have an E and absinthe for breakfast if you chose, and blunder through the day in a liquefying mirage of near-sexual affection for everything, and nobody thought you were at all unusual. The world become spectacle, hedonism, pure theatre. That, she loved.

That, and the fact that the streets and bars were full of beautiful, creative, talented, permissive, artistic, passionate people all wanting to sleep with each other.

'You're wrong. When the right person turns up, it won't feel like a compromise, that's the whole point.'

'You are such a fantasist.' Lola glanced at her watch. 'Oops. I have to get to Langan's, I am going to be so late. And Greg Burns is not the right person, by the way, in case that's what you're thinking.'

'Would you give it a rest with the Greg Burns thing. We barely exchanged two words.'

Lola frowned.

'The trouble is, I can see right through you. Are you going to stay here on your own and drink more?'

'While I'm waiting. Rhys is coming down in a minute. We're going to the piano thing at the Tate with that elk-faced bloke he's seeing, what's his name, the dresser –'

'Brett?'

'Brett, who is less interesting than this beer mat. Then we're going to a party at some club in Fulham that's a promotion for something, I forget what.'

'Rather you than me.' Lola wrestled her way into her coat and buttoned it across her considerable chest. Then she leaned on the back of the chair and looked at Sally. 'Eat some food, then. And make sure Rhys sees you home. Wouldn't kill you to have an early night for once, Sal.'

'See, that's the sort of thing James used to say.'

'That's why he was good for you. See you Sunday.'

'Do give my love to Lars, and raise a glass to the Fatherland.'

Lola failed to understand, Sally thought, as she fought her way to the bar; it was not that the quest was more important than its object, nor just her fear of boredom. The object of the quest was Platonic; reified, it could only ever be flawed. That much was given. But she was not such a perfectionist that she was running away from that. Sally expected people to disappoint her, not because she tired of them, but because, sooner or later, they would show weakness, they would do or say some tiny significant thing that proved you could not lean your full weight on them, and her trust in them would correspondingly recoil. But this did not mean she ever stopped hoping for someone strong enough. A principled man.

'I miss you,' she said suddenly, aloud, without knowing why she'd said it, or to whom.

6

'No – no, this simply won't do,' said the magnificently rich tarry voice of Dame Barbara Bathurst, one of the most distinctive in British theatre, as she carefully folded her script at the present page and levered herself up from the sofa to face Devraj Dutta.

It was the ur-expression for upper-class English understatement, Sally thought, smiling to herself, applied to everything from an undercooked roast to the Holocaust, but only by people like Barbara, who had always comported herself in a way commensurate with her title, long before the government had made it official. What wouldn't do in this instance was Dev's continual and alarming cough, a cough out of place in a boy of twenty, which seemed to ricochet around his thin chest and was severely slowing the progress of the company's first read-through. Even resting, his breathing sounded like a large motorbike idling.

'I expect you smoke a lot of marijuana, do you?' Barbara said, pragmatically.

Dev nodded, too awed for denial.

'And do you mix it with tobacco?'

Dev nodded again.

'Well, you see, there's the answer. That cough's not going anywhere unless you smoke it pure as God intended. It's up to you but we're not going to make any progress while you're hacking away like an old tramp on a park bench. I do insist that while we're here we do our best to concentrate on the job, otherwise we're wasting each other's time, which is simply bad manners.'

Dev looked at his trainers miserably.

'Now – I once had an Albanian taxi driver who told me the most wonderful cure for a cough – you won't believe it but I swear on my mother's grave it works. You need clear honey and freshly ground black pepper, do we have any?'

Lola, clasping her clipboard, glanced anxiously towards the door at the far end of the office that led to the small kitchen area which contained only depleted crates of cheap Chardonnay, as if trying to remember whether she might have picked up such unlikely ingredients on a recent non-existent shopping trip.

'I think probably not.'

'Oh. Well, not to worry – I'll pop down the road and get some.'

'Barbara, I can do that –'

'Nonsense, won't take a minute and I know what I'm looking for.'

Dame Barbara whisked her coat from the stand and disappeared.

'She's not like a film star at all, is she, nart I'm saying?' Dev, suddenly perky, hugged his knees and grinned, then buckled under another bout of coughing.

Sally had not been consulted about the casting of Dev, who was to play Allan Duddy's seventeen-year-old son, Sean. She had assumed that Rhys was jealously guarding the casting fee, but it had crossed her mind that allowing her to feel she had got her own way over the casting of Greg Burns as Allan was a pre-emptive sop. So she had been mildly, but not wholly, surprised the week after Greg's casting to encounter Dev, whose popular soap character Vikram had died a few months earlier as a result of a racially motivated attack and Dev's agent's advice about diversifying. Sally had been at great pains to point out that her concern was simply Dev's lack of formal training and any previous experience of stage acting, which Rhys had chosen to interpret as an implicit accusation of tokenism and quota-filling. Freddie placidly insisted that Dev's urban authenticity was just what the play needed to give it a sense of balance, and Sally knew this was one argument she could never win without exposing herself to all manner of unpleasant suggestions, which was why, the following week, she was perching on the windowsill at the river end of Avocet's office with a copy of her own, much edited script, assessing whether it was necessary to graft on some lines explaining how Greg's son and Barbara's grandson came to be from the subcontinent. She was aware that every time she looked up, she seemed to catch Greg's eye.

Rhys arrived late, fulminating, his black wool coat silvered with rain across the shoulders.

'*Days* of my life I've wasted in that fucking council office queue, while the Pooters of the parking permit department contrive ways of making my life even more difficult with their Byzantine application procedures, which I'm told – finally – are apparently down to *enhanced security measures*.' He shook his umbrella murderously, as if in the face of a local government employee. 'I mean, for Christ's sake, has the world gone *insane*? What – do they think Osama is going to apply to Camden Council for a permit before he parks his white van full of explosives? I could *weep*. Was that Barbara I saw walking down the road? Has someone upset her?'

'She's gone to buy honey and black pepper.'

'For the love of God. Is this more of her Ayurvedic quackery? The woman's a macrobiotic zealot.'

'It's for Dev's cough.'

'Has she never heard of Boots?'

'My granny in Derry used to put a spider in a brown paper bag and tie it round her children's necks when they had a cough,' Sally said.

Rhys wrinkled his nose. 'How fortunate, then, that we did colonize that benighted country with our advanced medical science, angel. Now, what have I missed?'

Freddie smiled his calming smile. 'We're at act one, scene five. Everyone's doing really well, considering it's the first go. I think things are really falling into place. Dev's been wonderful.'

'Ah, I fucked it up, man. But, you know, I never –'

'Hey, you're doing great,' Greg said, sitting suddenly forward and slapping Dev between the shoulderblades, jump-starting another Olympian cough. 'You've even learned your lines already, that's really professional. Better than Barbara, eh? She's still reading it off the script.' He nudged Dev gently, as if this were a little secret observation available only to the two of them. Dev looked up at him and smiled gratefully.

'I was a bit freaked out by her being a film star and that. Not by you, man, you're all right. But, you know, she's like – *proper*.' Dev leaned towards Greg confidentially.

Sally caught Greg glancing across at her and bit down a smile.

'I know what you mean,' Greg said. 'But listen, if it's any consolation, you got higher ratings as Vikram than anything she or I have ever done on telly. So in a sense you're more famous.'

Dev straightened to take this in.

'No fuckin' *way*! You reckon? Shit. Cheers, man.'

He gave a little unconscious strut from the neck up. Sally, watching this exchange, was impressed by Greg. That was a nice thing to have done. She threw him a quick smile as Rhys crouched beside her.

'And you – what's happening here? Don't over-complicate everything, Sal – just give him an Indian mother, it only needs a couple of lines, it's not as if she's appearing.'

'That's right, Rhys, if you want it to be really simplistic. Forget the finer shades of character, eh?'

'I do hope you're not planning to make a meal of this from now until the opening night, or I might have to rethink whether it's helpful for you to be at rehearsals.'

Sally, with great self-discipline, allowed this to pass.

'I was thinking maybe we should change his name,' she said, in a low voice.

'What, you think he should be called Sanjay or Salman so the audience are quite clear that we've noticed he's *ethnic*? Do you think it's asking too great a suspension of disbelief that an Asian man might be called Sean?'

'Don't start that thing, Rhys.'

'What *thing* is that?'

'The thing where you act as if you're the only one who can empathize with the marginalized.'

'Come on now, guys,' said Freddie. 'He's got an Irish father, an Indian mother, they live in London, he's called Sean. None of that needs lengthy explanation, not these days.'

'Am I supposed to be Irish?' said Greg, alarmed.

'Yes,' said Sally.

'No,' said Freddie, at the same time. 'My mistake.'

'I can do Irish,' Greg said.

'Bangladeshi,' said Dev.

'What?'

'My mum's Bangladeshi. My dad's Indian.'

There was a silence while everyone looked on encouragingly, then Freddie said, 'Great! Bangladeshi it is, then.'

'Sorry – can I – Dev, I don't want to seem, but – do you think he'd be called Sean, is that realistic?'

Dev looked at Sally and shrugged. 'I've got a mate called Sean, yeah.'

'And where's he from?'

'Leyton.'

The buzzer drilled an intervention and Barbara entered, barely out of breath from the stairs, with a Costcutter carrier bag.

'Miles, I had to walk, I don't know how you manage. Now then – have a spoonful of that with the pepper ground on top, no – more than that, lots and lots, until you can't see the honey. It's vile but it's like motor oil on your chest.' Halfway through hanging up her coat, she half turned to Greg and said in her magnificently rich tarry voice, as if the reading had never been interrupted (and entirely without reference to the page), '"Your trouble, Allan, is that you've never truly understood that there's a world beyond your own head."'

~·◦·~

Greg's first thought on being introduced to Barbara Bathurst was that no theatre audience would ever in a million years accept that she was his mother, not because she looked especially young for her age, but because he felt that, in comparison, he was looking especially old.

'Barbara – hello – it's really an honour to meet you. I'm Allan, by the way, I play Greg. Your son. No – other way round. Sorry. No, but it's really, I can't tell you, great, to be working with you, because I've always admired your work and I'll never forget you in' – his mind spasmed and blanked – 'you know, with Alec Guinness, *Sir* Alec Guinness, I should say – anyway, it's one of the really great British films, is that. So – it's really – an honour, is what I'm saying.'

'Well, thank you, Greg, that's awfully kind,' she said, clasping his hand warmly between both of hers.

'No, thank *you*,' he said, which was a ridiculous thing to say.

The reading had gone OK, though, he thought, considering. He was quite pleased with himself for having been seen to make an effort to jolly Dev along. Greg could well understand how he might feel daunted, poor kid, he'd never been on the stage before. Still, at least Dev had the bravado. And although Greg barely knew Freddie Zamora, he suspected that the decision to cast actors of such minimal West End repute as himself and Dev was firstly to throw Barbara's presence into relief, and secondly so that Freddie himself could take a greater share of the credit if it proved to be a success and shunt the blame if it didn't. Then there was the girl, Sally, the writer with the caustic remarks. She seemed less hostile towards him this time; true, she had not addressed one word to him directly, but she had seemed to approve that he'd been generous to the boy. Every time he looked across at her, their eyes had docked, although until that moment she'd tended to be wearing a kind of cynical half-smile that suggested she might find him laughable rather than funny. He was probably being over-sensitive. If there was one thing that age had taught him, Greg reflected, it was that he'd spent years of his youth worrying about the wrong things with regard to women, and still he had very few answers.

He had already decided that he found Sally more interesting than Lola, who was all soft hair and giggles and girlish charm in an obvious way (though he was not so vain as to assume it meant anything; he had seen her direct the same mannerisms towards everyone). She struck him as the sort that would want to comfort a man, and he did not want to be comforted, because he did not want to acknowledge the persistent nameless ache beneath his functioning surfaces. Part of the point of doing a play, for Greg, was that it furnished a rare opportunity for socializing outside the inflexible subset of couples that formed his and Caroline's circle of friends in King's Lynn, and thereby for flirtation, an added reason to look forward to going to work. In a bigger cast there would always be some chorus girl or understudy willing to reciprocate his attentions, in gesture if not in deed, but here, in a three-hander where the only woman present was playing his mother – not that Barbara was not a striking woman, but the margins of Greg's enthusiastically catholic interest in the opposite sex had to be drawn somewhere, and he felt that the over-sixties and under-sixteens should be out of bounds for reasons of decency – his eye fell instead on the only other females present in the company.

Sally was not his usual type, if a man with such wide-ranging and largely theoretical tastes can be said to have a type. She didn't bother to make her manner alluring or even approachable; during the read-through she had confined her attention to the play and, although Freddie did most of the talking, when she did offer a comment or a joke it suggested a broader intellectual frame of reference than Greg felt himself to command. She was clever and self-possessed, unlike the kind of needy girls usually willing to soak up a bit of targeted flattery. Tomboyish, too, with her uniform of jeans and boots; all hard edges, rangy and distracted-looking, she smoked hungrily, as if something urgent were waiting for her attention the second the cigarette was finished. Yet there remained the fact that every time he glanced at her he had caught her looking back, with that hot and dangerous unquantifiable charge in her look that reminded him still of Elena, the manic girl at drama college twenty-five years ago, who had nearly driven him crazy with her unpredictable peaks and troughs. He recalled how, before they had ever become involved, some rational part of him had instinctively known she was a bad idea; he heard the same candid warning bells now when he caught Sally watching him. And that, of course, was part of the excitement.

It was late afternoon when Freddie wrapped up his dauntlessly positive observations on the cast's progress. The rain had receded northwards and, between the clouds, a low sun streaked neon over the river and through the window.

'What's the easiest way to King's Cross from here?' Greg asked the room, with a quick glance at Sally. It was a straightforward enough question, but offering ample opportunity for anyone to suggest going for a drink.

Lola shrugged. 'Northern Line from London Bridge, probably.'

'If you have a death wish,' said Rhys.

'That'll take hours,' Sally said, and paused. 'I could give you a lift as far as Clerkenwell, if you want, you can walk from there.' She was looking out of the window, as if it didn't bother her one way or the other.

'That would be great, thanks.'

She looked him up and down for a moment, then went to a cupboard at the far end of the office and emerged with two motorbike helmets.

'Oh. I was thinking you meant, you know, in a car.'

'It's a bike, take it or leave it.' She held one out to him and grinned. 'Go on, I'm very safe. I've barely had a drink today.'

'OK.' He felt a sudden pulse of excitement; it was not quite canyoning in New Zealand, the kind of thing Patrick Williams did every summer, but zipping across London on the back of a girl's motorbike was the nearest Greg had come to living on the edge in some while (excepting one of his more vigorous recent rows with Caroline, when she had thrown a jug at him).

'I used to have a bike when I was younger,' he commented, outside, as the shadows of Clink Street debouched into a wider cobbled area where a virile sports bike was tethered with a chain the thickness of a man's arm. 'A Honda 125. I went all the way from York to

Devon on it when I was eighteen. Can't even remember why now – I expect it was a girl. Then it broke down and it was too much to have it mended so I had to hitch home. But I loved that bike. Blimey, is it this one?'

'Yes.' She coiled the chain into a recess beneath the seat.

'Big bike for a girl.'

'Do you want to walk?'

'Can I have a go driving?'

'Can you fuck,' she said, and swung her leg over. 'Remember not to put your feet down at junctions.'

Through the City in the fading light he held – not too tightly – on to her waist, face nipped with the damp air of an autumn evening, knees tilted awkwardly skywards at acute angles. She drove decisively, though his unfamiliar weight made them wobble at corners, but as much as he enjoyed the illusion of speed, he couldn't help wishing that he had been the one with the big bike taking *her* on the back. That was the natural order of things. Her blithe self-sufficiency unmanned him slightly. Instinctively he touched his feet to the ground every time they stopped at lights, until she flicked up her visor and shouted over her shoulder. He only caught the words 'fucking' and 'feet'.

She pulled off the Farringdon Road into a lane strewn with bags of litter and lined on both sides with the skeletal infrastructure of a street market.

'This is where I live.' She lifted off the helmet and laid it on an empty barrow. 'If you go up to the top and turn left you'll hit Gray's Inn Road, then you just follow it up to the station.'

Greg handed back his helmet and rubbed his numb hands together and waited while she chained the front wheel. They stood facing each other for a moment, wondering what to say. She looked away, hooking a helmet over each arm.

'Unless you've got time for a quick drink?'

'What, he just took off? Just like that?'

'Yep. Like a Country-and-Western song.'

Sally leaned forward and tilted her glass for Greg to refill. The bar was growing crowded but they had found a corner table with a wax-encrusted bottle holding a stubby candle; a bottle of Australian Shiraz was emptying at speed.

'Took the clothes he was wearing and a credit card, and instead of going to work he took the bus to the airport.'

'That's extraordinary.' Greg drank while he thought about this. 'I mean, I've thought about leaving home sometimes, I think everyone does, but not so – definitively.'

'No, well. Cormac McGinley doesn't do things by halves.'

'How old were you?'

'Thirteen.'

'Not a good age.'

'What's a good age for your father to disappear?'

'No, you're right.' Greg looked at the table. 'It must have been very' – Greg couldn't find a useful word. 'How did you find him?'

'We didn't. He was listed as a missing person for two years.'

'Where did he go?'

'Canada. The police searched for him, but once they found he'd caught that plane – well, he'd obviously gone voluntarily. Apparently he moved around taking casual work. Played the piano in a casino for a while, apparently.' Sally gave a small, bitter laugh, and drained her glass. 'He was having a belated adolescence. I believe it's called a mid-life crisis.'

'Was he having an affair?'

'No. Well, I imagine he had plenty while he was away, but that wasn't why he left. He was always very –' She paused, and frowned. '*Principled*, I suppose is the word. He grew up in Derry, you know, in a working family, but he got a scholarship to university to study law, and when he qualified he wanted to put something back. He had very strong ideals. At one time, anyway. He moved to London, he did a lot of *pro bono* stuff, legal aid cases, never made much money. Everything he did was for other people. They married young, and my mother said he was faithful to her until the day he left, and I'm sure he was. That was probably part of the problem. And then –' She shrugged, and subsided.

'He wanted more.'

Sally looked up sharply.

'Exactly. A sudden need for self-fulfilment.'

Her voice was ringingly contemptuous.

'And he was what, in his forties?'

'Yes. Forty.'

'Well, that makes a lot of sense. It happens. You start wondering if you're just going to carry on in the same old rut until you die.' Greg filled both their glasses to give himself something on which to concentrate, because various elements of the play and of Sally were falling into place just as he was becoming slightly too drunk to make proper sense of them. 'I wondered when I read the play – how you could know so much about how someone like Allan would think. I didn't realize he was your dad.'

'Now look.' Sally fixed him sternly across the table. 'Can you get it into your head that even if a character is based on someone real, it's never that simple. Allan may have been based on Mac to start with, but he's Mac filtered through me and then you.'

'Is that why it's called *Real*?'

'No. That's metaphysical. Freddie thinking he's Wittgenstein.'

This only confused Greg, so he said, 'And Sean is you?'

'You could say he's a seventeen-year-old Anglo-Bangladeshi male version of me, if you wanted to be that literal.'

'But your father did come back?'

'Mac? Oh yes. After three and a half years, just came back as if he'd got it all out of his system, whatever it was, like a kid having a gap year. And thought everything would be just the same and we'd be delighted to see him.'

'And you weren't.'

'We weren't there when he came back. I mean, we weren't even in London.' Her jaw was set tight. 'It nearly destroyed my mother, you know, those years. It was the not knowing – why he went, where he was, if we'd ever see him again. For a year and a half she was a wreck. Then she just kind of pulled herself together and decided to get on with her life as if he'd gone for good. So we moved to Surrey and started a new life. And two years after that he came back and seemed a bit put out that she'd sold the house.'

'Christ.'

'She refused to speak to him for months. But Mac doesn't give up. He kept wanting to explain and eventually she let him. She listened to him apologizing and self-justifying, and at the end she just asked him for a divorce.'

'Do you see him?'

'No. You don't abandon people like that and imagine you can just show up and say sorry. I have nothing to say to him. He lives in Dublin now with a fucking Father Christmas beard and plays in a pub band where apparently he's very happy. So good luck to him.' She raised her glass without sincerity.

'And that's the story of the play?'

'Pretty much. I wanted to look at how you go about forgiving someone for something that you consider unforgivable. For a betrayal of trust. Whether you can even begin.'

'And you think you can't?'

'That is my conclusion, yes. But it may not be true for everyone. Have you ever been terribly let down by someone you loved?'

Greg rummaged in his memory through the haze of wine.

'Not like that, no. My dad was always a bit of a hero to me. He was a fireman, he saved lives. He'd have liked me to do something manly like that, I think. He wasn't very impressed with the theatre. I always felt like the one that let him down.'

He flushed at such an intimate confession, one he wasn't sure he had ever made aloud before, and lit a cigarette to curtain his embarrassment.

'Is he still alive?'

'Oh yes. He's in York. I wanted him to move nearer to us when my mum died, but he's very proud. I always have to stop him climbing up ladders to check on his gutters.' He laughed self-consciously and, looking at Sally, realized why she disconcerted him; she was frank and unswerving in her eye contact, as very few people were. 'Did you always call your dad Mac?'

'Not always.'

'When did you stop calling him Dad?'

'When he stopped deserving it.'

Again, Greg sensed a kind of warning, a tension in his chest; perhaps a premonition of how it might feel to hear Daisy as an adult saying something similar about him. How fragile the trust we have from our children, he thought, and how easily it can be ruptured.

'Don't worry – I don't see you as a father figure,' Sally said, in a tone that suggested it was time to lighten the mood. 'I think we should get another bottle, and you should buy some more fags because I have in fact noticed that you're smoking all mine.'

Greg looked at his watch. It was already half past six, and the bar was filling with young people in big rustling trousers. He should have been on the train half an hour ago at the latest. Could he convince Caroline that the reading had taken longer than expected?

'Weird to be drinking so early,' he said, standing up.

'*Early?*'

She was smiling languidly, the nearest he had seen her to coquettish, and he found himself thinking about kissing her. Not about actually doing it, but about the idea of it. Such a teenage, innocent hobby, kissing; no one seemed to bother much with it after the age of fifteen or the first few weeks of knowing someone, and it was underrated, in Greg's view. He couldn't remember the last time he and Caroline had kissed properly, as an activity for its own sake. On the rare occasions when he attempted to kiss Caroline in bed, she would turn her face away, as if the intimacy such a kiss would imply was a falsehood. But he would very much like to kiss Sally, he thought, whose lips appeared artlessly untreated and soft.

'You're gorgeous,' he said suddenly, surprising himself, and immediately wished he were less drunk.

Sally stared at him for a moment, then laughed in a way that implied disbelief.

'You daft fuck. You're all right yourself. Go and get some wine.'

Greg wove his way back with a new sense of recklessness and a heightened colour in his face.

'It's a great thing, this play,' he began, setting down the new bottle and taking off his jumper. The heat of bodies was rising, coating the bar with the dank wall-sweat familiar to venues with inadequate air-conditioning.

'Thank you. It's been bowdlerized somewhat.'

'I don't mean that – not that it isn't a great play, of course. But as an opportunity. To work with Freddie and Barbara. It's the best break I've had for a few years, I don't mind telling you. It's not been a walk in the park since the end of *Vets*.'

'No chance of bringing back Doctor Jeremy, then?'

'No, sadly not. I've stuck my hand up my last cow's arse.'

Sally laughed suddenly, and with a pleasing lack of decorum snorted wine over the table.

'Could make your name as well,' he said, when she'd recovered. 'You must have thought about that.'

She twisted her mouth into an ambiguous line and leaned along the table.

78

'Doesn't really happen to writers. Anyway, I'm never entirely sure I want my name made, when it comes to it.'

'Why not?'

'Well. All the grief that comes with it. Look at Freddie. He can't buy toilet roll without there being a photo of it in some magazine or other.'

'Freddie's loaded though, isn't he?'

'There is that. I wouldn't say no to the money.'

'Why would you write otherwise?'

'Because I couldn't do anything else.'

'Oh, I'm sure that's not true,' he said, meaning to sound conciliatory. She shook her head.

'I don't mean I'm no good at anything else. I mean, if I did anything else I wouldn't really care about it, you know? It's the thing I should be doing, if that makes sense.'

'I always thought I couldn't stick a nine-to-five job,' he began, when his phone rang in his pocket with the specially designated Caroline ring tone. He contemplated leaving it, but only for the space of two rings. 'Sorry, excuse me a sec' – and he pushed his way through to the door.

Caroline didn't know she had her own ring tone, because Greg had banked on the fact that she would never be near enough to hear herself calling him, but he had thought it a good idea to have advance warning in case the call required some self-justification on his part, which was often the case.

'Are you on the train?' Caroline asked, in a distinctly peevish tone.

'Er – no, they're all a bit delayed, that's the problem.'

'So where are you?'

'I'm at King's Cross.'

'Well, what time is the train?'

'Er – I don't know, that's the thing, because there are delays on the line so they're all backed up. I'm just going to get the first one that comes in, but it probably won't be for half an hour or so.'

'You know I've got my evening class tonight, and Daisy's got Sophie staying? I can't go until you get back.'

Damn. *Damn.* He had forgotten, of course, or he'd failed to make it as important as getting drunk with a girl he fancied.

'I'm sorry, the reading overran a bit, he's very demanding, Freddie is, so I was late getting to the station –'

79

'Are you in a *pub*?'

'Er – I'm just in the bar at the station. While I wait.'

This was greeted with a chilly pause.

'Well, look, just hurry up, will you, and call me if you want a lift from the station. If you'd called when you knew the train was late I could have made some arrangements.'

'Sorry.'

'Life goes on outside your play, you know, Greg.'

Heavily, he pushed his way back through the bar to Sally, experiencing the unpleasant onset of sobriety and guilt. The cheeky sense of rule-breaching had dissipated, leaving him with a congealing resentment towards everything: Sally, for luring him on to a path he could not follow to its end, and Caroline for yanking him back to reality just as he was remembering the simple pleasures of getting drunk with no responsibilities. And the palpitations of anxiety were also oncoming; it was not beyond the scope of Caroline's suspicion or wit to phone National Rail Enquiries to confirm delays on the King's Lynn line.

'Was that your wife?' Sally looked up at him mischievously.

'Well, she's not *technically* my wife,' Greg said, and then wished he could recall it; few responses could have sounded sleazier.

'So, what does that mean? She doesn't mind if you behave as if you're *technically* single?'

'Not quite. It's complicated.'

'Ah, it's always complicated when there's a wife.' But she was smiling.

'I just mean we're not – Caroline, that's her name – we're not actually married.'

'Why not?'

Greg met her direct look, and shrugged. 'I suppose I don't really believe in it.'

'Good for you. Neither do I.' She raised her glass, and he lifted his, newly filled in his absence, to meet it.

'So what about you?'

'What about me?'

'Is there a boyfriend?'

'Many, and none. I broke up with someone in April. I can't be bothered at the moment.' She winked.

'You just haven't met the right man yet,' he said, which was meant

80

to sound joky but also missed the mark, he thought; she might take it to mean he were offering his own candidacy.

He wondered what kind of competition he was up against. She must have numerous suitors. Almost certainly, his circumstances disadvantaged him. On the other hand, though, how many of his competitors could claim the doubtful honour of being paid to impersonate the father she must on some level be seeking to replace?

'Is she telling you to come home?'

'Kind of. Look, I think I'd better get on my way. I'm really sorry, with the wine and everything –'

'Don't worry, it won't go to waste.'

'I'd rather stay, if that means anything.'

'Ah, but you can't, Greg, because you've chosen to be accountable to someone else. Whereas I can live in perpetual irresponsibility because there's no one to care whether or not I come home. There's pros and cons either way. Anyway, there'll be lots more opportunities, I guess.'

'I hope so. Really.'

Greg fought with the sleeves of his jacket with bad grace, reluctant to leave. She stood to kiss him goodbye, and in a badly choreographed stumble they made brief contact with the corner of each other's mouth. Gathering his bag, Greg had what he considered to be a stroke of blinding imagination.

'I was thinking – while I'm working on learning the part, it might be really helpful if I could give you a call, you know, if there's any questions I have about Allan. Mac. Allan.'

'Sure,' she said, with no apparent emotion, and wrote down her number on a piece of paper which she tore from her Filofax.

'Do you know if there's a phone shop near here, by the way? I need a new pay card.'

'On the corner of Gray's Inn Road. By the traffic lights.'

Greg thanked her, wondered about the wisdom of attempting to kiss her again, decided against it and left. On the corner of Gray's Inn Road, he found the shop and managed, in spite of noticeably blurry vision and speech, to conduct a conversation which resulted in the purchase, on his personal credit card, to which Caroline did not have access, of the cheapest pay-as-you-go service on offer.

On the train he gave the instruction booklet a cursory perusal, but found it to be like reading through 3D glasses. Emboldened by distance, and without having mastered the punctuation keys, he laboriously composed a message to Sally that read:@sc:thanks for drnik wish I was still tthere@scx:

A couple of minutes later the trumpeting of his new message alert drew aggressive exhalations from his fellow passengers. He ought to read the chapter on how to silence it, he thought, smiling victoriously around at having joined the ranks of the texted. Concealment was going to be important.

He clicked open the reply. It said, simply:@sc:well, your jumper is, moron. guess you'll have to come back for it . . . xx@scx:

7

Greg came from a down-to-earth family that did not recognize non-physical illness. Meaning exactly that: it was not simply that his father, Tom, viewed depression, stress, neurosis or breakdown as namby-pamby modern fabrications (though he did), more that such concepts had no corresponding reality in his experience; he literally would not recognize them. Of course there were, he would concede, some poor souls who were born not right in the head and could do no more than end up in the loony bin, and women could be expected to have their nerves on occasion, at certain times of the month and especially when they'd had a baby, but the notion that in this day and age you could be given paid time off work just for feeling a bit sorry for yourself – this was beyond his comprehension. Folk apparently didn't seem to grasp any more the basic truth that life *was* hard graft, and that it was no use complaining, you just had to knuckle down and get on with it. Greg was aware that there was enough of his father in him to effect an identical reaction at the most visceral level, even while his modern consciousness manfully battled it.

When Caroline had had her protracted episode of depression after the miscarriage, and had lain in bed day after day, eating nothing but dry toast and staring at the wall, refusing to get up, he had done his best to manifest support and sympathy, while beneath this mask of concern his every muscle was taut with the urge to grab her by the arms and shake her, slap her round the face and tell her enough was enough, it was time to clean herself up and bloody well snap out of it, he couldn't be expected to look after her and Daisy *and* put food on the table. His father had been quietly appalled at the way he'd indulged her ('If your mother had tried running rings round me like that, son, she'd have had very short shrift'), and more so at the idea that her doctor had actually given her some kind of medication for this performance, as if pills could stop you moping about and crying instead of looking after your family. Greg had felt obliged to defend Caroline's condition and by association his tolerance of it, but he was stung by the knowledge that his father thought he was being a soft touch, and more so by the covert guilt of knowing that privately he thought his father was right.

She had always been prone to exaggerated mood swings, but there was only one repeat of that kind of depression, though less severe and of shorter duration, triggered, it seemed, by the discovery of his 'affair' with Paula. Greg had felt at the time that her reaction was out of all proportion to the scale of the offence, but Caroline's depression demanded deference; it had to be tiptoed around and appeased, like a riled and dangerous animal, lest it be provoked to greater violence. Among other things, the pills had the side effect of comprehensively quenching any last flicker of sexual warmth. Even Greg could appreciate a certain irony in this; the side effect of this side effect was that her anti-depressants were making him extremely depressed. In fact, when he thought about it, Greg suspected that at several points in his life *he* might well have been medically depressed but, conditioned as he was to brace up and put his shoulder to the wheel, it would never have occurred to him during those times to give his feelings such a name, still less to demand *pills* for something so intangible as *Weltschmerz*.

Now, as he watched her crouching to stack the dinner plates in the dishwasher, an old fear began to clot in him. He had prepared himself, on arriving late and drunk from his impromptu evening with Sally the week before, to barricade his face with his arms before the lash of Caroline's anger, to endure it until it was spent and then ride its aftershocks for several days, but she had barely said a word. She had continued in this tired, defeated near-silence all week, speaking to him only when she required specific information, closing herself with a kind of ostentatious weariness inside the cyclic routine of household jobs and her two and a half days of teaching work, seeming to find him in her way wherever she went, like a large item of unwanted furniture awaiting removal. Greg was troubled; this kind of behaviour was not one of her usual tactics. The will to fight was the surest indicator of Caroline's robust mental health; its withering, the first symptom of unease. He felt that the onus was on him to pull them back from whatever emotional Waterloo they were hastening towards.

'We've got our first proper rehearsal on Monday morning,' he began.

She didn't turn around. Instead she balanced a plate over the bin, whose pedal mechanism was broken, so that she had to hold the lid up manually with an elbow while trying to scrape Daisy's leftovers with the other hand. A piece of boiled potato glanced off the rim and landed wetly on the floor; Caroline produced an apocalyptic sigh that convulsed her whole body, laboriously put down the plate and the knife and set about scooping up the potato with her fingers while Greg looked on helplessly. She had asked him weeks ago to see about the bin; that, he suspected, was the subtext of the sigh.

'OK.'

'I was thinking – we could all go.'

'Go where?' She crossed to the sink to rinse her hands.

'To London. On Monday. We could get tickets for *The Lion King*.'

He presented the suggestion like a dog offering up a fetched stick, expectant of praise. Instead Caroline continued drying her hands slowly, twisting the tea towel between them, until finally she looked at him with incredulity.

'Daisy's got school on Monday. You can't just take her out of school like that.'

'Why not? Just this once. For a treat. You could take her on the Wheel in the morning while I'm in rehearsal, then I'll come and meet you both for lunch and we'll go to a matinee. It's one day of school – she can make up whatever she misses. Come on. We'll say she's ill. We'll do her a note.'

He tried to summon an encouraging smile. Already some of the pleasure was leaching from his brilliant plan, formulated in the sleepless hours of the night, to win back a small amount of credit in advance of the vast deficit that going away would bring. He had expected Caroline to fall on the idea of a family trip with outpourings of gratitude and admiration for his worth both as partner and as father; Daisy's friend Sophie had recently been taken to *The Lion King* by her nan and Daisy had not stopped talking about it since. Now Caroline's reflex negativity was souring his goodwill.

'You expect a ten-year-old child to pretend she's been ill when she's actually been to London to see *The Lion King*? Which, apart from the fact that you're encouraging her to lie, would be impossible, and unfair. She needs to be able to tell her friends about it, the competitive thing is part of the pleasure.'

'Well, surely she can get a day off just this once? They're always closing the bloody school for their training days. It doesn't seem to trouble them that she misses lessons then.'

Caroline appeared to be weighing this up.

'But you're going to London on Monday anyway.'

'It's only for the morning. I'll be free in time for the show.'

'No, I mean, why does it not occur to you to suggest doing something as a family on a Saturday, when no one has to make a compromise? It's like – you've got to go to London anyway, so we might as well tag along.'

She folded her arms. Greg felt ambushed.

'All right, it was only an idea. I thought it might be nice for us all to do something together.' He stood up to leave.

'No – it *would* be nice, that's not my point.'

'What *is* your point, then?'

'My point is that why don't we go to London for the day on a Saturday so that Daisy doesn't have to miss a day of school?'

'I go sailing with Martin on Saturdays,' Greg said, as if this were self-evident.

'Exactly! So you only think of going to London with us when you're going anyway, *that's* my point. When it doesn't require any extra effort. Because it's always what suits you.'

He held up his hands in surrender.

'OK, forget it, it was just meant to be a bit of fun. I thought it would be fun for Daisy. I'm sorry – obviously I've misjudged somewhere along the way, but I don't understand why you have to turn it into an argument.'

'No, I know you don't. If you understood there wouldn't *be* an argument because you wouldn't have done it.'

Greg retreated to his office and shut the door; there could be no victory against such self-cancelling sophistries. But in his conscience a sediment of guilt was settling, had been settling for the past week, and he feared that Caroline had somehow, intuitively, tuned into this and guessed at the motives behind it, and that he was therefore directly responsible for nudging her towards what looked like incipient depression, which only added to his guilt.

In the shallowest cylinder of his blue desk-tidy, amid a tangle of paperclips, was a small silver key which fitted the bottom drawer of his filing cabinet, the drawer in which he used to keep his porn magazines. Unlocking it, he felt his heartbeats chasing one another in anticipation; beneath the files and economy packs of envelopes, the screen of his clandestine phone informed him that he had a waiting message. Through the week that had just passed, the presence of the phone in its locked drawer had seemed to burn towards him wherever he was in the house, like a lump of kryptonite. He had begun by sending Sally an occasional message, lightly joky, when either he or Caroline were safely out of the house; she had responded with dry one-liners, which he flattered himself might be flirtation cloaked in mock insult, but he noticed that she always left an opportunity for a comeback, as if it mattered that they continue the exchange. Now he was taking risks; diving for the office to check the phone every time Caroline was in the toilet or making a cup of tea, all his concentration bent on its tiny silenced square of light deep in the drawer while he affected concern with Daisy's homework or the updated headlines on News 24, with the present fear of being caught adding to the thrill.

The little pixellated envelope on the screen had become a kind of necessary fix for him in the airless confines of family life, promising another world that existed beyond it to which he would, in a very short time, be admitted for a stretch. Sally appeared to hurtle at speed through a blurring diorama of cultural, intellectual, artistic and hedonistic appointments, usually three or more per night – book launches in West End bars, gigs in unorthodox venues by bands he'd never heard of, talks at the ICA, previews of European films at the NFT, stand-up comedy, fringe theatre, performance poetry, jazz cafés, readings at the Italian Cultural Institute – all of which, she cheerfully informed him the following morning, would usually default to one or other late-opening Soho members' club where she and her metropolitan, culturally aware friends would debate art, consciousness and politics, fuelled by tequila, cocaine and cigarettes, like a scene from *fin-de-siècle* Paris. Or so Greg imagined it, as he sat in his living room in the evenings, watching repeats of *Dad's Army* with Daisy, the outside world muffled by the thick curtains, screened out by the electric light glancing off the sliver of dark pane visible between them. He liked the sound of Sally's life. It was a cooler, smarter, more high-octane version of the sort of life he'd lived at her age, before he'd been hobbled by responsibilities. He wondered that she could possibly find anything appealing about his mid-life stasis.

Two days earlier, she had not replied to the potentially double-entendred text he had sent in the early evening, and with every hour that passed his anxiety had swollen in his chest, like a pressure on his lungs – the fear that he had misread her and crossed an uncrossable line. At midnight he had gone to the office again with heavy tread on the pretext of a glass of water, and still the phone beneath its barrow of paper intransigently displayed its network logo and nothing more. His disappointment and sense of rejection had been more extreme than the situation warranted, and this too troubled him. In the morning he had found a message informing him that she'd been to a party in a basement club where there had been no signal, and he was surprised to find himself worrying about whether she was telling the truth, or had simply tired of his inexplicit advances, or whether she might be with someone else.

He would have been arguing from a weak position anyway, he recognized that, given that he was nightly, in the most literal sense if no other, sleeping with someone else. But when he thought about Sally, which was a considerable amount of the time now, he was not only thinking about having sex with her. Of course, he *was* thinking about having sex with her, in varied and creative contortions and locations; but he was also, frequently and inexplicably, picturing them walking on a shingle beach hand in hand, looking round secondhand bookshops together in a seaside town, or cycling along arcadian lanes before stopping for a cream tea. These romantic fantasies filled him with confusion, because they did not originate in any part of him that he recognized, nor had they pestered him on previous occasions when he had found himself slipping into an inevitable theatre flirtation. It was partly because he already felt a formless apprehension about these thoughts that he wanted to take Caroline and Daisy with him on Monday, as a kind of talisman.

'I've been giving it some thought,' Caroline said later, supine under the duvet, as he brushed his teeth in their tiny en-suite shower room.

'What?' He spat. Thoughts of Sally had displaced their earlier conversation.

'Monday. I don't see that it would hurt Daisy to miss one day. I'm going to write to Mrs Penny and explain that you were given free tickets and we couldn't go any other day. She can make up the work.'

'That's a *lie*, though, Caroline.'

'But only you and I will know that, so we're not asking Daisy to lie. That makes it all right, in my book. And Andrea thinks the school will be fine about them having a day off.'

'Them?'

Greg felt the last dregs of his enthusiasm for this trip swirl out of sight with the blue froth. He did not have a great deal of time for Caroline's sister, Andrea, largely because he had always suspected her of suspecting him of not being good enough in any capacity for her younger sister, and he suspected also that this suspicion of hers was justified. In addition, he found himself goaded on Daisy's behalf by Caroline's repetitive beatification of Andrea's precociously gifted and smug daughter, Molly, who, though a year younger than Daisy, had already passed her Grade 5 piano with distinction. He padded across the bedroom and burrowed his way into the close tunnel of bedding, catching a waft of fabric conditioner and warm skin, the familiar smell of what he knew, then switched off the light, taking care not to brush Caroline's body in any way that might communicate a desire for contact.

'Yes, I thought it would be more fun if she and Molly came too.'

'But it was meant to be the family.'

'Andrea and Molly are family. Anyway, you'll be in your thing all morning, so this way we'll have some company and we won't be hanging around if it overruns. You know rehearsals never finish on time.'

A sudden shaft of opportunity illuminated Greg's gloom.

'That's right, now I think about it, Freddie does tend to go on a bit. No, it'll be nice for Daisy to have Molly along. Good thinking.' Now don't overdo it, he thought.

'Greg?' She turned on to her side, sought his shoulder in the dark and gave it an elegiac squeeze. It was the way she always touched him now, most often when she was sitting next to him in the car; a spontaneous gentle rub of his leg, imparting a kind of sorrowful affection, as if in memory of something that had once existed between them.

'Hm?'

'It *was* a nice idea. Thanks.'

'No problem.' He always slept on his back, sarcophagal. He pinned his arms by his sides. 'We'll have a good day.'

'And – Greg?' She hesitated, deeply breathing.

'Yes?'

Sensing – wrongly – a rare invitation, Greg reached over and parked an opportunistic hand on her stomach. Instantly his wrist was clamped.

'Did you put the bins out?'

Defeatedly, Greg swung his legs out from under the duvet, scouring blindly for his slippers and feeling the bite of cold air on his ankles. But his thoughts were elsewhere.

8

Every weekday morning Sally was awakened by the unsubtle noises of the street market assembling for the day. It billed itself as a lunchtime market, but the business of mantling and dismantling, loading and unloading, lasted from approximately 7.30 a.m. until mid-afternoon, creating an endlessly rolling loop of noise that carried up and down the narrow road like a busker in the Underground, beginning with a grumble of vans and the teeth-jarring rattle of the downstairs café's reinforced steel shutter zagging upwards. After this came the clang of extension poles, the creak and smack of trestles, the hefting of plastic boxes on to pavements and, over it all, the unflagging cheerful Cockney banter of the traders (though none of them was ethnic Cockney), no matter how foul the weather; specifically, in Sally's case, the exchanges of Imran and Sam, who had the stalls immediately below her bedroom window. These exchanges were marvellous in their inanity and capacity for repetition. Imran, who sold imported leather goods all made, as far as Sally could ascertain, from goat, would daily offer up his observations on world affairs, bellowing to be heard above the thundersheet ripple of his candy-striped canopy unfurling. 'Phew, ask me, yeah,' he would shout, as he fanned out purses sporting pastiche Chanel or Gucci logos like a hand of cards on the blue felt cloth, 'get 'em all out the West Bank, you solve the lot overnight, yeah?' and Sam, who had facial piercings and sold her own handmade Aztec-look jewellery, would reply, 'Yeah, but my mum read this thing where all the terrorists in actual fact are funded by the CIA to keep themselves in work, yeah?' and Imran would shout, 'Not bein' rude, yeah, but your mum talkin' out her hole.'

Sally, lying in bed, could hear daily variations on these conversations even with the windows closed, as the smell of frying meat from the Turkish Cypriot café slowly rose and soaked the breathable atmosphere of her tiny flat. If, after a particularly frenetic night, she stayed in bed for long enough, she would hear the noise of construction segue into the noise of operation: vigorously competitive radios, all poorly tuned to different stations, and even more vigorously competitive hawking by the stall-holders; the heckling countercurrents of determined shoppers with an office curfew and distracted women with pushchairs, smacking and dragging while browsing the displays of promised bargains: indoor ferns, combat trousers, batteries, underwear, veg, bathtowels, enamelled candle-holders, suspect DVDs (starring Bruce Wiliss!), crystallized fruit and nuts bagged up with gold ties like stocking-fillers, mops and lipstick and aromatherapy burners in the shape of mascaraed hippos. Eventually, by late afternoon, the noise of transaction would pass into the noise of folding and packing, and as the last van grumbled away, leaving crushed boxes and pulped fruit in its slipstream, the whooping, flashing refuse trucks would follow, and then the squat lunar craft of the roadsweeper, with its dust-coughing brushes and monotone bleeping like the throbbing of a migraine. Occasionally, if the council was on strike, they didn't come, and the black sacks and cardboard would pile up in drifts in the doorways, threatening entropy. When the street cleaning was over, the bars with their roadside tables would begin to fill with after-work drinkers, and at closing time one of the bars would turn itself into a club, urgently kettle-drumming beats that rattled along the walls of all the buildings on both sides of the street. When it closed in the unspecified small hours, its patrons would spill out to the pavement, kick over the market barrows, shatter some glass, set off a car alarm or two and have a fight. Then there would be an hour of anxious, knife-edge quiet (apart from the cats) before the café concertinaed its shutter up again and the traders' vans grumbled back for another cacophonic replay.

None of this was especially favourable to sleeping or writing, the two things a writer might reasonably be expected to do during the working day, but when Sally was shown the flat by the letting agent she had been so charmed by the vibrant local colour of the market that, as with so many things, she had made a decision on impulse and thought it through afterwards, when it was too late. Besides, she was glad to be forced out of the flat during the day; even in a house like a morgue she could find herself endlessly sidetracked by nothing, and her computer was elderly and infirm and also apt to be distracted from the job in hand, so it was to everyone's advantage that she be elsewhere.

Wednesdays and Thursdays she spent in the Soho offices of a film production company where she read submitted screenplays and treatments and wrote reports on them. It was a dispiriting job, Sally felt; most of the scripts appeared to be written by people who had never been to the cinema, nor (in many cases) ever had or even overheard a conversation with another human being, and the small number that were bearable were still not as good (in her opinion) as anything she'd written. Still, it paid reasonably well if you were a quick reader, and because she'd been doing it for three years, the Head of Development trusted her judgement enough to let her keep the reports fairly concise. 'Unspeakable shite,' she would write across the top, or sometimes just '*Shite!!*' In this way she could furrow through enough scripts in two days to cover her rent and bills. One of the scripts she had recommended the year before was now, to her chagrin, in pre-production. Some days she thought about quitting, but she was nursing a secret long-term plan to dust off one of her own plays under a pseudonym and then give it a glowing report.

The rest of the week she left deliberately unstructured, because the whole point of not having a real job, she told office-bound friends, was to be free from routine, though, if they only knew, the theory was more enviable than the reality. She liked to see how she felt in the mornings, to see what the shape of the sky suggested to her. Sometimes, if the weather was appealing, she walked determinedly through occult corners of London, guided by battered copies of the novels of Iain Sinclair; at other times, if she felt she'd been neglecting her soul, there would be flurries of devotion to a season of unsubtitled Iranian films on the South Bank or some similar exercise in cultural self-improvement; sometimes she would spend a day driving to the coast on the bike or truffling through the secondhand music shops on the Portobello Road; once, a year ago, she had embarked on a project that involved travelling all London's bus routes from terminal to terminal, though this was abandoned after a wet afternoon in a Neasden bus shelter (on which someone had etched, in runic script, 'London is A Shit Hole') provided a little too much in the way of grainy urban realism. More frequently, though, her unstructured creative freedom meant that she found herself intimidated by the expanse of self-governing time in each day before she could legitimately start drinking, and so would gravitate towards Southwark, there to spend the mornings in the café behind the Cathedral, expertly eking out one large coffee and reading the papers (it was Ibsen who said a dramatist need only read the Bible and the daily papers to encounter all of life; Sally had already read the Bible and felt no need to repeat the exercise). The afternoons she spent lounging on Avocet's sofas. She went to the gym occasionally not because she was obsessive about her body, but because she knowingly did so much to abuse it that she often felt sorry for it, and thought that it deserved a chance to fight back; her interpretation of yin and yang was that if she did *everything* to excess, it might result in some kind of equilibrium. She went to the theatre as often as possible, and in the gaps between all these things she invented people and wrote down their imaginary conversations.

On weekdays she made an effort to book herself in for lunch or coffee with a friend, contact or acquaintance from one of the various circles that overlapped with hers in the Venn diagram: radio and television producers, theatrical agents, directors, magazine editors, journalists, publishers, scriptwriters, script editors, script developers, the odd inescapable publicist. Sally knew a lot of people. Most of them liked her, because she was good company and took the trouble to maintain contacts. They didn't know that she did this not out of native bonhomie or even a conscientious will to network for the good of her career, but because she was engaged in an ongoing battle against her own reclusiveness, in the way that other women struggled with their weight. She was an introvert masquerading as an extrovert, convincingly enough to remain undetected. Sally had a secret fantasy in which she retired at thirty to run a secondhand bookshop in a Suffolk coastal town and lived contentedly, untouched by success or failure, with only a lolloping dog which she would walk along wintry beaches while talking to herself; it was an idea whose whole appeal rested in the knowledge that she would never do it.

Sally had been a solitary child by choice, and a solitary adolescent by default. Only at university, feeling less of an oddity, had she grown into an ability to perform in company, but she remembered sharply exactly how it could feel to be lonely, so that now she compensated for her natural curve towards solitude by hurling herself into the thick of every gathering, even when bored almost to tears, because she was secretly afraid that there might again come a time when she didn't have the choice. As if you could somehow shore up human contact against future exiguity.

'Sal! It's your lucky day, girl,' Imran greeted her, as she backed through the door of her building, next to the café, and stepped into the street. His T-shirt said 'Viagra Is For Pussies'. 'I got a load of them baguette bags in. Do you a special.'

Sally, who, in the interest of neighbourly relations (and because she occasionally bought coke from Imran), already had more goat-leather bags and Aztec-look ear-rings than she strictly had use for, politely declined, claiming that she was rarely called upon to transport baguettes, and in spite of Imran's literalist explanations, she set off down the street towards her bike, swinging her crash helmet in good spirits, on the way to meet Freddie for lunch. It was the Friday before the first week of rehearsals. These days she seemed to be spending all her available lunchtime and coffee slots with Freddie, whose tweaking and poking of her script was verging on vandalism.

'It's crucial that we present a united front,' he said, over a creamy rare steak in a Soho brasserie. In his favour, Freddie did not cut corners with his expenses. These script meetings were the only time Sally ever saw the major food groups gathered in one place. 'If there are cuts and rewrites to be done, we have to make sure we're agreed long before we get to the cast. I don't want to be arguing with you in front of the actors. It's very bad form.'

Sally nodded and chewed. Encouraged, Freddie shunted across the table a well-used copy of her play, the printed lines choked by marginalia in red biro.

'Here. Barbara's made a few suggestions.'

'A *few*? Christ.' Sally gave the pages a cursory flick. 'Are there *any* of my words left here? Oh yes, look: "and" and "the", I recognize those.'

'Sal.' Freddie held up a warning hand. 'Barbara had already chalked up fifteen years experience on the stage before either of us was even *born*. She's not trying to take over, she just has a feel for what her character would reasonably say. You've got to respect that.'

'I invented her fucking character.' She lit a cigarette with exaggerated gestures. 'God, Freddie, it's my play.'

'OK, and it's also my play now. I've got a lot riding on this.' Freddie rubbed both hands over his face like a hamster washing.

'Whatever you may think, one Bafta does not a reputation make. There are a lot of people who would love to give me a kicking over this if it doesn't work out. It's not the same for you.'

'What, because I've got nothing to lose? Why don't you take my name off it then?'

'That's not what I'm saying. *Jesus*, Sally – Monday is the first walk-through – we should be over these kind of teething troubles by now. Instead I've got you opposing every edit, I've got Dev ringing up every five minutes telling me I've made a terrible mistake with the casting and he doesn't think he's up to it –'

'Hey, it was your choice to cast someone who hasn't been on stage since his playschool nativity play.'

'He's Hindu.'

'Don't be so academic. Look, it'll be fine.'

'I know it'll be fine.' Freddie paused to finish his wine. 'It's a good script. That's why you're still knocking around.'

'You're too kind.'

'Listen, Sal. I *want* your input. You know better than anyone who these characters are and what they think. I put enormous value on your contribution, and I've had to fight for it. You know what Rhys thinks.'

'Rhys thinks I should take my cheque and fuck off.'

'Exactly. Whereas I do think you have a contribution to make. But I don't want you making it in front of the cast. It leaves us looking extremely unprofessional. Whatever happens, you are still just the writer.'

'*Just* the writer.'

'That's right. You are not an assistant director. So whatever's involved in getting this down to the running time, we discuss it and we decide on compromises in private, and at the end of the day, what I say is final. I don't ever want to hear you questioning my authority in rehearsals in front of the company, is that clear?'

Freddie had been two years below them at university. By the time he arrived, blinking humbly around the door of the theatre in Freshers' Week, asking if he'd got the right place – he was very keen on directing, done some at school and so on, did they mind if he just sat in – she and Rhys and Lola were presiding unchallenged over the university's somewhat self-congratulating dramatic community. Everyone wanted to be in their shows; everyone wanted to be in their circle. Rhys was dandified and imperious, with an epigrammatic delivery; Lola had famous connections, and was beautiful like a Titian; Sally was the Dionysian element, the inciter to riot. Between them they commanded the best drugs, the most obscure music, the biggest group of hangers-on, the most innovative productions. Had it not been her idea, Sally thought grimly, to adapt a punk musical out of the songs of Tom Lehrer? And how grateful Freddie had been to assistant stage-manage on that one. Now Freddie had a Bafta and Harvey Weinstein on his speed dial, and she thought it was Christmas when she got an Afternoon Play on Radio 4. How had this been allowed to happen?

She nodded, subdued.

'And keep an eye on Greg.' Freddie lifted the uneaten half of Sally's steak from her plate to his between his knife and fork. Novel though it might be in small doses, food was, in the end, Sally felt, a necessary impediment to the business of smoking and wine for which restaurants principally existed.

'Greg? Why?'

'Ah, well.' Freddie pursed his lips. 'I've met his type before.'

Sally already knew that she was going to sleep with Greg. She had known it from the moment they looked at each other across the coffee table at his audition, with an oddly prosaic certainty. She didn't mean that she *knew* in the sense that she found him inexorably attractive and was planning an attempt to seduce him, nor that she sensed that he especially wanted her and would probably try himself, nor even that she experienced some kind of cosmic frisson when they had looked at each other. It was just that: a simple knowledge of inevitability, of predestination. Sooner or later, it was going to happen, without either of them needing to make much effort towards it. As if it was *meant*. On the cards.

'His *type*?'

'Yes. See – I don't mind Barbara offering suggestions on the script because she knows what she's doing, and she's not a prima donna. She's got a wider vision. And Dev's so in awe he wouldn't dare change a comma. But it's the mid-list actors – the ones who are desperate to make it before it's too late – they're the ones that like to start splitting hairs if they think their part is threatened. Allan's the character with the most lines, so if we need to cut the running time down – and it's looking increasingly likely – the obvious thing to do is slash a few of his speeches.'

'I'm sure he'll be fine about that,' Sally said mildly.

'Well, will he? I think he sees this play as being very much about making his comeback.'

Sally laughed, and snorted smoke through both nostrils.

'That's a bit unfair, Freddie. It's not as if the rest of us are doing it purely for the love of Art.'

'See, he's got to you already. This is my worry. He's smart enough to know that one of the oldest tricks if you want to save your lines is to worm your way around the writer. The writer never wants any of it cut, so if you can get the writer on your side against the director you've won half the battle.'

'I think you're attributing motives that aren't –'

'Lola said you'd been out for a drink with him.'

'She did?'

'I wasn't surprised. I thought he might try to get round you behind my back. I suppose he took you out so he could rave about what a great part Allan was and how it would be a travesty of your work to lose any of Allan's immortal words, did he?'

'No, not at all. I asked him for a drink, actually. I was just being friendly.'

'Well.' Freddie nodded wisely. 'He'll be building up to it. Just be aware, that's all I'm saying. They're canny, you know, these actors. They all know how writers are plagued by self-doubt and suckers for a bit of flattery.'

'Right. Thanks.'

'Apparently he used to try and shag everything that moved on the set of *Valley Vets*.'

'Even the goats?'

Freddie laughed.

'I'm just saying watch yourself. There's something about him I can't quite put my finger on. He's not –' He looked into the middle distance. 'That's it. He's not a team player.'

9

'You're wearing those shoes, then,' Caroline observed, as they were driving to the station.

It was pitched midway between question and statement. Greg braked for the traffic lights and glanced down at his old Hush Puppies; given that they were five minutes away from catching the train to London, as a question it appeared redundant.

In the back seat of the Land Cruiser, Daisy and Molly were plaiting the hair of their Bratz and applying sparkly clips. Over their soprano excitement, Caroline's sister Andrea was on the phone to her doctor's surgery on her hands-free, giving her the appearance of talking to her own reflection.

'It looks like I am, yep.' Greg checked the clock display and banged the sides of his hands against the wheel. If they couldn't park outside the station they would never make this train, and then he'd be late, and Dame Barbara would think he was provincial and incompetent and wasting everyone's time, and Freddie would smile in that annoyingly forgiving, Christlike way, and Sally would think – what? What would Sally think? And why did it matter?

'What's wrong with my shoes?'

Caroline didn't reply. Instead she twisted to crane over her right shoulder and offered a gleaming smile to the girls.

'Are you excited about going to London, girls?'

'I think *The Lion King* is my very best show *ever*,' Daisy said reverently.

'Oh, *duh!*' Molly paused, mid-plait. 'How do you know, you haven't even *seen* it yet.'

'Really, nothing until *Thursday*?' said Andrea to herself.

'I've got it on video though.'

'That's a *cartoon*, it's totally not the same thing.'

'Well, you haven't seen it *either*.'

'I never said I had.'

'What's your best show then?'

'It's a kind of on-and-off abdominal pain,' said Andrea.

'I've seen loads of shows. Haven't I, Mum? I've seen millions.'

'I saw *The Wizard of Oz* last Christmas.'

'Huh.' Molly was scathing. 'That was in *King's Lynn*. That doesn't count. Shows don't count unless they're in *London*.'

Ain't that the truth, Greg thought. He shot a quick glance at Caroline. She was staring straight ahead with flinty eyes.

'It feels like it's around the ovaries,' said Andrea.

Greg winced.

'What's wrong with my shoes?'

'I'll tell you what ones I've seen – I've seen *Joseph*, *The Lion, The Witch and The Wardrobe*, *Cats*, *The Nutcracker*, *The Secret Garden*, *Slava's Snowshow*, um – what other ones have I seen, Mum?'

'I keep saying you should throw them out. Or just wear them for gardening. They're disgusting.'

'They're comfortable.'

'I'm just suggesting you could have made an effort. We're going to the theatre, after all.'

'Dad, Molly's been to *loads* more shows than me.' Daisy leaned forward and tapped his shoulder accusingly.

'And I'm going to a rehearsal first. It's very difficult to get tickets for shows in London, Daze. It's a walk-through. I want to be comfortable.'

'It wouldn't have killed you to have dressed nicely. That's all I'm saying. I mean, I bought you that Paul Smith shirt for your birthday and you've worn it, what, twice?'

'No, it isn't, Uncle Greg,' said Molly knowingly, also leaning forward to tap his shoulder. 'My dad belongs to this thing where you're on the mailing list, then you get to book early for all the shows you want to see.'

'Well, I'm sorry if you're ashamed to be seen with me.'

'No, I've never had an abnormal smear,' said Andrea, loudly.

Greg looked at her in the mirror. Had she not noticed him, or was he just irrelevant?

'Dad, why aren't *you* on a mailing list so we can get tickets for shows?'

'Can you believe that, Caro?' Andrea ripped the earpiece out with indignation. 'You'd think the minute you suggest there's something wrong *down there* they'd make you a priority appointment, but no! *Thursday!*'

'Has your bleeding got heavier again?' Caroline asked, turning sympathetically.

'Right!' Greg announced breezily, executing a small handbrake turn as he pulled up outside the station in his haste to interrupt. 'Why don't you ladies get out here and be buying the tickets while I go and park?' He contemplated pretending the car park was full and leaving the car several streets away, thus missing the train and getting to travel alone, but the next one was not for half an hour and there wouldn't be time to get all the way to Bermondsey.

The rehearsals were taking place in a photographic studio off Southwark Park Road, a blinding high-walled space in a Victorian mansion block with locked gates and a grizzled security guard, who told him to wait, and conducted a lengthy and indistinct phone conversation vis-à-vis Greg's admittance without once blinking or swerving his scowl of suspicion. Inside, Lola was running in and out of the studio kitchen, brewing up vats of coffee and arranging fruit. Sally was smoking a cigarette on the fire escape; she regarded him without much interest, nodded, and returned to her pensive vigil of the middle distance. All the imagined intimacy of their text conversations appeared not to survive another encounter in person, and Greg was embarrassed by his rash double entendres. The stage manager, her assistant, the lighting designer and the set designer were all present, obediently waiting for Freddie. On a red chaise longue, one of the photographer's more suggestive props, Dame Barbara and Dev were huddled close together; Barbara wearing Dev's headphones and an expression of extreme concentration, Dev looking up at her anxiously.

Freddie pulled some chairs into an approximate semi-circle and the company drifted towards him.

'Are we all here?'

Freddie began his address. It was mid-November. They would rehearse for the next week and a half in the studio, the first three weeks of December, take a week off for Christmas and New Year, come back for a week in the studio, two days including the tech and the dress rehearsal in the theatre itself; previews would begin on January 12th, with the press night two days later. He expected to have all script edits out of the way by the beginning of the following week, and lines to be learned by the end of it. He hoped everyone was happy with that. They were blessed with an excellent technical team – here he introduced them individually, with a brief history of credits – and a magnificent cast; it was a privilege to have the opportunity to work with the most exciting young production company in the country and such an up-and-coming writer, and altogether he was looking forward to an outstanding production.

Greg was relieved to discover that, despite his youth, Freddie Zamora was reassuringly traditional in his rehearsal methods. You learned your lines, you paced through your scenes, the director told you how to do it better. As it should be, Greg thought. He had worked with directors who would spend weeks 'exploring' the characters in improbable improvised scenarios ('OK, I want you to imagine Nina and Konstantin are going on a skiing holiday in, let's say Val d'Isère, they've got lost, they have an argument because he's accused her of reading the map wrong. OK, off you go'), or shepherd their casts off on day trips to war museums or animal-research labs or mental hospitals, or force them to spend hours lying on cushions in darkened rooms musky with scented candles, dredging up some childhood trauma the better to produce real tears. Call him old-fashioned, but Greg was not a fan of the Method (he preferred to leave his unconscious undisturbed), nor of the notion that dramatis personae had any kind of life beyond the play that contained them. Acting was acting, he felt; that was the point. If you couldn't laugh or cry or look surprised on cue then you were in the wrong game. Besides, most of Greg's real emotions, except boredom, were buried so deep not all the scented candles in Neal's Yard could have dislodged them.

At half past eleven they broke for more coffee. Greg joined Sally on the fire escape; she lit his cigarette for him and they leaned on the rail in silence, contemplating the rooftop infrastructure of domestic audiovisual technology, its receptors, transmitters, decoders and amplifiers, etched against the dirty sky of South London. Sullen clouds mooched east, towards the estuary.

Greg had noticed that Sally always wore very small T-shirts, and that she had impressively perky breasts. Not too big, but a very pleasing shape. He hoped it wasn't all scaffolding – you could never tell.

'We're all going out for lunch at one,' she said, after a while. 'You should come. Freddie's booked a table at the Angel on Bermondsey Wall, up by the river. Pepys used to go there to watch the hangings. The tech crew are all coming. You should get to know them.'

'What hangings?'

'Pirates. It's opposite Execution Dock. You could have a pint and watch from the pub, in the days before pool tables.'

'You're very well read, you.'

Sally laughed. 'It's not as if I do anything else all day.'

Greg flicked his dog-end over the railing and glanced at his watch. 'Do you think it will be a long one?'

'Lunch?' She smiled. 'Oh yes. Is there any other kind?'

Greg hesitated. He had folded his women responsibly into a taxi at King's Cross, despite the girls' disappointed protests (but who would allow their wife and child on the Underground, in these volatile times?) and arranged to meet them at half past one at the Festival Hall, after their morning on the London Eye. The matinee started at 2.30. Either way, he wouldn't get there for lunch, but he could still make it for the theatre. And the reason for inviting Caroline and Daisy, he reminded himself, had been to show a willingness to spend time together as a family, an objective Caroline had chosen to interpret in her own way first. The surprise deployment of Andrea and Molly had already turned the family day out into an unequal battle (he was easily outnumbered), so he could hardly be accused of abandoning them if he were to go for lunch with the cast. No – fuck the cast, with *Sally*. That was the choice here. Sally, or his family. On the other hand, he did want to see Daisy's little face all rapt and shining with excitement at the show. On the *other* hand, though, he still held out hopes of seeing Sally's little face all rapt and shining with excitement, one way or another. But his ticket was already booked and paid for; however much Greg liked to believe that underneath it all he was essentially a free spirit, he had never been reckless with money and West End musicals didn't come cheap. Ah, *but* – the ticket was in Caroline's handbag; if he told her he'd been unavoidably held up she could try to get a refund.

'I'll just have to make a phone call,' he said.

Caroline, predictably, was brisk and unamazed when he explained that he wouldn't be making it to the Festival Hall. He didn't mention lunch. Instead he mentioned Freddie's implacable perfectionism, he mentioned the constant interruptions of the stage manager and the lighting designer, he mentioned the fussing and dithering and inter-minable improvisation exercises, he even mentioned (this was an imaginative touch, he thought) how the bloody writer kept kicking up a storm over every line of the script. Caroline listened without remark, then reminded him that *The Lion King* started at 2.30 and said that they would see him in the foyer. Once again, Greg sensed that his presence or absence was of no real interest to her or to Andrea; together they were self-sufficient. So it wouldn't matter if he cut it a bit fine. He could stay for an hour, he reckoned, and still make it to the theatre, providing he could find a taxi.

The Angel was listed and listing; black-beamed and tarry, with Alice-in-Wonderland doorways and bulging plaster. It would have reeked of riverside history even if it hadn't been stuccoed with plaques at every turn, commemorating the drinking of press gangs, buccaneers, smugglers, Hanging Judge Jeffreys, the Diarist himself, Daniel Defoe, Captain Cook. They had an upstairs table overlooking the rusty water and the industrial ghosts of Wapping on the opposite bank. Wine appeared in catering quantities. Away from the rehearsal room, Sally and Rhys laid aside their mutual antagonism and fell into a natural double act, feeding each other punchlines to anecdotes of university days, largely involving farcical bed-hopping at country-house parties, each (it seemed to Greg) growing camper by the other's influence. Barbara regaled the company with backstage tales of the theatrical giants she had worked and/or slept with, which were stagier still (sometimes, Greg thought, Barbara appeared very like a drag queen, or a parody of one), but delighted her audience, especially Dev who, inspired by Barbara's example, had announced his intention of working next with the RSC.

'God, and the hours we used to spend with vocal coaches, working on enunciation,' Barbara said. 'That's all gone by the by now. And I for one don't lament it. It's all progress, eh, Dev?'

'Nart you mean,' said Dev solemnly.

Greg was enjoying himself more than he had in a long time. The stories, the good-natured teasing, the like-mindedness, the fact that no one frowned at the number of bottles emptying, or even seemed to be counting, the fact that they laughed at his jokes. He liked the com-pany; he was thrilled to be part of it. He felt at home. That was it: he felt at home, in a way that he never did at home any more. He had smoked seventeen cigarettes already. He was himself again. His *real* self, he thought. In his jacket, his phone was ringing with the Caroline warning bell, but over Barbara's deep guffaws he failed to hear it.

In the baroque foyer of the Lyceum Theatre, Daisy Burns clutched her souvenir programme and a box of Maltesers to her chest, dolefully watching the door.

'Come on, Daisy,' Caroline pressed her lips into a white line and with a vicious castrating motion, snapped her phone shut.

'I don't understand.' Daisy looked up at her mother. 'Doesn't Daddy want to see *The Lion King* with us?'

'Of course he does, darling.' Caroline ushered Daisy towards the box office. 'He's got held up at his rehearsal, I expect. He'll be really fed up, eh? You'll just have to tell him all about it when he gets here. My husband's running late,' she told the flat-faced woman in the booth, as if it were her fault. 'Can I leave his ticket here for him to collect?'

'Latecomers won't be admitted until a suitable break in the programme. What's the name?'

'Burns. Greg Burns.'

'Mum, phone him one more time? *Mum*? He might be stuck on the Tube, mightn't he?'

'*Duh* – he can't hear his *phone* in the Tube. Auntie Caroline, we *have* to hurry *up*,' Molly urged, from the stairs. 'That's the three-minute bell.' She shook her head decisively. 'I don't know how anyone could *stand* to miss *The Lion King*.'

Daisy cast a last glance at the street, and followed as the final bell knelled them into an extravaganza of cabaret wildlife singing Elton John.

It was funny how drink could do that to time, make it elide and skip without warning like that, like an old record, Greg thought as he registered that it was twenty past three and he had four missed calls. Only five minutes ago it had been two o'clock and he was all ready to call for his taxi. It was a scientific phenomenon. Must be. The drink–time continuum.

Fortunately, he thought next, by logical progress, failure was not calibrated with Caroline. It was like the 11+ or the driving test in that regard: once you'd failed, the percentage by which you'd missed became irrelevant. He was drunk and he'd missed *The Lion King*.

There was no clawing his way back from that. In itself this was oddly liberating.

So when Sally said in an aside as they were all leaving, 'Do you want to come and pick up your jumper then?' – quite matter-of-factly, looking the other way, without a trace of seduction – he simply nodded, and at some point – he couldn't remember how exactly – they peeled away from the others and hailed a rare taxi.

He kissed her on the back seat. It seemed a good opportunity. She gripped a handful of the hair at the back of his neck and kissed him back with a ferocity that took him by surprise. Halfway up the stairs of her building he put a hand boldly on her bottom. She pushed herself against him. On the face of it, Greg thought, it was looking promising.

Sally's flat was small. The kitchen was in the sitting room. There were books everywhere, and on one wall a portrait photograph of Samuel Beckett glowered with fiery eyes over the room, an electrical storm of white hair against black shadows.

She undressed with a candour that was new to Greg; or rather, it was very old, lurking dimly on the edge of memory. Not the candour that came from twelve years of sharing the same bathroom, the naked candour of indifference, but a frankness that came from youthful firmness and an unselfconscious expectation of being admired.

Greg discovered that she wore matching underwear, which was also a novelty, though it didn't stay on long enough for him to make a proper assessment. He discovered that the enticing shape of her breasts was not down to underwiring, which was a relief. He discovered too that her pubic hair was scrupulously waxed (or plucked, shaved or otherwise depilated – he was hazy on the mechanics) into an extreme V; a slender arrowhead that seemed unnecessarily severe for anyone not taking part in a porn video. Caroline kept herself well tended in this area too, to her credit, but usually to coincide with taking Daisy swimming or having an aromatherapy massage. With Sally he had the sense that it was artistic rather than functional. She was used to having it looked at. The thought troubled him briefly, but only briefly.

More troubling was the fact that she evidently used the same fabric conditioner as Caroline; her bed, when she pulled back the duvet, smelled damningly of home. Here ended the similarities, however. Sex with Sally was like wrestling a crocodile (so he imagined; he'd seen a programme). It occurred to him, as it had occurred to him before, during his bouts with Paula Jackman (Jackson?), that there must be some code imparted to women of this generation that obliged them to motor through at least five different positions in the same session or be judged substandard; he felt permanently wrong-footed. At one stage, kneeling behind her, he saw for the first time three Chinese characters tattooed in the small of her back, right in the curvature between the two pelvic dimples, and considered pausing to ask what they signified, but decided he would do better to concentrate on keeping his erection. She bucked and reared alarmingly; she revved and purred; she was vital and whippy and of an unfamiliar plasticity. It made him think – and he was fully aware of the crass level of the analogy – of how it had felt when he first bought the Land Cruiser after years of driving a wheezing Sierra estate, before he grew accustomed to its throaty engine, its responsiveness; the merest touch on the pedal and it would go haring off with a vigour he didn't anticipate, being used to so much more effort for so much less reward.

He made her come three times. At least, he thought he did, though he wasn't entirely sure about the third one; she kept up such an extraordinary output of noise that he found it hard to differentiate individual peaks and troughs. He couldn't remember the last time he'd got a noise like that out of Caroline.

Caroline. Even by her negative properties she was constantly present. At every new experimental twist of Sally's he found himself thinking either, 'Caroline used to do that (better/worse/differently)' or, more frequently, 'Caroline would *never* do that', and he began to resent this intrusion, this suggestion that his entire amatory repertoire could only be defined in relation to Caroline. He supposed it might be a manifestation of conscience.

Sally rolled off him and staged a melodramatic collapse, flushed and giggling as if from a funfair ride.

'Blimey,' Greg said, with admiration, gazing glassily at the ceiling. For a moment they contemplated the cartography of its disrepair in silence.

'Same goes for Norvern Island,' said Imran's voice, through the window, over the clang of folding metal. 'They all wanna good slappin'.'

A siren howled by, several streets away.

She levered herself up, straddled his stomach and reached across to the bedside table for her pack of cigarettes. God, she looked like porn, Greg thought, sitting there with her shoulders back, pouting out smoke and grinning like a successful gambler.

'Caroline won't even let me smoke in the house,' he said. 'Can I ask you?'

'What?'

'How many times?'

'Three. Three–one to me.' She held the cigarette out for him.

'Caroline never comes. I mean, not that we – any more. We don't. But she doesn't.'

Sally seemed to be scouting his face for a subtext. After a while she said, 'Well, I think we've established that's not your fault.'

'She used to. She's not really had much interest for years.'

She shook her head with a show of indulgence.

'It's 95 per cent psychological, you know.'

'What is?'

'The female orgasm. Men lose so much sleep over this delusion that it's all about how good they are. That's horseshit. If you really want someone, if you really desire them, all they have to do is touch your elbow and you'll go off like a rocket. If you don't, they can be busying away there for hours with every trick in the book and you'll still be looking at your watch. That's what happened with my ex.'

Greg thought about this for a moment.

'Is that true?'

'More or less. There's a very delicate and finely tuned connection between here, here and here.' She motioned to her temple, her heart and her crotch. 'Once it breaks down –'

'I think she doesn't fancy me any more. She does love me, it's not that. But she just doesn't see me like – I used to take her out for dinner and then try to get her drunk because it was the only hope of getting any. This one time,' he said, carried away, 'we went to a Christmas party and she got so pissed that when we got home she had to be sick, and while she was there leaning over the bowl throwing up, I gave her one.'

Sally was staring at him as if he were criminally insane. He realized that he might have overreached with the confessional streak.

'I shouldn't have told you that.'

The stare flexed into a disbelieving smile.

'Jesus. You poor bastard.'

She tilted back and exhaled two wavering rings.

'Do you mind me talking about Caroline?'

She shrugged. 'Why would I?'

'I could say anything to you, couldn't I? And you wouldn't be shocked.'

'Yeah, I'm fairly unshockable.'

Greg lowered his head incrementally back into the pillow. Suddenly adrenalin and endorphins were treacherously fleeing on all sides, abandoning him to the remorseless advance of a red wine headache. Sally arched over to tip her ash into the ashtray, and as she raised her hips he could feel his recent deposit reclaimed by gravity, warmly glooping into his stomach hair. Panic bolted through him and he sat up again.

'Are you on the Pill?'

'Oh. There's a thought. Good thing you checked before you shot all that in there.'

'Well – I assumed that if you'd wanted me to use a – you'd have said. So I assumed –'

He could hear his own voice rising. Sally laughed, not altogether kindly, he thought.

'Of course I am, you daft fuck. Don't get defensive. Do you think I'm stupid?'

'Sorry.' He lay down. Then, almost as an afterthought: 'I've got a kid, you know.'

'I know.'

'Daisy. She's ten. I'm supposed to be at *The Lion King* with her this afternoon.'

As he said this, the dawning of sobriety revealed to him what a total shit he was, and what a total shit he must appear to her. Although it was technically her fault that he was being a shit, he reminded himself; had she not benefited (three times) from the ugly chasm gaping where his conscience ought to be? Sally looked, for the first time, properly surprised.

'You left her on her *own*?'

'Oh no – she's with her mother.'

'So you're going off to meet your *wife* now?'

'Not wife.'

'OK – your not-wife?'

She seemed caught between incredulity and amusement.

'Am I a total shit, do you think?'

She snuffed the cigarette and rolled over beside him on her front.

'You're not a shit, Greg. I wouldn't presume to judge you. You're a bit reckless, though, I'll give you that. And you made a bad call – *The Lion King* is not to be missed.'

'*This* was not to be missed.' He traced the outline of her tattoo with a finger. 'What does this say?'

'Says, "If you can read this you're too close."'

'I thought it might be "Made in Taiwan".'

'Very good. It's the Chinese sign for Imagination.'

'Why?'

'*Duh!*' She banged the heel of her hand against his forehead, laughing, and for an awful moment made him think of Daisy. 'I'm a writer, you fool. I had it done the day I first got paid for a play. I was twenty-two. I was paid a hundred quid by this shambolic educational theatre organization that worked with dyslexic kids. And it was the world's worst play. But that wasn't the point. See, when I was a kid,' – she looked down and picked at her nails – 'Mac – my dad – used to tell me I had an over-active imagination. As if it was a bad thing, you know, as if that was what got me into trouble. So when I finally made some money out of my over-active imagination, I wanted to commemorate it. I now realize, of course, that makes me sound like an arsehole, that's why I never tell people what it means.'

'So it means "Fuck You, Dad".'

'Oh, now you're a psychologist, eh?'

'It was a very thoughtful idea – gave me something to read from behind.'

Sally smiled. 'That's been said before.'

The thought of other men describing the strokes of the characters with their fingertips and making his joke disturbed him more than it ought. Already he found himself confused by his thoughts about her.

'I'd like to visit a secondhand bookshop with you,' he said.

'Why? What do you want to get?'

'No, I don't mean I want a *book*.'

Again, she gave him the look that spoke of concern for his lucidity.

'That's mostly what they sell.'

'I mean as a general thing. When I think of you, that's what I'd like to do. Hold hands and look round a secondhand bookshop. One day?'

She leaned in and kissed him hard just below his left eye.

'OK, now I'm shocked. You old romantic. Do you want coffee before you go to meet the not-wife? You still look pissed.'

'I feel like death after that.'

'That's what they all tell me.' She swung her legs over him to stand up, stretched and wrapped herself in a shirt. She turned back at the door of the bedroom. 'And you should probably have a quick shower. You smell of cunt.'

If asked to recount the afternoon's event, Greg would probably have used the word speechless in its figurative sense to describe the effect of one or two things Sally had done to him, but at this moment he was quite genuinely unable to produce a sound. He simply nodded obediently. He couldn't remember ever hearing a woman use the c-word before, not even as an insult (and Caroline had covered most available ground in the course of their arguments), but certainly not anatomically and so unselfconsciously. This, he would say, looking back, was when he decided that Sally was something quite extraordinary.

In her cubicle-sized bathroom, he glossed the racks of tubes and bottles with their rash boasts in search of something that would not smell too overtly feminine. Would Caroline even recognize the smell of cunt? Would her suspicions not be more piqued by the smell of unfamiliar (women's) shower gel? The flat was so small he could hear the pop of the kettle boiling in the kitchenette. He settled on something that promised him 24-hour moisturization and wasn't pink, and was under the spray trying not to get his hair wet when Sally put her head round the door.

'Greg?'

'Yeah?'

'I just wanted to say – I'm on the Pill because it stops me getting PMT.'

'Oh. OK.'

'Not because I shag lots of blokes.'

'Right.'

'I just wanted you to know that.'

'OK. Right.'

'There's a coffee on top of the loo.'

'Thanks.'

'And *The Lion King* will have finished ten minutes ago.'

He dressed while she sat on the bed, watching him with unreadable intent, holding a cup of coffee with both hands. Under her scrutiny he felt more self-conscious than he had naked. He couldn't usefully explain to himself what she might be doing with him, and tried through an encroaching hangover to see himself through her eyes. Was he just a curiosity?

'Sorry about my shoes,' he said, tying the offending articles with some labour.

Again, the frown of incomprehension.

'What's wrong with your shoes?'

Greg looked at her with renewed admiration, then laughed, and hugged her awkwardly, mindful of the coffee.

'Sally, I might just have to marry you.'

She twisted a corner of her mouth.

'Yeah, they all say that too, eventually.'

By the time he reached the ground floor of Sally's building, the whole episode was already taking on a sheen of unreality. Caroline was going to kill him; that was certain. This trip was supposed to have been an atonement – for what, he wasn't entirely sure; his general failure towards her, probably – and now he couldn't think of any way to up the ante. What further act of atonement could atone for having so decisively mismanaged the original one?

And yet he didn't feel guilty. He was surprised by this, since his conscience was permanently silted up a with a vague guilt always associated with infidelity, whether in thought or deed; but he didn't feel specifically guilty as he stepped out into the street over an oozing binbag, because he couldn't convince himself that any of it had really happened. It all seemed so unlikely. In one sense, of course, he knew it was real; he could feel the incipient protest of muscles brought out of retirement, and the eight messages flashing their icon at him from the screen of his official phone were unquestionably real, and at some point very soon, when he had summoned all his mental resources, he would have to listen and respond to them, if only to find out where Caroline and the girls might be. But he found that by the time he had formulated a natural-sounding explanation of how Freddie had extended the rehearsal into an afternoon session and how, by unhappy coincidence, his battery had run out, he was actually persuaded by his own revisionist version. It seemed much more plausible than the notion that a woman fifteen years his junior would without hesitation have taken him to bed on a Monday afternoon on their third meeting. And done all *that*.

Strangest of all, though, he thought – and this really did suggest some aberration in him, in his attitude – was this urge he felt to tell Caroline all about it. Because, in spite of everything, Caroline was his first port of call for news – good, bad, banal; she was the only one who could be relied upon to care about the small events of his day. I met a girl, he wanted to tell her. I met an extraordinary girl. I slept with her. *She* finds me attractive. Oh yes. Three times. I'm intending to do it again. He even wanted to impress upon Caroline how much she would like Sally. He wouldn't, of course (as he braced himself to press the voicemail key); he might feel the occasional kamikaze prompting as far as his home life was concerned, but it was never to be acted upon. And in front of him were three months in London, three months of the play, and freedom, and Sally. Three months of another life, without prejudice, if he played it right.

Caroline's recorded voice, tinny, accusing, said, without preamble, 'You'd better have a bloody good excuse, Greg, that's a thirty-pound ticket and I couldn't get a refund.'

END OF ACT I

ACT II

One month later. London, King's Lynn, Dublin, Edinburgh.

10

Sally stood aslant at the end of the stalls bar, half an hour before the first official performance of *Real*, squinting into the eye-watering soup of equatorial heating, smoke and damp coats. She knew this crowd well, by sight at least; she had been privately ticking them off as they came down the stairs. Those assailing the free bar as if they had never before been to the theatre were Avocet's guest list – backers, friends, associates and hangers-on. Those who looked as if they'd rather be anywhere else were the professionals, acknowledging each other with curt professional smiles. They were all here, functionaries of every publication she recognized and some she didn't. Although reviewers on the whole took very little notice of such peripheral detail as the words, Sally felt craven before their pending judgements; either way there was nothing more she could do now than spend her first West End press night investing in the kind of climacteric hangover she felt it deserved.

She stepped away from the bar and into the press of bodies in search of Lola, and found her talking to an unknown woman.

'Ooh, *hallo*, Sally,' Lola said, pre-empting her arrival, in the loudly remedial voice of entertainers at children's parties.

'I want to go home. Look at their faces.' Sally cast her cigarette to the floor and lit another with unsteady hands. 'I'd like to see them write a play.'

'Yes – um, Sally, this is Caroline, *Greg's partner*. Caroline, this is Sally McGinley, the writer.'

For a heartbeat, the room gave the illusion of falling into a waiting silence. Lola appeared to be bracing herself. But Sally, who had once dreamed of being an actress, rallied all her dormant theatrical skills, collected her thoughts and allowed only a momentary flicker of poise before forming a smile of innocent politeness and saying, 'Caroline. Well, it's very nice to meet you. Greg talks about you a lot.'

Then, unbidden, she received a mental montage of some of the contexts in which Greg had talked about Caroline over the past five weeks, and had to turn away to hide a guilty smile of dramatic irony. Did wives, she wondered (or even not-wives), possess a telepathic skill for discerning whether you'd been sleeping with their husbands? She had never persisted in any relationship long enough to have honed that particular talent for herself, and wondered if her secret history with Greg could somehow be read in her face.

'You too.' Caroline extended a small hand. Sally brushed it for a microsecond.

You too what? What did that mean? That Greg talked about *her*? Was he completely mad? Or simply that Caroline was fulfilling the social obligation to express equal pleasure at meeting Sally?

She was surprised to find that Greg's not-wife was considerably more attractive than she had been led to believe, and knew that she should not be. She had enough experience of men to have learned that, where sexual behaviour was concerned, none of the logic women wishfully attributed to them had any basis in reality. They did not cheat on their wives because the wives were unattractive or the marriage was unhappy; they did not visit prostitutes because they couldn't get it elsewhere; they did not hoard pornography and beat off to it in private because you, their wife or girlfriend, did not fulfil their needs (or rather, they *did*, but this was not down to any shortcoming on your part); they would sleep, with alarming frequency, with women whom other *women* would like to believe didn't stand a chance: fat women, hairy women, women with bad skin and unflattering clothes, women with huge arses and barn-owl voices. The only consistency Sally had ever observed regarding the sexual behaviour of men was that it was governed wholly by opportunism. She remembered how duped she had felt when this was first revealed to her empirically towards the end of her teens; duped into having squandered all those hours spent waxing and polishing, hours on sunbeds and Stairmasters, hours spent waiting ungrateful tables in order to buy the right jeans or bag in the belief that this was how men would judge you and find you wanting or not, when it transpired that, all along, this had been for the judgement of other *women*. But no one ever seemed to stop and say, oh well, fuck it then, I won't bother. Some had tried, briefly, in the Sixties, and had been branded hairy lesbians. Pretty soon they had stopped that particular manifestation of the fight. There was no alternative.

So she should not have been surprised, she told herself, to discover that Caroline was an attractive woman (for her age, Sally added, with pleasing malice). She was one of those exceptionally petite, doll-like women that seemed to make men feel protective and manly. Sally, who was of above-average height and more with her tall boots on, and had never excited feelings of protectiveness in any man, always suspected that there was some kind of paedo element at work in such situations – how could a man sleep with a woman the size of a twelve-year-old without that in the back of his mind? Caroline could not have been more than five feet tall. She had a shoulder-length bob with copper highlights and good skin. Yet there was something brittle about her, Sally thought, something defensive in the way she wrapped her arms around her chest and didn't meet Sally's eye. Perhaps it was simply the defensiveness of being launched into a room crushed with over-confident people she didn't know, people who would cant over her and say, 'So what do *you* do? Oh, you're a part-time *teacher*, how *interesting*', before turning away to someone more famous.

'Greg said it's based on your father,' Caroline said, without looking at Sally.

'Oh, well – yes and no. My father used to be a lawyer so if he ever asks, you say no, it's a complete coincidence.'

Caroline laughed politely and, Sally thought, slightly dismissively.

'Oh!' Lola clutched her arm. 'I've just seen Lars come in, I must go and make sure he's being looked after. Do you mind if I – will you be all right here?' She glanced from Sally to Caroline doubtfully, as if violence might break out without a referee.

'Heil, Lars,' Sally said.

'Sal – you're to be *nice* to him tonight.'

Lola made a face of weary reprimand and pushed through the crowd. Sally looked down at Caroline and caught the expression with which she was watching Lola's back. She had decided not to like Lola, Sally could see. Women (wives, girlfriends) often took against Lola as a first impression – especially Lola in full evening get-up, with cleavage adrift and gleaming curves – which was ironic, since Lola had not a particle of malice in her and was unfashionably chaste, despite her proudly Restoration display of bosom. It was doubly ironic in this case, Sally thought, Caroline feeling threatened by *Lola*.

In fact it was almost funny.

'Can I get you another drink, Caroline?'

'No, thanks.'

'Are you staying in London tonight?'

'Yes.'

A bell rang and was accompanied by an announcement. Sally tried to calculate how many cigarettes she could reasonably get in before the curtain went up, and reckoned on five. She lit the first and tried again.

'So, are you and Greg coming to Barbara's party?'

'Yes.'

Rhys scuttled past with a television executive in one hand and nodded a brief acknowledgement to Sally.

'No Brett tonight?'

Rhys pulled up short and the executive continued on his trajectory for a few paces before skidding abruptly to a halt.

'Certainly not. Do you know, he had this outré foot fetish? I mean, I found it quite amusing at first, but it was all he ever wanted to do – lick my shoes. Shoes, shoes, shoes – it's all he talked about. Apparently *Newsnight Review* are in. Hello, Caroline.'

Caroline looked delighted with Rhys. She probably finds gay men terribly exotic, Sally thought.

'And get to your seat, McGinley,' Rhys said. 'I am *not* having a late curtain tonight of all nights. The *Telegraph* want a quick interview with you and Freddie afterwards. That's not optional so don't get off your face in the interval.'

Sally turned back, meaning to include Caroline in the conversation, but she had gone. Wandering back towards the bar in search of an ashtray, she found herself headed off by the figure of Lars Faldbakken.

Lars Faldbakken, the Norwegian millionaire whose gift had enabled the play to become reality. Instinctively Sally resented being under obligation to anyone, and so instinctively she resented Lars because he expected her gratitude. He was tall for an old man, with eyes the colours of zircon, the bags under them ruched as theatrical drapes. Sally had met him only once before, and had thought then, as she now thought anew, that the only difference between eccentricity and madness was a few million pounds. He was wearing a surgical mask hooked over the ears with elastic.

'This city is afflicted by plague,' he announced, pulling it down to hang under his chin.

Sally gestured towards the smoke hanging in the lights.

'You'll be all right – nothing's going to get through the air in here.'

'Sally, you remember Lars.' Lola, at his shoulder, gave a look of stern warning.

'Thank you. Now please leave us, Miss Czajkowski. Would you mind holding this for a moment, Miss McGinley?' Lars handed Sally a slim black cane that looked to be made of ebony topped with a silver wolf's head. Elaborately he took from his top pocket a flat silver case, removed a dark cigarillo, replaced the case, extracted from the same pocket a matching silver lighter which ignited with barely a breath, inhaled as if tasting cognac and, when he appeared to be satisfied with the proper completion of this procedure, turned his attention back to Sally, who had twisted the cane to examine the wolf's head carving. To her alarm, the ebony shaft suddenly came away as a sheath, and as she grabbed to stop it falling, her hand closed around the blade of a rapier.

'*Jesus!*' Sally seized her hand as the weapon clattered to the floor. Blood was running down her palm.

Lars bent patiently, retrieved his cane and screwed the two parts back together.

'You must be more careful. It's extremely sharp.'

'It's extremely illegal, surely? Ow, *fuck*.'

'A gentleman should always be able to defend himself. Besides, Miss McGinley, so much of what we find beautiful in life is considered to be illegal – true, no?'

Sally found this on some level quite disturbing, but she was more preoccupied with her hand.

'It's a surface cut. You must run it under clean water. I apologize. It belonged to my father. I never leave home without it. Miss McGinley, I have a gift for you, in recognition of your excellent play.'

'Thanks. I should wait till you've seen it, though.'

'No need – I have read it. Every draft. Mr Zamora was kind enough to accommodate some of my further suggestions. It retains the kernel of a serious work.'

Sally was amazed enough to let go of her cut. She met Lars's stare. His eyes shifted colour in the light.

'Wait – what – Freddie let you *edit* it?'

'No, Miss McGinley, he let me *read* it. And the only suggestions I made were that he reinstate your original lines where he proposed changes. I greatly admire your turns of phrase.'

'I had no idea.' Sally attempted to process this. 'I didn't even know you'd seen the script.'

'Do you know many rich men, Miss McGinley?'

'Sadly, no.'

'Then I will tell you something about rich men. They do not become rich or remain rich by investing without caution. I would not put my money or my name to a piece of work about which I had no conviction, no matter how many beautiful young girls approach me with the, yes indeed, very pleasing embonpoint. But I am too old to have an interest in such things except as a passing aesthetic treat and, to tell you the truth, for that I prefer these days a painting. Those you do not have to engage in conversation. Worth a thousand words, hm?' He tightened the wolf's head one last quarter-turn and handed Sally a paper serviette from the bar for her hand. 'You are a fine writer, Miss McGinley, and this is an interesting play, but I ask myself – where is the message?'

'What message?'

'Precisely. This is about *people*, yes – very good, very well, but where does it fit in? In these troubled and complex times, a dramatist should be *engagé*.'

Sally shrugged.

'I write about people. That's what I do, I just tell stories. I've never tried to be political. Besides, everyone hates political drama.'

'Because so much of it is done so badly. One can never *just* tell stories. Do you not have a cause, Miss McGinley?'

'No. I really don't. I mean, I marched against the war. At least, I would have done if I'd got up in time. I meant to.'

'What is the purpose of drama, Miss McGinley?'

'Oh, please –' Sally was not in the mood to parry such large questions, but she glanced at Lars and found an unpredictable smile there. 'What do you want me to say? To hold the mirror up to Nature.'

'But so much of Nature is so very ugly, don't you find? Perhaps you need a larger mirror.'

'What?'

He laughed. 'I will explain. But first, open this. I was assured it would not offend you.'

He passed her a silver box with a clasp, the lid intricately worked. Sally opened it to reveal a fat and pungent lump of hashish on a bed of purple cloth.

'Oh –'

'I've just come back from Afghanistan,' Lars said, as if by way of explanation.

'How did you get it through customs?'

'That is your syllogism, Miss McGinley, I make no such boast. You are confused anyway, Afghanistan exports opium. I am building a school there, with the Red Cross. A school for girls. I say I am building it, naturally I do not mean literally.'

'Well, that's very – generous of you.'

'For an old fascist?'

'I never said –'

'I am an admirer of certain artists you would no doubt consider unfashionably illiberal, Miss McGinley, and I am fascinated by the artefacts of Europe's past. I owe you no justification for that. On the other hand, I will only buy fair-trade coffee and I consider leather trousers to be an assault on all manner of sensibilities. One man's terrorist, no? But Afghanistan. A wounded country. These girls, these women – they have many stories to tell. Someone needs to tell their stories before they are forgotten. Not by documentary, the world is tired of that. I mean, it has seen enough of war and it turns the channel to the wife-swapping illiterates because these things make no demands. These stories need less journalism and more – *story*. You see.'

'Right.' Sally was still staring at the hash and extrapolating its street value.

'You must write a play about these women. For the television, perhaps. Or perhaps for the cinema. I will pay for you to go there and to meet them.'

'To *Afghanistan*?'

'People forget so fast, Miss McGinley. One minute, all over the news – one minute later, another war, another crisis, and they are left to struggle on in silence.'

'You seriously want to send me to *Afghanistan* to write a film?'

'It is an idea of mine. I would like to see such a film, and I would like to see it written by *you*.'

'They offer a hundred thousand dollars for the head of a Westerner, you know,' said Sally, who spent a considerable amount of time in the public reading room of W. H. Smith keeping up with salient articles in *Time*, *Newsweek* and the *New Yorker*.

Lars smiled, in his disturbing way.

'Tales to frighten children, Miss McGinley. Besides, nothing ventured, nothing gained, no? What is life without adventure?'

'There's adventure and there's getting your head cut off.'

The five-minute bell was rung. Lola returned anxiously to assist Lars to his seat, and lingered behind as he moved towards the stairs.

'How did that go?'

'Oh, grand. He tried to slice my hand off with a sword, then he gave me a lump of dope the size of Kent and now he's sending me to Afghanistan to be beheaded. All in a day's work.'

'He *is* a bit eccentric.'

'He's *mental*.'

'He'll hear you.' Lola watched Lars heavily ascending. 'He's very serious about the charity stuff, you know. There's someone at the BBC who's keen, I forget who. But you should do it. Write a film, Sal, you could.'

'Oh, OK. And Kabul's lovely this time of year, apart from the certain death.'

'You're such a dramatist. Come on, put that out, you can't be late for your own play.' Lola tugged at Sally's smoking hand, then paused by the exit. 'By the way, I just popped backstage. I told Greg you wished him luck. I didn't tell him you'd met the wife.'

Sally stopped too.

'Do you think it was out of order for him to bring the wife?'

'What was he supposed to do, tell her to stay at home?'

'It's just that it's my big night too, you know? It seems – inappropriate.'

'Some might argue that you're not in the best place to comment on what's *appropriate*. Poor woman. I mean, she's a bit abrasive, but – I'd hate to be in that position. Not knowing. Look, Sal,' – Lola rubbed her cheek, concerned – 'it *is* just shagging, isn't it?'

'*Just* shagging?' Sally poked her tongue between her teeth and grinned.

'I mean, you haven't tried to convince yourself that this is your prince coming, have you? You're not expecting him to fall in love with you and leave her and live happily ever after like the cards promised?'

'Christ, no. You're the one who believes in the cards.'

'Not this time,' Lola said with conviction, and the three-minute bell excitedly trilled.

⚭·❖·⚭

'That's her there, don't stare.' Greg articulated with his head and looked the other way.

Patrick Williams rubbed a hand over his stubbled hair and craned across the bar.

'The blonde one? With the leather trousers?'

'Yep.'

'With her arm round the bloke on steroids?'

'Yep.' Greg closeted his expression away from his agent. There was no need for Pat to have pointed out that Sally appeared to be accompanied by a very well-built man with quite so much self-righteous glee; it had been the first thing Greg had noticed as he vaunted into the reception with a tilt and a swagger, his face still stinging from the make-up remover and all his synapses fizzing with the unfamiliar, the forgotten current of success. The performance had gone expertly. The audience of critics had whooped them back for two curtain calls. And had he not just a moment ago overheard, on the stairs, the woman from the *Observer* saying quite candidly to her companion, 'I was very impressed by Greg Burns'? Granted, in context what she had actually said was 'I was very impressed by Greg Burns, he was always so wooden in that vet thing', but even *so*, Greg thought. And in this mood he had entered the roped-off bar, where token thimbles of champagne had been arrayed for the guests, seeking out Sally to exchange congratulatory and suggestive winks, only to find her giggling into a drink with some bloke, which struck him as completely out of order.

He had not seen her for two weeks, and the crowded itinerary of a family Christmas and New Year had shouldered in, making communication with her almost impossible. Family Christmas was one of Caroline's highest priorities, even more so now that both her own parents were gone, in the interests of laying down a foundation of happy Yuletide memories and rituals for Daisy to pass on to her own

125

children one day. The urge manifested itself in various ways: choral music on the stereo all hours of the day and night; some kind of permanent spiced-apple-scented candle effect that fogged up the sitting room and made him gag; Caroline's Christmas Eve drinks party, which he quite enjoyed, because he got to make his customized mulled wine; and particularly in Greg's being dispatched to York on the day before Christmas Eve to bring back his father, about whom he had eternally mixed feelings.

Tom Burns, at seventy-four, begrudged any event that made him move outside the perimeter fence of his garden. 'I'd have been quite all right in me own house' was the only thing he'd said to Greg, as they loaded his suitcase into the Land Cruiser. 'You can't be on your own at Christmas, Dad,' Greg had said, with effortful festive spirit.

'I could have gone to the day centre for me lunch.'

'You don't want to go to the day centre instead of being with your family.'

'I'm always in somebody's way.'

'That's rubbish, Dad. We love having you.'

'Season of peace to all mankind. Why can't *I* get a bit of bloody peace?'

Greg, who would have been more than happy for his father to have stayed in his own house, couldn't provide a convincing answer to this. Tom had spent the first afternoon at their house loudly rereading the train timetable to see how soon he could leave on Boxing Day, but by Christmas Eve had grudgingly made himself at home sufficiently to undertake a tour of the Burns house with accompanying structural commentary: 'Call that grouting, son?' or 'You've put them towel rails in without rawl plugs, are you simple? Do you *want* your plaster cracking?' But between them, Daisy's oblivious chirruping and the Famous Grouse managed to mellow his mood enough to persuade him to stay until New Year's Eve, when Greg and Caroline had left him curled up with Daisy watching *Chitty Chitty Bang Bang*, and dressed up to see in the New Year as usual, at Martin and Kate Parrish's party.

The festive season had put a severe strain on Greg's conscience. Watching Daisy, in her pyjamas, kneeling with her stocking at the end of their bed on Christmas morning, bouncing and yelping with a childish delight that seemed at odds with the proto-sexual implications of the presents she was unwrapping – sparkly lip gloss, ear-rings, fishnet tights, diamante body jewellery – or curling up with her on the sofa for heart-warming Christmas films whose themes were always the triumph of kindness and love and family integrity, Greg was skewered with a fierce love for his daughter and associated self-loathing for his own errata, and vowed to put an end to all behaviour that might lead to a bleak future in which they spent Christmas mornings apart and she took to calling him 'Greg', if she spoke to him at all. He would be a *better* person, he determined; a less selfish person, a better example, a better father, a better husband. He would stifle his own needs and wants and thereby become more deserving of his family. But a week later, fifteen minutes into a new year, smoking a cigarette on Martin's and Kate's patio and clenched against the cold (did *no one* outside London let you smoke indoors any more?), he watched invisibly through the French doors as Martin, his sailing partner and accountant, led a roomful of people in their forties into a woeful exhibition of dancing to 'Suffragette City', and felt appalled both by them and *for* them. Then, he had looked up at the ultraviolet drifts of cloud and thought achingly of Sally. Later, Caroline had been drunk enough to make it apparent that she wouldn't resist if he attempted to have sex with her, which he duly did, in mechanical fashion, since his own enthusiasm was now conditioned to decrease in inverse proportion to hers; he couldn't stop worrying about where Sally might be; what exceptional party he might have escorted her to if he hadn't been stuck in King's Lynn; whom she might have taken home to her enviably dishevelled flat above the caff instead.

Now, as if to confirm all the worst imaginings of the married lover (and he had been so terribly predictable, he knew, during the weeks of rehearsal; always checking his watch or panicking his way into his clothes the minute he finished, or hiding in the bathroom while he lied grotesquely on the phone), here she was in the press-night bar with another bloke. And this bloke, Greg had to concede, with a small grinding of teeth, was a much better match for Sally than he could ever hope to be. You might argue, Greg thought, that it was fair enough, since he was there with Caroline, but that was completely different; Caroline was a given, a known factor in this equation. He had never lied to her about Caroline, whereas she – *she!* – had assured him that she was not seeing anyone else. Greg felt that to spring this on him, especially on press night, had to be outside the rules. If, indeed there *were* any rules governing this thing on which they were embarked; rules and futures had not been discussed.

'I hope you know what you're doing, mate.' Patrick shook his head.

'It comes back to you after a while, Pat, it's like riding a bicycle. Although it's more like a very powerful stunt motorbike in this case, you know what I mean?'

'I'm serious, Greg. She might be a bunny boiler, like your last one. And look how that turned out.'

'Paula Thing? Come on, that was a mistake. She's not even the same species. Sally's a really good laugh, you'll like her.'

'Lovely. Why don't we have you round for dinner?'

'I'm only suggesting you say hello, don't get all –'

'All what? I'm not going to lie to Caroline for you.'

'I won't ask you to.'

'Look, Greg – just think a bit further ahead than your next boff, that's all I'm saying. You've got three months in London with this play, and then what? You have to go back to your life. And think about your career, if not your family. I don't want to sound like your mother – enjoy yourself in London by all means, but remember you're here to do a job and you've got to be concentrating first and foremost. There could be a lot of projects lining up if this run is a hit, and God knows you could do with them. And it won't look very good if it gets out that you've been carrying on with the playwright.'

'*Carrying on?*' Greg laughed. 'That is what my mother would have said, actually. *That Mr Tucker from the brewery, he's been* carrying on *with her from number forty-seven.*' He affected a high-pitched, northern charlady accent.

Patrick didn't laugh.

'I'm just telling you to be careful. It's my job.'

'I don't remember signing you up as the voice of my conscience.'

'Well, it's not my job to tell lies on your behalf.'

'That's the whole of your job, old son. That's what it says under "agent" in the careers guide.'

'Not to your wife.'

'She's not strictly speaking my wife, remember.'

'You couldn't live without her, Greg. As you well know.'

Greg looked away and made a face. Patrick was three years younger than him but his sense of fun, Greg often felt, was prematurely arthritic. Frequently, hoping for a partner in crime, Greg would stay over in London with his agent after some meeting or other, anticipating a night of glorious freedom, *on the tiles*, as his dad used to say, and would end up feeling as if he had spent the evening with his dad. Without words, Pat had the ability to radiate an astringent disapprobation for anything that might betoken mid-life instability; an interest in drink, say, or younger women or staying out beyond the beginning of *Newsnight*. But Pat wouldn't understand the fissures of a stale relationship, Greg thought with some bitterness; Pat, with his beautiful half-Nigerian wife and his South London townhouse and his long-haul holidays; Pat, who was invited to film premieres and TV parties all the time, while for Greg it was a rare and special treat just to go to a *pub* in the West End; Pat, who mowed his whole head to a millimetre of bristle in order to pre-empt early baldness – and where was the logic in *that*?

Caroline returned from the Ladies and wrapped her arms appreciatively around his waist. Over her head he saw Sally watching him from the bar, and pointedly turning away. Good, he thought, and looked down at Caroline, who was stroking his back proprietorially. *Now* she was all smiles, of course; whenever he was being admired she wasn't slow to get in on the act. Perhaps he was too quick to judge Pat's life, he thought; you could never guess at what happened beneath the surface of someone else's life. Anyone – Sally, for example – seeing him and Caroline tonight might imagine they were very much in love and would be going back to their hotel to enjoy mutually considerate marital sex, whereas he could have put her straight; what would happen would be that they would go on to Barbara's party, he would drink too much and talk to other women, she would tolerate this briefly and then petition him to go home, whereupon they would have an argument, he would capitulate, they would get back to the hotel, she would tell him he stank of booze and in defiance he would blast through the minibar and most likely fall asleep with his clothes on. Nothing for Sally to worry about, if she only knew.

He looked for her over the heads of the guests; she and Freddie were having their picture taken in a less dense corner. She was laughing, pretending to elbow Freddie out of shot, all bright eyes and tumbling words from adrenalin and drink, and the absurd idea occurred to him again that she and Caroline would really get on, if it weren't for the circumstances.

In Dame Barbara's house there were many rooms, every one of which could comfortably accommodate Sally's entire flat. Barbara's third husband, Tibault, was a knighted architect, and although the house presented to the street a colonnaded face of Georgian solemnity, the front door opened on to a space odyssey of knock-throughs, split levels, atria, ducts, chutes, walkways and cantilevered galleries. A floor had been removed so that the main room was two storeys high, a gleaming basilica of glass and stark brickwork, walled with almost certainly original paintings of the Abstract Expressionist school.

In recognition of their friendship, Barbara had unwisely invited Dev to bring his decks, and the cavernous central space was juddering with unnavigable beats while Dev's girlfriend and her friend loitered either side of the table looking gorgeously bored with one hip thrust out.

'I've got a theory about you and married men,' Lola said, looking down, as they braved a suspended gangplank over a deep stairwell in search of a bathroom.

'Is this going to be father-related?' Sally gripped the handrails, feeling that the gangplank, cat's-cradled above a fifteen-foot drop and swinging alarmingly, was a flourish too far. She imagined Sir Tibault finishing his grand conversion of the house and not being able to stop tinkering with gratuitous improvements, in the way that her father had been halfway through taking up the floor in the bathroom for no reason when he suddenly decamped to America. It had been the first thing he apologized for when he returned, her mother said, as if this more than anything else had been giving him sleepless nights for three years. *I hope youse managed to get that floor sorted.* She'd put it in the play; the audience had found it funnier than she'd expected.

'Probably, on some level. But I think it's because they prove you right. It's a self-fulfilling prophecy.'

'Do go on.'

'Well, you secretly think all men will turn out to be cheats and liars and can't be trusted –'

'No one could ever accuse you of over-simplifying.'

'– and the minute they get involved with you, they *become* cheats and liars, even if they weren't before, so by the act of falling in love with you they've demonstrated your thesis, so that even if they really do want to be with you and leave their wives, you don't want them any more because by then you already know they have the capacity to lie and cheat and not be trusted. See?'

'Have you lain awake polishing this in the long watches of the night?'

'No, it just came to me. I was watching Greg and feeling sorry for his wife.'

'Well, don't feel sorry for his wife, you don't know anything about it. She's a bitch to him, by all accounts. Anyway, it's all over – they've been talking about a trial separation.'

'Oh, Sally.' Lola pressed her lips together like a disappointed Sunday School teacher. 'They *all* say that.'

The gangplank pitched with an unexpected distribution of weight. Sally turned and saw Dev launching himself on to it.

'Wennoff all right, dinnit, tonight?' he said, amiably.

'You were great, Dev.'

He did a kind of shrugging, lateral movement with his neck.

'Yeah, well, I dint forget any of it, that's the main thing. I was bricking myself to start with cause they kept laughing.'

'They were supposed to. You've got some funny lines. Though I say so myself.'

'Yeah, but it's different in rehearsal.' Dev looked accepting, if not impressed. 'Din expect them to laugh that much.' He grinned, and thrust down a foot so that the walkway jolted frighteningly to one side. 'All them awards and he can't build fuckin stairs.'

Beyond the swaying of the gangplank, Sally could feel the champagne taking hold, and was glad of it. Greg was behaving with a concentrated strangeness tonight, which she attributed to the presence of Caroline. After a pointed coldness towards her at the theatre, he had walked unavoidably into her on arrival at Barbara's; he had introduced her, looking candidly ill at ease, to Caroline, who had his arm in a pincer grip. Sally had shaken her hand again and said, with an edge she hoped Greg could not mistake, 'We've already met.' He had looked carefully away.

Rhys Richards was not a tolerant man, and at midnight, to widespread gratitude, he called a masterful halt to Dev's banging bhangra and hip-hop confection and replaced it with a selection of Barbara's albums of showtunes. Then he turned to Caroline, who was nearest to hand, and whirled her into the middle of the room in an exhibition tango to the opening bars of 'I Hope I Get It' from *A Chorus Line*. A number of other guests broke into applause and rushed to join them.

Greg, who was predictably to be found by the makeshift bar, turned to watch Caroline squealing with delight as she twirled with Rhys and idly thought how pretty she still was, how well she had kept her figure, feeling at that moment nothing but a deep irritation towards her. He wondered, not for the first time, if she might like *him* better if he were gay; not only would he leave her alone with his scrabbling fingers in the night, but as a bonus he would have better music. He considered how best he might extricate himself from his present situation; he was cornered by Lola's father, Anthony Czajkowski, with his arresting beard; a man-sized piece of bronze statuary depicting what might be either a pregnant woman or an owl, depending on how you looked at it (those two round staring globes – were they breasts or eyes?); and an elderly care-in-the-community escapee wearing a surgical mask which he refused to take off. Finding himself suitably drunk, Greg had decided that this was the moment to impress upon Tony Czajkowski how great an admirer he, Greg Burns, was of Dickens, Hardy, Jane Brontë or indeed any of those Victorians with breeches, and how irreplaceably perfect he would therefore be for whatever forgotten classic Tony was next planning to bring to general release. If anything was guaranteed to get you groupies, Greg thought, it was doing a Tony Czajkowski costume drama in breeches.

Tony was deep in conversation with the man in the mask when Greg approached, opting for the universal point of entry to a man's affections.

'You must be very proud of Lola, Mr Czajkowski.'

Tony accepted the interruption with a gracious nod.

'Your daughter. Lola.'

'Yes, yes, I remember Lola. I'm extremely proud, of course. She's worked very hard on this play – well, you all have. You deserve every success.'

'She's a lovely girl. I wish she was my daughter.'

Tony looked alarmed.

'I mean to say, I hope my daughter turns out to be as committed to – her' – he faltered – '*things*. As Lola.'

'How old is your daughter?'

'Ten. But I don't think she's interested in the theatre.'

'No? Well – it's a charming age, ten. Couple of years, she'll turn into an opinionated little bitch you can't even have a sensible conversation with, both mine did. They grow out of it, of course.'

'In my experience,' said the old man, through his mask, 'this is not a phase women ever grow out of. But – Anthony – *Afghanistan*.'

'Sorry, Lars. Carry on.' Tony turned back to his original conversation. Greg understood himself to be superfluous, but was unsure as to whether it would be better to melt away quietly without further imposing himself, or if manners demanded that he announce his departure with some kind of *it's been a great pleasure talking to you* sign-off. In the end he reversed away apologetically, kicking himself for not getting the breeches in more quickly.

He climbed to a mezzanine level above the main room and from there wandered through *Star Trek* corridors of mirrors and galvanized steel contrivances and expensive, ugly art, until a pair of glass doors brought him out to a balcony sheltered from the drizzle by a scalloped awning, from where you could see into the cathedral-like kitchen of the next-door house. At the far end he caught the firefly glimmer of a lit cigarette.

'Hey.' Sally was wadded into a coat on a curlicued metal bench, her legs pulled up to her chin. Greg felt a sudden skip of excitement.

'What are you doing out here?'

'Thinking.'

'It's bloody freezing.'

'That's mainly what I was thinking.'

'Budge up, then.'

He settled companionably beside her, close enough to share a ghost of warmth, and lit a cigarette. It was fairly unlikely that Caroline would find her way out here, he thought, glancing behind him.

'Your *wife* is quite a mover on the dance floor,' Sally said.

Greg decided to ignore the tone.

'She's in her element down there. She always gets on better with gays, for some reason.'

Sally shook her head.

'You can't say *gays*.'

She sounded like Daisy reproaching him for not knowing the name of some singer or other. Greg had never concerned himself especially with the flux of social change, but now he felt a momentary stab of cultural anxiety. He did not like to be patronized by Sally.

'I thought it was all right to say gay.'

'You can say *gay*, but you can't say *gays*.'

'What, you can't use the plural?'

'You can't use the *noun*. At least, *you* can't. There's a world of difference between noun and adjective. See – he's *gay* – adjective, neutral description – that's fine. He's *a* gay – noun – implies a label that's potentially derogatory. You're categorising people as *other*. Same goes for queer, and black. He's black – fine. *The* blacks – definitely not fine. See? She's Jewish – description, fine. She's *a* Jew – well, that's more complicated but essentially the same rules apply.'

'Do you ever think you're too clever for your own good?'

'You've got to be aware of these things, Greg. It's a minefield out there.'

'I live in King's Lynn, I never meet any gays, blacks or Jews. *Joke*,' he added, seeing her half turn sharply in the thin spill of light from the window above.

'You're living in London now.'

'True.' Greg had not yet properly assimilated the full meaning of this. 'Pat's found me digs. Some old dear in Primrose Hill.'

'Nice.'

'Right by the park. Her husband used to be in the theatre in some capacity. She lets her basement out to actors. Should be all right.'

'Does she let you have visitors in your room?' Sally was giving him a sly look, the cigarette propped at an angle in a corner of her mouth.

'We'll soon find out.'

He gave a sudden seismic shiver. From below them, sounds of the party surfaced, muted, and drizzle misted across the lights.

'Your agent doesn't like me,' Sally said, after a while.

'Why do you think that?'

'He gives me squinty disapproving looks.'

'Maybe he didn't have his lenses in.' Greg fought to reignite his cigarette in the damp wind. 'He thinks you're going to get me into trouble.'

'And what do you think?'

'I don't know. Really. When I think about you, it disturbs me. Like tonight – when you were talking to that bloke in the bar.'

'Which bloke?'

'The good-looking one.'

Sally appeared to struggle for clarity.

'What, Tim?' She laughed. 'I've known him since college. He writes for *Time Out*', as if that explained everything.

'I thought you were flirting with him.'

'I probably was, but it's meaningless.'

'Well, anyway. I thought you were with him, and I was jealous, if you want to know.'

'Well, I wasn't thrilled to meet Caroline.'

'No, I'd like to have avoided that. But it's not in the rules, is it, feeling this kind of stuff?'

'What rules?'

'Whatever this is we're doing. It's supposed to be casual, isn't it?'

Sally hunched forward and stared into the space between her knees.

'That's up to you, I'd say. You're the one with the wife.'

'I don't know what you're doing with me. You could be with any bloke. I can't offer you anything, really.'

'I haven't asked you for anything, have I?'

'That's what I don't get. I'm thinking it might just be a double bluff.'

She laughed again.

'It's an adventure, Greg. It's all a big adventure. What is life without adventure, eh? Do you want some coke?'

'No, I'm all right with the beer, thanks.'

'You are sweet.' She banged her head affectionately against his shoulder and rested it there. Greg checked anxiously behind him. 'Come with me to Afghanistan.'

'What?'

'A trip. Holiday. Come with me.'

'Thanks, but I think we're already booked into Centreparcs for this year.'

'Come on, Greg, do something crazy for once. Do you enjoy your routine that much? Don't you want to just say *fuck it*, and get on a plane to Kabul?'

'I might consider the Eurostar, that's about the limits of my adventurous spirit. Look, I'd better get back, I'm freezing my bollocks off.'

'OK, listen. In the main room, in the top corner behind the bar, to the left of the Warhol, there's a spiral staircase, you know it?'

'Vaguely.'

'All right, so you go up that and all the way along the minstrels' gallery and at the far end there's an automatic double door –'

'Yes –'

'– if you go through that and along the hallway with the glass floor and the Northern-Lights-effect lighting –'

'Yes –'

'– and at the end of that there's a stairwell with an Art Deco mosaic ceiling and a suspended gangplank and if you cross that and take the second door off the corridor that's got the Henry Moore at the entrance, you come into a Moorish-effect bathroom with a sunken bath full of aromatherapy gunk and a little fountain.'

'Right. And – ?'

'Meet me there in five minutes and I'll give you something to put a smile on your face.' She tapped her pocket. 'And if you get lost on the journey, don't whatever you do put on the magic ring.'

Later, in their hotel room, Caroline would lie awake watching the strobe lightshow of the television on the ceiling and wonder at the stamina of Greg's post-performance adrenalin; at how determinedly he sat, cross-legged, rocking and muttering in a soft voice at the silenced screen; at how meticulously he applied himself to the mini-bar shelves in strict order of display, regardless of compatibility; at how relatively few times he had attempted to jab her in the back with a half-cocked near-erection; most of all at how the unbending, face-chewing grin appeared to be welded on to his face since the latter hours of the party. She would eventually reason, as sleep purred over her and Greg poured himself another mini Drambuie and Tizer to accompany an early episode of *The Sopranos*, that it was, after all, his first West End press night and it was bound to make him a bit over-excited.

11

Girls' hips, thought Greg. You never used to see them at all, and now they were everywhere. Even here, in Brighton, at the end of February, surrounding him on all flanks; one glimmer of winter sun and everyone started dressing as if they were in Tobago. That was England for you. Trousers were receding, had clearly been receding for some time, at both ends, it seemed, and Greg applauded this stylistic development; there was something unapologetically stiffening about this expanse of female skin now delivered to public view: that mystical S-bend, tracing its undulation from the tense waist downwards and outwards to the teasing push of the hip-bone and back on its inward curve . . . At the back, too, when they leant forward, the generous cello swelling, the symmetry of the paired dimples, the nubbed spine . . . Even the fat ones, even those with raw gooseflesh rising like dough each side of the garrotting waistband, even their curves were fascinating, because these were the parts of women you never used to see unless you'd got to the point where you were seeing the full show anyway. Usually, with these trousers, you also got the twisted T-junction of lace and elastic riding up at the back for anyone who cared to look, which some people might find vulgar, but which Greg found exceptionally arousing.

:At the moment, Greg found everything exceptionally arousing. He had always *looked* at women, but now he *always* looked at women; all the time: fat, thin, old, young, grievously young. This he attributed to Sally's influence. Sex, he supposed, was like any other addiction; denied the substance for long enough, the cravings eventually weakened; conversely the appetite for anything was fuelled by being fed. At home, pandering to his instinct for pleasure required so much effort that he usually ended up deciding to leave it; smoking meant sitting outside in the cold, drinking had to be legitimized by inviting other people to do it with you, with all the cooking and washing up and wearisome conversation that *that* entailed, and sex presupposed hours of wheedling and self-abasement beforehand and apology afterwards. None of the rewards seemed worth the price. In London, however, all these treats and more were easily to hand at all hours other than the two during which he was required to be on stage, and he was beginning to be alarmed at the ferocity of his desires. There simply weren't enough hours in the day to smoke all the cigarettes and bang all the women he wanted to. Sally's artistry in the bedroom (and on the stairs, in a taxi, in the theatre dressing-room, in a park), her blithe lack of censorship, either of him, herself or anyone else, had untethered forces that he had believed long extinguished by his adult self (such as it was).

Now, in a hippy little café in one of the runnelled streets leading away from the wind-burned seafront, a teenage waitress wearing just such cleft-skimming jeans bent her head studiously to write down the two coffees. Her crotch was at the exact level of his head, Greg noted, wondering at the smooth convexity of her unblemished stomach before realizing with some confusion that she could not be many years older than Daisy. Sally, arranging the exoskeleton of her motorbike jacket on the back of her chair, caught the direction of his gaze, made a lascivious move with her tongue and grinned. Greg sat back and blushed.

Sally understood about men and sex, or she liked to give the impression that she did, which was not the same as being understand*ing*, though she seemed to believe it was. Caroline, for example: if they were walking down the street together and saw heading towards them a girl with unavoidable breasts, *Caroline*, knowing he wanted to stare, would pointedly watch him as he searched frantically for an innocent diversion – a dog, a child, a non-sexual cloud shape – on which to comment until the temptation had passed. Sally, by contrast – now *Sally*, knowing he wanted to stare, would pre-empt by poking him in the ribs and nodding at the oncoming phenomenon, saying, in a theatrical aside, 'Whoa, Nelly!' or something similar. This must be a generational distinction, Greg thought, but he was fairly convinced it could be only cosmetic. Women didn't like you to look at other women's breasts when you were out with them, full stop; that didn't change. So he couldn't decide whose approach was more self-deluding; Caroline's, for trying to convince herself that he didn't look, or Sally's for trying to convince him that she didn't care?

The play, *Real*, was nearing the end of its second month and was proving a considerable success. Fridays and Saturdays had been selling out since the beginning of February, and the mid-week nights, even Mondays, were respectably peopled; there was even talk of the run being extended. The reviews had been fulsome, and Greg's performance had been singled out for special praise in *The Times* ('surprising emotional literacy . . . Burns is an unintentionally intuitive comic foil'), the *Observer* ('shown himself to possess a wider range than *Valley Vets* would have led us to expect') and *Metro* ('by turns darkly funny and comically poignant'). Rhys and Lola were confident that Freddie and Barbara would each be nominated for an Olivier, and there was a good chance Sally might be shortlisted for the *Evening Standard*'s Most Promising Playwright category. No one had been heard to express the likelihood of Greg being nominated for any awards, but it was understood that any individual decoration was the achievement of the whole company, to which Greg said privately, *horseshit*. He had no interest in Freddie's gong, nor Barbara's, nor even in Sally's, unless he were in the running with them.

Over the preceding two months Greg had entered a churning, vampiric existence in which he had come to feel increasingly dislocated from exterior reality. The performance energy was high and the cast chemistry still strong; they had been through only two duff nights in as many months, which was almost unheard of for any production with Greg in it. Each night he would go straight from two hours of pretending to be someone else, for which he was being paid, to another night and day of pretending to be someone *else*, for which he was paying dearly (in every sense), except for Saturday nights, when he would take a hurried cab to the station for the last train back to King's Lynn, where he would spend Sundays with Caroline and Daisy pretending to be the person he used to be, for which no payment had yet been exacted, but surely would. Oh yes, it most certainly would. In fact, Greg thought, the role that demanded the least of his modest acting talent was the one he was performing on stage.

At night, when he was out with Sally and her friends, with the bars and the music and the Class A motivation and all the crazy, flashing sideshow lights of London, his home life felt untouchably remote and he believed himself truly free. He felt eighteen again, the hopeful would-be hedonist arriving at drama college with life still looking like an adventure. Sally had chosen to go on believing that life could be an adventure (though she was clearly old enough to know better, which Greg found impressive, on some level), and he was infatuated with this energy because he recognized the youthful shadow of himself in the (frankly ridiculous) conviction that the adventure lay wholly in seeing how far you could go beyond the extremes. Most nights they would fall into Sally's bed at three or four and after whatever acrobatics their punished lungs and limbs could be pushed to, would fall fitfully asleep. Then at seven, or thereabouts, with the first grating of the café's shutters, guilt would knee him awake with reminders that he was a family man, with a wife and child; bright images of Daisy tumbling and giggling in the garden with the dog, and Caroline patiently taking her to flute lessons and reassuring her that Daddy would be home on Sunday to look at her science folder.

Sally's invasion of his ordered life might have rejuvenated his spirit, but it was making his flesh feel pensionable. Each morning, while she slept the unconfined sleep of the young and single – her long body bisecting the bed, limbs comfortably adrift, squeezing him into a far corner against the wall, her unconscious clearly unconditioned to the presence of another body – he would flail urgently to his feet, fogged and blighted from the previous night, palpitating with a whirl of inner accusations and filled with an urgent need to flee the succubus and devote what remained of his day to something pure and wholesome. Fortunately Mrs Cudlipp, the proprietress of his rented accommodation, seemed to have little interest in his comings and goings (mostly goings), provided he didn't frighten the cats and provided she received her hundred and fifty pounds each week (Greg had already calculated the amount he would save if he didn't have to maintain, for Caroline's sake, the front of a rented room and could simply move in with Sally for the length of the run); better still, she did not allow her lodgers access to her telephone, so that Caroline's only means of reaching him was via his mobile. He had told her he couldn't get a signal in Mrs Cudlipp's basement.

Greg had read somewhere that guilt – indeed, all emotional flux – was merely the result of chemical disequilibrium in the brain; it followed, then, he told himself, that the strident paranoia and howlings of conscience that he now experienced daily through these barking hangovers were exacerbated by the amount of foreign chemicals he was putting into his system. Greg had little history with drugs, apart from the brief obligatory dalliance with pot at drama college (which had only ever succeeded in sending him to sleep), and he liked this new image of himself as someone who coolly tucked away a couple of lines of cocaine at the beginning of a night out better than he liked the actual business of doing it, which was playing havoc with his sinuses. He suspected this might also be true of Sally and her friends; he was dimly suspicious, too, during these nights out, that he was almost certainly less witty and entertaining than he believed himself to be, but again, this was probably also true of the rest of the company. But he was fighting a losing battle with guilt. He was a walking, living, breathing, fermenting *seethe* of guilt. Guilt was the whole of his life, except for those occasional flashes of bravado (as when, for the first three weeks of the run, he had come home on the Saturday night and attempted with some verve to have sex with Caroline, because he liked the idea of having two women on the go, but telling himself afterwards that she would find it suspicious if he did not at least try. In fact she found it *more* suspicious that he tried with such vigour.)

Sally had told him about a novel she had read recently, American, in which they had invented a drug that countered the effect of the guilt-inducing brain chemicals. In the book, the middle-aged middle classes took it to relieve the stress brought on by trying to conform to social expectations, and the young took it to have wilder sex. But it must be possible, Greg had thought, outside fiction, it must be possible in *real life* for someone to come up with a pill that would eliminate guilt, or at the very least, dull its edge; they had them for every other intangible condition. The pharmaceutical solution must exist. Presumably they didn't license it because without guilt and shame society would fall into anarchy. Still, he would be the first to sign up.

It was no reassurance, either, to remind himself on Sundays that these assaults of conscience were purely neurological. As if in response to the prompting of some territorial instinct, Caroline had pitched herself into an organizing frenzy of family-centric activities to celebrate Greg's one day at home. After a week of self-wrought atomic devastation on his mental and physical health, on top of the demands of six evening performances and two matinees and Sally's sexual requirements, when what Greg most desired was to huddle on the sofa with a pint of tea and watch a Western, or sleep, he found himself herded into the Land Cruiser for a family day out, regardless of the weather. There were barbecues for all their friends, where paramilitary units of other people's children mounted raids room by room until the house was laid waste; there were sleepovers for Daisy's friends, which he had to police; there were jaunts to reconstructed Iron Age villages, wildfowl sanctuaries, cottages-turned-museums that had once sheltered Oliver Cromwell, adventure playgrounds, zoological parks, ice rinks, where he would nod with grim empathy at the other Sunday dads being hauled around by their anorak sleeves and assailed with pleas for ice-cream, all the while still feeling, if he stopped to conjure it, the pressure of Sally's teeth and fingers on various outlying parts of his body. He suspected strongly that none of them was really enjoying these forced outings, in the company of other families aggressively enjoying their quality time; Daisy was not a good actress, and her pink excitement always wore the sheen of insincerity on these occasions. No doubt she would have much preferred to stay at home too, and no doubt Caroline had impressed upon her the importance of spending time together *as a family* to remind Greg of what anchored him in the face of so much temptation during the week. How much of his London life she guessed at, Greg was unable to tell; still, the thought that she could read him better than anyone only pressed another heavy layer on to the sediment of guilt that weighed in his stomach and the base of his skull.

Finally, the previous week, he had drawn the line at pony-trekking and installed himself obstinately in front of the television; Caroline had shouted, Daisy had cried, he had remained intransigent. On the Monday morning, as she drove him to the station, Caroline spoke to him for the first time in twenty-four hours only to tell him, with glassy voice and expression, that he might as well stay in London the following weekend as she had already made plans with Andrea. Affronted, in defiant self-vindication, he had taken a taxi from King's Cross straight to Sally's, where he had given her a good seeing-to for two hours before going to the theatre (usually he liked to preserve his energy for the performance) and asked her if she'd like to have a day out on Sunday. She had seemed almost childishly delighted, and it struck Greg that perhaps Sally deserved more effort and respect that he had been offering her (which produced additional and unexpected guilt and resentment). *Two* demanding women at the same time was not the Nirvana he had imagined.

'Ooh, *Mama*,' Sally said suddenly, gesturing towards the window where two teenage girls were passing, midriffs agape, wind-stiffened nipples rearing proudly under skinny tops. Greg glanced up and nodded, and quietly registered that in four, possibly three, years' time, men in their forties would be looking at Daisy the way he was now being invited to look at these kids; the way men looked at Sally, which partly made him puff his chest out in conquest and partly want to protect her. He knew only too well what men could be like. The trouble was, so did Sally. She seemed to have no illusions regarding the basest, most animal, most elemental currents of the male psyche; he imagined this was a father thing. She did not, unlike Caroline, expect the best of him. Which, on Wednesday, had made it easier to ... Which was why, on Wednesday ... He needed to make a confession. All this lying was undoubtedly furring up his arteries.

'They must be freezing,' he said.

Greg was freezing. He had begun to believe that his joints were permanently fixed by the cold into the angles of stoked terror they had assumed on the bike. As with many of Sally's suggestions, he had liked the idea of it better than the reality; not only did he feel embarrassed, when they pulled alongside other bikers at traffic lights, to be pillion to a girl (there were a lot of bikes out in Brighton, and not one of them with a girl driving), but as soon as the bike achieved its sixth gear he became rigid with a craven fear of death and lost all instinctive sense of balance, so that twice Sally had had to stop and ask him impatiently what the fuck he was playing at back there. It was fine for Sally, encased in her tight matching leathers (and looking more like a fantasy in her cladding than any of the half-naked girls wandering the pier, he had to admit, which had been one of the main incentives to agreeing to the bike – that and not wanting to appear a middle-aged coward), but Greg's leather jacket, which he had worn on her strict instructions, was more in the Seventies detective-show style, thin and pliable, so that as he watched the tarmac streaming under the wheels at unimaginable speeds (he couldn't see the dials over Sally's shoulder without standing up on the footrests, which he was not prepared to attempt), he could only visualize how tenderly it would shred and pulp, like his poor skin, if they were to capsize. And there was still the return journey to complete; it had occurred to him fretfully that if he were to sustain serious injury in an accident it would be impossible to hide from Caroline the fact that he had come off a girl's motorbike on the road from Brighton; naturally she might have some questions about what he had been doing there in the first place.

For some years now, more or less since the birth of his daughter, Greg had nursed a small but persistent anxiety that he had not slept with enough women, and that time was running out. A late starter, he had enjoyed a short-lived bloom of promiscuity in his final year of drama college, then a succession of unsuccessful but largely monogamous relationships through his twenties, then Caroline and the six last-ditch flings. His conquests totalled twenty-six. He was forty-four. Sally was twenty-nine, and claimed, with neither boast nor apology, to have slept with twenty-nine people, which had pricked him again with that vague unease he sometimes felt around her; not that he was morally troubled by the figure, more a sense that things were the *wrong way around*, just as they were on the motorbike.

Sally was deploying a clever strategy, Greg had decided, though he also recognized the possibility that it was only his narrow assumptions about women that led him to imagine there was a strategy in play at all. She gave the impression that, as far as she was concerned, their affair was exclusively about sex; he remained unconvinced, largely because he had never, even at his best, been the kind of man women took on purely for sex. But Sally only ever referred to their adventure in those terms; therefore, the perversity of human desire (human *male* desire) being what it is, the focus of all his energies immediately became that which was deliberately withheld. Most women, in Greg's experience, squandered unasked-for affections on you and used sex mainly as a kind of currency, to be bartered for dec-larations of love. Sally pointedly avoided any suggestion of romance and projected only coolness and indifference; conversely, and logical-ly, Greg was becoming obsessed with coaxing, wheedling, seducing and baldly lying some soft words out of her, which, he half suspect-ed, was probably her intention all along. The nearest he had come had been during one potentially charged and tender post-coital moment, with her hair lightly draping his damp shoulder and his ebbing blood throbbing in time to the beats of the street, when he had touched her face and said, with maximum caveat, 'I could probably quite fall for you, you know.' Sally got up swiftly after that; standing naked by the bed with one hip forward and a cigarette propped in the corner of a smile, she had winked over the cocked lighter and said, 'Well, you're only flesh and blood.'

She was establishing her credentials, Greg imagined, as the polar opposite of Caroline. Then, presumably, once she had him, the performance would end and she would reveal the hidden capacity for nagging and unreasonable demands, because surely – *surely* – it was impossible for any woman to have such a male approach to the business of love and sex. It had to be a double-bluff, arch with womanly cunning. Only the week before, she had offered to take him to a strip club. At the end of her narrow market street was a broad-faced pub, whose calligraphic sign invited patrons to enjoy the large patio garden and non-specific good food, and gave no hint of its attractions apart from the darkened windows. As they passed its doors one night on the way home, the neckless doorman had greeted Sally by name like an old friend, she had cheerfully saluted him in return, and told Greg, quite matter-of-factly, that it was a lap-dancing bar. 'We can go there some time if you want,' she had said, as if recommending an Indian. It had taken only a second for Greg's pulse to quicken at the audacity before it dawned on him that visiting a strip club with Sally was unequivocally what he did *not* want. The sole pleasure afforded by strip clubs (though it was a good decade and a half since Greg had seen the inside of one) was the element of transgression. Well, perhaps not the *sole* pleasure, but a good deal of it. A strip club was where you went when you'd all told your wives and girlfriends you were somewhere else; the solitary punters you saw staked out along the bar, those at liberty to visit whenever they chose, because they had no one to lie to, never looked as if they were getting much out of it.

Why can't a woman be more like a man?

Greg had auditioned for the part of Professor Henry Higgins in *My Fair Lady* during the dry years after the demise of *Valley Vets*, but his singing voice had let him down. Nevertheless he remembered thinking what shards of truth were in those lyrics, now considered by everyone else who heard them to have gained a sheen of archaic irony. Because now they were, of course, women; those of Sally's generation were just like men, and as with so much of life, Greg felt, it had turned out to have been better in the wishing than the reality. Not that any man wanted a clingy, helpless bim without a thought of her own in her head, who just did whatever you told her (admittedly he wanted that at times, but only on a temporary basis), but there was something not only unconvincing but disturbing, in his view, about a woman who wanted to invade and experience every nook of manhood. It was possible that the men of Sally's generation were undergoing a parallel evolution, to the extent that they were comfortable with their womenfolk joining them as equals in terrace, casino and strip bar (the mere suggestion to Caroline that they watch porn together would be enough to send her scuttling to the nearest women's refuge), but in him such forthrightness inspired a niggle of fear, and it was the fear of his identity being undermined. This, in its turn, seemed to be fanning a latent anger, towards women in general for their contradictions and double standards, but concentrated, in unguarded moments, on Sally herself. Which was why, last Wednesday . . .

As they left the little café and walked, not arm in arm, exactly, more *netted* in one another's limbs, towards the sea wall and its neat rows of whiteboard beach huts, he thought it very likely that he *could* fall for Sally, in spite of the bike and the strip club. If he didn't care about her, he reasoned, he wouldn't feel this prodding need to explain what happened on Wednesday. In the light of the fleshless winter sun, with its optimistic glitter, amid the smells of kelp and vinegared chips that salted the air, Greg ran a hand down the slope of her back and looked up towards the pier, considering, with renewed appreciation, that he had not expected to see days like this again; the simplicity of free time, without constraints. There was such a post-war innocence about English resorts, even one as made-over as Brighton, that brought him back to the family fortnight in Scarborough, every July through his childhood and adolescence, saved for all year by his mother and father with resolute self-denial. As a teenager, he had both dreaded and longed for this annual exodus in his father's tobacco-jaundiced Renault 16, its boot piled high with the flaking leather-look luggage set his parents had had as a wedding present. In spite of the mildewed guesthouse with terrible curtains, in which he'd finally been granted a separate room from his parents when he reached fourteen, though he remained under obligation to return each evening for a compulsory and sullen family meal, the days were long and occasionally warm; a young man could mooch through the arcades, watching with envy the older lads with scooters who could afford to play the machines, and talk to the girls who hung around the fish and chip booths on the promenade (better accomplished in theory than in practice), while his parents engaged in uncharacteristic holiday activities they couldn't possibly have enjoyed (minigolf and bowls). In his fifteenth summer, he had met a girl named Alison, who was very pale, with braces on her teeth and no breasts, and spent every day of the holiday walking with her, holding hands, gazing into her eyes as cinema had taught him. On the evening of his last day, she had let him put his hand up her top on a bench beside the Old Harbour. It had hardly been worth the effort, but he had embellished it later in the telling. She had written to him for months afterwards, but as soon as he was back in York she had receded into memory; he had written back twice and then grown bored and forgotten. Even so, (now that he thought about her for the first time in thirty years), he remembered Alison with fondness for offering his first innocent summer of intimacy with a girl; oddly (perhaps it was the coastal wind and its associations), today he was feeling primed for the same rush of discovery and hesitant romance with Sally.

'So, you know Wednesday?' he began.

'COCKSUCKER!'

Sally shook his arm away and furiously fisted the air in the wake of a oversized 4x4 that had whipped them out of their ambling reverie as it smugly hurtled far too fast along the narrow street, forcing a couple of elderly pedestrians to leap for the kerb.

'Are you all right?' she asked the old man, who seemed startled but unharmed. 'Jesus, I fucking *hate* those things,' she added, turning to indicate the vehicle's passing, to which the old man's wife looked politely shocked, then nodded a fervent agreement.

'Seriously,' – she looked at Greg for back up – 'I don't know why anyone has those in towns. Or anywhere. You have to be such an unreconstructed *cocksucker* to want one. Just wear a shirt with your fucking salary printed on it, that's a far more responsible way of showing off how much you earn. *Jesus.*'

He could at this point have kept his mouth shut, but something about the frankness of the sea had put him in a confessional mood.

'Actually we've got one at home.'

'Oh.'

'We bought it secondhand. It's only a P reg.' He hoped it sounded placatory. 'You know, because the dog fits in the back.'

Sally faced him with a total failure of recognition, and the pause that followed reminded Greg of those silences that happen occasionally on stage, where everyone knows that somebody is supposed to be speaking but is fairly certain that it isn't them. It struck him that in the giddy ripple of seaside sounds and smells he had been on the verge of declaring a love of sorts to a woman who, through no fault of her own, knew almost nothing about him. The picture she had of him, he assumed, must be that of someone who drank too much, cheated on his family, tried – absurdly – to pretend he was still eighteen, and who, in spite of all this, she still wanted to sleep with, and it seemed terribly sad to him at that moment to think that she only knew him at his most despicable. She didn't know, for example, how he stood in the kitchen each night making Daisy's packed lunch for school the following day while Caroline irrigated her face in the bathroom, carefully cutting the crust off her sandwiches, choosing the crisps, putting in a little surprise – a fun-size Mars Bar, perhaps – tucked away behind the forbidding packet of dried apricots that Caroline insisted she took because he could picture her smile when she found it. Neither did Sally know how patiently he looked after Caroline when she was ill, nor how he would sit for hours stroking Daisy's hair and singing old Sinatra tunes when she was scared and couldn't sleep; she didn't know that he spent whole Sundays lacerating his fingers with chicken wire and unplaned wood to build a run for the guinea pigs, nor did she have any idea how demolished his confidence had been when his television work ran out, nor how much he missed his mother and how afraid he was of his father dying nor, worse still, and unconfided to anyone, how much more afraid he was of his father *not* dying, but fading slowly and interminably past his century as everything he owned ebbed away in care-home fees, nor quite what a profound sense of loyalty he was only now realizing he had to Caroline. Sally couldn't even muster the imagination to see him as someone with a family car. Suddenly he wanted her to know all this, wanted her to see that he was a better person than she thought, but he was aware that insisting how much he cared for his family as his greatest selling point might in these circumstances come across as a little insincere. He also wondered, with a degree of dismay, whether it was his worst side that Sally found appealing, and whether she might in fact go off him if she were to discover that from time to time he did attempt to be decent.

'The dog *fits* in the back? What, it has a special dog-shaped boot or something?'

Sally, to his relief, was laughing, so he joined in, until he saw that her eyes were not. He knew why; he had spoken the unforgivable word. He had reminded her that he was part of a 'we' that came before her, and which she worked hard to exclude from her consciousness and from the time they spent together; this was a far worse crime on his part than owning a Land Cruiser. She was jealous and trying to hide it, which Greg considered an overreaction and at the same time quite erotic. So, perversely, he decided to push his luck.

What had happened the previous Wednesday was that Sally, who had given up sitting through the play night after night and only now turned up to the bar to meet him afterwards, had been given a ticket to see the Magnetic Fields in Shepherd's Bush by a friend called Dan who worked for the record company. Greg was not familiar with the Magnetic Fields and had attempted to cover his ignorance by making an ill-judged joke to the effect that she hadn't mentioned this Dan before, and he wasn't sure he liked her going on dates with other men, which Sally had – quite irrationally, in Greg's view – failed to understand as the humorous aside it so clearly was, and instead taken as a display of possessive behaviour to which he, for obvious reasons, had no right. The argument had ended with Sally telling – not inviting or suggesting, but *telling* – him to come and meet her afterwards in a bar in Hammersmith, and adding before she signed off that actually Dan was someone she used to sleep with but was now just a friend, not that it was any of his business.

Greg was no expert on the etiquette of affairs but he felt sure that when your mistress started behaving like your wife, you were not obliged to put up with it; that was the beauty of the system. So when he arrived in the theatre bar after his shower, feeling less than pleased with his own performance and therefore in a heightened state of tiredness and irritability, he was ready to find some distraction that would prove to Sally that he was not at her beck and call. Of course, he could simply have gone back to Mrs Cudlipp's and gone to bed, but he was growing increasingly superstitious; he feared that if he admitted even once to himself, to Sally, to London, which he sensed watching him constantly with its billion eyes and judging, that he

149

was forty-four years old and frequently yearned to be in bed before midnight, the charm would be broken and he would be flung back into the life of provincial middle age that he was fleeing. In London he not only felt young, he *was* young, by objective standards; in London, men with twenty years on him stayed out until the small hours drinking with beautiful women. In King's Lynn, people asked him whether he'd considered becoming a school governor. It was unfortunate that in the theatre bar he had run into Gonzo, the assistant stage manager.

Greg didn't actually like Gonzo. There was the self-conferred nickname for a start, no doubt meant to suggest Thompsonesque abandon but more pertinently reminding Greg of the scrawny shrill Henson puppet. Gonzo was a pushy, bragging kid in his mid-twenties with bleached hair and an obsession with gadgets. Greg appreciated the allure of a good gadget as much as the next man, but he couldn't see the mileage in buying endless magazines that informed you that the state-of-the-art Blackberry or iPod you bought last week was no longer state of the art; that was just self-flagellation. Added to this, since Gonzo spent all his money on gadgets and gadget-related magazines, he was forever poncing fags and drinks off everyone else on the grounds that he'd return the favour as soon as he was paid, which annoyed Greg further; you can forgive a man many faults if he only stands his round, and Gonzo never did. But on Wednesday Gonzo had been looking for someone to drink with and Greg, in a momentary spirit of rebellion and self-assertion, had agreed to accompany him on a picaresque journey which saw them turned away from the doors of almost all Central London's private clubs while Gonzo barracked with doormen on the grounds that, OK, he wasn't *technically* a member but he did come in there all the time, with John, he was a mate of John's, surely they knew John, and so on. Finally they fetched up outside an emphatically democratic, non-exclusive club off Regent Street called Viva Cuba! which Gonzo assured him would be peopled entirely with ropey old foreign slappers. It had cost them ten pounds each to get in, a further seven pounds per drink, which they were quickly cornered into providing for two giggling and incoherent Danish exchange students who were not especially attractive but were nevertheless Scandinavian, which Greg found hazily exciting, and who invited them back to their hostel to share a bottle of vodka.

By the time they were crushed haphazardly into the back of a cab, with one of them half sitting on his knee, Greg had long exceeded his modest capacity for drink and could barely see. Slamming the window down and gulping grateful mouthfuls of night air, his tongue flapping like a retriever's, helped the nausea abate briefly, and in the psychedelic whirling lights of traffic he thought he saw images of both Caroline and Sally and wondered, with a detached curiosity, as he might of a stranger, or as a stranger might of him, why someone with not one but two infinitely more desirable women in his life should be in a taxi on the way to Bayswater drinking warm wine from the bottle with two raucous girls neither of whose names he could remember. The answer, obviously, was that sometimes you wanted someone you had no respect for; it was thinly disguised misogyny. He was mildly surprised at himself for formulating such a sophisticated thought in his present state, though his inner voice couched it in cruder terms. Unfortunately, whatever dim and base intentions he had harboured towards either or both girls were dashed almost immediately when he fell out of the taxi, into the lobby of their hostel and threw up noisily on the stairs. By the time he had voided he was more than ready to comply with their shrieking insistence that he and Gonzo should leave, but Gonzo was not prepared to have his prize snatched away at the last moment and became equally insistent on being admitted, at which point two rectangular New Zealanders emerged from a room along the corridor and swooped gallantly to the girls' aid by physically heaving both him and Gonzo on to the street, where Greg discovered that somewhere along the way he'd lost his second phone, the one he kept for Sally.

Having regaled Sally with this story, uncensored, he now took a step back and turned to gauge her reaction. They were halfway along the pier by this time and had stopped to buy candyfloss. Wind badgered at the awnings of the kiosks and he realized that Sally was simply staring at him with unreadable eyes, apparently oblivious to the cat's cradle of hair and pink sugar the wind had whipped around her mouth.

'I thought you'd find it funny,' he said.

'Hilarious. And if you hadn't been sick? What – you'd have done what, exactly? With these girls?'

'I don't know. Have a drink.'

'Were you going to have sex with them?'

He looked at her again. There was a definite jut to her lower lip, a new glisten in her eyes, though she was fighting it, and the sight of her suddenly vulnerable, clutching her candyfloss, made his heart tighten a little. *She makes love just like a woman, but she breaks like a little girl.* Good old Bob, a line for every occasion. All the cockiness was gone, he thought; she needed him, at that moment, to make some gesture of conciliation and warmth. It would have been so easy too, just to put an arm around her and reassure her that he had no desire for anyone else, even if this was untrue. But the newness of her need and of his unprecedented position of power inspired a perverse impulse to the contrary. He thought about New York.

'Why?'

'What do you mean, *why*?'

Her face suggested that for once she was not au fait with the rules of the game, and this pleased him. Sally had spent a lot of time in New York – she had various friends and ex-boyfriends there – and she could drop its exotic topography into her anecdotes as naturally as the names of her family. Bleecker Street, the Village, the Lower East Side – words that to Greg rang with a cinematic glamour that bore no geographical correspondent, as real to him as Gallifrey. Less so, in fact; he had, after all, once been in an episode of *Doctor Who*. When he told Sally that he had never visited America, she had looked at him with an expression of such disbelief and pity, as if this were inconceivable, as if New York were simply another Tube stop that all right-thinking people knew like the back of their hands, that he felt as foolish and rustic as if he'd told her he couldn't read or didn't own a television. She hadn't meant to, but a man doesn't like to be continually humbled, even unintentionally.

'I didn't think you were the possessive kind. Not that you would have any right, anyway. See, this is the kind of conversation I'd expect to have with Caroline. I thought you were different. I thought I could say anything to you.'

Sally turned away.

'There's not much I can say to that, is there? The last thing you want is someone behaving like Caroline, eh.'

'Well, it's a bit hypocritical, isn't it? Coming from you.'

'It's also horseshit, Greg, because you actually want someone exactly like Caroline, otherwise you're out of your depth.'

'So you think it's fine for me to be unfaithful to Caroline but not to you?'

She sighed, with the unmistakable female undertone of patience in the face of stupidity.

'You're not listening to me. You don't want someone else, you don't really want me, you just want Caroline to want you again. And because she doesn't, this is all a big cry for attention. Me, this whatever with Gonzo. You don't really want to leave Caroline because it's safe.'

'Thanks, Freud. I never said I did want to leave her, since you ask. I don't even know if I could.'

'I didn't fucking ask. It's not that complicated, Greg. You just want to have all your cake and eat it, like every other fucking bloke. If you don't want to leave her, go back to her, and on the way back ask yourself why you're here if your life with her is so fulfilling.'

'What are you expecting, then? I've never promised you anything, have I?'

He was shouting, partly to overcome the wind and partly because he felt himself indefinably to be in the wrong.

'Fine. Get the train back.'

She started walking away, her candyfloss stick held at an angle to shield it, and for a moment Greg imagined the pleasure of a safe, warm train carriage and a newspaper before once again measuring safety against risk and realizing how close he was to pushing Sally away. She could find someone like him, shot through with insecurities and paranoias and misplaced arrogance, in a second. She could destroy ten more threadbare marriages before the end of the week and barely notice, while his chances of finding someone else like her were – well . . .

'I'm sorry,' he shouted. She didn't turn.

He broke into a heavy run and overtook her, barring her path and putting his hands on her shoulders. She was so much taller than Caroline, he thought, and he missed the easy superiority of talking over someone's head. Sally demanded to be looked in the eye, like an equal.

'Sorry. About what I said.'

'Which bit?'

'All of it. And the girls. I don't want to go back to Caroline.'

'But you don't want *not* to go back to her, do you?'

'I don't know.'

She was half smiling, but there was a tiredness in her eyes and he realized that, if they were to carry on, that tiredness would only grow and grow until it bleached all the animation from her face, and he would know that it was because of him.

'You know your problem, Greg?' She began walking again, slowly this time, picking sticky strands of hair from across her chin. 'You don't know how to be wanted. It's especially acute in your case because you've had to watch her stop wanting you, but it's universally applicable. Blokes – you're all told from your teens that it's a battle to get women into bed and you have to be prepared to use all kinds of bluffs and stratagems, so you're conditioned to believe it's always going to be your job to coerce and her job to resist. So you don't know what to do with the notion that a woman might desire you. And not just desire a good fuck either, finally the idea that women like a good fuck is allowable, but I'm not talking about that. I mean the idea that *you* might be desirable. You, Greg. You're so used to the idea that you're undesirable that you don't know how to respond to anything else. So if you'd rather have what Caroline offers you because that's easier to understand, or you'd rather have some skanky little tart in a youth hostel because you can dismiss it afterwards, then it's up to you. But don't expect to have me as well.'

She threw the pink-tinged stick over the rail and it helicoptered out into the spray.

'So I have to choose?'

She shrugged, yes and no.

'Not definitively. Not yet. But I'm telling you I can't do this skulking part-time thing for ever.'

'I'm the one who has to do the skulking.'

'And it's boring to watch. Come on, let's find somewhere to have sex.'

'What?' Greg whipped his head round in alarm, as if she might be expecting him to drop his trousers right there in full view of the promenading grandparents and ice-cream-smeared toddlers. 'Where?'

'Don't know yet. Come on,' and she grabbed his arm.

That was the moment when Greg knew what his choice would have to be. The impish gleam in her eyes, the breathless giggle – anyone else would have found her face at that moment arousing beyond words and he did, intellectually, but for the first time his caution was stronger than his desire. And it was bloody cold, to boot. He couldn't keep up with her, even though he guessed that in part she was only making the suggestion because it was so evidently something Caroline would never do. He couldn't keep this up indefinitely; it would kill him. When the play finished, then. That was when he would tell her. No sense in cutting off his nose to spite his face any earlier. He had given so many hours' thought to how this might be made to run in parallel with his real life, when he had to return to King's Lynn; he had asked Patrick to book him auditions for jobs that would give him the maximum time in London for the rest of the year. Caroline would never accept that without some kind of showdown, though, and he already knew that continuing with both lives would be impossible. Greg believed he had come to the conclusion that in a few weeks' time he would, reluctantly, have to stop acting.

12

For the third day running, the fat tramp was missing. Sally craned further out of her streetside window in case he had unaccountably chosen a different berth, knowing in her heart that he had not, while the morning smell of frying bacon from below contorted her stomach in an extreme fashion which added to the general sense of unease.

The tramp usually slept on one of the permanent market trestles under the awnings on the cobbled area at the end of the street. He arrived with his bags just as the council cleaning robots were honking their way home, and left when the first vans rolled in the next morning. He looked unexpectedly well fed for a tramp – it was a wonder his wooden bier held him all night – with a Himalayan belly and a sheep of a beard; he was also genial, with an educated voice, smilingly called Sally 'ma'am' when she passed in affectation of a Dickensian beadle, and because he never asked, she often bought him a cup of tea from the caff on her way home. But he hadn't slept there for three days now, and Sally was experiencing a fearful anxiety and culpability that was all mixed up with the other, more immediate anxiety. The tramp had become a kind of Gideon's fleece test; if he's back tomorrow, she had told herself, everything is going to be all right. But he wasn't back, and the idea that he might be gone for good and that he might have fallen victim to something terrible – violence or hypothermia – and that she would never know filled her with sudden dread and tears, and when the next bacon-and-onion updraft came she had to rush into the bathroom and be sick for the second time since standing up.

On the bike, on her way to the surgery in Primrose Hill, she was aware of being more careful than usual, overly cautious of the traffic, its feints and ambushes and above all its fearsome tonnage, and she was not oblivious to the irony of this caution, which, paradoxically, led her to think too much and therefore ride without the kind of fluid instinct that had so far kept her out of trouble. As if – what – she were somehow more fragile now, more easily crushable? She was keeping the visor up because inside it the smell of the rubber seal made her feel sick. With it open, the fumes of the buses made her feel sick.

Sally didn't enjoy visits to Dr Cavendish on the whole, and she suspected that Dr Cavendish felt the same. It didn't matter what you went in for – contraception, shin splints, cholera – every visit began and ended with a mandatory declaration of your weekly alcohol units and although she usually remembered mentally to decimate the original estimate before naming a figure, it still caused Dr Cavendish to wince as if stuck with a hypodermic. Likewise, Dr Cavendish always seemed disappointed when Sally's blood pressure reading turned out to be not just adequate but, in her own reluctantly muttered phrase, 'very good'; it was as if this patent failure of the laws of cause and effect was illustrative of a greater and more general injustice in the universe. When Sally proudly informed her that at college she had completed a triathlon, tenth out of twenty-seven, while never smoking fewer than thirty Camels a day, Dr Cavendish had given a sigh of Sisyphean magnitude and Sally had felt bad in case the aberration had caused her to resign, but on her next check-up, Dr Cavendish was still in place, like an NHS fitting, shabby and worn and wearing the same face of well-intentioned disappointment.

Like the doctors, the waiting room reflected the general murk of pessimism in the Health Service, its olive paintwork scaling away and the children's toys in the corner bearing an air of abuse, a riot of bacteria where their fur had been chewed and dribbled on. Amid the international babble in the room, all of it in tones of complaint, Sally acknowledged the half-hour minimum delay with forced equanimity and tried to concentrate on *Unholy Wars: Afghanistan, America and International Terrorism*, recommended to her by Lars's contact at the *Guardian* (who had merely laughed at the suggestion that she wanted to go there, but was now lending her reading material and treating her with amused indulgence, as you might a child who nurses fantasies of being an astronaut). A production company had shown considerable interest in the idea of an Afghan drama, according to Lars, and it seemed that a trip to Kabul might become a possibility. One stick could feasibly get it wrong, Sally thought, juggling significant dates of the Soviet invasion, but four suggests a definite trend. Looking up, she caught the eye of an elderly woman in black, her swollen legs stuck straight out in front with skin like the rind of a Serrano ham. She glared at Sally as if she could read her sins on her face, and Sally felt a sudden heat of defiance and protectiveness and wondered if that was what was meant by instinct. Beside her was a woman in a burka, gently rocking a swaddled bundle in her lap. Sally couldn't see the child's face among the sweep of the woman's clothes, only hear the tiny emery board rasp of its cough and intermittent mew of protest. That woman didn't have a choice, presumably, Sally thought, as Dr Cavendish opened her door enough to lean her head through and spoke the words 'Sally McGinley, three o'clock' (the intercom was permanently out of service) flatly to the damp air.

'And what can we do for you today?' said Dr Cavendish, as she always did, as if the choices were infinite, as if she were a cosmetic surgeon and Sally's budget no object.

Bigger breasts and whiter teeth, I think, Sally wanted to say, as she always wanted to and never did.

'I seem to be pregnant.'

Dr Cavendish barely even twitched.

'I see. What makes you say that?'

'I did four tests and they all said I was. They can be wrong though, right?'

'Wrong. In that they're not wrong, usually. So is it good or bad?'

'What?'

'That you're pregnant.'

'Well, it's –' Sally realized she hadn't really considered it in such terms. 'It's just ridiculous. It shouldn't have happened.'

Dr Cavendish narrowed her eyes. Sally wondered if she were picturing any child of Sally's as a small smackhead requiring unending attention from Social Services.

'You were using contraception?'

'Yes, but – I don't know how. I guess I must have forgotten it.'

'It's not uncommon. That's why they put all those warnings on the packet.'

'I didn't do it on purpose.' Sally heard the snap of her own defence, and realized this was a rehearsal for telling Greg. 'I thought the pill was supposed to make you less fertile. It was in the papers.'

'Not necessarily. You obviously have very healthy ovaries.' Against all the laws of physics, she might have added. She looked up and, unusually, met Sally's eye. 'Have you been pregnant before?'

'Nine. But the Sisters of Mercy took them all to the workhouse.'

Dr Cavendish merely looked at her.

'No,' Sally said.

'No,' Dr Cavendish repeated, slowly, and typed something. 'And how does your partner feel about it?'

'He doesn't know yet.'

'Have you thought about telling him?'

'I wanted to make sure.'

'And how do you think he'll feel?'

'I don't know.' She left an entertainer's pause. 'I shouldn't think his wife'll be too pleased though.'

There was a chilly little silence. Sally felt her attempt to lighten the mood had fallen short of the mark. There was every chance, given Sally's knack for offence, that Dr Cavendish's own husband had knocked up a younger woman and run off. She would look so much less worn if she just dyed the grey out of her hair, too, Sally thought, and then felt bad; Dr Cavendish's frayed and raddled appearance was surely a direct consequence of underfunding. Suddenly it seemed to matter that Dr Cavendish didn't despise her.

'No, I'm joking.' Pause. 'She's not technically his wife.'

'Do you know when you were supposed to have your period?' Dr Cavendish said curtly.

'The week before last, I think. I can't really remember.'

'Do you have any idea when you might have conceived?'

'Some time between that and the one before, I'm guessing.'

'You *are* taking this seriously, aren't you, Sally? Because very soon you're going to have to make a decision that will impact your whole life.'

Sally stared at her with some surprise for a moment, as if they'd both just got their lines wrong. She wondered when doctors had started using 'impact' as a verb.

'Oh God, there's no question. I mean, there isn't a choice. I can't possibly have a baby.'

Dr Cavendish's eyebrows rose with perfect symmetry, as if on hydraulics.

'Because you're afraid you would be on your own?'

'Because – well, everything. I can't have a baby. It's just not in the plan.'

'Then we must discuss your options. But are you sure you don't want to talk to your partner first?'

The window of Dr Cavendish's small room backed on to the railway line and jittered in its frame whenever the trains shuttled past on their way to Camden and Kentish Town. Sally could see a snapshot of sky etched with pylons and cables like a musical stave. She wanted this to be like pulling out a tooth; something quick and sharp and irreversible that you could clench your fists against, brace yourself with squeezed eyes and acknowledge the pain later, at leisure, once the worst bit was over. If Dr Cavendish had produced a shot of morphine and offered to do it there and then, Sally would have planted her feet and said, come on then, let's get it over with, and it would be as if the whole thing had never happened, and that life had never –

She caught herself; that was the wrong word. *Life* was a word that belonged to the world outside her blood. *Life* was what she would be giving up. *Baby* was a word that had to be kept even further away from this situation, and talking to Greg would give it substance, inevitably, turning this into a discussion, a two-person debate in which the phrase *our baby* might be used by either of them and some acknowledgement not just of the future but of their present would be called for, some nod to reality and the possibility that there might be an element of choice after all, a thought which made her shiver and feel inexplicably aroused. But she had not lied to Dr Cavendish; there was no question. Not really.

'Let's look at this another way, Sally – how do you think he would feel if he found out that you'd taken this decision without telling him? What would that do to your relationship? I only ask you to consider because I see a lot of young women who think this is an easy option that can be got over quickly and then discover that it's not so simple.'

'There's a pill for it, though? You don't have to have an operation, these days?'

'That will depend on your dates. At the moment I would estimate that you're in plenty of time. Does the idea of a pill make it feel less of a serious decision?'

'Than the Hoover, you mean?'

Dr Cavendish made a tutting expression and turned back to her computer. Sally shrugged.

'It's less messy, I suppose.'

'Not really.' Dr Cavendish capped her pen in a conclusive fashion.

'It doesn't require general anaesthetic, so it doesn't have the connotations. But it's not magic. It won't just make it disappear – whatever you do is a question of ending the pregnancy and that's not something you can do without noticing. It will require a day in hospital, and don't be deceived – it will be, effectively, a miscarriage, and it will be painful and bloody. Now, if you decide you do want to make an appointment, you'll need to call this number and you'll need someone with you.'

Not Greg, was her first thought. For him to see her in a hospital gown, bloodied and unappealing, what would that do to his image of her? Despite the intimacy of everything she let him do to her during sex, she was careful to maintain a level of dignity and privacy with regard to her body's non-erotic functions. She suspected that Greg was the kind of man who would become helplessly squeamish in the face of gynaecological detail.

'You're quite sure there isn't some kind of mistake? With the tests?'

Dr Cavendish handed her a note card with a number, underlined. Sally wondered why she had felt the need to underline it. Perhaps she thought Sally was quite capable of forgetting she was pregnant (and then, presumably, nine months later, of thinking, while in the throes of unusually severe stomach cramps, bollocks, I knew there was someone I was meant to ring).

'No. But when you go for the first appointment they'll probably do a scan to establish your dates, that'll make sure.'

'I don't want to have to see it. The baby.' She winced at her own slip. 'The thing.'

'Don't worry, you can ask them to turn the screen away. And you might want to think twice about riding round on that,' she added, nodding towards Sally's crash helmet.

Sally's jaw set. 'Why's that, then?'

'Well – it's dangerous.'

'But I'm getting rid of it.'

'Probably wise.'

'I meant the – baby. So it's fine for me to risk death on the roads but not with a baby to think of, is that it?'

'It's not uncommon to experience dizziness and fainting as your blood pressure changes. That's all.'

'Right. How about if I don't go out of fourth and I get one of those Baby on Board signs?'

Dr Cavendish passed an arch glance over her and turned back to the screen.

'You should expect some erratic mood swings, too. More than usual.'

Outside the surgery, the sky offered only the blankness of March, a residual damp suggested on the pavements despite weeks without rain. Pausing by the bike, Sally placed her helmet on the ground and lit a cigarette as a seal on her decision. After the first drag, she felt her stomach rising again and snatched another lungful of smoke defiantly before stubbing it under her boot. On her phone there flashed a message from Greg which, when opened, revealed a couplet in pidgin French:

@sc:je te manque

je veux un bonk@scx:

Sally wondered if this was touching or just childish, or in some way touchingly childish, then erased it. *Tu me manques*, she thought, that's what he means, and felt unaccountably irritated that even Greg's poor French unwittingly reinforced his egocentrism. He was clearly not working very hard on his script. For a moment she weighed up calling him, and instead called Lola.

'Have you got time for a coffee? I need a quick chat.'

'Where are you?'

'Primrose Hill.'

'I'll be home by five, then I'm going to yoga at six. Come over before that if you want.'

To pass the next hour, Sally decided to go to the Zoo. Not because she had any special affection for the Zoo, or found it conducive to serious thought, but because it was to hand and struck her as a suitable backdrop. If this were a scene in a romantic comedy, the Zoo was exactly the sort of place she would go to kill time. And the trouble with their relationship, she reflected, as she waited at the traffic lights on Regent's Park Road, was that she and Greg both spent far too much time imagining they were in a film; making sure they got the colours right, the light, the dialogue – and never enough attention to the plot.

At the gridded entrance to the Zoo, she was reminded that it cost twelve pounds to visit and decided this was too high a price for ambience, so instead she turned into the park and took the walkway that ran alongside the animals' enclosures. The hyenas were sensibly in their shelter, it seemed, but there were the ostriches, burying their heads in the sand in supportive metaphor. Except that they weren't; they didn't have any sand, only peaty woodchips, and they stared back motionless at Sally with meaningless eyes, as if they'd already been stuffed. She stopped and leaned on the railings, uncomfortable in her stiff jacket.

These wintry afternoons, with their stark vaulted light, were the special domain of children. There were hundreds of them, it seemed, bunched in twos and threes, dangling from the Maharishi combats of their mothers on their way home from schools that demanded comical miniature blazers and ties, the cold air carrying their imprecise shouting to all corners of the park. This time she watched them more carefully; took in their shiny faces, their clumsiness, the particular gloss children in this part of London seemed to acquire that might be to do with accent, uniform, expensive haircuts, their overwhelming blondness.

She wondered if she would be able to look at these children in the same way after this undebatable thing had been done, or whether she would be tortured by the idea of what its finished face might have looked like. Would she look at small boys, for example, like this one here with his collar awry, pounding his comic repeatedly with the back of his hand as he walked and talked in his effort to make his friend understand his point, and imagine what colour eyes her boy would have had? Or little girls, like this one on the pink bike, her flared jeans flapping dangerously around the pedals, and wonder if her little girl would have been a tomboy? Or did she have the discipline not to let this spill into the rest of her life? Though by no means proactive (she was too lazy for that), Sally had always considered herself a good feminist and had often argued, to neo-conservatives or Christians, that a woman's right to precisely this choice was one of the cornerstones of an equal and civilized society. Once, at college, she had been corralled into an organized debate in which she had posited, without much scientific sophistication, that you couldn't call it a person until it had a proper face. Now she found herself questioning the specifics, if not the principle. Already – and her rudimentary calculations suggested it could not have been conceived more than six weeks earlier – it was indisputably one or the other, and she felt an unexpected pang of loss at the thought that she would never know which.

Sally didn't really like children. They seemed to require patience in measures that no normal human being could be expected to achieve. A couple of autumns ago, when she had been between flats, Sally had stayed for a month at Lola's, during which time Hallowe'en had fallen. Lola lived in a street popular with young families, and Sally had been intrigued when the doorbell rang as they had been preparing dinner.

'Leave it,' Lola had said. 'It'll be kids trick or treating.'

'Fucking extortion,' Sally had replied, on her way down to the front porch where she had encountered two girls dressed ineptly as witches.

'Trick or treat,' they trilled, eager little faces uptilted.

'What's that?' said Sally.

The girls had looked nonplussed, exchanged glances, and the brasher one had said, 'It's Hallowe'en. You give us sweets or we play a trick on you.'

'Doesn't have to be sweets, though,' said her placatory friend, quickly.

'Right. Then tomorrow, can I come round your house and you give me your pocket money?'

'No, that's not how it works.'

'Why? That's fair, isn't it?'

'No, but it's just tonight. Because it's Hallowe'en and we're dressed up.'

'You've drawn a mole on your face so I have to give you sweets for no reason other than if I don't you're going to do something nasty to me? Have you heard of the Mob?'

'It's the tradition,' said the diplomatic one, as if this were unassailable.

'It bloody isn't. We're not in *America*. Do your parents think it's all right for you to come out and threaten people?'

At this point Lola had arrived and given both children a Kit-Kat.

'See what you made me do?' she said, on the way back up the stairs. 'I don't like the principle of it either, but no eight-year-old deserves one of your Socratic dialogues. I feel sorry for your kids.'

The next morning, at seven o'clock, Lola's downstairs neighbour had come up to complain about the use of the word 'bloody' to her daughter, for which Lola had uncompromisingly apologized. Sally, who had been forbidden from answering the door, distinctly heard

164

the words 'harmless tradition', and wondered if this lobotomy was a cause or effect of becoming a mother.

To the south, over the trees at the edge of the park, a pale half-moon hovered in the still-blue sky, awkwardly, as if it had arrived too early and now had nothing to do. It was cold, and none of the other animals in the parkside enclosures had bothered to come out. Sally put her hands in her pockets and began walking. She was finding it genuinely difficult to picture Greg's reaction. Sometimes she believed that Greg was in love with her, and she with him, and even that they were in some way designed to be together and that fate would deal them some means of bringing this about without too much paper-work. In more prosaic moments, she felt that Greg was in love not with her but with her life and was hoping – understandably – that she would save him from the tedium of his own. At other times, she was quite certain that she was a distraction, a dose of caffeine to a flagging ego, and that (though he may not even be aware of it himself yet) Greg didn't have the stamina to leave Caroline, and at these times, when she found herself on the verge of despising him for his lack of courage, she then began to pity him for having to carry the weight of a dead relationship and almost wanted the responsibility of saving him. In these moments she was also uncomfortably aware of how convenient it was for her to blame all the aberrations in Greg's behaviour on the way he had been treated by Caroline, how much easier it was to explain away those odd glimpses of a less than admirable character by telling herself that his true self had been crushed and warped out of all recognition by the weight of Caroline's unreasonable demands, and aware too that men, by somehow per-suading women to blame other women for men's faults and failures, had been getting away with outrageous behaviour for centuries.

Her phone rang.

'Hello, foxy,' said Greg. 'What are you wearing?'

'I'm totally naked except for my socks,' she said, rounding the corner by the porcupines' enclosure and causing two passing mothers to double-take. In the background, the gibbons began to yelp porno-graphically.

'Did you get my poem?'

'It was very moving.'

'I'm bored. Can I come round? We've got time to cop off before the show tonight.'

Sally felt that, in the face of such irritating buoyancy, this was not the right time to make the announcement.

'I'm not home, I've got to go round to Lola's.'

'Where are you?'

'I've just been to the doctor.'

'Not ill, are you?'

'I'll tell you about it later.'

'Ooh. Sounds ominous. Should I be worried? You haven't got Aids, have you?'

He laughed self-consciously and Sally almost wanted to take the phone from her ear and stare at it in disbelief, though she suspected that this was the sort of gesture that would appear with depressing frequency in Greg's comedy drama. Sally had two acquaintances who were HIV positive; it was another mark of the gulf between their lives that, for Greg, it was so far beyond the bounds of experience that he could make such a joke with total confidence. She wondered what he would do if she were to say yes.

'No, Greg.'

'I did tell you, didn't I, that I've got these friends coming to the play tonight?'

'What friends?'

'The Parrishes. Martin and Kate. They're friends from King's Lynn. Family friends.' He paused. 'So, you know, if you're going to be at the theatre, if you could just act like –'

'Like we've never met.'

'Well, no, that would be stupid. But obviously, bear in mind they're Caroline's friends too. Don't give anything away, will you? For my sake.'

What about for my sake? Sally wanted to ask. Then she wondered briefly whether, if she stayed with Greg and had a baby, she would enter a world where it was normal to refer to people as 'the Parrishes'. Presumably in King's Lynn there was a collective noun for Greg and Caroline. The Burnses. If he were to leave her and set up home instead with Sally, would they then become the Burnses? And what would Caroline become? She felt suddenly very tired.

'I'm not going tonight, I'm not feeling great.'

'Well, I'll come round later then. But they'll want to have a drink and meet Barbara and Freddie and all that first, so, you know, it'll probably be late.'

'Fine.'

'Are you all right?'

'I'm fine. We'll talk about it later.'

'You've got me worried now.' His voice had changed register slightly.

'Forget about it. Go to the theatre and don't fuck up my play in front of your friends.'

'Okey dokey, kid. Catch you later.'

Sally stirred herself and began to walk south, around the perimeter of the Zoo when, directly ahead of her on the path, her way was blocked by a woman of about her own age leaning on a Land-Rover-sized buggy, whose attention was all twisted backwards over her shoulder to where a small toddler was lying on his face with his bottom in the air and making a noise that was far beyond screaming, approaching perhaps a kind of elemental, choric protest at the universe. The baby in the buggy was howling too, and Sally heard the woman say, '*Please*, Milo, come on, Mummy's got to get home, we haven't got *time* for all this messing about.'

It was said not as an admonition or a cross assertion of authority, but as a kind of despairing plea, with the threat of tears in her voice, as if all she could hope for now was clemency, in the way that one partner might say to the other after a night of weeping and recrimination and fruitless argument, 'Can't we just *stop* all this fighting?' Sally felt a sudden flush of relief, and with a unworthy lack of sisterly feeling, took some pleasure in the thought that this woman would not be travelling to Afghanistan to write an award-winning film any time in the near future and felt, too, that she had no need to apologize for such sentiment; this woman had made her choice (and good luck to her), but she, Sally, was making a different one, for which she silently thanked the woman and pitied her.

Lola owned a split-level maisonette in the leafiest part of Little Venice, with a roof terrace and no mortgage, which ought to have been unforgivable ('To those who have, more shall be given,' Sally had commented with some bitterness when Lola inherited it from an unlamented relative immediately after university), were it not for Lola's generous hospitality with her space. The soft furnishings bore the scars of the early years of parties, many of them at Sally's instigation. These days Lola still gave parties, but the guests tended to be potential financiers and advertisers, and there had been a corresponding downturn in the amount of broken glass and vomiting in the plant pots.

'Do you want a glass of wine?' Lola asked, disappearing through the kitchen door as Sally bowled her crash helmet into a corner of the sofa and hurled herself beside it.

'No thanks.'

'Course, you're on the bike. Stupid.'

'Yeah, and I'm pregnant.'

There was a thud in the kitchen and Lola stood in the doorway with the face of someone who's been goosed.

'Did you really just say that?'

'Mn-hmn.'

'Well – Christ. I mean – how did that happen?'

'A man put his penis in my vagina,' Sally said with affected boredom, reaching for the copy of *Vogue* on Lola's coffee table.

'Is it Greg's?'

Sally snapped her head up and stared.

'Sorry.' Lola shook her head, as if to dislodge a troublesome strand of hair. 'I don't know why I said that. I'm in shock. How are you feeling?'

'Sick as a dog.'

'Have you got an appointment?'

'I've got to call them tomorrow.' Strange, Sally thought, the immediate assumption that there wasn't even any question about it.

'Have you told Greg?'

'Not yet.'

'Good. Don't.'

'Well, I've got to tell him at some point. It's his as well.'

'It's only his if you keep it. What are you going to achieve by telling him?' Lola poured herself a glass of wine. 'Unless somehow his response is going to affect your decision.'

Sally turned her attention back to *Vogue*.

'Sal? Is that what you're thinking?' Lola leaned forward. 'Oh, Sally. He's not the one you're going to stay with, you have to see that. Don't you?'

Sally said nothing.

'Do you think this is going to be the thing that makes him leave her? He's not going to leave her. Whatever he may say to you – it's such a goddamn trope, you're the writer, I don't believe you can't see it. They never leave the wives, fact. And Greg is such a fantasist, I know what'll happen, he'll get all sentimental and tell you he wants you to have the baby, and you're such a romantic as well underneath it all that you'll agree and five minutes later he'll come to his senses and go back to her and your life will be over.'

'Thanks for your yogic wisdom.'

'Someone's got to talk sense to you. Tell him afterwards, if you must, but don't let him be part of your decision.'

'I want to tell him. He's got a right to know.'

'I can't believe you're being so obtuse. Do you know the battles some women have put themselves through to establish that he has no rights at all while it's in you? What if he says he wants you to have it?'

'Then we'll talk about it.'

'Jesus, Sally, you're not seriously even considering having a baby? With *him*?'

'You've just got an irrational problem with him.'

'No, you have. I mean, being blind is par for the course but I'd always thought you could spot a –' She stopped, and sucked in her bottom lip. 'You and I see two completely different people when we look at him. You told me yourself what he said the other night, about Julie, and then you try to tell me that's normal. Anyway, he's already got a kid and he's not exactly devoted to that family, is he?'

'That's not fair, Greg loves his daughter.'

'As long as she doesn't get in the way of him doing what he wants.'

'Why do you want to give him such a hard time for getting stuck with the wrong person? Can't people make mistakes and have a second chance, in your world?'

'Do you believe that? I don't think he's with the wrong person at all, I think he's with one of the few people that would put up with him for that long. You wouldn't, that's for sure. But he knows her too well so he's bored.'

'But we have this connection –'

'No you don't. You only think you do because your entire relationship consists of getting drunk all night and shagging. It's always like that with married men – he thinks he has a connection with you because he never has to have those conversations about bills or school or whatever. That's why marriage is such a con – almost anyone else is more exciting than the wife just by virtue of not being the wife. Ninety per cent of domestic life is boring, that's why people have affairs. You can't be so deluded as to imagine that if you lived with him, and ironed his shirts and brought up his kid you'd retain any of the appeal you have for him now. He's into you because you're exactly what he doesn't get at home. The minute you asked him to get home early or smoke outdoors because of the baby, he'd look for the exciting stuff somewhere else. That's what marriage does.'

'And you're such an expert?'

'My dad's been married three times. And both times he got divorced he said exactly the same thing – I've met the woman I'm meant to spend my life with. Except that after he'd been with her a couple of years, she turned out to be just like the last woman he thought he was meant to spend his life with. In other words, the gloss wore off.'

'Not everyone's the same.'

'OK, Sal, you know best. I've got to get changed.'

Lola went upstairs to her mezzanine landing. Sally flicked through pictures of shoes and thought about the week before, when she and Greg and Lola had gone to a late bar and run into Julie, an actress friend of Lola's, a prolix, melodramatic girl with an operatic bust, the kind of girl (Sally thought) who couldn't help latching on to any man present as if her career depended on it, as, presumably, it often did. She had turned the whole of her force and coke-driven monologue on Greg, leaning over him, touching his leg at every opportunity; only the fact that Julie was not particularly attractive meant that Sally's reaction was scaled down from real anger to minor irritation. Later, in bed, she had asked him, 'Did you fancy her?' and he had replied, with untroubled frankness, 'No, she was a nutter. I just kept thinking that I'd like to rape her, you know.'

When Sally had ventured that she might have misheard this, he had said, 'You know, hold her down and give her one good and hard, just to make her shut up for once.' Seeing Sally's face, he'd tried to shape it somehow into a joke, by saying, 'So are you up for a three-some, then?' but it was clear to her that any indication that she found his remarks disturbing, or even out of the ordinary, would only pro-voke accusations that she was prissy, uptight, just-like-Caroline when he thought she'd been different.

'He's given me such an insight into male sexuality,' she had said breezily, having made the mistake of relating this episode to Lola, 'it's going to be a huge benefit in writing characters, I think. He has this extraordinary honesty. That's the kind of thing that men really think about women, and most of the time they hide that dark side, so we have no idea. That whole animal, predatory thing – it's refreshing to find someone who feels comfortable enough to be open about it.'

Lola had not spoken. When Sally had finished she had said, quietly, 'I can't believe you want to carry on sleeping with this person.'

Now, Sally had to admit, as she went to the loo once again, it was possibly self-deluding to imagine that this kind of openness was a positive quality in Greg; civilization was, after all, the collective effort to sublimate these impulses. It probably wasn't a good thing that your lover considered it normal to tell you that he wanted to rape drunk women in bars, no matter what contemporary sexual liberationist gloss you put on it.

She looked at her stomach. Was it already more domed than usual, or was that just her imagination? Maybe the whole thing was imagined, she thought, with a brief thrill of delight; perhaps this was an instance of the phantom pregnancy phenomenon – although, on reflection, from the little she knew about it, that tended to be a wish-fulfilment hallucination. She didn't know if a psychological term existed for the antithesis. Laying a hand on her stomach, she fancied she could feel a distant fluttering.

From above she could hear the sound of drawers being banged shut.

'I think I felt it move.'

'It's the size of a fucking lentil,' Lola shouted, from deep inside her bedroom. 'You've probably got wind.'

'What if I can't ever have another one?' Sally said rhetorically, cupping her stomach, but loud enough for Lola to hear.

With a great deal of thumping, Lola hopped to the top of the stairs, half in and half out of a pair of Christie Turlington yoga trousers.

'Another what?'

'Baby.'

'Don't be daft. Why wouldn't you?'

'You hear all these stories. About it going wrong.'

'In *The Cider House Rules*, maybe. Not in London hospitals. They won't be using a rusty coathanger.'

Sally looked up, her hand still low on her stomach.

'What if this is it, Lo? What if this is my chance to be a mother, and I don't take it?'

'You don't want to be a mother.'

'Not right now. But I might, some day. What if, in ten years' time, I do want one and I find I can't? How am I going to feel?'

'And if in ten years' time you lose both your legs in a bike accident, are you going to be gutted that you never ran a marathon while you had them?'

Sally frowned.

'Yes, obviously. Among other things.'

'But the chances are you'll always have two legs and you'll still never run a marathon. And the chances are in ten years' time you'll be with someone decent and have twelve children, so don't make plans based on the most unlikely thing ever. Plus, now you know you can get pregnant, you don't even need to worry about it.'

'I might get cancer.'

Lola threw her hands up and retreated to her bedroom.

'Then stop smoking, don't have a goddamn baby.'

'I just feel like – this has happened without being forced, without anyone expecting it.'

'Well, exactly.'

'So, it's like Fate has just handed it to me. To me and Greg. Maybe this is my adventure, maybe this time I should just see where it takes me.'

'It'll take you to your life being over, Zen master.' Lola reappeared, took a scarf from the bannister and wrapped it three times around her neck. Then she stopped and looked at Sally. 'Where's all this come from? You seemed to be on top of it when you got here.'

'I'm supposed to have a choice, though, aren't I? That's what the struggle's supposed to have been about, that's what freedom is. And I don't feel like I have any choice. That's all. And that's not right, is it?'

'Do you want me to tell you that you do? Is that what you want to hear? Oh, Sal.' Lola sat beside and laid a hand on her arm. Sally sensed that Lola would have liked to have hugged her, but Sally was not someone who invited hugs, even from old friends, and at that moment she wished she were a softer, more embraceable person. 'I can't tell you that, because I don't believe it. It's just the wrong time and the wrong person. You know that, really. Look – if you rush Greg into any kind of decision based on this, it'll be a disaster. If you do end up together – talking of outside chances – you can have a baby, then, when it's all a bit more black and white.'

'Why does everything have to be black and white? Who tells us we have to live like that?'

'Common sense. Otherwise it's all a big fucking mess that you leave for your kids to clean up. Who knows better than us? Look what our fathers have left us – if you're going to have a baby, don't you want it to grow up in a normal family?'

'I wouldn't want it growing up in a family that only accepts one definition of normal.'

'Good, if you're so bohemian be a lesbian and adopt a Chinese orphan but don't have this one, Sally, seriously. Don't persuade yourself even for a second that this could be a clever idea. I've got to go, are you going to let yourself out?'

'No, I'll come now.'

'Are you sure you should be riding that?' Lola said, on the porch. 'You know, with the –' She patted her stomach.

Sally's expression was hidden behind her visor, but she revved the engine unnecessarily loudly and took the corner much too fast, as if to make a point.

She had just stepped out of the bath when the phone rang, and was slathering body lotion over the imagined convexity of her stomach and the undeniably empirical bulge of her breasts, looking down at their unfamiliar contours and feeling surreptitiously weird for enjoying their new size and the sensation of the moisturizer, rubbed in mirroring circles, as if they were someone else's, when the phone went off like an alarm and she remembered Greg. It was ten past ten; he would just have come off stage. The audience would be filtering up the tight stairs impatiently, emerging into the snap of cold air, deciding whether or not they had liked the play, and Greg would be sitting in his dressing room, waiting to shower and meet his friends, his and Caroline's friends, and what she had to say was going to destabilize him entirely.

'Hello.'

'Hi. Look, I've been worrying about this, about the doctor thing, are you going to tell me?'

'How did it go?'

'Fine. You haven't *got* something, have you?'

'No, I haven't. Have you been to see your friends?'

'No, they're waiting downstairs. I wanted to talk to you now because I don't want to be fretting about this all night, if I'm going to have to get myself checked out –'

'Will you shut up about that? I haven't got anything.'

'So what then? You're not pregnant, or something?'

Sally left a silence while she considered how to follow this up.

'Oh my God. You *are* pregnant?'

'It seems I am.'

'Well,' – she could hear him spluttering, moving around the room – 'how did you let that happen?'

This time, the silence was of disbelief.

'How did *I* let it happen?'

'Yes. You're the one supposed to be on the pill.'

'What, you think I was lying?'

'No, I don't know, I just – isn't it foolproof?'

'Apparently not. And I didn't hear you clamouring to be allowed to wear a condom.'

'So it's my fault?'

'Fault is a stupid word, we both contributed. Look, these things happen, we'll deal with it.'

'How do you know it's mine?'

Sally put the phone down. It rang again immediately.

'I'm sorry I said that. I'm in shock. I feel a fool. I thought we were having, I don't know –'

'Having what?'

'Just a light-hearted, you know, affair. Just some fun. This makes –'

'Forget about it, Greg, I'll deal with it myself.'

'Look, I'll pay half, of course.'

'Fuck you.'

Sally put the phone down again and waited for it to ring. When, after five minutes, it hadn't, to her great disgust she felt the back of her throat thicken and tears burning her eyes; she sat on the bed and tried to force them away. Another five minutes passed and the phone rang.

'Sally? I just had to have a shower and take it in a bit. You know. Anyway, I have to go down and see Martin and Kate so, we'll talk later, shall we?'

'Whatever.'

'Well, don't be like that. What did you expect me to say? Am I supposed to be pleased or something?'

'No, but you could try being less of a cunt.'

'This is a bit of a bombshell, Sal.' There was a long pause, in which she could sense him wanting to end the call. 'How are you feeling?' As an afterthought.

'Oh, top of the world.'

'Look –' He sighed, the wrenching outbreath of a man shouldering an insurmountable burden and wanting everyone to know how heroically he was bearing it. 'You won't have to go through it alone.'

The insincerity of this, the tone of having said what was expected of him, was almost political.

'Don't lose any sleep over it, Greg, I'll sort it out.'

'I've got to go down, they'll be waiting. We'll talk later, OK?'

For a while, Sally stood by the window with the lights off, watching the couple in the loft opposite through the giant plasma screen of their floor-to-ceiling windows; coverless windows made from one single pane of glass and lit like a tourist attraction, inviting spectators. Sally often found herself transfixed by the detail of their lives: the kitchen appliances banked up in chrome and white like the bridge of an ocean liner; the small repeated gestures of their arguments. The woman always folded her arms across her chest like a child; he would take off his glasses and pinch the bridge of his nose. Sally was overtaken by the urge for a ham and cream cheese cracker, but possessed neither ham nor cheese; she tried to push the thought aside, remaining immobile in front of the real-life reality television of her neighbours' late supper, but the craving was as persistent as the pitch of disappointment deep in her chest. Eventually she pulled on a coat and in the chill and drizzle walked the half-mile to the all-night convenience store by Holborn station, where they stocked neither the cheese nor the ham she'd had in mind, and to her shame and confusion this appeared a personal attack and made her cry. Instead she bought a party-size bag of Jelly Babies and ate all the black ones on the walk home.

Had she really imagined Greg was going to be pleased? Of course not, she argued, in the face of the genuine distress she was experiencing and could not explain to herself, but there had always been such a softness in the way he spoke about Daisy, a unique sheen of pride and devotion, that part of her, perhaps, had understood these emotions to be Caroline's unanswerable weapon. It would always be an unequal duel; Caroline had the advantage of her not because of their history or because she made Greg happier than Sally did – Sally was certain that, temporarily at least, this was not the case – but because of the way he felt about their daughter. Whatever Lola might think, when he told her about his daughter, Greg appeared to Sally to be moved by the experience of fatherhood in an almost mystical sense, so perhaps, after all, she was unsettled to find that he had not treated her announcement with the same reverence.

It was twenty to one when Greg called back, and he was audibly drunk. Sally had been lying in bed, furiously awake, listening to a CD of Westminster Cathedral Choir singing Christmas carols as a kind of audio self-mutilation; the music was a beautiful pain that made her lonely and homesick and justified the unstoppable crying that she still couldn't understand and could only attribute to hormones.

'I'm going home because I think it's probably a bit late now,' Greg said, unevenly. 'I'm in a cab.'

'Your friends stayed a long time, then. They must have kept the theatre bar open late.'

'Well, no – yes – but then I went out with some of the – you know – the crew.'

'OK.'

'Tell me it was a joke.'

'If that's what you want to hear, it was a joke.'

'Are you really pregnant?'

'Don't worry your pretty head about it, Greg, just go home.'

'I think I'm just really fertile, I think, because Caroline was using a thing, you know, when she got pregnant, so I think I must just have really powerful sperm.'

'Well done, you.'

'Yeah, so it's not your fault.'

Sally could hear the low murmur of the driver's voice over the engine.

'I couldn't honestly tell you mate, I think it's left,' said Greg. 'I'm going to go home now, because it's getting late.'

'Yes, you said.'

'I'll see you tomorrow. We should talk, Sally, but not now because it's late.'

'Whatever you want.'

Sally had to get up to go to the toilet again, conscious that through the thin plasterboard her next-door neighbour could hear her urinating; she had often wondered whether he got any kind of kick out of this. If so, the past couple of weeks would have been a gift to him; she was up at least five times a night. So Lola was right about Greg; he was a coward, and it would have been wiser not to tell him. It was better to have evidence, though; now she could proceed on her own with a clear conscience, and this thought prompted another round of crying.

As she pulled the duvet around her chin, she recalled suddenly Greg's offer to pay half, and the resulting anger burned away all threat of tears. Traditional gallantry (she knew, she had seen enough films) demanded that the gentleman offer to facilitate the removal of the problem. And Greg, quite unsolicited, had offered to pay half. *Half.*

'You utter shit,' Sally said aloud, into the dark, and immediately felt better. 'Not you,' she added quickly, in case her neighbour was still awake.

13

'Excuse me.'

'. . .'

'Ex*cuse* me –'

'What?'

Greg was not sure how long he'd been standing in the middle of the pavement outside Regent's Travel smoothing out a laminated wallet, but he lurched suddenly back to the present to face the impatience of a blonde woman with a brace of matching toddlers in a buggy whose path he was blocking.

'Sorry. Miles away.' His automatic thought, as he looked down and stepped back, was: *Jesus. What if it's twins?*

In fact, Greg had no recollection of the transaction he had just completed; it seemed to have taken place in some unreachable part of his cortex, perhaps the part which takes over after drinking, where it is possible to perform certain basic functions, such as getting home or, in this case, booking two flights to Dublin, with such bravura and confidence that you only realize afterwards just how greatly you put yourself at risk, and that the minute-by-minute detail is entirely absent from the record of memory. Even if he really tried, now, he couldn't remember any part of the conversation he had just had with the girl in the travel agent – it had been a girl, he was fairly sure of that, though he could not have described her if a murder investigation had depended on it – but here he was with a wallet containing return tickets to Dublin, one in his name and one in the name of Sally McGinley, leaving on Friday, the day after next. He re-read the itinerary, which looked as if it had been printed out on one of the old dot-matrix printers, and a convulsive shiver surprised him; he was vaguely aware that this was probably a terrible idea and that it was not too late to do something useful about it.

He remembered the events leading up to the purchase of these

tickets, of course. The night Sally had announced that she was pregnant – only the previous Friday, though he felt as if he'd been worrying about it for at least nine months already – he was aware that he
had not behaved well. He had not behaved like a man. Or, rather, he
had behaved like a man, in all the worst senses that the word might
connote; he had got drunk and run away. Perhaps he would have
responded with more pragmatism and support and – he supposed
the word was maturity – if it had not been the evening that Martin
and Kate had come to the theatre, but he had been obliged to meet
them afterwards and introduce them to Barbara, and then Martin had
insisted on buying a bottle of champagne from the theatre bar, and he
couldn't very well have excused himself on the grounds that he'd just
learned that his younger lover was accidentally pregnant and he
ought to go and deal with that small matter and by the way, could
they please *not* mention it to his wife who was at that moment at
home in blissful domestic ignorance while she looked after their collective children overnight? So by the time Martin and Kate went back
to their hotel he was already quite drunk and it just seemed easier
somehow to go on drinking with some of the tech crew than to sober
up in the night air and discuss the fate of a child who frankly should-
n't even have come into being if Sally were responsible enough to
bloody count or read the days of the week properly, so he'd ended up
quite persuaded that he was in the right, and that somehow if they
didn't talk about it straight away, that first night, the problem would
lose its urgency and perhaps even cease to exist. Sally had seemed a
little uptight, but then you'd have to expect that.

The following morning, Saturday, he had awoken with the same
cold dread that had accompanied the death of his mother, the grey
certainty that something terrible and permanent has happened,
something that has not, for once, been put right by a good night's
sleep. Though it was included in his rent, the prospect of a breakfast
with Mrs Cudlipp, a dedicated reader of the foreign affairs pages and
always keen to discuss the Middle East over a silted coffee, was not
what Greg needed most, so he had taken a spiral-bound notebook
(Why? Did he imagine he was going to make a list of pros and cons?)
and gone to Starbucks, where he sat for an hour staring at his phone
as if daring it to launch another life-shattering assault.

He had wanted to talk to someone, and had briefly considered
Martin Parrish; one glance at the latitude of Kate's hips and her blunt

eschewing of cosmetic artistry suggested that she could not possibly be the sole provider of Martin's erotic pleasure these days, and that Martin might therefore hold out the hope of empathy and advice. But Greg, to his own present chagrin, was inept at male friendship; with Martin he talked about cars and sailing, with Patrick he talked about work and the perfidy of heads of programming; with the lads at the theatre he fumbled inexpertly through conversations about football and digital cameras; with his father he talked about spirit levels and the council, but there was no one to whom he could say, 'I've made the most unspeakable fucking mess of things, help me.' There was only one person in his life who truly understood his ability to make a mess of things, and who could always be relied upon to listen with sympathy and useful advice and, with the most exquisite of ironies, it was Caroline.

Eventually he had called home, partly in the hope that Caroline would find a reason to launch an argument with him, and that this might cauterize his feelings of guilt and tenderness towards her and fortify him for the conversation with Sally which he could not with any decency postpone much past lunchtime, but instead the phone was answered by Daisy, who announced with all the brimming pride and gusto of a newly elected pop idol that she had just been fitted for her first bra.

Greg had thought at first that he might faint. He felt oddly off-balance, and it seemed that this was the result of some hideous cause-and-effect of his own making, as if by impregnating Sally he had unleashed a tide of fecundity into the world, whose first catastrophe had been the innocence of his daughter. He suspected too that his attempt to put himself at ease by saying, with misguided humour, 'What do you want a bra for, Daisy, what are you going to keep in it?', being met with a huff and a wounded clattering of the receiver, was not the congratulation she had expected on becoming a woman. (A woman, he thought. At *ten*?)

After a brief and predictable argument with Caroline over Daisy's precocity, lingerie-wise, he had called Patrick, who at least had some sort of professional obligation not to let him fall apart. Patrick had explained briskly that he was taking the kids to the Aquarium while Ashana went to her spa day and that this was non-negotiable but that Greg was welcome to accompany them if he wanted; so Greg had found himself dwarfed between monstrous floor-to-ceiling vitrines gurgling with exotic marine life, explaining to Patrick the potential fissure even now opening up beneath his own existence, as Barnaby and Thea skittered back and forth whining, in the way of urban middle-class children for whom the ante has been upped to its limit, that the myriad wonders of the marine world gathered here for their entertainment were something of a let-down. 'Those sharks are so gay they don't even *kill* people,' Barnaby had sniffed, and Greg had wanted to punch him; eight-year-old Barnaby, who had his own agent and had already appeared in an advert for grape juice and an episode of *Midsomer Murders*.

'So what's she going to do?' Patrick's face, rippling in a plasmic turquoise light, creased with ill-concealed irritation. Greg noted with some pleasure that Patrick was beginning to show deeply scored crow's feet.

'I don't know.'

'What are *you* going to do? If she keeps it?'

'She won't keep it, will she?' Greg turned, struck by this new horror. A transparent jellyfish undulated behind Patrick's head like a babydoll nightie. 'She wouldn't want to keep it. She's only twenty-nine. What would she want with a baby?'

Patrick shook his head and kept walking. Eventually he turned and, as if venting the cumulative provocation of their fifteen-year working relationship, clamped his hands to his head and said, 'You *fucking* idiot.'

'I didn't do it on purpose.'

Patrick continued to shake his head.

'And what about her?'

'She wouldn't – what, on purpose?'

'Not a bad way to force the issue with Caroline, if you were a bit slow making a choice.'

'There was no question of a choice – she never asked – Caroline doesn't need to know, does she?'

'Why are you even here, talking to me? Why aren't you sorting this out with Sally? You're a fucking adolescent sometimes, Greg.'

'I just wanted some advice.'

'How can I give you any advice when you haven't even asked her what she's going to do?'

'To be honest, I'm not sure I can face her.'

'I wouldn't presume to tell you how to handle women, but in my experience if you run away from talking about things, they just go ahead and make a decision anyway, and it's usually one you don't much like.'

At this point Patrick's daughter Thea had come triple-jumping back to ask if she could have her allowance because she wanted to buy a dolphin rubber in the gift shop, and Patrick had asked, with discreet malice, whether she might like to buy one for Greg too, as a present. Thea had scowled and said, emphatically, 'Can't Greg buy his own rubber?' to which Patrick had replied, looking over her head at Greg, 'No, sweetheart, apparently he can't.'

Greg had left wanting to punch Patrick as well. On the plus side, he was stopped for an autograph by a woman herding grandchildren through the entrance hall, who exclaimed, beaming and unaware, as she handed over a gnawed Bic, 'Ooh, you used to be my favourite!' He was not certain of who it was that she imagined him to be, but he signed the back of her entry ticket, wondering what it signified when women of a certain age had already moved on from him to a new favourite. Did it mean he was ageing at twice the normal rate? Over the past few days he had begun to believe it.

By this time, of course, the afternoon was half over, and since he had to be at the theatre by six there hardly seemed time to get to Sally's. He meant to call her but it seemed quicker just to send a text suggesting they meet in the green room after the show. She didn't reply, which he had taken to mean 'yes'. That night they had sat side by side on tall stools at the far end of the theatre bar, not speaking for some minutes, until Greg had held out a packet of cigarettes and said, 'Come on, have one, let's smoke the little bastard out.' Her reaction had been much the same as Daisy's earlier in the day; how was it that women could lose their sense of humour so instantly?

That had been Saturday. After a lot of apologizing, he had taken her home and even had sex with her in the hope of showing her that he was still on her side, that he was not running away, although he couldn't deny feeling oddly discomfited by the idea of the child, his child, inside her still-taut stomach, which had put him off his stride a little. Neither could he deny a certain chest-beating male pride, and who wouldn't (forty-four, everything still working, thank you)? And then Tuesday had arrived – was it only last night? – and Sally had informed him (by text message, as if she were discussing nothing more important than a lunch arrangement) that she had already been to the clinic and had the blood tests and filled in all the forms and would be having the procedure the following week. That was her word, procedure. And overnight this formless child, which until that moment had been at best a severe irritation and at worst a threat to his family, his career, his life, took on a face, a future, a name, all of which Sally was selfishly and irretrievably about to snatch away from him. Because it would be a him, Greg felt it instinctively; he saw him in fitful sleep and when he closed his eyes. A little blond boy with wide eyes, like the photo of himself as a little boy that his mother had kept on her dresser and which his father must have put away with the rest of her things; a little blond boy, and he would be called Thomas, Tom, because it was about the least he could do for his old man after having been such a disappointment to him for the past forty-four years. He had always been secretly convinced that the baby Caroline had miscarried would have been this son, this Thomas (Caroline had favoured Gabriel, but that was just ridiculous), and he understood that another lost child would not be simply forgotten; he would exist as a shadow behind Daisy, and with every year that passed he would look at children in the street of approximate age and know the ache of regret, of having deliberately undone his own last chance, and he felt that somehow he must make Sally understand the magnitude of what she was about to do.

Which was how he came to be standing, dazed, in the middle of the pavement outside Regent Travel with two return tickets to Dublin leaving on Friday afternoon. If you want to solve a problem, his mother used to say, you have to step away and look at it from the outside. At least, he thought his mother used to say that. He might have imagined it.

～•～

One of the minor details that now struck Sally as significant about the sex she had with Greg was that he had never needed to use his hands when entering her. She had thought it noteworthy in a small way the first time, but with hindsight she realized that it had happened every time he was on top and that seemed to take on a kind of symbolism. Usually there was so much inaccurate scrabbling involved in the moment of penetration; most men would wield it in a fist like a cosh, stabbing optimistically, or would expect her to do the tricky business

183

of docking, guiding them in as they hovered nervously above. But with Greg it always seemed effortless, even after quantities of drink; as if there was a kind of homing instinct between them such that he could cup her face in both hands and look her in the eye while gliding in with barely a stumble. There might be one gentle nudge as a kind of reconnaissance, but she would only have to tilt her pelvis slightly to effect that perfect, magnetic connection. And this, she reflected, was the first casualty of the present situation.

The first time he had tried to have sex with her knowing she was pregnant had been the first time in their three months of sleeping together that he had failed to manage an erection. She had tried to encourage him without letting him see that she was aware of his disgust and that she took it as a personal rejection; she had made all the jokes about oysters and parking meters and he had got out of bed to smoke a cigarette in gulps asthmatic with anger. She could have protested at this, because it made the sickness clutch at her with a frenzy, but she kept quiet and waited for him to come back to bed, where his frustration at his own failure became increasingly directed towards her. The truth was that she repelled him. Her body had not even begun to change but already the mere fact of carrying his child had robbed her of any appeal she had once held for him; she knew this, and so did he, and neither of them could say it.

Instead he said: 'Give me a minute, I'll be all right. I'm a bit preoccupied.'

He said: 'Seems wrong, doesn't it, with a baby in there.'

He said: 'Your tits have got bigger. Looking on the bright side.'

He said: 'The thing is, I know we have our problems, but I do love her, you know. And she loves me.'

He said: 'I'll be all right in a minute. I'm a bit preoccupied. As you can imagine.'

He said: 'Did you have a bra when you were ten?'

He said: 'I can't just throw away twelve years like that.'

He said: 'If you have a baby, you won't want me any more. That's what happens.'

He said: 'This is the hardest decision I've ever had to make.'

He said (finally): 'The thing is, I feel like my job's done here. It's time to move on to the next cave. You can't blame me – that's just biology, isn't it?'

He didn't say any of the following: How are you feeling, do you want to talk about it, come here to me, whatever you choose I'll be there with you, I'm sorry for behaving like an asshole, I love you. But then, she hadn't really expected him to – although the fact that she was troubled by his failure to have said as much clearly suggested that on some level she had expected it.

So she had gone to the hospital by herself, without telling him, because what else would she have done? It would not be a place for togetherness; she could picture the incongruity of them sitting side by side in a stark waiting room, clasping hands in a facsimile of solidarity to do the one thing which, if they genuinely had been together, they would not have dreamed of doing. The irony was, as she discovered when she found the place after lengthy errant journeys down unmarked corridors heavy with the plaited smells of bleach and urine common to hospitals and music festivals – they couldn't signpost the ward, she assumed, in case of pro-lifers with homemade explosives – the irony was that in the waiting room were a number of couples sitting in just such bowed symmetry, because the waiting room was shared with the Early Pregnancy Unit. And whose smart idea had that been, she wondered. Half of us here in mortal fear of going forward, the other half terrified of going back – how must they feel, the pale fearful ones for whom the first sight of blood shatters their future, how did they feel when they looked at her, single and jittery with impatience, one knee jigging uncontrollably in her anxiety to be out of there and back to normal? The answer, apparently, was that they just didn't look at her. Not the most diplomatic of floor plans, Sally thought, but perhaps there was no spare budget for tact.

It was not that she hadn't thought it through. It was more that thinking it through seemed to be the sort of thing more appropriately indulged in after the fact; if she could treat it like an exam, or a cross-country run – something to be endured with eyes fixed straight ahead, but finite – she could wrestle with the questions of conscience afterwards, when it was too late for a whimsical volte-face. She had always asserted that it was better to regret the things you'd done than the things you didn't do – though she acknowledged that in the present situation that could be made to apply either way. In any case, the nearer she got to thirty, the more she began secretly to doubt the wisdom of such a maxim.

Eventually the bullish Eastern European nurse called Sally's name and she was motioned past the silently weeping woman on the end of the row to a room where a tiny Indian doctor peered at her with faint impatience from behind a desk.

'What are your dates?'

'My dates?'

'How many weeks is the pregnancy?'

'I don't know. Seven, maybe. Eight.'

'When was your last menstruation?'

Sally explained. The doctor frowned.

'This suggests to me nine or ten.'

'Yes, but it can't be more than –'

'We can't proceed without an accurate date because this will determine the options available to you.'

Sally appreciated the terminology; it sounded like shopping for a loan.

'Fortunately for the first twelve weeks the foetus grows at a standard rate so it is possible to date the pregnancy very accurately by measuring it. I'm going to send you downstairs for a scan and we can discuss your options when you come back. Room 9. You'll need to take this form. There may be a wait.'

In the corridor she passed a young girl in a white-paper gown being led along by an older woman. The girl's face – she could not have been more than sixteen – was fixed in a kind of soporific horror, as if she'd been stunned at the very moment of witnessing an act of terrible violence, and she walked gingerly, as if barefoot on glass, making Sally think of the Little Mermaid and how every step she took on land was like knives in her feet. That, too, had been a sacrifice for a man, and the Little Mermaid had not done too well out of it, if she remembered correctly.

The sonography department was at the far end of the oncology floor. Sally sidestepped her way through trying not to look at the dying people, trying not to make the comparison between the cluster of cells feeding and growing inside her and whatever was budding inside them. There was indeed a wait.

'This is a dating scan,' the woman explained when she was finally admitted, oozing a gel that looked like KY on to Sally's still flat stomach.

'I know.'

'Which means I can't answer any questions relating to any other aspect of the pregnancy.'

186

'OK.'

'People sometimes ask, you see. The experience of the scan can make it seem more real. Do you want to look at the screen?'

Out of sight, out of mind. Seeing is believing. As long as she didn't actually see it, either on the screen or later, it could remain imaginary.

'Certainly don't.'

The sonographer tilted the screen away and swirled her light sabre in cold patterns on Sally's skin, breathing through her teeth.

'Ah. There we are.'

With her left hand she reached across to the console and clicked the mouse twice, and at that moment Sally figured, why not – she was, after all, a writer of drama and therefore experienced enough to know that nothing you saw on a screen was ever straightforwardly real. So she leaned forward and twisted to look into a world of hissing static, and in its centre a cone of clear darkness, and in the midst of that, a small paisley shape, like a 9, caught between two pixellated crosses with a line stretched between them. Behind her a printer began clearing its throat.

'Take this form back to Dr Agrawal.'

Sally was still staring at the 9.

'It's not moving.' She noticed a rising note in her own voice.

'What? Oh, I've frozen the screen.'

'But it's all right, isn't it?'

The sonographer looked down and removed her latex gloves finger by finger, with as much ceremony as if she were in a Regency drama.

'I can't give you any more information.'

'But the baby – is it healthy? You can tell me that – I have a right to know that, surely? Because – I didn't know I was pregnant at first so I was still smoking and I probably had a drink or two and it might not be – has it got all its arms and legs and – I don't know, bits in the right place?'

'That's not a question I can answer for you.' She lifted a sheet from the printer and – unnecessarily, Sally thought – folded it inside a sealed envelope. 'Take this to Dr Agrawal, I'm sure she'll be able to provide more information.'

On the way back through the cancer patients and up the stairs, Sally opened the envelope. '9 wks, 3 dys,' it said. That *was* specific. Nine weeks was more than two months. How could she not have noticed in two months? And it was now the end of March, which meant that he had impregnated her some time in January, when he had barely been in London a month and they had only really known each other for two. If blame was to be apportioned – and this seemed unjust in an enterprise that so self-evidently depended on the equal participation of two parties – then, according to the letter of the law, it had to be hers (she was, after all, the one in charge of the contraception), but when you looked at the time frame like that it seemed grossly presumptuous of Greg to have knocked her up after less than a month of sleeping together. And she knew only what she had culled from the Internet, but she had a nasty suspicion that nine weeks was too late for the tablet option.

Dr Agrawal laid her small hands flat on the file in front of her.

'This is a consent form for surgical procedure, it requires you to give your medical history and your signature. You are too late for the RU-486, the pill, so we are talking about a general anaesthetic. You will need someone responsible to accompany you.'

'That rules all my friends out,' Sally said, feebly.

'Take it with you to fill in and bring it back to me when you've seen the counsellor, then we can discuss a date for the procedure. You can have this one anything up to fourteen weeks, so you do have a little time in hand.'

Sally sat up.

'What, you're not going to do it today?'

'This is a preliminary appointment. You will need to make a further appointment for surgery if you are certain that that is how you would like to proceed.'

'Of course it is, that's why I'm here, if I didn't want it done I'd be at home knitting bootees, you have to do it today, that's why I'm here –'

'This is something you can usefully discuss with the counsellor. You will be called to see her in a moment. Meanwhile, you can be filling in the green form.'

'I don't need to see a counsellor.'

Dr Agrawal shrugged.

'It's compulsory. I can't authorize surgery unless I am satisfied that you have been properly advised as to the possible consequences.'

Sally tried to bite down her irritation; she felt that Dr Agrawal's idiom was shifting from managerial to gently hieratic. What were these dire unspecified consequences that required a professional caution? Were they, as in the best Victorian melodramas, purely physical – a gangrenous uterus and certain early death – or were they, as the religious opponents still believed, further-reaching – the countless eternal torments shored up for the mortal sin of taking a life? Or did she just mean that one might, in years to come, get to feeling a bit down if one dwelt too long on the fact that one had deliberately Hoovered one's child into a plastic bag?

She found her way grudgingly to a small room with a frosted-glass door. The counsellor was rope-thin and wore an inoffensive white shirt and navy skirt, but Sally noticed that her fingernails were painted black. So she was to be shrunk against her will by a weekend Goth.

'How do you feel about the decision you're about to make?' said the counsellor, with such an undisguised lack of interest that Sally was suddenly conscious of the long queue of women who must have traipsed in here before her, each sick with fear and worry about what their body had unintentionally allowed to happen and how best to undo it, and how many times already that day the counsellor must have asked the same question, and the overwhelming sadness of the probable answers (no one, after all, was going to say 'Fine, can I go now?'), and that was when, to her own surprise, she put her face in her hands and began to weep until her hands were slick with snot and tears.

14

Greg realized beyond doubt that he had made a monumental mistake at that first moment of absolutely no return: as the plane began to taxi towards the runway. He was no great fan of flying at any time – it was a process that made no sense to his rational mind – and was often seized by this feeling during the preparations for take-off; the sensation that he still had time to do something, but that in a very few minutes it would be too late and he would not be able to get off until the plane had gone up and come down again in another country, assuming that it were able to do so without bursting into flame over a residential area or shattering on impact into a freezing black sea. During this time, as the plane began its leisurely stroll through corrugated buildings, he always wondered what would happen if he were suddenly to leap out of his seat shouting, 'I've changed my mind, I want to get off!' just as the air hostesses were commencing their synchronized gesticulation to the doors. Probably, on a more significant flight, these days he would be shot down by air marshals, but today, on a budget flight to Dublin, there was a good chance that, for the sake of a quiet life, they might just stop and roll up a flight of steps and let the madman out. Except that on this occasion, the rising panic clawing at his chest and throat was nothing to do with the prospect of taking off and everything to do with the conversation he had lined himself up for once they were in Dublin. You couldn't call them that any more, air hostesses; you had to call them cabin crew. Most of them were shirt-lifters, anyway, it seemed to be a particularly shirt-lifter-friendly profession. Greg wondered why that should be; because they were more like women at being comforting and cheery *in extremis*?

'I'm going to be sick.'

He turned to Sally, whey-faced in the seat beside him, and tried to mask his irritation. All at once it disgusted him, a woman's physiology, with all its oozing and churning and secretions, and he wanted no responsibility for tending to it. With immense effort to muster sympathy, he said, 'Do you want some water or something?'

She nodded, mouth pressed tight. Greg looked around. The plane was still sauntering idly past rows of other planes; the cabin crew were rooting in mysterious drawers and cupboards, presumably checking their guns were loaded. He pressed the call button and a harassed but smiling woman appeared, and Greg heard himself say, without embarrassment, 'My girlfriend's pregnant. She's feeling sick.'

'Oh, you poor love. I remember it well. You'll want some dry crackers, I'll see what I can find.'

Before she returned, Sally had retched decisively into the bag provided. Greg turned his face to the window and tried to cover his mouth and nose discreetly with his hand.

'Congratulations,' said the flight attendant, with beaming warmth, handing Sally a glass of water and a biscuit.

Greg was tempted to respond that chucking up was not really an achievement worthy of congratulation, until he realized that he was included in her admiring smile, apparently for still having a dick that worked, and in spite of himself he felt a budding pride.

'Thanks,' he said, squeezing Sally's arm in a protective way. He didn't miss her sideways glance.

Already the scaffolding of fiction he had been obliged to construct around this trip was threatening to obscure the point of it. After the impetuous booking of the tickets, he had called Caroline and told her that, with the play finishing on Thursday night, Patrick wanted him to stay in London over the weekend for a new play reading on the Monday, and invoked the usual argument that he always needed a few days to decompress after the end of a run; the transition back into full-time home life always afforded him a few moments of acute difficulty, as she knew from experience, and it seemed much the best idea for him to come back on the Tuesday with his head duly straightened. She had said, 'What about the christening?'

He had forgotten about the christening – the child of Caroline's cousin – and for a moment he thought she was gathering breath for an ultimatum, but she suddenly subsided and said, simply, 'Do what you like, Greg, you always do.'

It was not the tone he'd hoped to take away with him, but whenever a job came to an end it always seemed to occasion in their relationship what counsellors would call 'a rocky patch'. It was growing worse as he got older, he noticed, perhaps because these days the promise of work was unreliable; the end of a run, particularly one as significant to his career as *Real*, pitched him back into the dismal round of auditions and readings, with all the attendant uncertainty and the prospect of days confined to the house, where he was expected to atone for his absence by devoting himself to the domestic grind . . .

And how to explain to her the desolation that stole over him in the middle of the night at the prospect of giving up the hospitable squalor of Sally's studio or the Edwardian comfort of Mrs Cudlipp's basement to return to the home in which he felt increasingly like a tiresome relative who has outstayed his welcome? How to make Caroline understand the anxiety, the sense of loss, at leaving the gaudy crowds of London and returning to the silence of King's Lynn, a silence in which he feared he might disappear? How to tell her that, essentially, he didn't want to come home?

Although there were moments, of course, when he wanted nothing more than to come home, as if slipping back into his routine of provincial family life – the school run, the packed lunches, the Wednesday flute lessons, the Saturday sailing with Martin and the two pints afterwards in the Cross Keys, the Sundays with Andrea and Philip – as if all this might make Sally and the past three months disappear. He watched her as she stared into the smeared circle of sky beside them. She appeared to have lost weight, if that were possible; her face was fragile, the stubbornness around the jaw was no longer there. You'd think that the prospect of becoming a mother might have lent her gravitas, he thought, but it seemed to have had the reverse effect; she looked to him like a child herself. As the plane tensed itself for the big push, he began to understand his own motives; what he had secretly wanted was not a weekend away with Sally, but a means of prolonging the experience of *Real*, of not letting it end quite yet. Sally *was* the play, for him; what he had been with her belonged to that world and this weekend, he now realized, was only a way of hanging on to something that had already reached the end of its natural life. If he could have brought Dev, Barbara, Freddie, Rhys and Lola along, he would gladly have done so, particularly since Sally was not shaping up to be a great deal of fun.

And the logistics were beginning to worry him. Patrick had been furious at being asked to lie for him again, but given the extreme circumstances (he had assured Patrick that the weekend would be devoted entirely to sorting his life out in time to audition for a new thing at the Royal Court in a fortnight) he had reluctantly agreed. But there was already the question of money; he had booked the flights on his own credit card, not the household one which was in Caroline's name, so it was theoretically possible to pay it off without her ever seeing an itemized statement, but she would be sure to notice the transfer of over a hundred pounds from their joint account and query it. He foresaw the same problem with the hotel; he had taken out a hundred and fifty pounds from the cashpoint in several smaller, non-alarming withdrawals which he had changed into euros at the airport, but that wouldn't cover two nights, and it was too late to take out more, because any withdrawal in Dublin would be registered on the statement, but if he paid for the hotel with his credit card, could he guarantee that Caroline wouldn't, given the present hostilities, seek out his bill as evidence? He wondered if he might persuade Sally to put the hotel on her card and pay her back in increments. It seemed the most sensible cover, but he suspected she might find it less than romantic.

'Do you think phones work in Ireland?'

Sally lifted her head with some effort.

'I doubt it, Greg, I think they still make them out of potatoes.'

'I just mean, will I be able to get a signal? Caroline thinks I'm at Patrick's, she'll be down on the first train if my phone's off all weekend.'

As soon as he'd said it, he wondered if there was a small chance that Caroline might attempt a surprise visit. She'd done so once before, when he was filming *Valley Vets*, dressing up her obvious suspicions as an affectionate and spontaneous gesture. It must have been so easy to have an affair thirty years ago, he thought, when all you had to worry about was the neighbours spotting you. Now life was all surveillance; you could be traduced by inanimate objects which tracked your every move and would snitch to your wife at the first opportunity. Only the previous week, he and Sally had been out for lunch and he had left his phone on the table at the restaurant. Sally had tried to call him in the afternoon, to be answered by the Italian proprietor, who explained where he had found it; she had offered to drop by and pick it up later in the day, which would have been fine, had Caroline not attempted to phone him five minutes after this exchange, to be told by the Italian that the person she wanted to speak to was not there, but that his girlfriend would be coming to get his phone later. He had been obliged to fashion a story in which Rhys and Lola had taken him out for lunch and he could only assume that the bloke in the restaurant had got the wrong idea. Plausible, certainly, to most people – though Caroline had been uneasy as to why anyone would have thought that Lola was his girlfriend; she must have been touching him? – but it had been a close shave.

Sally twisted to face him.

'You get a European ring tone in Ireland.'

'What's that?'

'You know. If someone calls you, it'll go, beeeeep, instead of brrr, brrr.'

'You're kidding? So she'll know I'm not in London regardless?'

'If she's that savvy.'

Greg assimilated this, and was constricted with regret. Sally shifted in her seat and watched him.

'Are you good at lying, then?' she said.

He considered the weight of this, all its barely submerged subtext.

'It's easy to lie when you know you'll be believed.'

'Funny, isn't it?' She turned back to the window. 'There's nothing you can do to make someone faithful, is there? Doesn't matter if you trust them or not, it's out of your hands. Fidelity has to be freely given, like love. You can't coerce it out of someone. Have you slept with Caroline since you started sleeping with me?'

Greg was caught for a moment.

'I haven't slept with Caroline for a long time,' he said, because it seemed like the answer she would want.

Without a reply, she folded her jacket into a bundle, tucked it under her right ear and cradled her head for sleep. Greg read the duty-free magazine and wondered whether, if he were to switch his phone on for ten seconds, just to check the bars, it would actually make the plane nose-dive into a cliff.

~·❖·~

There was a lot of gilt in the hotel lobby, and heavy velvet drapes; huge mirrors in carved frames, and all the staff in livery; it felt like the interior of a Hollywood Arthurian musical. Sally thought about pointing out to Greg the abundance of gilt, but he tended to be a bit slow picking up a pun, and the idea of making the remark and then having to lay it out flat for him wearied her.

She was beginning to suspect that this weekend, which had seemed such an impulsive and tender gesture, just the kind of expression of feeling she had been hoping for, had no chance whatsoever of living up to its promise. For a start, Greg seemed to be treating it as if he were away for a stag do; after she had pretended to sleep, he'd spent the flight trying to make himself interesting to the girl across the aisle on the subject of Dublin pubs. When the girl had mentioned the International, described by Joyce in *Dubliners*, he had sprung into such a eulogy of Joyce ('to me he just captures what Irish writing is all about') that Sally had felt obliged to open her eyes and say, 'Which Joyce exactly have you read, Greg?' This had irritated him, she could see; she also saw him flash an unmistakable eye-roll at the girl, an eye-roll which said see-what-I'm-stuck-with-but-I'd-much-rather-be-going-to-Joyce's-pub-with-you. So we've got here already, she thought; not even three months since she had conceived his child and already she had become a Mark II Caroline.

Dublin was wet. In Sally's experience, and she had been many times, Dublin had only ever been wet, but Greg had huffed and stamped as they waited for a taxi as if the rain were also the result of her carelessness and stupidity and determination to lay speedbumps in his path. The taxi had been overheated, the driver garrulous, and when Sally had laid her coat over her lap, Greg had reached under, unzipped her jeans and slid his finger inside her.

It was uncomfortable, and Sally was hotly aware of the driver's proximity; the taxi was an ordinary car, with no partition, and if she could smell the sharp tang of herself then he almost certainly could, but he carried on chatting about the knock-on effects of the smoking ban, never removing his cheery smile from the rear mirror, as if this kind of back-seat floorshow happened all the time with holidaymakers. She made a small motion to push Greg's hand away, without much conviction, and in response he pulled her left hand under the coat draped across his legs, where she discovered that he had his cock out, alert and straining against the material.

Only a few weeks earlier, she might have found it thrilling in an adolescent kind of way to wank Greg off in the back of a taxi without a partition, but tonight it had irritated her; she was tired and nauseous and had a headache from the flight, and she needed the loo and something to eat, but she had caught the look on Greg's face as he chatted to the non-pregnant, non-demanding girl on the plane. That was what she had been when they met: someone with whom he could be without responsibilities, someone who thought about sex as often as he did, who was outrageous and flirtatious and daring and all the things that Caroline was not, and if she wanted to keep him, which she now believed that she did, she must continue to be that person. So she half-heartedly jerked a few strokes before she was distracted by the sight of a garage approaching on the left and asked to stop for a packet of biscuits. Greg had quietly put himself away without looking at her, but his annoyance at being thwarted by the practical needs of her present state bristled off him.

At a junction, a soaking couple on a squat black motorbike had pulled up alongside them.

'Look, that could be us,' Greg said.

'Except I'd be driving.'

'Not if you have a baby you won't.' It sounded unexpectedly vehement. 'Have you thought about that? You can't take a baby on a bike.'

'I had no intention of trying. Obviously I've thought about it.'

'Right, and you'd miss the bike, though, wouldn't you?'

It seemed such a feeble effort at manipulation that for a moment she thought of simply getting out of the car and waiting for the next taxi back to the airport. Except that Greg had the tickets. If his intention was to impress upon her how much he didn't want her to have this baby, it hardly seemed worth travelling all the way to Dublin to do so.

When they reached the hotel, Greg seemed distracted, in spite of having ascertained even before the seatbelt signs in the plane were switched off that he did indeed have four bars of signal and was therefore, in theory, untraceable. Looking around the lobby, Sally saw a door that led through to the bar and restaurant, an exuberance of Oirishery, with Guinness barrels stacked beneath murals of leprechauns and cast-iron farming tools proudly bracketed to the wall. On a stage just visible through the door, a fiddle band was setting up for the evening influx; with a sudden jolt of horror, she checked to see that it was not her father's band.

'Do you think that having an Irish theme pub in Dublin is self-reference taken to its logical conclusion, or does the fact that the self-ref-erence is so knowing mean that it's actually more authentic?'

'What?'

'The bar, in there. With the leprechauns.'

'Not everything has to turn into a fucking essay, Sally.'

'Sorry. Just making conversation.'

Greg's face slackened. He glanced at the door as if expecting Caroline to walk in.

'Look, can we check in under your name?'

'If you like.'

'I mean, with your credit card. I'll pay you back when we get back to London, it's just that it'll show up on my card and Caroline thinks –'

'You're at Patrick's. I know.' She nodded. 'I would, but I'm nearly up to the limit. I don't think it will go through.'

'Can't you write a cheque?'

'My, you're so gallant, Greg. I suppose so. It might bounce.'

'Haven't you got any money?'

'Not very often. I'm a playwright, I only get paid when someone sees fit to produce one of my plays. *Real* was the first decent advance I've ever had, and most of that was clawed back by the bank.'

'So how are you going to support a child?'

'I don't know if I am yet.'

He looked stricken.

'I can't leave her, Sally. I don't know what she'd do.'

There was an American couple stationed between them and the reception desk. The wife was remonstrating loudly and the Australian receptionist was placating with an air of condescending boredom. Sally watched the light twinkling off their matching plastic raincoats.

'If we're going to have this conversation, maybe we should get into the room. Plus I need something to eat or I'm going to throw up again.'

'I need a pint of Guinness. Let's go into the bar and listen to the whining Celts. "Oh, Paddy, don't steal me goat, me potatoes are dead and gone, pass the whiskey mother, diddle-de-dee."'

'I wouldn't mind a lie down for half an hour.'

'We're in fucking Dublin, Sally, and you have no idea how much work I've had to put in to get this weekend, so let's try and enjoy ourselves at least a bit of the time, eh?'

'OK, but I'm fucking pregnant, Greg, which I thought was kind of the point. If you wanted to drink your face off you should have come with Gonzo.'

'Maybe I should.'

'Yes, maybe you should.'

'Do you have a reservation?'

They both turned, embarrassed.

'Yes. Burns. Double room. But if you could put it in the name of McGinley.'

'Right!' The receptionist simpered hideously with complicit intrigue. 'McGinley it is. If you could fill this out, Mr McGinley, and I'm going to need a credit card.'

Greg pushed the pen towards Sally. Reluctantly she wrote her name and address.

'The credit card will need to be in the same name as the form.'

'Oh, that's all right.' Greg beamed. 'I let her have her own credit card. It gives her a sense of independence.'

In a beige room with a pained heating system and a reproduction of John Lavery's *Blessing of the Colours* opposite the bed, which struck Sally as potentially inflammatory for visitors, she hung on to the headboard and made a great effort to come with as much noise as possible, twice, as Greg slathered her in baby oil and went at her from behind, although it was causing unexpected pain from which she distracted herself by thinking about the bath she was going to have when he was finished. If she was slightly troubled by Greg's premeditation in packing baby oil for a weekend away – it was on a level with satin sheets – she cheered herself with the thought that Greg had a sheltered life in the provinces and no doubt considered it a principal accessory to erotic abandon. She imagined Caroline didn't bring out the baby oil too often. Well, she would indulge him.

Afterwards, Greg sat naked on the windowsill and smoked a cigarette.

'They're going to a christening.'

Sally sat up and pulled the sheet over her breasts.

'Who?'

'Caroline and Daisy. Tomorrow.'

He sounded wistful.

'Oh. Can you open the window a bit more, it's really making me feel sick.'

'Daisy'll be all excited because she'll get to wear her posh clothes. She got these boots for her birthday. I should phone.'

Sally considered the optimum response. Failure to show an interest in Daisy would only damage her own stock; on the other hand, she didn't want to encourage endless reminiscence born of guilt about the family for the rest of the weekend.

'She sounds like a great girl.'

Greg turned.

'She'd really like you, that's the daft thing. In a different world. You'd be like her dream big sister.' He appeared to realize the implications of this and gave his attention back to the orange reflections in the window and the smoke gusting back through the open half-inch.

'Maybe one day I'll meet her.'

'That'll take some preparation. She's a highly strung kid, is Daisy – she gets these imaginary illnesses if something upsets her. And she picks up when things aren't good with Caroline, so I can't really see: "Daisy, this is Daddy's new wife and this is your little brother." Can't see that she'd cope too well with that.'

Sally looked down at her hands, allowing what had just been said to settle into her consciousness, anxious not to contradict it.

'Kids can be surprisingly adaptable.'

'How would you know?'

'I've heard.'

Greg laughed, in the manner of an initiate.

'Yeah, you wait.'

For what, then, Sally wanted to ask, but instead she went to the bathroom and began to run the hot water.

She heard the click of the door as she eased back into the bath amid gusts of hotel-scented steam; Greg had gone down to the bar to phone Caroline and make a start on the Guinness. Watching the water spill and separate over her unrecognizable breasts and the fractional curve of her abdomen, still no more pronounced than in days of pre-menstrual bloating, she raised her knees and noticed, unmistakably, a thin film of scarlet dispersing in the water.

Fear gripped her by the roots of her hair; in her haste to get out of the bath she almost fell, and landed in a half-crouch by the toilet, pressing tissue between her legs, heart scudding. There was blood. This meant she was going to lose the baby, and in this moment she was blinded by instinct; pushing the tissue, and then a towel, harder against herself as if this might stop it escaping.

Still shaking, half crying, she managed to dress herself, her underwear stuffed with toilet paper, and run down the two flights of stairs to the bar, where she found Greg glaring at the fiddle band across his pint, a shamrock leaf ironically twirled in its surface by the Australian barmaid, shredding his beermat with fingers impatient for a cigarette. The music combined with the smells of food and beer made her think briefly of childhood Sunday lunches, and it occurred to her again that her father was somewhere in this city, perhaps only a few streets away. Everyone else in the bar appeared to be on a hen weekend. This was not a place to leave Greg on his own.

'Did you have a nice bath? Here, I'll get you one of these. They used to give Guinness to pregnant women, you know – it's full of iron.'

'I have to get to a doctor. It's an emergency. I'm bleeding.'

'Christ.'

She had been so afraid he might have put on the face of cruel amusement he used sometimes to make her think this whole business was her problem alone, or made some kind of quip to the effect of this saving them the trouble, but Greg responded with uncharacteristic efficiency, Sally thought; he abandoned his pint and sprinted through to the hotel reception, pushed to the front of the queue and demanded a taxi to the nearest emergency hospital. Then he sat her on a banquette by the door, told her to stay put, as if she had Alzheimer's and might just wander away unpredictably, and sprinted back to the room to get their coats and passports, which he thought might be required if she needed treatment. He seemed suddenly galvanized and, to Sally, supremely competent; in her present confusion she felt crushable among the people milling in the hotel lobby, childishly lost, and infinitely grateful to have Greg there to take charge. She was taken by surprise by this surge of need for him pushing its way up to her throat; this need to hold on to him and his baby, the one depending on the other, and when she saw him emerging again through the doors from the stairs she lifted her arms to him and in spite of herself began hopelessly to cry again.

In the back seat of a cab, under the smeared lights of the wet city, he wrapped her up and muttered into her hair that it was going to be all right, and even then she wanted to ask, all right for whom? But she dared not risk making him angry in case he left her alone to deal with it.

There was at least a three-hour wait at Accident and Emergency. Greg ran a hand through his hair and exhaled between his teeth; Sally saw him calculating that this would take them past closing time and totting up the lost pints of Guinness. His mouth was set in a way that suggested an effort to suppress any comment, and she knew that he was seeing her once again as an inconvenience, an obstacle to his enjoyment, and feared his resentment.

'You don't have to wait. I'll be fine. I can sit here, if you want to go back to the bar.'

He turned, disbelieving.

'Do you think I want to go back to the bar? Is that what you think of me, that I'd rather do that while you're in here?'

'No, I just – it's a long wait. If you want to get a drink or something.'

'Christ, Sally, I may not be the most perfect human being but I do have some feelings. It is my baby as well, I'm not just going to leave you here. I really can't believe you said that.'

He half turned away from her, with difficulty, because all the rows of orange and blue plastic chairs were crammed with Dublin's wounded, in varying degrees of severity. A considerable number looked to have injuries sustained in the course of stag and hen revelries, and Sally felt a brief indignation; she ought to get in before them, because it was entirely their own fault that they'd fallen out of a window or walked into a lamp-post or had a pint glass broken in their face, whereas she, through no fault of her own, was being viciously mocked by nature, which was threatening to take away a baby she hadn't yet decided to keep. Then she acknowledged her own hypocrisy; she had complained bitterly, the previous New Year's Eve, about the apparent lack of sympathy on the part of junior doctors for those with quite reasonable damage that could have happened to anyone who felt moved to dance on a beer-slick table in heels.

She touched Greg's arm.

'Sorry. Of course I want you here. I just don't want to feel like I'm being a burden to you.'

'Maybe you should have thought about that before you got pregnant.'

This time Sally turned away. On the television screen bolted to the wall above their heads, a popular hospital drama was playing with the sound off and subtitles. Most of the bloodied, shuffling crowd in the waiting room seemed engrossed. She smiled to herself, and was tempted to point out to Greg the postmodern comedy of this (why didn't they just look around them?), but was afraid he'd accuse her of trying to be clever.

Minutes passed. Eventually Greg shifted in his seat, pulled her head against his shoulder and said, gently, 'Go to sleep, baby girl. I'll wake you up when they call. You can't do any good by worrying about it.'

Greg woke the next morning with a bouncy, air-cushioned feeling in his chest; the jaunty sense of disaster averted, of having got away with something. It took him a moment to remember where he was; the homogenous fittings of the room, the coughing of gulls, the thin sunlight straying over Sally's head, crooked heavily against his chest, traces of the previous day's make-up smudged on her cheekbone where she'd wiped her eyes with the back of her hand, and he experienced a sudden gulp of affection for her, and for the child inside her who was, apparently, in perfect health.

There had been a slightly odd sensation of detachment as, after nearly four hours in the waiting room, which had come increasingly to smell of stale beer and chips, they had been ushered into a ward and behind a curtain where he had stood by, trying not to get in the way of the brusque, older doctor who prodded around inside Sally where, only a few hours earlier, he himself had been prodding around with less professionalism but a considerably better response.

'It's quite normal to experience a bit of bleeding from the cervix during the early weeks. You've been having intercourse, I take it?'

'They tell me that's how it got there, yes.' Sally had attempted to smile. The doctor pretended not to notice that a joke had been made.

'If the cervix is raw, over-vigorous intercourse will cause bleeding.' He had looked pointedly at Greg, who had felt grossly shamed, as if he had been reprimanded by a priest. 'But your pregnancy is fine. You might want to avoid intercourse for the next few days, let things calm down.'

There had been no taxis but Sally, radiant with relief, had claimed to feel fine, so they had walked back to the hotel along the Liffey, through the rain and the closing-time crowds with her leaning on him, her face tucked under his chin. He would have been lying if he said that he hadn't felt a momentary leaden thud to his stomach at the doctor's parting advice; not only could his girlfriend not drink or smoke any more, she could now no longer fuck, on medical recommendation, and it seemed to him that all the things he had enjoyed about Sally's company were being stripped away one by one. He might as well have come for a weekend with Caroline.

And yet, as he stretched out on a crisp hotel bed and curled a strand of Sally's hair around his finger in the unexpected sunlight, he admitted again the panic he had felt the night before at the idea of her losing the baby, as if the horizon had suddenly gone dark and he had run off the road. The baby was already a unique entity that could never be re-created; even if it were never born, and he were to leave Caroline to be with Sally, and they were some day to have another child, it would still not be this one, and the thought of this child, its one-in-however-many-billion chance of having come this far, filled Greg with optimism and tenderness. She *should* have the baby, and he would somehow square things with Caroline; Caroline, after all, would never have another and this was his last chance, at forty-four, to sire the son he was now convinced he had always wanted. Even another daughter would have been fine; the more he thought about it, the more he felt that one child was an insufficient memento mori, a poor legacy for a man to leave behind him. He should fill the earth with his offspring – he suddenly felt very biblical about it, and was by now possessed of a raging hard-on which, mindful of the doctor's words, he thoughtfully did not attempt to poke into Sally, but instead woke her up and very gently eased her down the bed until she was in a position to comfortably suck him off. That she was sick immediately afterwards he did not take as a personal slight but rather celebrated as a sign of the continuing good health of the baby, towards whom he was now feeling quite protective.

He carried this optimism with him throughout the day, which began with a double visit to the hotel's full Irish breakfast bar. Sally sat opposite him and picked at a piece of dry toast.

'Here.' He cut a piece of sausage and dumped it on to her plate. Her mouth twisted slightly. 'It'll be good for the baby.' He winked, and Sally grinned weakly. It seemed immensely liberating that they were now talking about it as if it were real.

Yesterday's rain had left only a bright sheen of petrol rainbows on the streets, the sky was a dirty blue and as they walked out on to the quay, Greg felt that Dublin and its cheery citizens were all doing their best to make him happy. After the uncertainty of the previous night, home seemed more remote than ever, and Greg walked with his arm tightly around Sally's shoulders, shielding her with his body where the pavements became crowded, feeling an unprecedented warmth and magnanimity towards her; this morning he was glad to be here, with her, in spite of her not being very good company. She was trying, after all. She'd even bravely attempted a drag of his first cigarette, just to show that some vestige of her old self remained. She had thrown up immediately afterwards, but it was a nice gesture, none the less.

In a spirit of generosity, he indulged her desire to show him the Abbey Theatre and the bullet holes in the General Post Office; with more pleasure he allowed her to show him a number of pubs associated with James Joyce, though he vetoed a suggestion that they should visit the Joyce Centre (a suggestion he belatedly realized was a mocking reference to his professed interest on the plane). They walked through Temple Bar and stopped for lunch in a restaurant with literary connections, where Greg had a Guinness and six fat, phlegmy oysters which he mauled and slurped while Sally watched with the kind of rapt horror with which you might greet a surgeon showing you your own appendix.

After lunch, she insisted on taking him to the Dublin Writers' Museum; Greg's first response was that he would prefer to have his testicles slammed between two hardback dictionaries, but he realized that saying so would make him sound both selfish and illiterate, so he rallied a smile of enthusiasm and trooped after her. He had known that Sally was bookish, but this side of her was partially neutered by her appetites for excess; without the drink and the drugs, he thought, she was turning out to be a bit of a swot. What he had envisaged as a wild and dirty weekend, or as near as you could get to one with a pregnant woman, was rapidly becoming a school trip.

The smile lasted about ten minutes into the exhibitions before it spasmed into a grimace of endurance. Noticing this, Sally said, 'You're hating this, aren't you?'

'Not *hating* –'

'Come on, I'll show you something cool.'

It wasn't yet spring-like outside, but the sun was unclouded and between buildings, where the wind dropped, Greg felt a whisper of warmth on his face. Sally led him down a narrow residential street, flanked by boxy houses of brownish brick that debouched into an open space fenced with spiked railings and fronted by a pair of high black ironwork gates.

Inside, a path of rigidly squared grey slabs bordered a large artificial lake, ruffled by the wind and the silent-movie skiddings of ducks and assorted waterfowl. Bright shrubs skewed out of crevices in the surrounding wall. On a bench next to a raised border of tentative daffodils, out of the wind, Greg sat down beside Sally and she rested her head on his shoulder; watching the sky fracture in the water's surface, he experienced an unusual tranquillity, and placed his free hand on her stomach.

'This used to be part of the Royal Canal in the eighteenth century,' she began.

'Shh. Stop talking, eh.' But he didn't say it unkindly.

They sat like this for minutes watching the swans' procession. He couldn't have said how long, and at that moment he felt quite certain that somehow it was all going to be all right. Caroline would understand. She might be a bit aggrieved at first – that was to be expected – but in a short while she would forgive him; they would have an amicable separation and remain friends. Daisy would adore her new brother (or sister, if it came to that) and would spend weekends with him and Sally in London. Where they would live in London with a baby, and how they would pay for it, he was not yet sure; perhaps Sally would sell a screenplay, or perhaps he would land a lucrative sitcom role. Maybe they could sell the house in King's Lynn, since he had, technically, paid for most of it himself, though it seemed unfair to uproot Daisy from her home as well as shattering her nuclear family. Anyway, but – and people would understand that it was not that he'd stopped loving Caroline, but that they had outgrown their relationship, which happened to plenty of people, and no one would judge him for it. Above all, Daisy would understand that, in time. Lots of people moved on to second families and managed it without tempests and vicious lawyers. People moved on. He had a right to that. He understood that he had responsibilities – in several directions now – but he was also a man with a right to choose his future.

'I always thought, you know, that I'd be someone who had lots of different wives and children all over the place, like, uh –'

'Saul Bellow?'

'Mick Jagger.'

'And?'

'It's not as easy as that.'

'No.'

'Part of me wants to leave Caroline. But then there's twelve years of history – you don't know the pull that has. And there's Daisy, her whole life to think of. And part of me thinks it's never going to get better with Caroline, so I should just get out now before it gets any worse, but I've been twelve years with the same woman, would I really want to go straight into another family? I might feel, you know, if I left her, that I'd need a bit of –'

'Fucking around?'

'Freedom. Time on my own. And when all's said and done, I do love her, and she loves me. In our way. You can't understand that unless you've been married for that long.'

'You're not married.'

'Doesn't mean I can just pack my bags tomorrow. It's the same difference, in the end. She's the mother of my child.'

'Well, she's one of them.'

He laughed, without much conviction. Then he took her face between his hands and scoured it with his eyes, looking for – what? – the kernel of a belief, a faith that matched his, that somehow this could be made to resolve itself without anyone being lost? A promise that she would make sure this happened?

'Do you want to have my baby?'

Sally's eyes twitched away from him, although he was still holding her head.

'That's not fair. Do you want me to?'

'I asked first.'

'I'm not answering that until you tell me what you think. Although it's my choice in the end anyway. In case you'd forgotten.'

'Yes.'

'Yes what?'

'Yes, I do. Want you to.' He was looking at his shoes.

Sally exhaled and leant forward, elbows on her knees as if she felt faint.

'Fuck me, Greg.'

'Not allowed. Doctor's orders.'

'Are you serious?'

'I'm always serious. I don't believe in humour.'

'Do you even know what you're saying? If we do this, it's for the rest of our lives. And his life.' She gestured to her stomach. 'You can't change your mind when we get home.'

'I won't change my mind.' He pulled her tighter into the nook of his arm. 'Was this what you wanted to hear?'

She spoke into his jacket.

'Yes.'

'You really want to do this?'

'As long as we're doing it together. I guess this is the big adventure.'

Silence again, under the reprimands of the gulls and the splash and flurry of the ducks. Greg looked out across the blue expanse of water, incongruous in this neighbourhood of housing estates, trying so hard not to look urban, and felt a sudden elation, a sense that for once, in longer than he could remember, he had just made a decision that mattered. He wondered when it was that decisions of consequence had been taken out of his hands. He could think of nothing significant in his life over the last twelve years – his domestic situation, the birth of his daughter, the houses he lived in – that had actually been decided proactively by him. He had been drifting for so long, and now he had made a decision that would follow him for the rest of his life, and it felt good. He was going to be a father again, and he was seized by an urge to stand up on the bench and shout it to all the people in the faceless houses around the park. This was the unexpected. This was being alive.

'Thomas,' he said.

'Who?'

'Can we call him Thomas, after my dad?'

'It might be a girl.'

He kissed her hair.

'It'll be a boy. I've got a gut feeling. Sally, you're going to have my son. It's amazing. My *son*.'

He repeated it, just to try out the words again. When he looked down at her face, he saw that she was crying and smiling at once, and suddenly he was doing the same, and they clung on to each other and rocked back and forth on the bench with as much emotion as if one of them had been pardoned on death row. A realist might have attributed this on Sally's part to hurricaning hormones and on Greg's to the two and a half pints of Guinness he had had with lunch, but at that moment, he could not have been more convinced of his own sincerity.

～·◆·～

What Sally should have taken away from the weekend in Dublin was the memory of that conversation at the Blessington Street Basin; Greg's unprecedented tenderness, the knowledge that they were now bound together, however unpredictably. But later, when she looked back, what stuck in her mind more than any of this, more than Greg telling her, as he left her at Liverpool Street Station on the Sunday evening to pick up his bags from Mrs Cudlipp's before getting the train back to King's Lynn, that he sort of loved her, more than this historical breakthrough she remembered the episode with the fortune-teller.

She had spotted a faded card in the window of a bric-a-brac shop in one of the narrow lanes behind Trinity College. Gypsy Rose, Palms Read, 20 euros. It was a test, like one of the sacrifices laid out by Old Testament prophets to prove the existence of God; if by some chance the fortune-teller was open on a Sunday, and if by some chance she confirmed the predictions of the Tarot-reader all those months ago, if she found, without prompting, any sign of Greg or the child inscribed in Sally's hand or her tea leaves, then Sally would know that she was vindicated. She wanted this external corroboration, even while she knew that it only indicated the insecurity of her own decision.

'Yeah, you could go in there,' Greg said, when she tugged on his sleeve and bounced on her tiptoes with anticipation, 'or you could just flush twenty euros down the bog for the same effect. Or you could spend it on beer and *then* piss it down the toilet and that would be a much better use of it. She's called Gypsy Rose, for Christ's sake. You're asking to be fleeced.'

But he relented, and even handed her the money as a treat, on the condition that he could stay outside and smoke a fag.

Sally felt stupidly hopeful as she pushed aside the thick fringed curtain that looked, as did all the furnishings, as if it had been stripped from a down-at-heel saloon.

Gypsy Rose was an unabashed fraud. She had no crystals, no tuning forks, no charts and laminated cards. Her face was a grooved map of years of poverty, and white spume gathered at the corners of her mouth. Sally felt reluctant to let her take her hand.

'Aye, you'll have luck,' she said through her cigarette, after long perusal.

'Can you be more specific?'

Gypsy Rose looked almost annoyed.

'You'll have a long life. Full of luck.'

'Good. Anything else?'

'You've a member of your family with an illness.'

'Not really.'

'No, but you will. But it won't be serious.'

'Well, that's good news.'

'You'll find love and happiness. With a foreign man.'

Sally was surprised at her own disappointment, and tempted to ask for the twenty euros back. Instead she tried to think of it as charity.

'What about children?'

Gypsy Rose appeared to considered Sally's palm from a number of angles. Eventually she said, 'No children for you. Not for a long time.'

Sally stood up.

'Well, thanks. Actually I'm pregnant.'

Gypsy Rose shook her head with regret, as if Sally were only fooling herself.

'I see no children. 'Tis a bad sign.'

Three months ago, Sally might have retorted with a quick lash of sarcasm, or simply told her to fuck off, but through the gauze of her new hormonal compassion, she looked and saw, instead of a shyster, a poor sad old woman who had no doubt had an unbearably hard life, and was almost moved to give her a tip.

'Thank you. Have a good day,' she said.

Gypsy Rose creaked into something like a smile.

'You're a lovely girl. Luck will be with you.'

'Let's hope so.'

Outside, Greg had his collar up against the wind and his hands folded into his armpits.

'Are you going to be rich and famous?'

'It was horseshit. Apparently I'm going to find love and happiness with a foreigner.'

'So I've got to look out for some greasy wop after you, have I? You're right, it's horseshit. You're going to find happiness with me.'

Sally laughed, but she couldn't quite shake off a sense of unease, an anxiety that perhaps her destiny wasn't as clearly written as she wanted to believe.

15

Sally deliberately didn't watch Greg walking to the Underground entrance at Liverpool Street when they returned from Dublin, because she didn't want him to see her watching, and when she turned around at what she judged a safe distance to catch a last glimpse of the top of his head sinking slowly down the escalator, he had already been subsumed by the crowds. She had stood at the bus-stop, alone for the first time in three days, and felt a cold kind of falling, as if she had stepped out of a plane without first checking that her parachute was in full working order. Or, indeed, if she was even wearing it.

In spite of this, there was an unchallenged instinct in the centre of her that told her this decision felt right, in the same way that she had felt a profound sense of wrongness on her first visit to the hospital, less than a week earlier; as if, by taking her away to consider the situation, Greg had held up a mirror and shown her for the first time her own desires. She hadn't known whether she wanted this baby until she heard *him* say that he wanted it, and now it seemed extraordinary to her that they should ever have considered it anything other than a miracle. In the midst of this euphoria, however, it hadn't escaped her notice that the hotel in Dublin had been paid for on her credit card and that Greg had not mentioned any reimbursement. It had seemed churlish to remind him, in the face of the turbulence he was about to introduce into his life on her account.

And while she waited for him to untangle his world, she had to return to hers and announce herself as somebody else. She had planned not to tell anyone until after her second visit to the hospital, until everything was official, but the day after she returned from Dublin, Lola phoned her and said, without preliminaries, 'Do you still want me to come to your abortion with you?'

'Oh. No.'

Sally put a hand reflexively to her stomach, as if the baby might hear and take offence.

'Oh, good. Greg's going with you then?'

'What? No.'

'Well, you can't go on your own, you'll be all Mogadoned up and fall under a bus. I don't mind coming, someone's got to get you home. When is it again?'

'I'm not going.'

There was a crackly pause.

'What did you say?'

'I'm not going. I'm not having it. Or rather, I *am* having it. The baby.'

'You're having a baby.'

'Yes.'

'God. You've really thought about this?'

'I've done nothing else.'

'But Sal' –

Sally could hear Lola gathering breath for a speech, and then releasing it, as if defeated by the magnitude of the arguments she wanted to make.

'Come to the office tomorrow for lunch. We can talk about it then.'

'Don't tell me I'm being crazy, Lo. I know it. But it's an adventure. That's what life should be about.'

'Yes. But usually when you use the word adventure you end up arrested or in hospital or stranded in Morocco with no money.'

'Once. That happened once.'

'All right, I'm not trying to be a wet blanket. If you've made your decision, then I'm proud of you. You're not taking the easy road. Anyway, you know we're going to support you, whatever happens.'

Sally had never really doubted Lola's support; in fact, by the time they met for lunch in BarCelona! the following day, Lola was already talking effusively about the cutest little puffa jackets in DKNY Kids and how you could get really tiny little real Birkenstocks for babies in powder blue and pink, and Sally was privately reassured that Lola would be an assiduous godmother as a happy displacement for any biological stirrings of her own.

Rhys made no effort to hide either his distaste or his opinion that she was making the worst mistake of her life. His face was pinched, as if he were permanently swallowing down a vinegary comment through sheer good manners; three times he attempted to pour her a glass of white Rioja, and three times he made a little moue of disapproval when she waved it away. While they waited for the food, he lit a cigarette.

'You can't smoke near the baby!' Lola half rose, as if to escort him from the table.

'I'm in the smoking section. If pregnant women are upset by it, they can go and sit in the non-smoking section. I'm legitimately exercising my civil liberties. This isn't fucking New York.'

'Don't say *pregnant women* like that, Rhys, it's Sally. It's just not very thoughtful.'

'It's fine,' Sally said, trying to look unbothered. 'Would be a bit hypocritical of me to complain now, eh? And Greg's still smoking.'

'Greg's smoking sixty miles away in King's Lynn, nowhere near you or your baby,' Rhys pointed out.

'What's he going to do?' Lola folded her hands anxiously. 'Is he going to move down here?'

'Or is he just going to build you a granny flat on the side of his house?'

'It's pretty complicated for him,' Sally said, ignoring Rhys.

'I shudder to imagine. Someone should introduce him to the world of condoms.'

'You'd think the earlier he breaks it to her, the easier it would be,' Lola said. 'He does want to be with you? I mean, I'm assuming that's why you've decided to go ahead?'

'Yes, of course. But it might not happen immediately. He's got a lot of ends to tie up and he needs to be gentle about it, especially with Daisy. It's a question of finding the right time.'

'But at present, leaving aside diplomacy' – Rhys poured himself and Lola another glass of wine – 'neither his wife nor his extant child have any idea that he's even been dallying with you, never mind got you in the family way?'

'Pretty much.' Sally looked at her mineral water with resentment.

'Do you want to know what I think?'

'I know what you think, Rhys.'

'I doubt it. You *think* that I think you're being a fool because, as a non-breeder, I presumably feel my urban family threatened by the onset of middle-age bourgeois conventionality heralded by our imminent thirties, in which you'll all settle down in traditional family groups leaving me to grow old alone with my poodles, and that my objections to your having this child are therefore entirely selfish and founded on a fear of turning into Quentin Crisp.'

'And aren't they?'

'Only partly. Mainly my objections are that Greg Burns is a self-involved little sack of shit who doesn't care about you, doesn't care about the family he's already got, will be bored with you the minute you ask him to show some responsibility and is not even a particularly good actor. And I think you're being a fool in that the only reason you want to be with him is because you can't be. And finally, may I remind you that the pram in the hall is the enemy of promise. Why don't you write down everything you like about your life, Sal, and then put a tick next to all the things you'll still be able to do with a baby.' He put his glass down and turned to face Lola's reproachful stare. '*What?* Someone's got to tell her, someone who's not turned to mush by the thought of baby fucking Manolos.'

'I can get babysitters,' Sally said. 'I'll still be writing. I work from home anyway.'

'Do you know what a nanny costs? About twice what you earn, angel. Even if he gives you some money towards it, which by the way I would suggest you get him to put in writing as soon as you possibly can, just in case he doesn't show his face again. And I mean properly in writing. Get a solicitor so he can't back out.'

'You've got to be joking.' Sally felt again the background unease of not having checked the parachute. 'We can't start talking about money and solicitors, that's terrible. What would he think of me?'

'It'll be a lot more terrible if he fucks off and you've got to raise a kid on your script-reading fees and whatever piss-poor child benefit you get out of my taxes. Think about it.'

'Greg wouldn't do something like that,' Lola said, hastening to reassure. 'Not without providing for his child.'

Later, when Rhys went outside to take a phone call, Lola leant across and rubbed the back of Sally's hand.

'Rhys doesn't mean to be so harsh. You know how he gets about the idea of the group breaking up.'

'He doesn't know Greg,' Sally said quietly, and fought to keep out the question that was forming at the margins of her thoughts: what if she was the one that didn't know Greg?

Three weeks passed and, without warning, she woke up one day to find that the nausea, the bone-weariness, the headaches, waterlogged limbs and unpredictable episodes of weeping had vanished, along with the frankly inconvenient compulsion to give money to all homeless people, *Big Issue* sellers and Hari Krishnas that approached her in the street. Instead she felt a zestful equilibrium, and noticed a novel blush to her usually gaunt cheeks, a gleam to her hair. The underlying anxiety, however, remained. Even after her second visit to the short Indian doctor at the hospital, who (with a brief expression of congratulation) had issued her not with a procedural consent form for surgery but with a chart showing her prospective progress over the coming weeks and ending in a red-circled date – October the twenty-third – which would apparently be her baby's birthday, Sally felt it was somehow presumptuous to make plans, or even to speak of the child as an objective fact, without Greg's guaranteed involvement; indeed, that to do so might very well push him in the opposite direction.

The adventure so far was proving depressingly prosaic. She tried to focus on work, but was faced with unstructured days, stretched into unwieldy masses of empty time in the gap left by the end of the play, and by Greg's absence. Afternoons drifted; determined to write something significant in order to prove Rhys wrong, she would end up spending hours peering into a mottled April sky through the windows of her studio, electric with anticipation of the phone's teasing message tone that no longer came with anything like the same frequency now that Greg was back at home. The two ideas she'd been toying with as follow-up pieces to *Real* both seemed facile and, at the same time, too self-conscious. She was supposed to workshop both with two theatres over the next month and neither idea was even close to a piece that could be cast or read. All the books and articles she had read on Afghanistan grew dusty in the corners of her flat, mocking her with the knowledge that she would never make the journey now, and the film would surely be written by someone else. She started going again regularly to readings of new plays and fringe productions to remind herself of current tastes, and each time came away with a leaden sense that even the most graceless, rehashed *mise-en-scène* was a thousand times better than anything currently surfacing in her own imagination. At one such reading – an ensemble piece set in Iraq (during which she could think only of how easily she too could have written something of international impact, if she hadn't been pregnant) – she bumped into Patrick Williams at the bar. Radiating disapproval, he came over to speak to her, fidgeting his hands like a Parkinson's sufferer and not really listening to anything she said; she wondered whether she should put him at ease, though she wasn't entirely sure whether Greg had told Patrick about the baby, or whether his obvious discomfort was merely down to a general malaise in her presence. Eventually he said, 'Are you taking *care* of yourself?'

She hesitated.

'Well, I've given up smoking.'

'Yes, I – uh – guessed you might have done. Greg mentioned that you – uh – might have to.'

He appeared to be assessing her expansion in the breast and stomach areas; still not enough to draw attention as anything other than a bit of healthy weight gain.

'They're a handful.'

'My breasts?' Sally said politely. Patrick coughed and looked desperately around the room.

'Kids. I've got two.'

'Really. I've just got the one.'

She thought of asking him if Greg had any forthcoming auditions in London, but realized immediately that this would betray Greg's failure either to visit or to give her any indication of when he might visit, and she preferred Patrick to take away an impression of her as blithely self-sufficient.

'You look well, anyway,' he said, after a while, as if in response to someone suggesting otherwise. 'Greg is –' He stopped.

'Is what?'

'He's an impetuous character. He might mean what he says, but he doesn't always think things through. This comedy drama, you know, that he says he's working on. He's talked about it for years, always talking about what he's going to do with the money when he's sold it to Sky. But does he ever sit down and write any of it – no. Do you see what I'm saying?'

'You're being a little oblique for me, Patrick.'

'I'm trying to say – he likes the idea of his life changing more than he likes putting in the work to make it happen. And changing his life in that regard' – his eyes flicked to her stomach and back – 'would take considerable work, believe me. I'm just wondering if you're absolutely sure. Because, if it's not too late, it might be simpler –'

'Thanks. I'll bear that in mind.' Sally felt a sudden need to remove herself from this conversation before Patrick pronounced a hex over the whole enterprise by speaking aloud to the thought that circled in her mind every night: that Greg, even with the best of intentions, did not have the revolutionary spirit necessary to upend the *ancien régime*.

She had known, of course, that Greg's ability to communicate would be severely restricted after his return to King's Lynn, but she had anticipated that he would bring the same energies to engineering opportunities and stratagems that she would have done, had their situations been reversed. After three weeks, she had to concede that, even if all the elaborate excuses she invented on his behalf and presented to herself had been true, he was still not making much of an effort. He had a dog that could be taken for walks, the school run twice a day (both journeys involving one direction without Daisy), he could go running or cycling or shopping or simply shut himself in his office to create a few private minutes in which to phone her and ask how she – and his child – were faring, but he had not managed more than once every three or four days. One proposed meeting in London had been abandoned at the last minute because Caroline had apparently decided to come with him. After three weeks, a second meeting, this time at a discreet halfway point, was nearly cancelled because Daisy apparently had a stomach ache; Caroline was working and Greg was afraid to station himself too far from home in case the school rang demanding that he pick up his daughter – how would he explain himself if it took over an hour to drive back?

But Sally, by purposefully adopting an attitude she knew to be the direct counter to Caroline's modus operandi – not wheedling, threatening or nagging, affecting a dismissive indifference – had succeeded in making him feel sufficiently guilty that he did in the end agree to meet her, providing the day out was pared down to lunch. He picked her up at Cambridge station and drove for a few miles out of the city, towards Newmarket, until they came to a garden centre, where he tried to impart to her the humour of taking her to the café and then made a disproportionate fuss about the price of a baked potato. She liked to think that he'd chosen a garden centre for its wry connotations of suburban domestic mediocrity – the values she had spent her life avoiding and which he had protested to abhor about his life in

King's Lynn – but the way in which he paid attention to the carpentry of patio furniture, the little noises of approval with which he greeted a well-finished table, suggested to her that any irony was only surface and was a deliberate double bluff; he obviously did this regularly, with Caroline, and quite probably enjoyed it.

Tearing into a lasagne (her appetite was back and redoubled), she asked if he was any nearer to clarifying the present situation for his family. He became preoccupied with a string of melted cheese that would separate neither from his fork nor his potato.

'The thing is –'

'What's the thing, Greg?'

'You have to understand how difficult it is when I've been away working. To adjust. Daisy gets very – she's having trouble at school. And it's difficult enough for Caroline to get used to me being at home again without introducing something like this straight away. I've got to choose the moment. And to be honest, I've no idea where to even start.'

'Some might argue that it would be easier if she didn't get used to you being at home again.'

'What do you think I'm going to do, just scoop all my things into a bag and come and live with you?' Greg lifted his elbow level with his head. The cheese distended further to follow it.

Sally shrugged. 'Why not?'

'You just don't seem to have any idea of how much I've got to deal with. There's all the legal – I paid for that house, but I don't know how much she could sting me for. And I don't know what legal rights I'd have with Daisy, if Caroline decided to make it nasty. That's why I can't just get in the car and drive off into – even the car's registered in her bloody name, for a start, for the insurance. So I've got to make sure it doesn't get unpleasant.'

'So what do you have in mind? She doesn't even know you've met someone else and you're actually having another baby in October, so how do you plan to make that news *pleasant*?'

Greg had attempted to bite the cheese in half and was now picking elastic threads of it off his chin. Sally stifled a sudden desire to slap him.

'By doing it in my own time.'

'Yeah, but you don't seem to realize how much I've got to deal with – I'm expecting a baby in six months and I have to think about where we'll live, and how I'll manage without work, and you promised we were doing this together and at the moment I feel like I'm completely on my own.'

'I know. And I've said I'll support you – I understand what my responsibilities are. But it might not be as simple as we thought – I might have to get somewhere on my own at first, nearer home, just to make the transition easier. Then we can think about what happens after that.'

'After what? There's a deadline – I'm having a baby and I live in a studio with no washing machine above a fucking market caff, I've got to move somewhere else and I thought it was going to be with you.'

'Well, I don't know where you got that impression.'

'I got it in Dublin, when you took me on holiday and asked me to have your baby, if you remember. And you still owe me for the hotel.'

'Now wait a minute, I didn't ask you –'

'I said, do you want me to have it, and you said, yes.'

'OK, but you're making it sound like I begged you against your will to have it.'

'Against my better judgement, maybe.'

'Shh, it'll hear you.'

She looked up at him, and his impishness, the fringe in his eyes and the twinkle of deliberate troublemaking softened her again, and hardened her belief that he had chosen her and was doing his best to make it happen with as little collateral damage as possible, and instead of resenting what she had been coming to see as weakness and procrastination, she felt that she loved him for his consideration and gentleness.

'So when, though, Greg – you can't wait until it's born to tell her.'

'I was thinking – when do you have another scan thing?'

'Twenty weeks.'

'Right. Is that the one where they check all its bits?'

'Apparently.'

'Right, because obviously you're not going to have it if there's anything wrong with it, though, are you?'

The warm feelings began to dilute and erase.

'Don't say *obviously* about any of this when you barely talk to me about it.'

'No, OK, sorry – but you wouldn't, would you? You wouldn't

want that responsibility, of a handicapped kid?'

'I don't think you can say handicapped.'

'For God's sake, Sally, just reassure me that you wouldn't put that burden on anyone.'

'On you.'

'On yourself, on the kid, on anyone who's got to look after it. Come on, there are limits to being a liberal.'

His voice had gone squeaky with panic. Sally was strongly tempted to say precisely what he didn't want to hear, because she felt that his attitude deserved it, but instead she sighed and said, 'I probably wouldn't, no.'

'Fine. So – I was thinking I would wait to tell Caroline until we're absolutely sure that it's all OK and it's definitely going ahead. Because it will save a lot of – you know, if there's –'

'What you're basically saying,' Sally picked a mushroom off his plate, and then wondered whether she was allowed to eat mushrooms; according to the first baby magazine she had bought, the number of seemingly innocent foods that could potentially morph the foetus into a gibbering, limbless, inert, freakshow mockery of humanity were legion. Who'd have thought cured ham, for example? And mushrooms were a fungus; surely that wasn't good. 'What you're basically saying is that you don't want to upset the apple cart just yet in case there's anything wrong with this baby, because if there is I'll just deal with it and Caroline will never need to know, and you'll breathe a sigh of relief and go back home and it will be as if the whole thing never happened. You still think there's a get-out clause.'

'Now that's your hormones talking. I'm looking at that rhubarb crumble, do you want some?' He stood up with her tray. 'Sit tight. Look at me, I'm providing for you. I'm feeding you both. And when you've had crumble, I'll write you a cheque for the hotel, if that'll keep you quiet.' He smiled. 'Come on, I'm not the monster you think I am, Sally. I'm just a bloke trying to keep too many people happy.'

'Maybe that's the problem. Maybe sometimes you've got to be cruel to be kind.'

'Yeah, that's exactly what Caroline's going to say. Except she'll mean you.'

They had a half-hearted grope in the car, but Greg was too preoccupied with how many bars of signal he was getting in case the school should phone to say that Daisy was ill to show much conviction; there was something demeaning, Sally felt, about someone having one hand inside your knickers and tilting their phone towards the window with the other.

'You never really say what you feel about all this,' Greg said, gesturing vaguely to her stomach.

'You don't really want to listen.'

'Crap! I've driven down to see you, haven't I?'

'You haven't really seen me at all.'

They drove back to the station in silence; Greg's relief when he kissed her goodbye was palpable. Sally rested her head against the juddering window as the train lurched back towards London and felt that, not only was she not reassured about Greg's intentions, she was infinitely less certain than she had been that morning.

From the moment Greg returned from Dublin, stepped through the front door of his house and set his bags down on the mat, he felt like a criminal. Caroline had picked him up from the station in the Land Cruiser, leaning towards him without undoing her seatbelt and offering her cheek for the most token of kisses, so fleeting that he was not even sure that he had made contact with her skin.

'Decompressed, are we?' she had said, through lips so thin he had replied with the instinctive home reflex.

'Ah, it's always a joy to be back in the bosom of my family.' They had not spoken for the rest of the journey.

But the moment he walked into the smells of toast and warm laundry, the unfettered affection of his dog and his daughter, both leaping on him with wild hair and scantly controlled limbs, the particular atmosphere and history of his family written into the scratched doorframes and absorbed in the upholstery, he felt, as surely as if he'd suddenly noticed that he was drenched head to foot in shit, the extent of the filth and shame he was traipsing into this place of sweetness and softness and lovely, unsoiled things.

The guilt which in London had been a kind of abstract theory of guilt, hovering over him like smoke skeins over an empty bar, now assailed him as a physical presence. It dogged him through the house and garden, it stood at his shoulder as he made too bright conversation with the mums in the school car park, it brooded like Banquo's ghost at the dinner table when Caroline cooked a meal for friends. He became convinced that it was visible to those around him, this spectre of what he had allowed himself to become, and was perpetually amazed to find that his outside betrayed no trace of the corruption of his soul. What would they think, the twittering mothers in the car park, with their Espaces and their Voyagers and their pleated jeans, if they knew what he'd been doing for the past three months, if they knew how much he drank, and how much coke he'd taken, and how many extravagant sexual positions he had foisted on a girl fifteen years his junior who was not his wife, because she'd let him? What would Daisy's teachers think? Would they be so keen then to have him as 'special adviser' on the end-of-term production of *Oliver!*?

As the days passed, the memory of Dublin and those three unforgivable months in London began to recede, and he was left with a consuming remorse. What had he been thinking? *This* was his life, his home, his family; he had never intended to leave them, not in his heart. In London, he had been an abomination, and he now saw, with wrenching clarity, what he would become without the civilizing influence of Caroline and Daisy and the role in which other people in King's Lynn saw him; how quickly he could spiral into disaster without this anchor.

Every minute detail of his home taunted him with how close he had come to losing it and brought him brimming to the edge of tears with renewed affection: Daisy's flute case in the hall; the watercolour Caroline had painted on a family holiday in Cornwall, hung at the foot of the stairs; the rusty swing in the garden; the fresh flowers in the kitchen, thoughtfully replenished before they could wither; the way the fridge was always plentiful with fresh fruit and fair-trade chocolate (unlike Sally's fridge, he could not help thinking, which had contained only vodka and a year-old tube of tomato paste). Or the morning he came into the kitchen and found Caroline standing by the open patio doors, and saw her turn to him with a light in her face and say, 'Greg, I think there are bluetits using the nesting box!', that he felt overwhelmed by the sheer *goodness* of someone who could find such joy in something so innocent, and had hugged her as if some of that sweetness might transfer, as if such goodness could save him. His conscience was clogged with silent repentance, and because he couldn't confess, he turned instead to self-imposed punishments in a desperate bid to scour his soul, to become once again someone who could look on his family without dissolving in a red fog of self-loathing. He stopped drinking; he stopped smoking. He took up running every day, as if hurting his aberrant body might prove purgative; he cooked dinner voluntarily, and helped Daisy with her homework, and offered to forgo a Saturday sailing with Martin to take her ice-skating, until he caught Caroline eyeing him with concern one evening and realized that he was demonstrating the classic symptoms of someone having an affair.

It was almost working, the penance; he could almost believe that, like the prodigal son, with enough self-discipline, he would be able to put his crimes behind him and learn a valuable lesson from them, were it not for one thing. Sally was still in London, having his baby. In the afternoons, when he shut himself in his office affecting to read the scripts that Patrick sent, he would take out the glossy programme of *Real* from his desk drawer, turn to the short biographies at the back (*Sally McGinley: Writer. Sally McGinley has written a number of successful plays for stage and radio . . .*) and stare for a while at the black-and-white head shot – the planes of her face, with their deep shadows, the subtly sexual mouth, the dangerous eyes – and remind himself that she was having his baby because, instead of leaving her to get on with a decision she had 90 per cent made, he had bought her a ticket to Dublin and told her, in a fit of holiday optimism, that he wanted her to have his baby.

But as two weeks passed, and then three, it became increasingly difficult to assimilate this version of events into his present reality. He was not that person; he was *this* person, and *that* person had been a kind of madness, a kind of playing out of a fantasy double life. There was probably a medical term for it, Something Something Displacement Syndrome; at any rate, it could not strictly be called his responsibility, and he was not even really sure that he had ever said that he wanted her to have the baby. It seemed like something she had said, and he had maybe not disagreed with. He wondered what his father would say to that.

Over the years, Greg had experienced frequent surges of a manly, protective instinct towards his family (mostly towards Daisy; Caroline, he always felt, would be more than capable of looking after herself), though he was aware that these were largely sentimental. Privately he wondered just how strong that instinct would be if faced with a genuine emergency; would he really run into a burning building to save Daisy? Would he throw himself into the path of a run-away truck for her? Would it make a difference, in such a situation, if he could hear her calling for him, trusting him to save her, or if he could not? He liked to think that blind instinct would take over, but he also knew himself well enough to know that the instinct for self-preservation was very strong in him. His father had tried to impress upon him that it was a man's duty to protect his home and family; this, and this alone, was what it meant to be a man. Greg had never asked his father whether he had remained faithful throughout his marriage – it was a question to which he did not especially want the answer – but he knew beyond doubt that if there had been indiscretions, during his national service, perhaps, or after the children were born, they would have been scrupulously discreet indiscretions. The old man was biblical in that regard; he would surely have cut off the offending member with his army-issue penknife before he would allow it to threaten the security of his family. He would never have got himself into Greg's situation, and at some point Greg was going to have to present him with the situation and watch, yet again, the old man's expression of disappointment and pained, quiet disgust at his only son's inability to be a halfway decent man.

And gradually, Greg came to understand that the indistinct, name-less threat that he had always feared with regard to his family had arrived, and that he had introduced it himself, and that it came in the person of Sally; it was this last realization that stuck. Slowly, out of the spinning zoetrope of images in his conscience, this one emerged with the most clarity: Sally was the enemy. Yet, when he lay in the dark beside the inert form of Caroline, even her breathing impercep-tible, he was racked with images of Sally's long, ductile body, reminding him of those paper fish you got in crackers when he was a boy, which would unfurl and writhe in all directions in response to the warmth of your hand, and in those moments he wondered if he was making the right choice. It should have been such an easy choice. With Sally he would have had a future of fun and shared interests – travel, theatre, books, drinking, fucking – and with Caroline, a future of arguing over bills and being told to pick up dirty washing. He had reached the point in his middle years where he had grown out of his first wife and into his next one. So it had seemed in London, but Sally had muddied the simplicity of the choice by getting pregnant. Now both choices involved the demands of families, and he could appreciate the advantage of the known over the unknown.

One night, feeling utterly divided, he got out of bed and went down to his office to make a list of pros and cons – the sort of practical measure his father might have advised, if he had ever been in a position to seek his father's advice on such a question. It was more difficult than he had anticipated.

Caroline, for example, had thrown out a number of his favourite old shirts and pants while he'd been away, because Caroline was constantly letting him know that she was embarrassed in public by the way he failed to make any effort in the way he dressed. Sally, he knew, would never tell him how to dress; she didn't seem to notice, or if she did, she didn't care. On the other hand, Sally did tell him how to speak. Not overtly, of course; she had a way of subtly ridiculing his vocabulary by picking out a word and repeating it back with the one-eyebrow tilt of amusement that she kept for the congenitally stupid, in a way that made him feel provincial and clumsy and subliterate. There was the time when he'd asked her, before a party, if she was going to get any charlie (he'd heard it used), and she'd just looked at him with a twitching smirk and said, 'Charlie, is it?', as if he were someone's dad who'd casually tried to throw out the name of a hip-hop group; he'd been inexplicably hurt by that, even though no one else had been there to hear, and he hadn't felt able to tell her why. So maybe on that count she and Caroline were even.

Of course, he had a history with Caroline. On the other hand, he didn't have a history with Sally. He wasn't sure how to rate this; it seemed to him that both could be considered a pro or a con, depending on how you looked at it.

Caroline didn't see him as a man; didn't *want* him as a man. She wanted him to fulfil basic roles around the house, but she no longer saw *him*. Sally wanted him more – and more often, and more imaginatively – than he could strictly cope with, but then she hadn't yet had a baby, and he'd seen how that could change a woman. So the jury was still out as far as scoring that one was concerned.

If he left Caroline, he would lose the house, he felt sure; at any rate, he would no longer be able to live in the house, which amounted to the same thing. More importantly, he could lose Daisy. He wasn't sure of his legal rights, given that they weren't married on paper, but he knew that he couldn't come out of it looking good; he was the one who'd had the affair, he was the one having a baby with a younger woman, he suspected any court's sympathies would lie with Caroline, should it ever come to questions of parental responsibility, and access – and the mere thought of having to involve solicitors to fight for the right to see Daisy clubbed him in the stomach with dread. Sally, on the other hand, was much more tolerant, less extreme in her demands, that was what he liked about her. Of the two, if he had to live with one and see the other intermittently, Greg felt that Sally was much more likely to accept the part-time option. She would probably even prefer it in many ways, he felt; she was a young woman who valued her independence, and writers liked time alone. He could see her and the baby every other weekend, maybe, or once a month, and he felt a reassured glow as he contemplated this scenario: driving down to London, and Sally at the window of her flat saying to the little boy, 'Daddy will be here any minute', and the little fellow stumbling across the room with his arms thrown wide when the door opened. After all, she'd have a lot of friends around the rest of the time to help out. He felt quite pleased with that arrangement, and was able to go back to bed concluding that he'd clinched it. Obviously it was not going to be *nice* explaining the situation to Caroline, but once he'd calmed her down and shown her that he had it all worked out, and that he was not going to leave her, he felt convinced that it could be resolved with the minimum of disruption to all parties.

He had meant to explain all this to Sally when he met her in Cambridge, the first time they had met since returning from Dublin, but she had seemed so – *odd*, so unlike herself, and he had felt buffeted by such an unexpected storm of conflicting responses to her, that they had only been able to communicate haltingly, and he had not managed to say any of the script that he'd planned. In London, Greg thought, home had not been an imminent presence, therefore it had been easy for him to feel that he was not having an affair. Now that he had to worry about returning home on the same day, and whether he would somehow smell of her, or give away something in his eyes, or whether he might at any moment be called by the school to pick up Daisy – who had begun to suffer from a series of psychosomatic ailments as she often did when she could sense stress at home, as a means of seeking attention – and have to explain why it had taken him an hour to get there, he was acutely aware of his own shiftiness and transparent lies and the tawdriness of a couple of snatched hours (even though they were spent in the cafeteria of a garden centre, not a roadside travel lodge), and wondered how it was that Sally didn't despise him as much as he despised himself.

'I feel like you're the person who knows me best in the world at the moment,' he'd said, laying a hand over hers at the garden centre, 'because you're the only one who knows about you and the baby, so in a sense you know me better than Caroline.'

'So when are you going to tell her?' she had replied.

And when he'd tried to suggest that, on reflection, it seemed to him more sensible to wait until things were more settled at home, and she had made sure that the baby was well and truly green-lighted, she'd accused him once again of finding excuses and failing to stand up and face the music, and he'd been so disproportionately irritated by her, as if what he needed in his life was another woman bleating about his responsibilities, that he had been seized by a frightening urge to slap her in the face, just to remind her that – well, what, exactly? That he was in control? When he was so laughably not in control of any aspect of his life? What, then? To remind her, perhaps, of how angry he was that she'd backed him into this corner in the first place. And the days slipped by, and still he didn't tell Caroline about Sally, and still he didn't tell Sally what he thought about the future, and it occurred to him that he was in part still hoping that if enough time passed it might all just go away.

When Sally was fifteen weeks pregnant, she decided that the time had come to tell her mother.

Elizabeth Greaves, formerly McGinley, was a woman who had borne abandonment and betrayal with dignity and courage, and whose principal goal in life thereafter was the avoidance of pain. Sally knew this, and she also knew how much of her own life, being so entirely at odds with her mother's morals and standards, was apt to cause her mother pain; her mother knew this too, and preferred not to acknowledge it, so a mutually agreed filter was laid over the lens through which Elizabeth viewed her daughter's life, and amicable relations were more or less maintained, based on a wilful deception on both parts.

This meant, in practical terms, that when Elizabeth came to visit,

Sally washed all the ashtrays, hid them in cupboards and sprayed Pine Fresh Glade around her flat, thus disguising the fact that she smoked; she removed her pills from the bathroom shelf and put them in a drawer, thus masking the fact that she had a sex life; she took the empty bottles that amassed outside the front door to the recycling, and took any unopened bottles out of the fridge and hid them under the bed, thus implying that she was not a drinker. It was not that Elizabeth had no notion of her daughter's lifestyle, but there was nothing to be gained by rubbing her face in it. Neither did she ever go to any of Sally's stage plays, because the first and only one she saw, when Sally was at university, had been so full of immorality and bad language that they had both felt acutely uncomfortable trying to have any kind of conversation about it afterwards; in fact, the only meaningful discussion they had managed was when Elizabeth had said, 'Did you need to have so much swearing, or is that just a lack of imagination?' and Sally had replied, 'I didn't write it for you, Mum.' Even as she'd said it, she had been aware of how much of a put-down it must have seemed but, unfortunately, it was also true. From then on, it was agreed by omission that her work became one more aspect of Sally's life that, for the sake of *entente cordiale*, her mother chose to pretend did not exist. She did make the concession of listening to anything of Sally's that appeared on Radio 4, because they, at least, operated within the bounds of decency and, as if to compensate, Elizabeth always made a great show of how proud she was of Sally's *Afternoon Play* broadcasts, far in excess of what the work deserved, and made sure all her friends listened to them, which only made Sally want to swear more.

So Sally felt she could predict with a certain degree of accuracy how her mother would react to the news that she was having a baby with a man whom she not only had no tangible plans to marry, but who was also, to all intents and purposes, already married to someone else.

But at fifteen weeks she had been to the doctor's for a check-up, and had heard for the first time the baby's heartbeat – terrifyingly fast, like static on the microphone – and she had cried with the shock of it, the evidence that it was a separate being. On the strength of that evidence, she had decided that, as she had been advising Greg, it would be easier, if only slightly, to break the news sooner rather than on the eve of the birth.

So she had invited herself for a Sunday lunch and taken the bike down to Crowbourne, the small Surrey market town where she and her mother had lived since the year following her father's unexplained departure, when her mother had suddenly decided that life must be got on with as if he didn't exist. This was Elizabeth's way, Sally reflected; if it's uncomfortable, or it doesn't fit the pattern, pretend it isn't there. She wondered if Elizabeth would choose to do this with the baby.

April was almost over, and the past couple of weeks had seen a softness steal over the sky, in the outlines of the clouds and the edges of the wind; Sally caught scents of grass and warm tarmac through her visor as she moved south out of the suburbs and into green, and felt suddenly inspired by the season's optimism and the sensation of speed. She sang loudly inside her helmet, the words immediately snatched, although, she thought, the baby would be able to hear her singing from the inside. But every time she swung her leg over the bike now, and kicked back its stand to feel its sprung and poised bulk beneath her, it occurred to her that this might have to be the last trip. She was already wearing a loose top to hide the fact that she could no longer fasten her trousers, and she felt sure that the same vigilantes who were said to report a woman to the Social Services if she was seen with a glass of wine while pregnant would almost certainly have something to say about riding a motorbike at seventy miles per hour with a budding foetus of fifteen weeks on board. Nevertheless, Sally felt strangely invincible now, as if the decision to keep the baby had rubber-stamped its existence and predestined it for life; it had survived the greatest threat of all, therefore it was meant to be, such was her logic.

In the drive of her modest semi-detached house, Elizabeth came out to embrace her daughter and tried to mask a shudder that followed a glance at the bike she made a point of never criticizing, in the hope that Sally would one day grow out of it and the knowledge that any evidence of maternal disapproval would naturally delay this process.

Sally had been a recalcitrant and rebellious teenager, and in many ways was still, though she only became aware of it when she saw her mother and realized again how far she was from being the daughter her mother would have liked, and, more importantly, deserved, after everything she had been through. This was why Sally found it so troubling to visit her mother; not that they didn't get on, but that they only got on providing whole chapters of her life were left untouched – in other words, she felt that her mother only accepted her on the condition that they both pretended she was someone else, and yet they could have been friends, if only her mother's values in the superficial things (sex, language, intoxicants) were less Little England. It especially distressed her because she wanted her mother to understand that in the big things (justice, loyalty, kindness) Sally's values were exactly those that Elizabeth had always impressed upon her, but she always felt that Elizabeth's ideas of morality obscured anything else. Years ago, at university, she had nursed a fantasy version of her ideal relationship with her mother, based largely on Lola's father, Tony Czajkowski, who would arrive at college with great pomp and armfuls of bottles, take them all out to dinner, scattering bonhomie and regaling them with anecdotes about the movie business, then sit up with them all in Lola's room into the small hours, guffawing at his own incapacity to roll a decently compacted joint. That was the kind of parent you wanted to be able to show to your friends, Sally used to think, before she grew up a little and understood just how much Tony's behaviour – particularly his tendency to hit on her contemporaries in the college bar – made Lola cringe.

Now that Sally had stopped wishing for her mother to be different, she felt aggrieved that her new tolerance didn't seem to be reciprocated. And Sally wanted her mother to like her because Elizabeth was such a *good* person, a much better person than Sally herself could ever hope to be. She expressed no bitterness over the past, she lived with no complaints about her small means but instead was careful and generous with what she had, and three evenings a week she volunteered at a refuge for victims of domestic violence; by contrast, Sally felt, her own life was shown up as selfish, hedonistic and lacking in moral compass, and instead of inspiring her to be more like her mother, any acknowledgement of this polarity only helped to convince her that she was doomed to be, in her mother's eyes, a disappointment and a failure. She knew that Elizabeth would have dreamed of this announcement, the arrival of her first grandchild, and that the context in which she, Sally, was about to deliver it was entirely wrong in every detail; Elizabeth would be horrified by the mess of Greg's life, and the likely mess of Sally's life by association, and the awful responsibility of having, once again, to spoil her mother's modest dreams (Elizabeth would have required only a decent, caring husband in the picture, and a nice little house somewhere out of London) swamped Sally with remorse and self-contempt. During her adolescence, in moments of utter despair, goaded beyond her considerable patience, Elizabeth would scream at her daughter, *You're just like your father!* This was true, Sally thought; it was as if they had both been preordained to stain Elizabeth's life with disappointment.

'Did you have a safe journey? Isn't it a lovely day – I thought we might have lunch in the garden as it's so warm, but then I realized we haven't had the patio furniture out since September and it's all covered in cobwebs from being in the conservatory, so I've just asked Jeff to give it a good dust while I do the vegetables. Take that great thing off and come in – we haven't got any wine as you were on the bike and we don't like to drink at lunchtime, we just want to fall asleep in the afternoons otherwise, I expect that's our age, but I've got cranberry juice. You can have it in a wineglass and pretend it's wine, eh?'

'I'm not an alcoholic, mother.'

'No, I'm just joking. Now, I'm going to change out of these old trousers, I've been weeding this morning, I thought I'd better make the most of it, you never know how long the nice spell is going to last, do you? Come on through. Are you all at a loose end now the play's finished?'

'Jeff's here?' Sally followed her mother through the door and hooked her jacket over the end of the bannister. Jeff, her mother's second husband, a retired academic ten years older than Elizabeth, was the sort of person described as 'very involved with the local community', meaning that he wrote twee editorials for the local magazine and organized sponsored cycling events for the 'Crowbourne in Bloom' campaign; Sally privately detected a spirit of condescension behind all this, and then hated herself for her metropolitan snobbery and cynicism. Elizabeth had married Jeff, whom she had known for years through the hospital book-donation scheme, shortly after Sally left for university, and Sally was pleased that her mother had companionship; she deserved to be cared for properly. If her father and Jeff had been Top Trumps cards, Sally used to think, Mac would have scored maximum points for brio and charisma while Jeff would languish on zero, but Jeff would have trumped him into the ground in the fields of reliability and attentiveness to Elizabeth. So in the end they would come out about even, and Sally suspected that for her mother, approaching sixty, brio probably counted for a lot less these days.

'Of course he's here – he'd hardly go out when you're coming to visit, would he?'

'Mum, after lunch – there's something I need to talk –'

'Well, hallo, hallo!' said Jeff, entering the room brandishing a dustpan and brush. 'And how's the great playwright?'

'Dead, most of them,' Sally said, shaking the extended hand. 'I'm afraid you're stuck with me.'

'Ha, *ha-ha*! Rather good reviews, this time round, eh? Chap in *The Times* liked it enormously, didn't he? They're doing an Ayckbourn at the Jubilee Theatre here in a couple of weeks, that should be jolly, eh?'

'Are they? Great.'

'I thought we might get tickets, if you'd like to come down. Bit of a treat. Your mother enjoys the theatre.'

'No – I'd love to.'

There was a silence.

'I'm just going to look at the casserole,' said Elizabeth. 'Why don't you go through to the garden and I'll bring you a juice.'

'I'll just go and wash my hands, eh?' Jeff said, and tramped off up the stairs in a squeaking of corduroy.

Sally found herself alone amid the birdsong of her mother's garden. Three white-painted, unbearably uncomfortable garden chairs gleamed with sudden cleanliness around a small table spread with a red chequered plastic cloth, and the realization of the pleasure her mother took in her visits made Sally swallow hard with the nearness of tears. She had been half banking on some maternal intuition leaping into action, whereby her mother might smell the impending motherhood of her only daughter and pre-empt the business of having to say the actual words, or at least on Elizabeth, who was obsessed by Sally's usual gauntness, noticing her anomalous fuller figure, but in this most crucial of moments her mother seemed to have developed a perverse obliviousness to her appearance. It was only now, as she was faced with the prospect of shattering her mother's peace of mind, that she began to understand Greg's need for procrastination.

Lunch passed in a succession of Jeff's well-intentioned and unaccountably chafing questions – which novels had she enjoyed recently? what did she think about the Iraq situation? did, in her opinion, whoever-it-was deserve their recent Best Actor Oscar? if one were thinking of writing a memoir about life in a small town, not that he was, but one day he might, would she perhaps know of any publishers who might like to take a look? – in response to any one of which Sally was afraid she might blurt 'I'm pregnant, pass the broccoli', and had to concentrate to such a degree on not saying this that she found she had been having a conversation for an hour and had not listened to any of it. In the whirr of an electric mower from beyond the back fence she fancied she could hear the rhythm of the baby's heartbeat.

'Well, I'm off for my constitutional,' Jeff announced, when lunch was over and Elizabeth began urgently removing plates, as if disease might spread if they weren't all washed up by the time everyone had finished chewing. Jeff didn't specify his constitutional *what*; Sally suspected he meant nap, but it might equally have been walk, dump or wank – Jeff took a more than healthy interest in the body's flows and sluices and would often talk cheerfully of the benefits of keeping everything moving, which always made Sally wince.

When she and Elizabeth were alone at the table, Sally folded her hands together seriously, found she couldn't look her mother in the face, and said, 'There's this thing, Mum, that I have to tell you.'

Elizabeth looked grave and understanding, as if she might be anticipating the words 'gay' or 'drugs' to follow.

'I've met someone. A man.'

'Go on.' Some mothers might have shown enthusiasm here; Elizabeth's face remained sceptical. She did not have great faith in Sally's choices.

'So – he's nice. He was in my play. Uh – so, yeah. He's a bit older. But nice, you know.'

'How much older?'

'Forty-four.'

'Oh, Sally.'

'He's a very young forty-four.'

'Is this because of your father?'

'Don't try and shrink me, Mum. I don't know. Anyway, that's not really the important thing that I have to say.'

'Which is what?'

'The thing is – the *thing*. Is that. Oh, God. Mum, don't be cross.'

'*Cross*? What is the matter with you, Sally?'

'The thing is that we're having a baby.'

As soon as she'd said the words, Sally was not sure if she'd imagined them; they sounded like words someone had said on the television, many times.

Elizabeth's face took a long time to shift into a different expression. 'When?'

'October.'

'I see.'

Another silence.

'Don't just look at me like that, Mum.'

Elizabeth got up slowly and stood in front of Sally. For the first time in what might have been years, Sally leaned into her mother and felt Elizabeth's arms around her shoulders.

'It must have been a very difficult decision.'

Sally nodded into her mother's shirt.

'Does he love you?'

'He says he does,' Sally answered, because she couldn't say 'yes' with enough conviction, nor could she bear to hear herself say the word 'no'.

'It's very, very hard work, having a baby. It's bad enough when there are two of you.'

'I'll manage.'

'I know you will. You're very determined. But it seems very –'

'What?'

'Well – impetuous, Sally. How long have you known this person?'

'Greg. He's called Greg. Since the play was cast. Before Christmas.'

'About four months, then. Well, it's none of my business, but do you people not use contraception these days? After everything you read?'

'I was, I did. It just didn't – I don't know how it happened, Mum, it just did, and we weren't going to have it but then we went away and it seemed like the right – it might be a terrible mistake, I know, but – this is the person I want to be with.'

Elizabeth shook her head.

'You don't need me to tell you that's not the best reason to have a baby. You're an exceptionally clever girl, Sally, but – I've always said this – you have no common sense. Whatsoever. I sometimes wonder how you came to be so completely without any notion of the real world. But then, people have babies in much worse circumstances, I suppose, don't they? And of course we'll always support you. Are you going to tell your father?'

'Why would I?'

'Well, it's his first grandchild. He might want to see it.'

'He's the last person I want around.'

'Your father's never tried to force his way into your life before, he knows what you think of him. He'll be shocked, of course. But he'll want to be told.'

'You can tell him if you like, but I'm not seeing him.'

'I'm sure he'll respect that. I'll write him a letter.'

Elizabeth straightened and rubbed at the small of her back; Sally looked up and smeared her damp eyes with the back of her hand.

'Mum?'

'What, love?'

'Do you hate me?'

'Sally.' Elizabeth almost laughed. 'I can't begin to understand you, but I'll always love you. And the baby.'

But there was something a little strained in her voice, Sally thought, and she pictured Elizabeth having to phone around her friends and family in the coming weeks, putting on a bright, making-the-best-of-it voice. 'Sally's having a baby,' she'd say, but the pride and pleasure would be so diluted. 'No, I haven't met him,' she'd have to go on. 'No, they're not getting married. No, she's only known him a few months. I don't know if they're going to be living together.' And just wait until she had to add, 'Oh, and by the way, he already lives with someone else who had no idea about it, and they have a child.' The congratulations would be muted, to say the least.

'Mum, there's one more thing I have to tell you, since you're in shock anyway.'

'Oh, Sally, there's more?'

Elizabeth looked actively frightened, and Sally realized that it would be too much, at that moment; perhaps if she left it, and Greg got on with leaving Caroline, her mother would never have to know that he had another family, or at least not that he'd had them concurrently. That was the best solution, she thought, and then realized that this was precisely Greg's avoidance technique. Even in their most cowardly moments, she thought, they were the same.

'Uh – yes. I've got a tattoo. On my back. It's the Chinese symbol for Imagination. I had it done the first time I sold a play and I never told you because I thought you'd think it was cheap.'

Elizabeth laughed, with nervous relief.

'Is that what it means? I thought it might be something to do with John Lennon. Of course I've seen that – you have those ridiculous trousers that do up round your knees so that everyone can see your knickers. It's always popping out. You silly girl – you didn't think I'd mind about that?'

'Do you mind about the baby?'

'You're an adult, Sally. You're not practising for your life any more. This isn't something you can change your mind about, you know – this person is going to be part of your life for ever.'

'I hope he will be.' Sally allowed herself to look a little misty-eyed.

'I'm talking about your child. Your decisions are yours – it's not for me to tell you any more whether I think you're being wise.'

'But you think I'm not, clearly?'

'I think you've almost certainly romanticized the picture of you and this chap and your baby. It can seem a lovely, intimate thing – well, the most intimate, really. But I think you have absolutely no idea of the reality of childcare – it isn't very romantic when you've got stitches and cracked nipples and you haven't slept for weeks and you're washing poo off vests twenty-four hours a day. I'd guess you haven't spent too much time thinking about that, between you.'

Sally had thought about this, briefly; rather, she remembered having heard such complaints from women with children, but privately she was sure that the extreme hardship was usually exaggerated out of envy for the childless, and that she, Sally, had the physical stamina to make light of such trials. After all, she was used to staying awake all night.

Elizabeth turned back to the table and began to gather crockery again.

'When you were a little girl, Sally, you used to throw yourself into so many hobbies – think of all the musical instruments – and what excited you was the preparation, getting all the kit. When you found they required a bit of hard grind, you'd usually get a new interest. You can't do that with a baby.'

'I'm not stupid, Mum. And I'm not fifteen.' Sally sat forward, jaw set, then her defiance crumpled. 'I'm going to be a terrible mother, aren't I? How can I be any use? I don't know what I'm doing.'

'None of us does, love.' Elizabeth smiled. 'We have to learn as we go along. You'll be lovely.'

If Sally had been hoping to pick up a greater degree of conviction in her mother's tone, she was going to be disappointed. She sat alone while Elizabeth cleared the table and watched two sparrows capering in the bird bath. From the kitchen Elizabeth shouted, 'If you want to be a good mother, you can get rid of that bike for a start. A lot of your old life is going to have to go, Sally – that's what sacrifice means.'

Sally had always thought that words such as sacrifice and duty belonged to the generation before her mother's, to unenlightened women who didn't realize that motherhood didn't have to mean the obliteration of the self. Now she was beginning to suspect, with a creeping panic, that perhaps these words belonged intrinsically to motherhood itself, throughout the generations, and no amount of theory would ever splice them.

16

Anyone looking on would have assumed they were a normal family. Out beyond the sand dunes, the Wash nibbled inoffensively at the edge of the beach, sequinned by a fresh June sun, and the dog buffooned around them in its manic circles; at staggered points along the beach, other Saturday afternoon families – mothers, fathers, daughters, sons, grandparents, dogs – were chasing, ambling, conversing or arguing with expressions pitched at varying degrees between pleasure and duty. Greg was willing to bet that none of them was having a conversation as painful and impossible as the one that he was trying to conduct in an adult fashion with his ten-year-old daughter.

'*Why* not?' Daisy planted her feet apart and squinted at him.

He hesitated and chewed the skin at the side of his thumbnail, hoping to find some purchase on a fraying cuticle that he might have overlooked in all the frantic chewing of the past five days.

'Thing is, Daze, sometimes it's easier to talk things through when there's, you know, a bit of space between you.'

'*What* things?'

'Well, me and your mum have to talk about one or two things, but I don't want you to worry – it's nothing to do with you. And I'm not going anywhere, I'm still here.'

Daisy screwed up her mouth.

'You're living in the *pub*.'

This was not an exaggeration; for the past five nights, Greg had been staying in one of the rooms above the Cross Keys. He was sharing a bathroom with a travel writer from Sutton called Clive, who was writing an article (for whom, he never said; Greg suspected it would not turn out to be a household-name publication) on Norfolk's Historic Coastline, and who left a lot of body hair in the sink and the toilet bowl spattered with guano. Part of Greg was grateful; in some way he felt he deserved Clive and the deliberate abasement of a room above a pub; it threw into relief the squandered femininity of his former home. Clive epitomized the rootless world of divorced middle-aged men. He gave off the kind of stale smell that Greg associated with old men, and which reminded him of his father; not an absence of hygiene, as such, but something more intrinsic, an odour of decay that came from within. Greg was beginning to fear that he might absorb it through his own pores or, worse, that he might already be generating it himself. This was what happened when you got thrown out for cheating; it was domestic lore, and Greg felt it somehow right that cohabiting with Clive should be part of his punishment and rehabilitation. Martin Parrish had apologized for the apparent absence of solidarity: 'Of course, I'd offer you the spare room in a flash, old son, but Kate's terrified of appearing to take sides, and you've got to admit, from her perspective you don't look too sweet at the moment. I'm sure it'll blow over, though.'

Greg appreciated his optimism, however insincere, but Caroline did not have the temperament that permitted things to blow over.

'Look, Daisy –' Greg rearranged his limbs in the sand and watched the minimal progress of the small boats out in the bay, static triangles struggling against the stillness of the air. The sun was warm on his back, and the gulls yipped in their summery way; he would have liked to have felt happy, but the accumulation of guilt, regret, fear and a five-day hangover was wrenching and twisting his stomach, and he was anxious about the possible recurrence of the anxiety-induced diarrhoea that was blighting his days. He tried to remember how it felt to be happy, which only made the failure worse. Daisy was sitting a little way off, concentrating on stripping bark from a stick, which she sometimes also used to flick sand in the air; there was a clenched anger to these activities, a brittleness in her movements. 'You're old enough to understand that people sometimes have arguments. That's what's happened with me and your mum. It doesn't mean –' He stopped. What didn't it mean? What *did* it mean?

'You're always having arguments. But you don't usually go and live in the pub, so that means you're getting divorced.'

'Well, technically we can't get divorced,' Greg said, and then stopped again. Was Daisy aware that her parents were not legally married in the way that other people's parents most likely were? Had anyone ever sat her down and explained this, or had she just absorbed it?

'I *know*, because you have to be married. But it's the same thing if you go and live in another house and marry someone else, it's the same as being divorced.' Daisy stabbed the stick fiercely into a small mound of sand she had heaped between her feet. 'Kelly Hunt's mum and dad got divorced and then her dad went to live in Disneyland and now she gets to go there for all her holidays.' This was said defiantly, as if daring Greg to fail to produce a compensation package as advantageous as Kelly Hunt's dad's.

'Well, that won't happen, I promise. Did Mum tell you I was going to marry someone else?'

'No, I'm just saying. *Are* you?'

'No!' Greg heard himself squeaking. 'And I'm not going to live anywhere else. I'll be back at home before you know it. We just need to sort a few things out, me and your mum.'

'Have you had an affair?'

Greg snapped his head up; Daisy was still poking at the sand. He could distinctly hear his own heartbeat.

'Is that what Mum said?'

'No. She just said you'd had an argument. But Sophie said you wouldn't have gone to live in the pub unless you'd had an affair.'

Damned Sophie, too much the connoisseur of soap plots; for the first time, he felt the weight of his daughter's potential disgust – not only in the present, but for the rest of her life, this episode being branded into her tender memory. Oh yes, she would tell her friends at university, or possibly her therapist, I was ten when my dad left home for having an affair. What would it do to her, that memory, he wondered; would it propel her, as it had Sally, into the arms of men like – well, like himself? This only compacted the fear and completed the picture of himself that he was trying to avoid looking at full-frontal. The thought of anyone with thoughts as dark as his own ever laying their hands on Daisy's skinny body made his fists bunch and whiten.

'Do you really understand what an affair means?'

'It means you love someone else instead of Mum.'

'Not instead of.' How simple it was, at ten; affection was finite and had to be parcelled out. An excess here automatically meant a deficit there. For someone to be promoted to Daisy's Best Friends list in her pink vinyl diary, another ersatz friend would have to be relegated. Although in this case it seemed that Caroline had adopted the same logic. 'Anyway, I don't love anyone else except Mum.' The miseries of the past week had pretty well convinced him of the truth of this.

'It means you got off with someone else.'

'Daisy, *got off* is not the kind of language I want to hear.'

'Well then you won't have to hear it, because you don't live with us any more.' Her lower jaw was pushed out, but she was biting down on the tension in her lip.

Greg looked at her thin arms, cramped around her knees, and loved her; he wanted to hug her, but his physical affections had not been welcome since long before the past week, since the machiavellian Sophie had convinced Daisy that, at ten, they both stood on the threshold of adolescence. He wanted to clear his name, but what he wanted to tell her was not the truth, and all he could think of, all he wanted to say was: You have a brother.

Five days earlier, on a pale Tuesday evening, he had, to all intents and purposes, taken a knife and plunged it into the chest of the person he loved most in the world and to whom he had, barring his mother, the most reason to be grateful. He had chosen that Tuesday because the morning's post had brought a plain brown envelope with his name in Sally's slanted capitals containing a square of glossy paper. He had removed it from the envelope in the privacy of his office, as tenderly as if it had been a fragile banknote of impossible value. Its background was inked in the deep indigo of cheap photocopiers, and in the centre was a cone of white; nestled between its parameters was the unmistakable curled-up figure of a baby, and this baby was his son. Bowed over his desk, he had traced one finger over the infant profile; the snub nose, large forehead, the bones of one tiny hand lit up like a fin, the beads of light that made up the spine, and he had cried for an hour. Sally had included a note with the photo; it said, 'See how clear his spine is? At least we know that, unlike his father, he's actually got one.' She was still angry that he had not turned up to the hospital with her, after he had promised. He'd been stymied by Patrick, who had organized an audition for an Edinburgh play the day after Sally's twenty-week scan; the audition could not be missed, and his creative mendacity had run dry; he simply could not think of a convincing reason to keep him in London for two days without rousing Caroline's suspicions. It might have been better, he thought with hindsight, not to have left it until an hour before Sally's appointment to let her know that he wouldn't be there; she had listened to his explanation with seething calm and then hung up. An hour and forty minutes later she had called him back with the words, 'Your son is perfect.'

He'd held the photograph of this submerged, perfect child between his fingertips for most of the morning, while Caroline was at work, as if it had voodoo properties, as if creasing it might bring ill fortune, and when he heard Caroline's car roll into the driveway later in the afternoon, he had rustled through papers in search of somewhere to hide it. The only secure place in his office was the drawer that held his recently revived library of porn, and he balked at the idea of shoving his perfect son in with the plastic women, but if he put it in his wallet there was no guarantee that Caroline might not one day be short of petrol money, innocently pick it up off the bedside table and everything would be –

And then he looked at the photograph again and it struck him that this child was over halfway there; that he would not remain a shiny photo that could be hidden indefinitely in a drawer, and for a moment all he could hear was the timpani of blood inside his ears. He worked so much better from a script, where emotions and responses were preordained and structured towards a satisfactory ending, but whenever he tried to prepare the script of this scene with Caroline, in which he announced that someone else was having the second child she had craved, there was only ever a blank where her words should appear. In the end, he decided the only possible action was to say his own lines and try his best to improvise around a reaction he found he could not begin to second guess.

Daisy had gone to bed, but her music could be heard from upstairs. Sitting at the kitchen table with the patio doors ajar to let in the ghost of early summer air, Greg poured himself a glass of Merlot and offered one to Caroline, but she waved it away, head bent over the *Radio Times*.

'I've just had a couple of Nurofen, I've got one of those sinus headaches.'

'Caroline. There's something I need to talk to you about.'

She looked up sharply.

'Did you see that note I left? That Martin called about the cheque? Did you ever ring him back, or are you putting it off again, like you did with the bill?'

Greg winced. There was a small matter pending of a fine on a tax bill from the previous financial year which had accrued because Greg had genuinely forgotten to send it off; Caroline was especially furious because she hated to see money thrown away on the kind of careless mistake that she would never have made herself. She would have sorted it out herself in a moment, but because it was Greg's mistake, it had become a matter of dignity that he put it right himself (and not let her see how far the fine had crept up); he just hadn't got round to it. This was the difficulty with one's accountant also being a family friend; such details could not be kept confidential.

'He's called three times about this now. That's why you pay him.'

'It's not about that. It's – Caro –' He leant forward, penitent. 'I don't even know how to start telling you this.'

The irritation in her face changed slowly to alarm, but he could see that she still had no idea. She might be thinking illness, work, money problems. But not this.

'What is it?'

'When I was in London. With the play.'

'Yes?'

'I –' Cowardly, he put the heels of his hands over his forehead. 'I met someone. A girl. And this one time – well, a couple of times – I was drunk and we –'

He looked up. Caroline was staring, thunderheads of hatred beginning to gather in her eyes, daring him to finish the sentence.

'I slept with her. With this girl. I know it's useless to say – but I do – I mean, I was drunk, and it wasn't – and I am, you don't know how much I am. Sorry, that is.'

He tried to reach a beseeching hand across the table, but this was a gesture too far.

'Fuck off, Greg,' she said, in a voice barely held together, and as a mark of the gravity of the situation, she actually took one of his cigarettes out of the packet on the table and lit it, right there in the kitchen, without even opening the door fully. 'The one with the tits and the hair, was it?'

'No. Lola? God, no. It was – she's – she was the writer. Sally –'

'I DON'T WANT TO HEAR HER FUCKING NAME IN THIS HOUSE.'

'Sorry.'

Caroline breathed shallow gusts of smoke and drew her mouth in tighter.

'And is she – do you –' The arm that held the cigarette was tensely perpendicular, up by her mouth, its elbow supported by the other, which was wrapped defensively across her body. 'When your text message goes off in the middle of the night, is that her? Is it?'

'It doesn't go off in the night. Does it?' He thought he had always made sure to turn it off before going to bed.

'You don't hear it because you're asleep. I've heard it, but I always assumed it was advertising, you know, because I didn't really think your FUCKING WHORE –'

'Caro, it's not like that, it was just a drunk thing, it was just a couple of –'

'How old is she?'

Greg knew that this was going to be the killer blow, and felt like an inept matador; he had no idea how to deliver it in the cleanest way.

'Twenty-nine.'

The pressure seemed to abate in Caroline; she sat, heavily, and looked at the end of her cigarette with her head down, but he could see the onset of tears.

'So, good. She's twenty-nine and she writes plays in the West End. Very glamorous. I'm sure you have a much better time with her, I'm sure she's a great fuck, no wonder you never wanted to come home. So why don't you go and live with her, then?' This was all said through closed teeth.

'I don't want to live with her, Caro, I love you, I really –'

'No, you don't, Greg.' She looked up suddenly and met his eyes, coldly sensible. Her make-up was smudged, but her voice was steady again. 'If you loved me, you'd have thought about how much it would hurt me, and you'd have maybe thought that was more important than your dick. But you didn't, so you don't – it's just another way of trying to say sorry once you've had your fun. If you loved me, you wouldn't have done it.' She began to cry again.

'Caro –'

'God knows why you even needed to tell me, although I suppose it's better I know what kind of person you are – were you afraid I'd find out? Is she stalking you? Or is this because you want to leave, is that what this is? Are you telling me you're leaving?'

Greg stood up and moved towards her, but realized that it was impossible for him to touch her while he delivered the next lines. He wondered if he would ever touch her again.

'I'm not leaving. Unless you want – the thing is, I'm telling you now because I don't want to leave, I want to be with you and Daisy more than anything.'

She had the look of someone bracing themselves for impact.

'I'm telling you because –'

He swallowed.

'There's no easy way to do this. And I had no idea it would –'

'*What*, Greg?'

Caroline's hands were shaking. Greg almost hoped she would hazard a guess, so that the words didn't have to come out of his own mouth, but she continued to look at him with real fear.

'She got pregnant. She's having it.'

Silence hung between them, bright and vivid. Caroline moved a hand slowly in front of her mouth as if she had witnessed an accident. Greg saw the details of his kitchen – the wooden clock, the dried flowers – as if in close up, and didn't dare to breathe. She stared straight ahead, her eyes glazed. After a long time, she said, 'That's it then, isn't it?'

'What do you mean, it?'

'I think you should go now.'

She levered herself up gingerly, as if it hurt to move, and rounded the edge of the table, holding on to it for support.

'Caro, please, it doesn't have to be – can't we talk about it?'

'I can't even look at you, Greg. I need to take this in. Please leave now.'

He reached out uselessly, his hand groping in the space between them, and tried to speak; he felt suddenly afraid for her, that she might harm herself if he was not there to watch over her. Caroline stopped at the kitchen door, facing away from him, she looked so vulnerable as she held on to the doorframe; Greg felt as if he had just beaten her.

'I mean it.' She was barely audible. 'Just get out.'

'I don't want to leave you on your own.'

'Get out of this house.'

'What will you tell Daisy?'

'I don't know. I don't know. What will I tell anyone? You've made a fool of me. All of us. This was my *life*.'

She went upstairs then, haltingly, without any slamming of doors, and he had not dared to follow, even to pick up a jacket. Instead he did as she asked and got out, into the rain, and walked the mile and a half to the Cross Keys, where he fell into a corner, shaking and incoherent, so that Rod, the landlord, could only assume he had been assaulted and, in an awkwardly male gesture of kindness, laid an oily-smelling jumper across his shoulders and poured him a large Scotch until, half an hour later, Martin Parrish rolled up in his BMW X5 to make some sense of him.

'Bloody hell, old son. Better have a large drink,' Martin had said, with mildly surprised eyes, as if Greg hadn't clearly already had several, and Greg inwardly blessed him for his public-school veneer and slowness to judge. Sally called him twice that night; both times he watched her name flash on the display and enjoyed the coldness of not answering, as if, by deliberately spurning her need for him, he was somehow deflecting the pain she had caused back towards her. This was how he thought of it now; the horror of that night, and the days that followed, the tears and shattered glass and shattered hearts were all Sally's fault. She had done this.

The following day he had gone back to the house when he thought Caroline would be at work – aware once again, as he turned the corner into the drive and saw not only her car but that of her sister, Andrea, that it was men who went stoically to work when their worlds were falling apart, as if nothing had happened. Caroline, in the state he had left her, would naturally have called in sick – and was met at the door by Andrea with a face of such concentrated and vibrant anger that he didn't even bother to request an audience with Caroline, or a short trip upstairs to his own wardrobe, and instead he walked to the coast for an hour and stood looking over the sea, confecting in his head local news reports of his clothes being found at the water's edge and picturing Caroline's remorse. Except that of course he didn't have anything like the balls for that sort of act, and even if he were to fake it in order to make Caroline see how much she would miss him, the dog-walker or coastguard who stumbled upon his pile of abandoned clothes would find first a polyester East Norfolk Darts League 1987 jumper and assume that Rod was the casualty.

For the rest of the day he'd mooched around the shopping centre, realizing how long days could be when you didn't have a home and wondering why, given the extraordinary length of days, he'd achieved so little with all those that hadn't involved trying to find somewhere to sit, until he found he'd spent over twelve pounds on cappuccinos. During one of these extended sojourns on a metal swivel stool, moving his eyes over the same page of a discarded *Express* for an hour without seeing any of the words, Patrick had called to inform him with some delight that the producers of the Edinburgh show for which he had auditioned – a new play, a modern farce, by some little smart-arse who was about twelve – wanted to offer him one of the leads, and that there was a good chance it might move to the West End afterwards. He'd had to tell Patrick that he could no longer guarantee his availability, that he'd just blown his life into a zillion horrific fragments and that while he was attempting some kind of restoration, it might not be the wisest time to announce a further month away from home, that in fact that might look, from Caroline's perspective, as if he couldn't wait to get away again; although, on the other hand, if he really had been definitively thrown out of his house with no chance of being readmitted, it would at least give him somewhere to go over the summer, but there was no way of knowing how things would unfold. (It occurred to him that Sally might also be in Edinburgh, and he felt in no condition to understand whether this would be a good or a bad development.) Then he had embarrassed himself by crying on the phone to Patrick, who had barely made the effort to muffle a weary and irritated sigh.

After office hours, Martin had turned up at the Cross Keys at Greg's request with a collection of clean clothes – pressed shirts, and trousers that seemed to be made of cashmere and silk and other materials derived from impossibly rare and expensive creatures, and made Greg feel as if he were in costume, impersonating Martin or someone with a similar stable and remunerative profession. Martin had even brought him a tie, just in case, though why on earth Martin imagined he might have need of a tie in the Cross Keys or mooching the shopping centre, he couldn't fathom; perhaps it was ingrained, perhaps someone like Martin couldn't conceive of a man *not* needing a tie. Still, he was grateful for Martin's kindness, particularly since Kate was apparently severely disapproving of his fraternizing with the guilty party – the Parrishes, in her view, ought to be presenting a united front of sympathy for the innocent – and still he had not called Sally but, more oddly, he found he had barely given her a thought and didn't feel too bad about it.

By Friday, Caroline had decided that she was prepared to speak to him, and Andrea was despatched to pick him up from the Cross Keys; Greg wished, although he appreciated that in the circumstances he was in no position to dish out criteria, that she had given him a bit more notice. The previous day, he had reached such a nadir that the prospect of traipsing through the town for a second empty day actually caused him physical pain in his chest when he contemplated it, although that might also have been the legacy of the two packets of cigarettes he was smoking per day, partly because they passed the time and partly because they gave solace, they were small white friends that kept him company and didn't judge him; so rather than tramp the streets of King's Lynn he had decided he might as well spend the whole day in the Cross Keys; after all, if he was going to spend endless money frittering away these open-ended, wrenching hours, better to give it to Rod as a gesture of thanks than to a faceless coffee chain, he reasoned. He hadn't drunk all day, from opening time to lock-in, since he'd been at drama college, and as long as he lost sight of why he was there, in the Cross Keys, he found he was quite enjoying it. But it did mean that he was not at his best when he was summoned on Friday morning to begin peace talks with Caroline; in fact, as he buckled himself into Andrea's car and felt his face flattened by the tundra wind of her disgust, his vision was strobing and his limbs shivering and occasionally convulsing in the manner of someone who has recently had ECT.

'I warned her about you,' was all Andrea said to him as she drove, and Greg, humbled, looked at the floor without replying and wondered why no one had warned *him* about him, and whether he would have listened if they had.

It seemed that Caroline had been doing some maths; perhaps, Greg thought, she had even made a list of pros and cons and weighed them up. Either way, he had inadvertently come out on top; Caroline appeared to have reached the conclusion that this situation could be resolved with minimum disruption and grief if it was established that the battle was not between her and Greg, but between her and Sally. If Sally could be cast as the enemy, and she and Greg could close ranks, he could be accepted back, with a long list of caveats and conditions, naturally, and in time possibly even forgiven, and for Daisy's sake there would be no need to shatter the status quo. Greg had not fully realized until now how strong the territorial instinct was in women, how strong the desire to defend the nest, even at the price of a certain level of self-deception. In order for this restoration work to begin, Caroline needed to be convinced of a number of facts about Sally and Greg's interaction with her, and in the interests of damage limitation, Greg found it surprisingly easy to guide Caroline towards the following assumptions:

That he had only done the deed of darkness with Sally on two occasions, that he had been very drunk both times, and that she had more or less jumped on him when he was barely able to resist.

That she had told him she was on the pill (this, at least, was true, he thought, and felt himself vindicated slightly).

That he had told her categorically that he wanted her to have an abortion and had even offered to pay for it.

That she was the one doing all the chasing, and that he had insisted all along that he would never leave his family, so she knew that she was making her choice without his support.

That she drank too much, was very temperamental and neurotic in the way that writers can be, and quite possibly a little unstable and given to making things up.

He was surprised at how calm he'd felt, saying all this, and how easy these assertions, once they had been voiced, were to believe. Caroline stared at him from dry and puffy eyes over her coffee mug and nodded, once, grimly, as if to signify acceptance. She didn't rush to embrace him, nor did she tell him that he was forgiven or invite him to come home, but she did nod, and she didn't shout. Instead she said, 'I've been to see a lawyer.'

Greg's heart clattered to the floor of his chest cavity. He pictured (he didn't know why) bailiffs carrying furniture out of the house and Daisy being driven away in a van, out of his reach; he pictured himself growing old and pouchy and stubbled in the room above the Cross Keys, with Clive.

'Well, why? There's no need for – is there?'

'Apparently you don't need to do anything at all until it's born. You just deny it. Then if she wants to, she can organize a DNA test.'

'What?'

Caroline faintly smiled.

'She sounds like a slut, Greg. It's probably not even yours.'

This was a thought that had crossed Greg's mind on several occasions, but to hear it from someone else, as such a malicious accusation, made him instinctively rush to Sally's defence.

'To be fair, Caro, Sally's quite smart, I don't think she'd say that if she wasn't –'

'Fine, if she's so smart, off you go to London and live with her and her whore's bastard.'

'I didn't mean –'

'And don't ever, *ever*' – there was a climactic pause – '*ever* say her name in this house.'

'Sorry.'

'Greg, right now we've got to deal with the fact that you've slept with someone else, don't get me wrong for a minute, I'm furious and I'm hurt more than you could possibly realize, but I've had to do a lot of thinking, and there's Daisy, and if what you're telling me is true then I've got to think about whether our family and our relationship is worth more than how angry I am with you.'

'It was a mistake –'

'No, crap, Greg, you don't have sex with someone by mistake, it's not like falling down a hole because you didn't look where you were going, that's a mistake. You knew what you were doing, I don't care how drunk you were. But if I can believe that it would never happen again –'

'God, no, Caro – of course not –'

'– then we can talk about where we go from here. Because I don't think I'm going to let that slut ruin my life and my daughter's life.'

'Well, that's – no –'

'So let's try and d eal with that part of it first. And forget about the baby until it's been proved that it's definitely yours.'

In this moment, Greg conjured an image of Sally – her open laugh, her shrewd eyes, her dry asides – and acknowledged that he had had his own doubts on this point, but that he had put them down to innate biological anxiety (it had even crossed his mind when Caroline told him she was expecting Daisy: how did you *know*?), because he knew, somehow, that Sally would not have deceived him about something so apocalyptic; he had seen her face in that Dublin hospital, and the way she clung to his shirt. Yet there was always something so studiedly offhand about the way she responded to him, and the way she spoke (or, rather, didn't speak) about her feelings for him, that had made him wonder on occasion about the parts of her life that he didn't see; if there were other lovers. Paradoxically, the suggestion, now that it came from Caroline, seemed implausible, a diversionary tactic.

'I honestly don't think she'd –'

'So you won't have any more contact with her.'

'I won't – ?'

'Speak to her. No, you won't. Any communication you have with her basically says that you do think it's yours, and she can use that against you. And if she tries to call you, I'll have some words to say to her.'

Greg could not even summon the imaginative resources needed to picture this conversation.

'There's a good chance she will call me, though, because –'

'Fine, then we'll get the solicitor to write a letter saying that you deny paternity and you'll consider any further contact from her to be harassment until it's been proved that you're the father. And then we'll think about what we're going to do.'

Greg could not remember seeing Caroline so coiled for battle; even the outline of her shoulders trembled with determined energy.

'Caro –' He hesitated. 'I really don't think she'd have said this if she wasn't sure it was mine. Which means I am going to have to face it some time.'

Caroline laid her hands flat on the table with a terrible calm.

'You don't seem to understand. Whether it's yours or not, there's no way you're setting foot inside this house again or ever setting eyes on Daisy unless you swear to me that you will never see or speak to this girl again. Whatever happens. You've got a straight choice. And tomorrow I think you should take your daughter out and remind yourself of what your choice is going to involve. She won't go to bed at night complaining of stomach pains, which is all about you being away.'

'What have you told her?'

'Nothing about this. I told her we've had an argument but we're making it up. There's no way she's going to know about this, Greg. Not ever, OK?'

'Well, but if she finds out later in life, won't it be worse?'

'I don't know, Greg, will it? I can't really see how you could make it much worse, at the moment. But I don't want you back in this house until you can promise me that that bitch is out of your life.'

'I can't make someone disappear.'

'You can if you want your family back, and you will, because that's the only deal. Understood?'

Greg nodded, but if Caroline had expected him to agree without reflection, she was disappointed. He got up from the table without speaking and went upstairs to collect some clean clothes from a bedroom that already felt foreign. What would their lives be like if she took him back, he wondered; would it be a lifetime of walking on eggshells, pretending that this never happened, that Sally and the boy – the *boy*! – didn't exist? He was stuffing pants into a Sainsbury's bag when he heard Caroline shout up the stairs, 'You'd better bloody well decide whose side you're on, Greg.'

You have a brother, he wanted to say to Daisy, who sat hugging her knees, rocking with the unique pent energy of children. He wondered how much they would look alike, his children, ten (nearly eleven) years apart. Daisy had his colouring but her mother's small features. Would his boy look like him? Would there ever be a family photo of his children together, of Daisy holding her little brother (half-brother, he had to keep reminding himself) proudly and awkwardly on her lap? – and he understood then the magnitude of this choice, because there would not and could not be such a photograph. From now on, all his family snapshots would be characterized by absence – summer holidays, Christmas, school plays; as real as the child in the photo would be the absence of the one who was not. He couldn't even bring himself to make a mental list for and against: Daisy, nearing her teens, would have less and less need of him in the years ahead; he had done the bulk of his fathering with her. On the other hand, how could he give up a child he had known for ten years of his life, and the whole of hers, for one he didn't yet know, and one whose life might even be better for not knowing him, or knowing him only in snatches and fragments, even assuming Caroline ever mellowed enough to allow that?

'Do you still love us?' Daisy had twisted her head to look at him, unblinking.

'Oh, Daisy – you have no idea how much I love you. Of course I do – you must never think that, whatever happens with me and mum, and I know we argue sometimes, but that doesn't change anything about –'

'Do you still love Mummy?' Her voice was harder this time. At ten, she never used the childish version of her parents' appellations; it was a mark of distress.

'Of course I do.' He did, but did he sound convincing enough to a ten-year-old?

'So why don't you come home?'

'Well, because –'

'Mummy says you'll come home when you've decided if you still love her.'

'Did Mummy really say that?'

Daisy nodded. Greg looked away to disguise a sudden rush of anger towards Caroline; that was unspeakably low, to use such emotional leverage on their daughter, especially after she was the one urging diplomacy.

'If you don't come home, can I come and visit you in the pub? It's got a snooker table.'

'How do you know that?'

'Martin said. He said he went to visit you.'

'When did Martin say that?'

'When he came round.'

'Has he been round this week, then?'

'Yes.' Daisy had closed up again; she drew spirals with her stick and didn't meet his eye. 'He and Mum went on the Internet in your office.'

A number of possible images presented themselves to Greg's overwrought and paranoid mind's eye: Martin showing Caroline how to root through Greg's emails (and he was the sort of canny bastard who would know how to unearth the ones he thought he'd deleted); Martin looking innocently for tax records and discovering his cache of porn; Martin popping round to comfort Caroline over a glass of something reassuringly expensive and ending up –

'Why were they doing that?'

Daisy produced a grand shrug. 'Dunno.'

'I'll be home after the weekend, Daze, I promise.'

Daisy glanced at him with a moue of cynicism.

'Yeah, but you always promise stuff, Dad, and you probably mean it, but it just never happens.'

～•～

Sally was afraid that she was becoming another person. In the obvious sense, of course, she was becoming an *other* person, or at least another person was in the process of becoming within her, to a degree that she could no longer ignore; there was a self-aggrandizement, she felt, to the vigour and resolution of his acrobatics. He seemed to be constantly seeking attention, and never to sleep; well, she thought, that figures.

What troubled her was the enforced retreat from the person she had thought of as herself. She was a dramatist. For the past ten years, she had fed her imagination on extremes of engagement and solitude. In every photograph from university onwards she could be seen clasping a glass in one hand and a cigarette in the other, or with a glass and a cigarette in one hand and a bottle in the other, and quite often with a further cigarette in her mouth; her head would be looped in smoke like bunting, that was her thing, in the way that Lola had her hair and Rhys had his wry archness, with a hint of camp. It wasn't even that she couldn't give up either – she regularly took a break from both the drink and the smoking – but she always came back because people didn't seem to recognize her without the props, and when that happened, she became nervous about recognizing herself. She always seemed a bit less like Sally without the attendant kit, even to herself.

Now the props were really gone, and there was no margin for recidivism; the prospect of relapsing was still months away, and at the time when she most needed the reassurance of them purely as accessories, rather than for any chemical value. When she went with Rhys and Lola to BarCelona! at lunchtimes, she wanted more than anything to smoke a cigarette, not because she imagined she would enjoy it (the smell still prompted ripples of nausea), but because she felt bulky and clumsy and tired and weepy and needy and a collection of other unappealing traits that felt as if they belonged to someone else, someone more girlish and clingy, and the idea of smoking felt, in its new transgressive condition, as if it might bring her back to herself. But she didn't smoke. Instead, she sat and watched Rhys and Lola anxiously, suspecting that Rhys's patience with her constant presence in Avocet's Southwark office was thinning but unsure how to explain that, along with her sense of alienation from her own life, she had developed a fear – no, *horror* was not too strong a word – of being alone. This was harder to anatomise: she was a writer. Solitude was the sine qua non of her job, and her desire for it had always been fierce; it had been the breaker of a number of relationships, but now, whenever she found herself alone, she felt the early waves of a panic attack breaking at the edges of her chest. She had tried to convey something of this to Rhys to justify her permanent residence on the sofas by the window, the feeling that the presence of other people was the only buffer between sanity and its alternative, but he had merely allowed the curve of a smile and said, with obvious relish, 'But you're never alone, are you, with little junior? And you'll never be alone for the next eighteen years, so enjoy it, angel.' And she couldn't explain that it was this, of course, this ineluctable *presence* that was making her most afraid.

'You do look lovely, Sal,' Lola said, over a lunchtime glass of chardonnay. The fogged breath of condensation around the bowl of the glass, and the amber glow of the liquid as Lola tilted it into the sunlight, seemed to Sally almost sexual; she desired it with an intensity known only to addicts. She looked down at the desultory wink and fizz of bubbles in her own water with resignation; she would have had orange juice, but she thought she remembered something in one of the waiting room's worth of magazines she had bought on the subject saying that orange juice contained levels of mercury that might be harmful to the growing baby. On the other hand, she might be thinking of liver, or she might have got it wrong altogether; her state of mind was such that she read words without really processing any kind of information through them. Mostly she just looked at the pictures in these magazines, which seemed chiefly to be adverts for chrome-sprung, four-wheel-drive buggies that converted into a light aircraft at the flick of a switch and which she would never be able to afford, or photographs of chiselled men smilingly massaging the feet of a delicately pregnant model, or tenderly pushing teats into the faces of unblemished Botticelli infants.

'You're blooming. Your skin is amazing.'

'I look like a blimp. I want a drink.'

'How was your yoga class?'

In company, Sally had determined not to speak about the baby ever, if possible; she needed the rest of the world to see that her brain had not been turned to jello by the process, and to this end she made efforts to engage her friends in conversations about the Arts Council or the Turner Prize or American foreign policy with an enthusiasm she had never previously displayed, but Lola had launched herself into the business of Sally's pregnancy with vim, as if to compensate for Sally's own apparent lack of interest, and would not leave the subject alone. She had signed Sally up for a pre-natal yoga class in Hampstead recommended by her sister; 'bourgeois' was the word that had occurred to Sally, together with the words 'you've got to be joking' but to keep Lola's good will she had agreed to go.

She drank the water.

'Am I boring?'

'No, angel, you're a riot,' Rhys said, lighting another cigarette. Sally watched it as if it were as gorgeous as a firework display.

'I guess there's my answer.'

'No, Sal, of course not, God, you're pregnant, no one expects you to be the life of the party any more,' Lola said, rubbing the back of Sally's hand. 'It's just that we're incredibly busy at the moment, so –'

She left it unfinished, but what she meant, Sally extrapolated, was that their working life didn't easily accommodate nursing an unemployed pregnant playwright, and that the attention they did give her – these lunches, for example – were carved out of time that should have been more profitably used, and that they saw it as a duty of long-standing friendship rather than any kind of pleasure for its own sake.

'So how was the yoga? Did you make any friends with the other mummies?'

'Who are you, my mother? I didn't go. I was too tired. I'll go next week.'

Lola looked serious.

'But you have to go, Millie said it was fantastic. She shows you how to do all the breathing and everything. Plus it would be great for you to meet some other pregnant women, you know, because they'll have a much better idea about what you're going through. We're not much use, I'm afraid.'

Sally heard: *Please, for the love of God, find some other friends to cling to; your presence in our non-pregnant world is a continued nuisance.*

'I will go. But fuck the breathing, really. I'm having drugs.'

'Oh, no, Sal – you should try and have a natural birth, it's much better.'

'*You* have a natural birth. In what way can it be better? It's pain.'

'But it's good pain.'

'Pain is pain, it's amoral. That's like choosing to have the flu.'
Lola shuddered.

'Anyway, look, we wanted to tell you about our plan, didn't we, Rhys?'

Rhys, at the first mention of yoga, had drifted away to a barman-based reverie. He turned his attention back with hooded eyes and no visible urgency.

'Yes, Edinburgh,' he said. 'Freddie's taking a flat for a couple of weeks, he's got to do some thing at the film festival, so we thought we'd all go up and have a bit of fun, maybe a bit of talent-spotting, in every sense. You must come, it'll be your last chance to get out for God knows how long.'

Rhys always managed to make it sound like an interminable sentence. While she was counting down towards the end of this period of blimpishness and deprivation in terms of weeks, Rhys would remind her that the end of her confinement would only be the beginning of a much, much longer incarceration, and it troubled her that the faint sourness in the way he spoke about it echoed something in herself.

'It's two months away. I'll be the size of a shed. I'll never get up the hills.'

'Well, take taxis.' Lola upended her glass; Sally felt a pang of loss. 'Seriously, it would be so good for you to have a break, see old friends, check out some shows.'

'I'll be sober.'

'Sober in Edinburgh will be a kind of altered-consciousness experience in itself,' Rhys said. 'And you'll have a chance to get some sense out of Greg Burns before it's too bloody late.'

Sally sat up. Lola glanced quickly at Rhys.

'I saw Patrick Williams at the Garrick the other night,' she said, 'he mentioned that he's got a few clients going up, but you probably knew – apparently Greg's got the lead in Paul Breton's new thing.'

Sally's heart skidded into her throat. Greg had not called her for two days; he had left longer spaces than this before, but she had an intuitive fear that this time the silence was denser, more deliberate. She didn't say this to Rhys and Lola.

'Sure, yes. Paul Breton, you'd have thought Greg would set his sights a bit higher.'

'I believe it's *Madame Bovary* as a farce,' Rhys said, smiling.

'Oh yes, good Christ. How does he ever get the funding?'

'He sucks a lot of dick.'

'*Rhys*.' But Lola was looking at Sally with concern. 'Did you not know?'

Sally shrugged. 'We haven't talked about Edinburgh. Other stuff to think about.'

'But, aren't you making plans? I mean – he is still moving to London? He does come and see you, doesn't he? Has he told her yet?'

Sally yelped; the baby had pinballed himself from one side of her to the other and wedged a heel or some extremity hard into her bladder.

'He's been busy.'

Rhys gave an equine snort and pushed his chair back. He placed his hands on the table and leaned in towards Sally.

'I've got to get back and make some calls. Sally – for God's sake, get a fucking solicitor. He's under her thumb, as we always knew. I'm serious, angel – I've never pretended to like him, but that's by the by – you've got a child to think about, and I'm telling you, if he's got no interest now, he's not going to suddenly materialize once you've had it. Be fucking ruthless. Get something in writing.'

Sally looked at Lola, who made a face that was meant to imply both agreement with the content of Rhys's speech and disapproval of his delivery. But they didn't understand, she thought. It was a question of time. Greg needed time, and she would show him that she was willing to give it. She and Greg understood each other; after all, had he not been the first one to say he wanted this baby? Had he not cried on the phone when she told him it was a son? My son, she thought, putting a hand gingerly over the lurching mound. There would be no need for solicitors; if nothing else, Greg had a sense of duty. They would be fine. Everything would be fine.

In truth, she had been to the yoga class, for about three minutes. She had walked through the door of the modestly carpeted alternative health centre and seated herself amid the semi-circle of serenely swelling barefoot women who leaned with proprietorial grace against their earnest partners, and the aromatherapy burner in the middle of the floor had chimed with her direst expectations.

'Let's go round the circle and introduce ourselves,' said the class leader, implacably, 'and then we'll begin some exercises.'

'Hi, everyone, I'm Elise and I'm a barrister,' said the woman to her left, whose Juicy tracksuit looked newly unwrapped. 'This is my husband, Nathan. We're twenty-six weeks pregnant and we're having a boy called Elliot.' She smiled, a smile of unperturbable certainty.

'We're very excited,' added Nathan.

Sally found it hard to imagine that Nathan had ever been excited; his face was entirely inexpressive. She wanted to ask Elise if she'd ever woken up on the floor of a pub and not known where she was, although she could guess the answer. She also wanted to ask if the child's name, declared with such a ring of predestination, had been handed to Elise and Nathan at the scan; had the sonographer read the picture and announced, 'Ah, yes, here we are – it's a boy. He's called Elliot'?

'Hi,' said the woman to the left of Elise and Nathan. She made the word last several long beats. Sally thought she could *hear* the smile; it made a kind of hum. 'I'm Pippa and I'm a strategy consultant. This is my husband, Christian, and we're thirty weeks –'

'Sorry, is there a toilet?' Sally had asked at this point, scrabbling for her shoes, and had run from the building. It wasn't Elise and Nathan, nor Pippa and Christian, nor the maternal kindliness of the teacher, nor even the incense; it wasn't, as anyone who knew Sally might have guessed, a cynical distaste for the self-indulgence of the business, nor was it as simple as the unavoidable fact of her own isolation. Beyond all of these was an aversion to so much femaleness in so compressed a space.

Sally had never been very comfortable with the appurtenances of womanhood; this was neither political, nor symptomatic of any suppressed gender confusion. It was not that on some level she didn't want to be a woman; rather that she wanted it not to be especially noteworthy or important. In that room, where the air was thick with unfettered oestrogen, she had been overwhelmed by the reality of her present state, and terrified by it; this most undeniable aspect of being female. And the other women, unequivocally resplendent in their fertility – they didn't need to be afraid because they had the necessary balance. They had the male counterweight to lean against, the yin–yang effect, and Sally saw now why that was necessary; without it, how did you know where to define your own limits? How could Lola have imagined that she would find anything in common with these women? She was a refugee from both states of being: too unlike the women apparently sharing the same condition for them to understand her, and too unlike her old self to belong to that life any longer. All she had was Greg, and since she didn't actually *have* Greg, the loneliness was becoming painfully insistent.

For five days, Greg failed to call. After two days of throwing out the odd text designed to effervesce with cheeriness and independence and avoid any undertone of panic or grasping, none of which received a reply from him, she withdrew for the sake of self-preservation, and waited for what she already knew.

On the sixth day, a Sunday, he phoned her. She was standing in the check-out queue of Sainsbury's Local in Holborn with a basket full of organic vegetables and chicken fillets at her feet; she was feeling especially tired, her back was aching and she needed to go to the toilet; the basket was heavy and she would have to carry its contents half a mile home before she could relieve any of these problems, and Greg phoned her and said, 'Hello. It's Greg here.'

If her stomach had still been capable of lurching independently, it would have done so, but it was crushed by the permanently lurching presence. Greg never bothered to announce himself – not only had they almost immediately fallen into the 'it's me' greeting, confident that for the person being called there was only one 'me' in the world, but surely everyone, even Greg, knew that phones already announced you, like a butler? He sounded as halting as he had on the day of his audition for the play, and Sally realized immediately that there was someone listening. Caroline, specifically, and this would be for her benefit.

'I know.'

'I have something to say.'

'Can I ring you back? I'm in the supermarket.'

'Look, it won't take long – I've told Caroline.'

Sally waited. It seemed to her that the whole shop had fallen silent in sympathy.

'And?'

'We're working through it. It's been – a very difficult time for us.'

Sally said nothing. Greg said, 'So – the bottom line is, I love her. And we're staying together. And I can't see you again. Sorry.'

'*Sorry?*'

'And – obviously – we want you to have a DNA test before we're prepared to discuss this any further, so – obviously – that can't be

260

done until it's born, so, uh, we can get – you know. Solicitors and so on. When the time comes.'

One of the universe of thoughts that passed through Sally's head was, sadly, that Rhys was right. Greg was a reasonable actor, but not a great one; a great actor would have made such a speech at least a little more fluent, a little less as if every word was being hauled up out of his gut on a piece of cotton, and she loved him more for his inability wholly to conceal how much he was hating saying it. The queue edged forward. She was three people away from having to buy groceries and the ground had opened into a gaping chasm beneath her.

'You've got to be fucking kidding me. There is no *way* –'

'You can't expect me to do anything until I know it's mine.'

'This is me you're talking to, Greg. *Me*. How can you even think that I – ?'

In his stiff silence, she imagined she heard the heavy wrestling of duty and feeling. Then she wondered if she had only imagined it. Perhaps he really meant all of this.

'Sally, I've got to go. Sorry.'

He spoke her name, and she heard in that a resistance to all that had gone before; these, she convinced herself, were only words. Greg was acting.

'I know she's there.'

'Erm. That's all I've got to say. Bye.'

'Checkout number four, please,' said the electronic voice, with its roller-coaster cadence.

'Oh, love, you shouldn't be carrying all this lot in your shape,' said the large red woman behind the till, ramming cauliflower into a bag. 'You want to tell *him* to get off his behind and give you an and.'

'Who?' Sally looked around nervously at the man behind her, wondering if he would feel shamed into carrying her shopping.

'*Him*! Your feller. One what got you in that state in the first place. Don't know they're born, men, do they? Give him a talking to, I say. Seventeen pounds thirty-seven.'

She didn't cry until she got outside, but her face was glass, vibrating with the effort of control. She sat down on the ridged orange plank of a bus shelter with two plastic bags spilling vegetables on to the pavement at her feet, and heaved vicious sobs into her empty hands. People pretended she wasn't there, while walking an extra wide arc around her, as if around an accident victim. A taxi pulled up beside her and a woman got out, slamming the door with one sharp report like a shot, and the baby jumped.

Sally took her hands from her face, and watched the taxi pull away, in disbelief. The baby had unmistakably jumped at the sound of the door, which meant that the baby could hear. The baby could *hear* the world. He was a separate person; separate from her. He could hear car doors. Maybe he had heard the phone call. And now they were all separate people, all three of them. As she contemplated the reality of this, a boy ducked past in a hurry and trod on one of her tomatoes that had rolled out of the bag, and it seemed to Sally so ineffably sad, so unbearable, that she let out a muffled howl of pity: for herself; for her fatherless baby, with his new world of sound; for the tomato, so easily crushable; for all the abandoned people in the world who couldn't be comforted; they were all in it together, couldn't something be done? People looked at her from the corners of their eyes and moved away. Only an old lady carefully and tenderly picked up Sally's scattered shopping, item by item, placed the bags upright, and laid an arm around her shoulder. But her coat smelled like a jumble sale, and to escape the weight of the kindness of strangers, Sally boarded the next bus that pulled up and sat on it all the way to Waterloo, because she was too defeated to get off.

At the station, she attempted to use the toilet. It cost twenty pence to get through the turnstile; she didn't have a twenty-pence piece. The assistant in her blue nylon shook her head mutely and pointed at the little neon arrow indicating the coin slot.

'Listen,' Sally said, very quietly, and heard herself sounding like a gangster. A gangster with the jagged breathing of a recent sobbing fit. 'If you don't let me in, I'll piss on the floor right here for nothing, and I won't be the one who has to clear it up.'

The assistant looked back, unmoved; it was probable that she didn't speak English.

'Look.' Sally indicated her stomach. 'I'm pregnant, you have to let me in.'

The assistant looked doubtful.

'And I'm a single mother.'

The metal gate was slowly swung open, and Sally shuffled through it with her bags, thinking as she did so that the memory of this moment would not be erased for the rest of her life. She found it hard to imagine ever being sadder.

'I'm a single mother,' she said again, to her blotched and puffy reflection, when she was washing her hands. 'I'm a *single mother*.' But she didn't really believe it. Greg had been acting.

It was only when she was halfway home on the bus that she realized she had left the shopping in the toilet at Waterloo station, but by then she was too exhausted to cry any more.

17

The landmarks of Edinburgh – by which she meant not the Castle or the Scott Memorial, but the camber of the cobbles, the curvature of the many steps, the precise walking time for a moderately drunk person between any given theatre and bar – were mapped more prominently in Sally's psychic geography than those of London or her university town, as if extra effort had been committed to recording their details to compensate for the fact that she usually registered the city without the full use of all her synapses. If you totalled up all the hours of all the Festivals, she had lived in Edinburgh for over a year of her life, and was seeing it for the first time through eyes unclouded by any chemical agent; eyes that were also programmed to scan for Greg Burns on every street. Ten days had passed since she arrived and he had neither called her nor sought to find her, though he knew she was in the city; pride dictated that she could not call him first, so instead she spent the days climbing the endless hills in order to watch the first halves of plays she then gave up on, either from boredom, discomfort or envy, of all the laughing people who were not weighed down by seven months of pregnancy and the permanent search for someone whose face grinned at her sideways from posters but appeared to be nowhere. It was also the first time she had been to the Festival without work of her own, without the frustrations and camaraderie that attended a production, and she felt defined by her own redundancy, her distance from the heat of things.

With pointless extravagance, Freddie had rented a flat in the New Town that could have housed an orchestra; its cathedral-like entrance hall involved a stairway with brass bannisters that swept a curving line down two storeys and seemed to demand the wearing of evening gowns and fur stoles. Freddie himself was rarely seen; his sole activity at the Festival, it appeared, was to have lunch meetings. He had lunches that began shortly after breakfast and ended after midnight, in members' clubs so exclusive Sally had never before heard their names; whether these were the same lunch, or an overlapping series of shorter lunches, she could not be sure, but American television networks featured heavily. Lola was diligently attending five or six fringe and international shows in the hope of truffling out promising actors or writers, and Rhys spent most of the days shouting into the phone and then reeling home in the small hours with crowds of people, whose singing ricocheted off the high ceilings and whose smoke lingered palely in the mornings, reminding her of how she used to be.

There were a million visitors in the city, and yet it seemed to her impossible that she had not once seen Greg, even at a distance. She had taken to – not *lurking*, exactly, but placing herself fortuitously in and around George Street at the precise times when his play was beginning and ending, in the hope of giving coincidence a small nudge, but it seemed that he must enter and leave the theatre by some secret subterranean passage. The one person she stumbled into without fail, everywhere she went, was Patrick Williams, who greeted her with an expression of pained uselessness, palms outstretched, as if he'd like to offer to help her carry something but wasn't sure of the etiquette. The second time she saw him, in a sandwich shop in Teviot Square, he took her awkwardly by the elbow and said, shuffling, 'Have you seen Greg's play yet?'

'No.'

'Only, it's –' He performed a small dance of embarrassment. 'I wasn't sure if you knew, but his – uh – family is here. For the month, you know, so –'

'So he doesn't see me?'

'Well,' Patrick looked down at Sally's front. 'It's a bit difficult for him at the moment.'

'Mm.'

'I mean, I appreciate it must be difficult for you, too.'

'No, piece of cake.'

'Right. The thing is, she's been threatening him.'

'*Threatening*? With what?'

'Um. I don't know, really. But as you can imagine, she's very distressed by the whole thing. She's on Valium or something.'

'You're looking at me as if that's my fault.'

'I'm not interested in apportioning blame, that's not my business.

I'm interested in my client not having a breakdown while he's working.'

'Which would also be my fault, presumably. Not his fault, in any way. But you're paid 15 per cent to see things his way, aren't you?'

'I'm not interested in talking about sides. I'm just letting you know the situation so you're prepared. And I know he would like to talk to you.'

'He's got my number.'

'Yes, but – I think his phone's being monitored.'

'*Monitored*? What, by MI5?'

'As good as. Look, let me give you my number, that way if you need to get a message to him, you can always call.'

'That's very kind of you, Patrick, but that would be a bit fucking demeaning for both of us, don't you think?'

'Just trying to help.'

'Sorry. Appreciate it.'

'I know it's not easy. My wife's had two.'

I'm not interested in your wife, Sally was tempted to say; this information seemed largely irrelevant, but she understood it to be a lumbering attempt at empathy. She punched in Patrick's number just in case, but the information had been another quiet blow. Caroline was in Edinburgh. With Daisy. Well, of course she was, Sally thought; had she really imagined that Caroline would let Greg roam free for a month in a distant city that also contained his pregnant lover? Walking the streets searching for Greg's face among the bunches of other faces now entailed searching for Caroline's face too, and the nervous worrying at an internal script that might allow any such encounter to pass off without blood or the rending of garments. The standard Festival greeting – 'Seen anything good?' – might, Sally felt, prove inadequate.

On the morning of the eleventh day, a Friday, she was padding effortfully around the marbled kitchen in a vast shirt, making coffee; circumstances had conferred on her a domestic role in the flat with which she was not entirely at home. (It consisted largely of making hot drinks. 'Put the kettle on, Sal,' people would shout as they arrived, in a way that they never had before she was pregnant. In the past, it had always been, 'Sal, where's the corkscrew?') She accepted these duties without complaint, however, conscious that her presence in the flat was a gesture of kindness on the part of her friends:

kindness, or pity, she thought. Sunlight fanned through the high windows; Lola was seated at the table, neatly marking up her day's schedule in a notebook ruled carefully into rectangles for each hour of the afternoon and evening, and opposite her, a shirtless blond boy in jeans was colouring in the letters on the front page of yesterday's *Guardian* with a biro, trying not to make eye contact. Rhys, who sat smoking on the counter, had not introduced him, which meant that he couldn't remember his name. Freddie had apparently already gone out for lunch.

'My first show's at twelve,' Lola said, underlining her notes with resignation. 'I'm seeing four plays this afternoon, and one of them's from Latvia, with puppets. Imagine. Anyway, tonight I'm taking the evening off, and I'm going to *Tristan und Isolde* to treat myself.'

'I should treat yourself by getting trepanned, angel, it'd be more of an occasion.' Rhys was flicking through the fringe programme without looking up; it was clear, except to the boy, apparently, how much he wanted the boy to dress himself and leave. 'My hangover is Wagnerian today. Stay in and watch that.'

'I can't believe', Sally said, handing Lola a cup of coffee, 'that you're shamelessly trawling the streets looking for other writers and then coming home to me and expecting me to make you coffee. After all these years. My writing no longer excites you, is that it? You have to go whoring after the novelty of Latvian puppetry?'

'It would excite me if you were doing any. Are you?'

'Yes, actually.'

'Well, you shouldn't be. You should be preparing for the baby. Anyway, the Latvian puppets are very highly regarded. They've toured the courts of Europe. What are you doing today?'

'I'm in Footlights,' said the boy, suddenly, looking up. He had written 'Andy' across the top of the Guardian in bubble letters. Sally wondered if this were his own name.

'Today, since you ask,' she said, 'I thought I'd go and see the Paul Breton at the Assembly Rooms.'

The thud of an awkward silence; Rhys and Lola exchanged raised eyebrows, as she had known they would.

'Paul Breton was in Footlights,' the boy offered, brightly.

'Yes, and he's a very average fuck, too,' said Rhys. 'Sal, if you want to have it out with Greg, call his agent, go round to his flat, don't do him the favour of sitting through his play. And don't do Paul Breton the favour of paying money for a ticket, for Christ's sake. The critics have shat all over it.'

'I don't care. I'm going to sit in the front row and put him off. Then we'll see how much of an actor he is.'

'Oh, Sally.' Lola laid a hand on her arm. 'Do you really think that's the best way of doing it? What if Caroline's there?'

'You think she's sitting through the performance every night in case he talks to any girls while he's on stage?'

'Nothing would surprise me. Come on, you've got more dignity than that. Think of the baby.'

This had become Lola's mantra, usually in situations in which thinking of the baby was inapplicable.

'The baby can't see anything. It's not born yet.'

'*He*. Don't call my godson it. He's a *he*.'

'I read an article in which studies have proved that being made to sit through a Paul Breton play in the womb can cause internal bleeding in the brains of unborn children,' said Rhys, turning back to the programme.

'We've still got to think of names,' Lola said. She had switched on her baby-reverie face, an expression Sally seemed comprehensively unable to muster. She wondered if it was the exclusive preserve of those who were not actually having a baby.

'How about Andy?'

The boy's smile expanded; he put a hand over his scribbles.

'That's funny – my boyfriend – well, sort of boyfriend' – he glanced at Rhys – 'is called Andy.'

'Really.' Rhys lit another cigarette. 'And is he in Footlights too?'

'No, he's in the Met.'

'The opera company?'

'No, the police force.'

'Fabulous.' Rhys hopped off the counter and checked his watch. 'Right, I'm off to squander my bons mots on Americans.' He leaned to kiss Lola on the cheek in passing. 'Enjoy the Lithuanian puppets, angel, but if you decide to bring them to the West End, I shall professionally divorce you. If you get a chance to pick up another crate of that Merlot, I'd be indebted, I've got people coming later. Sally, maybe you could do it? The place in Morningside Road.'

'She's seven months pregnant,' Lola said. 'Of course she can't do it.'

'She can get a taxi, she's not doing anything else. Look,' – he took a note from his wallet – 'here's twenty, this'll get you there and back and you can give the guy a fat tip to carry it up the stairs.'

'Sal, why don't you come to the Latvian puppets with me this afternoon?' Lola said, taking ten pounds from her purse. 'Go on, it'll be a laugh.'

'That is the first and last time any of those words will ever appear in the same sentence.'

'Come on. And here, take this for a taxi too, I hate to think of you walking up those hills.'

'Then don't think of it. I don't need your money – if I want a taxi, I'll get one.'

Lola sighed.

'You've got to stop getting so huffy. We're your friends, we only want to help you. You're having a baby.'

'Is that what it is? If I want help, I'll ask.'

'Yes, but you won't, though. That's your problem.'

Lola left the money on the table with a final glare and a pointed finger. The click of the front door exploded around the vaults of the hall. Sally looked at the boy across the table.

'What time's your show?'

'Half past four.'

'Is it funny?'

He shrugged.

'Well, I think so. But it depends on the audience.'

Sally laughed.

'Good attitude. Maybe I'll come and see it.'

'Should I leave Rhys my phone number?'

He stood up, still toying with the pen, and looking absurdly young. He had no chest hair, and his nipples were tiny. Sally felt his embarrassment.

'I wouldn't have thought so. Here,' she picked up Lola's money and held it out. 'Do you want that? Get yourself a taxi home.'

The boy looked momentarily outraged.

'I'm not a hooker.'

'No, son, you're a student. You'll get three bottles of wine for that, take it.'

It was only after he'd gone that Sally realized she'd called him *son*, in the context of briefly caring that he should be all right. It was just possible, then, that she was capable of entertaining maternal feelings after all.

The sky was light and high, with the kind of clean summer warmth that only happened this far north; on a day like this, Sally thought, London would be clogged and gassy, unbreathing in its own cladding of heat, and she was grateful to be away. She felt fit, in spite of her cargo; the walking was creating ridges of muscle along her thighs and, although her eyes looked tired, she was assailed in every bar by old friends and acquaintances exclaiming how well she looked. 'I didn't know you were married,' some of them said, as if this were the only possible context for her appearance. To pre-empt the necessity of biographical information, she had taken to wearing her grandmother's ring on the third finger of her left hand, turned inwards, so it appeared as a plain silver band, and she hated herself for doing it. They told her how much pregnancy suited her; she did-n't bother to disabuse them, but it gave her some hope that Greg might see in her some buried trace of the appeal he had once found, if she could only see him alone.

But the acting was exhausting. Greg's leaving had unmoored her; she was numbed. Her body continued to function; it processed food, slept with difficulty, and went about its present business of building a person, but her consciousness had retreated. In company she could hold conversations, and make jokes, but they came from somewhere outside herself; words plucked from a ready stash that she had shored up for just such an emergency, but how long would it last? She had read somewhere that third-degree burns hurt less than first-degree burns, although the wound was graver; often didn't hurt at all, because the nerve endings were seared away. This was how Greg had left her; the blow was such that she didn't even feel pain, yet. She was ashamed of her own vulnerability: to being perceived as a vic-tim, as abandoned, which in turn meant that she could no longer dis-tinguish between acts of friendship and acts of pity. A lifetime of learning to protect herself had made her afraid of showing weakness, with the result that she needlessly pushed her friends away when they tried to offer help. She wondered how long their patience would last. She was watching life – not just her own life but the rest of life – from a distance of several feet, until she was no longer sure how much of it was actually happening.

She wasted time around the flat until the early afternoon, half reading, and then walked up through Princes Street Gardens, among the cheerful holiday crowds splayed on the grass with sandwiches, flyers and newspapers; through the bobbing heads of toddlers on their fathers' shoulders (everywhere, fathers and children; as if they'd all been sent out to step in her path and remind her), instinctively shielding the weight in front of her when the crowds began to press. A cloud drifted singly above the Castle. Two girls with dreadlocks handed her a leaflet, both dressed in identical black T-shirts that someone's dad had paid for, emblazoned with the name of their student play, a Greek revival. The baby hiccupped and lashed out at her ribs. She accepted the leaflet, smiling, dropped it into her bag, and walked on to the Pleasance.

The courtyard, with its picnic tables and primary-coloured umbrellas stickered with beer logos, was just as it had been in her student days. She knew everybody; they sat in the same groups, drinking warm beer from plastic cups, except that now most of them had given up smoking and had expensive clothes, which they washed. They worked in television, theatre and radio; they wrote sitcoms and films, or they made other people's happen. Here, they were self-consciously holidaying in a time-warp, summer after summer, as if their adult lives were fitted in elsewhere. Sally bought a ticket to the Footlights show, for something to do, nodded to a couple of people and sat down at the corner of a bench to read the paper with a Diet Coke. Then she looked up and saw Greg.

He was crossing the courtyard alone, wearing his shapeless denim jacket. She watched him, pulse hammering, and wondered if she should go after him, but before she had to make the choice he saw her, stopped instantly, and glanced wildly around. She followed the frantic motions of his head – was Caroline somewhere in his wake? – and realized that he was moving towards her.

'Hi.' He put his hands in his pockets, and took them out again.

'Oh. Hi.'

'I was going to call you.'

Sally looked up at him.

'Only Caroline's been here. You heard.'

'I saw Patrick.'

'She came – she decided it would be – you know. Can I sit?'

'Be my guest.'

271

He took in her appearance.

'Christ, it's enormous.'

'Yeah, they do that.'

His eyes moved across her face for a long time, as if assessing structural damage.

'I don't know what to say to you.'

'No, I can believe that.'

'It's been – you can't imagine what my life has been like. If I'd tried to call you –'

'Don't bother.'

'How's my son?' He tried to smile.

'Well, we don't know that he is your son, apparently.'

'Come on, Sally. I had to give her that. It was a gesture of apology.'

'What about me? You chose this, Greg, all of it, from the beginning. And I have to pay the price for it?'

'See it from her side. If I give you money, that's money that's being taken away from her child, as she sees it. So you could be lying, she thinks.'

'Right – I could be putting myself through this just to get my hands on your millions. Fuck the money, it's about you and me. And, what, you didn't have the balls to stand up for me?'

'There's nothing wrong with my balls.' He gave a slight swagger with his shoulders.

'You know, you should be on the stage.'

'Sally.' He reached across the table through a pool of beer and touched her hand. 'I think about you every minute. Both of you.'

'Well, that's a massive help. I'm touched. But we need to talk about things – you can't just pretend this isn't happening. There are things to discuss –'

'Greg Burns, Good Lord!'

Sally turned to see a large man in a baroque shirt and flip-flops approaching them, arms aloft. He looked like someone trying too hard to look like an actor. Behind him was a dapper woman in sunglasses.

'How are you, you old bugger!'

'Eddie! Good Lord, you old bugger,' Greg said, rallying himself without enthusiasm.

'Seen anything good? You're doing one, aren't you?'

'I'm in the Paul Breton at the Assembly Rooms.'

'Selling, is it?'

'Pretty much. Critics could have been nicer.'

'Oh, fuck the critics.'

'Eddie – this is' – Greg glanced at Sally with transparent intent – 'Sally McGinley, who wrote the thing I did in the West End.'

'Ah! *Hallo!*' the man said, as if she were four tables away, or foreign.

'This is Eddie Craig, he played Dai in *Valley Vets*.'

'My daughter died of leukaemia,' Eddie Craig said, nodding.

'God, I'm so sorry.' Sally looked at the woman in sunglasses.

'No, in the show. In case you didn't remember Dai. She died just as we were hit by foot and mouth.'

'Oh. Never saw it, I'm afraid.'

'This is my wife, Rhianne.'

'When is your baby due?' Rhianne asked, kindly, settling herself on the bench and lifting her sunglasses. Sally caught Greg's eye. His face was an entire conspiracy theory. For a moment she desperately wanted to drop him in it.

'October.'

'Ahhh.' She rubbed Sally's arm. Sally shrank slightly. 'Is it your first?'

'First and last.'

'Oh, we all say that, but you just wait.' She beamed. Sally suddenly wanted a cigarette more than anything. 'I'll give you one piece of advice, though. Get a girlfriend or a sister to be there at the birth. Because, I don't know if your partner's planning to be there –'

'No, neither do I.' Sally looked at Greg. He was picking splinters from the table with his chin in his collar.

'– but even if he is, they're worse than useless when it comes down to it, doesn't matter how many good intentions they have. Show them a dilated cervix and they just pass out. In China – I think it's China – they don't let men near new mothers from the last month of pregnancy until the baby's three months old, which strikes me as very sensible. Maybe it's Tibet.'

'How old's your little one now, Greg? Shift up.' Eddie wedged himself alongside Greg.

'Ten. Not so little.'

'You've got it all coming. Ours are twelve and fourteen now, and they're royal pains in the arse, both of them, but I tell you, I wouldn't

273

want to go back to all that with the shite everywhere and the endless screaming, eh, mate? I mean, you'll enjoy it all with hindsight, love,' he said, nodding to Sally, 'but it's a relief when they can sleep through the night and wipe their own arses, eh? Makes you glad to be middle-aged, Greg, doesn't it?'

'Mm.'

'It was very nice to meet you, I'm afraid I have to get to a show,' Sally said, complicatedly levering herself out from the table. 'Good luck with your play, Greg. I must come and see it.'

'Yes, uh' – Greg held her look for a few seconds, but seemed compelled to return his attention to the table. 'Good luck with your, uh, baby.'

'Well, thank you very much, Greg.' As she passed, she allowed her bag gently to swing the remains of her Diet Coke into Greg's lap. 'Oh, sorry. I'm such a klutz these days.'

Five minutes later, Greg panted up to her as she stood in the queue for the show.

'You seem to have wet your pants.'

'Fair enough, I deserved that. Thanks for not – you know. I've known them for years, they know Caroline.'

'Good. As long as Caroline's all right.'

'OK, I know how it must seem, but if I can get Caroline to come round, which means walking on eggshells around her at the moment, then we've got a better chance of all this working out.'

'Working out? And how do you see it working out, exactly?'

'Of her accepting it.'

'That you want to have two families?'

Greg pushed both hands through his hair.

'Look – she's going home tomorrow for a couple of days.'

'Is she leaving you with a babysitter?'

'Daisy's missing her friends, she doesn't really want to be here. They're going back so she can go to a party on Saturday, then Caroline's coming back on Monday. But we could meet tomorrow.'

'I might be busy tomorrow.'

'You're not, though, are you? Come on, Sally, I really want to talk to you, properly. It might be the only chance.'

'What, you don't think you'll manage to get in touch again before our child is born?'

'I don't know.' His face was growing anguished. 'You don't know

274

what it's like at home. It's a fucking nightmare.'

'Then why are you still there?'

'It's not as simple as that. Look, we can't talk here, we know every-one. Meet me tomorrow, up at the National Monument.'

'Edinburgh's Disgrace. You have such an acute feeling for place, Greg.'

'Well, you know. It's out of the way. Two o'clock?'

Sally hesitated. He looked so anxious, she didn't know whether she wanted to cuff him or hug him.

'Fine.'

'Great.' He grinned, and reached into the pocket of his jacket, smoothed out a crumpled ten pound note and handed it to her. 'Get a taxi up there tomorrow, it's too far for you to walk in that state.'

Sally turned it over and examined it, as if for counterfeit markings.

'You're sure you want to give me this without the DNA test?'

'Come on, Sally. Don't give me a hard time. I'm doing my best.'

'Well, thank you. I could make a living here off taxi fares.'

'Least I can do.'

'Yes, you're right there.'

~·◆·~

It was not until he arrived in Edinburgh, and knew that they were both in the same city at the same time, that it dawned on Greg how much he needed both Caroline and Sally in his life, and how much work it was going to take to keep them there. They provided a natu-ral counterweight to one another, and both sustained him in separate ways that he now found difficult to contemplate losing, but the key was in their equal and opposite force. Both met a need in him; too much of one or the other would leave part of him bereft, and it seemed to him significant in this context the way in which he had fathered their children: with Caroline, a daughter in her own image, with the same streak of hard-headedness, the same no-nonsense determination, and with Sally, a boy who – they didn't yet know, but he imagined this son to have the same fearlessness as his mother, the same wilful quest for adventure. And where was he in all this? In what did they resemble him, these children, the one familiar, the other all potential? And would they – could they – find reasons to be proud of him?

When Caroline had first announced her intention of coming to Edinburgh, he had been horrified, but he was tightly aware of the need to placate, and quickly saw that this was the only condition under which he would be permitted to do the play, which had a chance of transferring to off-West End in the autumn. Another thought had occurred to him: he knew it appeared unrealistic, but he felt that if he could somehow choreograph a meeting between Caroline and Sally, if Caroline could be persuaded that he was not going to leave her, and that it was not Sally's intention to steal him away, then, in time, some kind of amicable agreement might be reached. They had so much in common, after all – him, for a start – that it would be absurd for them not to get on. He put this theory to Patrick Williams one evening after he came off stage (he was allowed one beer with Patrick before his curfew, unless Daisy had been granted a special dispensation to stay up and Caroline was meeting him later).

Patrick simply stared, with the same expression he always used for Greg now.

'Why don't you just cut your bollocks off yourself and miss out the middle man?' he said. 'You're going to throw them into each other's path and hope they'll sort it out between them? I know Caroline better than that and I don't even live with her. She will never accept a time-share deal, Greg, not if you live to be a hundred.'

'She'll come round. Once she gets used to the idea that I'm not going to leave her, it just needs time.'

'It just needs someone other than Caroline. And Sally McGinley's no pushover, either. Don't underestimate her – she won't let you get away with bailing out over this.'

'She'll be fine. They'll both be fine.'

'Greg – do you even *know* either of these women? Do you know anything about women at all? You're living inside your own head.'

Greg had concluded that, because Patrick was naturally a worrier with pessimistic leanings, none of this was to be relied on.

He had seen Sally once at a distance, in the High Street, when he was on his own; she had stopped to listen to a string quartet and was standing half in profile, wearing a white shirt and jeans, with one arm curved gently across her stomach. Her hair was longer and she had not gained weight, except for the baby; watching her as she dropped some coins into the cello case and moved on, he felt a sudden uprising of tenderness and guilt in his chest at the sight of her alone, and wanted to go after her and kiss her and make her promises, but lack of resolve and useful words dragged him back. Impossibly, he had not seen her again; more impossibly, neither had Caroline, who, he knew, walked the streets every day like a bounty hunter, with a magazine of ready insults to fire off the minute she registered Sally's face in a crowd. What Caroline wanted most of all, he knew, was for them to encounter Sally together, the two of them, forces joined arm-in-arm against her, so that she could watch him spurn Sally at first hand, for her satisfaction. That, he thought, would give her some reassurance; worse still, he knew that, if the moment came, he would be able to do it, even if it wrecked him inside. He was, after all, a reasonably competent actor, whatever the *Scotsman* said.

The only part of the Festival that he was enjoying was spending time with Daisy, although she seemed to be enjoying it less than he was. Nevertheless, she was an astute child, enough to realize that her participation here was a requirement in whatever moves were being made towards détente between her parents, and the effort she put into pretending to be OK with this touched him deeply; she would do whatever was demanded of her to make things all right, and he loved her for it more than he could tell her. He had taken her to children's theatre shows and Latvian puppetry, they had listened to a band and eaten hotdogs in Princes Street Gardens, they had climbed up to the Castle and pretended to fire arrows from the battlements, but he knew that her patience with the city and its novelties had been exhausted after a few days; she missed home, her friends, the dog, her own things in her own room, and he wished that Caroline would relax enough to take her back where she wanted to be. The rest of it was not enjoyable. The Paul Breton play he was in seemed to exist on the brink of mania; most of the cast did not like each other, though under Caroline's diktat he spent so little time socializing with them that he seemed to have escaped the shifting factions and backstabbing, which meant that everybody else deposited their bile with him; the reviews had not been positive, which was making the London backers nervous, and this in turn filtered down to the producers, the director and the actors; in addition, the requirement that he return early to the flat every evening, where Caroline put all her energies into creating meals for the two of them that neither had the inclina-

277

tion to eat, was beginning to erode his sense of contrition, and the knowledge that Sally was somewhere, perhaps a few streets away, and that he couldn't reach her to say any of the many things he needed her to understand, meant that the pressure in their small flat was building, unavoidably, into the intimation of a storm.

Then he had bumped into her, in the courtyard of the Pleasance, and had been unseated by her coolness and the way she seemed to be contained within herself. She was angry with him, he recognized that and understood it, but he had expected her to show more need of him – perhaps a small display of tears or helplessness, something girlish to show that she had not already written him out of the story. It had occurred to him then, with a degree of alarm, that she might be even more self-possessed than he had given her credit for, and might be intending to punish him by calling his bluff and deliberately shutting him out, which, if she had understood him better, she would know had never been his intention. Sally, like Caroline, was resolute; he had seen in her attitude towards her father how she did not forgive easily, and the thought of losing her and the child irrevocably filled him with a sudden dread. Nobody must do anything hasty, he decided, although he knew that, if he had suggested such a resolve to Patrick, horses and stable doors would have been invoked.

So it was armed with a spirit of aggressive reconciliation that he saw Caroline and Daisy on to a train at Waverley station and then took a taxi to the top of Calton Hill, to try to restore the balance between his two lives. In the shadow of the doomed monument, the hill kept an aura of remoteness. People were walking dogs, and tourists with bright backpacks grappled with maps as they pointed out spires and rooftops to one another from above. Sally was nowhere to be seen, so Greg settled himself on a clump of grass and pretended to read *How to Write Television Drama*. Beyond the fringes of the city, the sea flung light back at the sky, and a warm wind scrappily undid his hair; already the reality of Caroline was beginning to fade, and the imminent presence of Sally excited him. He kept his attention to the roadway where a taxi would pull up.

She was walking now with a slight sailor's roll, he noticed, as she came down the path towards him, canted backwards for balance, and he tried to imagine, as he had done when Caroline was pregnant, what it must be like to make room inside yourself for another person. Where did all the organs go, for a start? Caroline had made him read a number of books on the subject, but he had not taken much in at the time and certainly could not remember now. Seeing Sally, the set of her jaw as she attempted to look as normal as possible, he experienced a complicated combination of pride and revulsion. She had been so expertly muscled, all planes and smooth surfaces, and her body would be irretrievably marked by this, and it would be his fault.

She approached him warily, without speaking, as in a bad spy film.

'Look at this view.' He gestured pointlessly.

'I've seen it before.'

She sat down, a couple of feet from him, as if they were unconnected.

'Sally.'

He manoeuvred himself behind her, so that she sat between his legs, leaning back on him, and he placed his hands on the dome of her stomach. For a moment her shoulders tensed, as if she wanted to move, but the tension subsided and she allowed him to put his face in her hair.

'I've missed you so much. It's been – I don't need to tell you how it's been.'

'You could have called me. I sent you messages.'

'My number's changed.'

'Just like that?'

'She put my phone in the dishwasher. I had to get a new one.'

Sally half turned, then burst out laughing.

'You're a whole sitcom all by yourself.'

'You wouldn't have laughed if you'd been there.'

A rook landed near by and began to pull at a discarded sandwich. They watched it in silence. The baby rearranged itself vigorously, making Greg jump.

'Blimey. He's really in there.'

'Yes, it's not just the beer.'

Greg sighed.

'All that time we were together in London. It was wonderful, but – it wasn't real life.'

'This is real life, Greg. *This*. It's actually happening, look.'

She laid a hand over his and guided it to a place where something hard jutted, like a corner.

'Is that his foot?'

'That's his horns.'

'Can I ask you something?'

'As long as it's not whether it really is yours.'

'Don't go on about that. It's just a formality.'

'It's not just a formality, Greg, it's a fucking insult.' She turned to face him, sitting back on her heels. 'You seem to think it's nothing. Don't you see what it says about how you think of me? Can you imagine how I'm going to feel, walking into a doctor with a baby and asking for a DNA test because his father thinks I'm a slut?'

'I had to agree to it, Sal. Caroline was threatening to kill herself and stop me seeing Daisy. You don't know what it was like.'

'Well, she hasn't thought that through – she could only do one or the other. And if you knew anything at all about the human psyche you'd know that the people who threaten to kill themselves in moments of high drama are not the ones that do it.'

'It was pretty frightening at the time.'

'I've never made demands on you, have I?'

'No. And I'm grateful, really.'

'But that's what you respond to, clearly. She screams and stamps her foot and gets her own way. So if I start making threats too, will that work?'

'Jesus.' Greg put both hands through his hair. 'You have to see, I owe her something, she's the innocent party here. We're the ones who have wronged her.'

'*Wronged* her? What kind of word is that – are we in *The Crucible*? Don't ask me to carry part of your guilt, either – she was never my responsibility. I never promised to be faithful to her – that was you, and you started this thing, you came after me, you bought tickets to fucking Dublin and told me you wanted me to have your baby.'

'I know.' He began to pick blades of grass from the area between his feet. 'That's what I wanted to ask you – if I hadn't done that, if we hadn't gone to Dublin – would you have gone ahead with it?'

'Knowing you were going to do all this? Don't be crazy. Do you think I wanted a child?'

'You mean you don't want it now?'

She was looking down and he couldn't see her face.

'I don't know what I feel about it most of the time. I wanted *this* child, when I was under the impression we were in this together.'

'We are. We will be. Some time.' He tried to pat her but she flinched. 'I'm not running away. I know it looks like it, but – one day we'll look back and laugh about all this.'

'Will we? Oh, good. What, when the three of us are drinking Chablis on your patio furniture as the kids run round the garden?'

Greg was silent. Sally shook her head.

'You really believe that might happen, don't you? You think it will all resolve itself without you having to do anything.'

'I think, if you could just talk to each other –'

'You're out of your mind.'

Sally turned away to look at the sea. He could no longer see her face. They sat for a moment listening to the wind.

'In this play I'm doing –'

'The Paul Breton?'

'Yes. In this play –'

'The Paul Breton that got one and a half stars in the *Scotsman*?'

'Yes, all right. In this play, my character is a bloke who's lost his child. It's been incredibly hard.'

'I'd have thought it would be incredibly easy.'

'I don't want to lose you, Sally. Either of you. I think about you all the time.'

'Then you have to do something. All these nice sentiments are not enough. I need more than that.'

'Money, you mean? I can give you money, of course I will. I'm not trying to get out of it.'

As he said this, he thought of what he had learned about Caroline's secretive meetings with Martin Parrish, and marvelled again at the reach of his own duplicity.

'Would you shut up about money?' She turned back to him, her face dark. 'I don't give a shit about that, it's about you and me and this child, and how we work it out.'

'How are you for money, though?' It occurred to Greg that he had no idea how much she earned, or how much babies cost any more.

She shrugged.

'I sold the bike.'

'That must have been hard.'

'It was just a bike. I can get another one.'

'I'll get you another one.'

She snorted.

'I just need to get writing again. I'm moving when I get back from here.'

'Moving? Where?' Greg was struck by a sudden improbable thought that she might decide to take the baby to Australia and start a new life.

'Crowbourne. Surrey. To be near my mum. Just for the first few – I don't know. It made more sense, you know, to have some help.'

'Yes, you'll need some help. With a new baby.'

'Thanks for pointing that out.'

Another silence.

'Sally.' He shuffled closer to her, moved to touch her arm. 'We only have one day together, I don't want to fight with you.'

'Ah. You want to have a day of skipping through the streets hand in hand and eating ice-cream, before you have to go back to your real life, is that it?'

'I love you.'

She looked at him for a long time.

'No, Greg. You only think you do. Anyway, you love Caroline. You said so.'

'I love both of you, in different ways. Is that impossible?'

'Not for you, maybe. But in the world outside your head, yes, I think it is.'

'My home is with her. That doesn't mean I don't love you.'

'Your house is with her.'

'All right, so I don't want to lose my house, is that so bad?'

Seagulls made urgent announcements overhead. An elderly couple passed them with indulgent smiles. People think we're happy, Greg thought. Anyone looking at us would see a happy couple expecting a baby.

'Actually, do you want an ice-cream?'

Sally arched an eyebrow and ineffectually tried to smother a smile. Greg recognized the expression; he had used it himself when he tried to tell Daisy off as a toddler and she always succeeded in making him laugh in the middle of it.

'Ice-cream works for us,' she said, patting the bump.

'I'll call a taxi.'

'Would you ever give it a rest with the taxis? I haven't had a hip replacement. Let's walk.'

'You know what we could do this afternoon?' Greg said, his arm round her back as they negotiated the downward incline. 'We could jump in the car and go across to Gretna Green and get married.'

Sally stopped and doubled over; he looked around in sudden panic.

'Are you OK?'

She straightened up, her face knotted in laughter.

'Yes, all right, Greg, let's do that. Be a nice surprise for Caroline when she gets back.'

'We could though, couldn't we? There's nothing to stop us.'

'I don't think they let you just turn up.'

'No, they do, I've seen it in films.'

'Ah, well then, it must be true.'

'I just proposed to you and you just accepted. That's official.'

'Whatever you say, Greg.'

'Do you want to be Burns-McGinley or McGinley-Burns?'

'Either way sounds like a company that lays asphalt.'

They spent the afternoon wandering the city like a couple on holiday; ice-cream, pavement cafés, street bands. Greg was conscious of the looks he got from other men as he stood with his arm around Sally, ripely swelling with his child, her face radiant in the sun; she seemed happy, and he realized that the simple fact of his presence was having this effect. He was troubled by the thought that he didn't deserve her. Or Caroline, for that matter. Only one moment marred the idyll; waiting to cross the High Street, he said, unthinking, 'You know, I could just push you under a car right now and solve all my problems.'

The way she unhooked her arm from his and looked at him, without anger, but with total coldness, informed him that his humour had not fallen well.

'It was a joke.' He ruffled her hair too boisterously, as if to demonstrate playfulness.

'Only partly,' she said. 'Like getting married. In your head, all these things are possible endings, aren't they?'

She walked on ahead of him; finally, he had to buy a rose from a street vendor to break the silence. Sally brandished it in his face and said, 'You're lucky I don't shove this up your arse.' The flowerseller smiled benignly.

Later, after his play was finished for the night, he went to Sally's flat and undressed her for the first time since Dublin. He had been doubtful about whether he would want to fuck her – his instincts now were more protective than rapacious – but there was something extraordinary about her body, its extra curves in the movement of light and shadow; not sexual exactly, but aesthetically moving, like a sculpture. She kissed him with such voracity, though, that his doubts were quickly eclipsed. She was about to straddle him when his phone rang.

'I have to take this, it'll be Caroline,' he said, rolling off the bed in search of his jacket. He saw Sally's face tighten; wordlessly, she wrapped herself in the sheet.

'I just called the flat and you're not there,' Caroline said, through static.

'No, I'm just having a few beers with the rest of the cast. I'm going back in a minute.'

'Is your whore there? Have you seen her?'

'She's not there, I haven't seen her.' He glanced at Sally. She turned her back to him.

'It doesn't sound like you're in a pub.'

'I'm outside.'

'Are you lying to me, Greg? Are you with her?'

'No. How's Daisy?'

'She's fine. Don't change the subject. So how long are you planning to stay out tonight?'

'I don't know, Caroline, I'm just having a drink, you have to trust me. We can't live like this.'

'How can I possibly trust you? You go to the pub for an hour, you'll have seven more children by tomorrow.'

'Please. Can I go now?'

Caroline hung up. Greg looked across at Sally.

'Sorry.'

'Are you going to be happy, living like that? How long will it go on?'

'I don't know. But I can't leave her, Sally, I've realized that. I can't just throw away twelve years. You're not even thirty. Your life will go on fine without me, but I don't know if hers would.'

'There's someone else's life to consider now. Tell me something – were you happy this afternoon?'

'Yes.'

'Are you happy now?'

'I'd be happier if I didn't have to sneak away in the middle of the night.'

'So, QED.'

'But I do have to, so.'

'You don't have to do anything, Greg, you choose these restrictions.'

She was putting a shirt on as she said this, so Greg deduced that the moment for intimacy had passed. Sally poured him a glass of wine in the kitchen while he smoked a cigarette, but he was already anxiously anticipating Caroline's next call to relax.

'She'll phone again in a minute – if I'm not home, there'll be hell to pay.'

Sally appeared to suppress a gesture of impatience.

'Listen – there's a party tomorrow. Something to do with the Film Festival. Freddie's got us all tickets, will you come? She's not back until Monday, right?'

'Do you want me to come?'

'Of course, that's why I'm asking.'

'Then I'd love to. We could have lunch tomorrow, if you want. I have to meet Patrick in the afternoon, but I'm free until three.' He leaned across and kissed her warm forehead, then lifted her shirt gently and kissed her stomach. 'Goodnight, wee man.' He straightened. 'Do you think he knows I'm his dad?'

'No, Greg. I don't think he knows anything, he's in a bag of whatever in the dark. He doesn't have ESP.'

'I think he knows. Goodnight.'

In the entrance hall he collided with Rhys Richards in a cloud of black tobacco and violent cologne, who looked him up and down with open disdain.

'So, Greg Burns, back on the scene, then?'

'I don't know about that –'

'You don't *know* if you're back on the scene? Hm. So sorry about your reviews, by the way.'

'Oh. Well –'

'Patrick mentioned he was going to put you up for the new Tony Czajkowski thing that's casting in the autumn. *Mayor of Casterbridge*, isn't it? For the lead, no less.'

'Yes.' Greg tried to bypass him, but Rhys matched his steps and blocked the way.

'Fancy yourself in breeches, do you?'

'Well, who wouldn't want to do a Tony Czajkowski?'

'Quite. The thing is – Tony's very fond of Sally, you know. We've all known him since college. She's like another daughter to him.'

Greg felt the subtext beginning to emerge. Rhys had a disabling way with eye contact.

'In fact, now that I think of it, a lot of people in our business are very fond of Sally. And it's such a small world, the acting profession, don't you find? So much depends on word of mouth. And you know how fussy producers are – they like to know they're working with people who are, oh, what's the word' – Rhys twirled his fingers in the air and looked to the middle distance, as if tasting wine – 'reliable. Not the kind of people who run away from responsibilities.'

'I understand.'

'Oh good. I hope you do, because frankly, Greg, so far you've behaved like a cunt, and no one I know wants to work with a cunt. You see what I'm saying?'

'I'll never work in this town again, is that it?'

Rhys affected affront.

'Gregory, you flatter me. You imagine I have that kind of influence? Not at all.'

'I get it. Thank you.'

'You don't piss about with children, Greg,' Rhys said, suddenly dropping the camp and poking him in the chest. 'And not with my godson.'

'What?'

'Oh, she didn't tell you? Don't look so alarmed. Poofs make excellent godparents, everyone knows that. On account of all our disposable income. I hope we'll see you at this party tomorrow, I think it would mean a lot to Sally. You know, not to have go alone.'

'Looking forward to it,' Greg said, absently, as he opened the door. She had already chosen godparents without consulting him, he thought, as he made his way down the stairs to the street. She was within her rights, he supposed; he had been absent for weeks. Had she chosen a name? He had meant to ask her again what she thought of Thomas, but in the carnival atmosphere of the afternoon he had forgotten. And Rhys Richards – to have Rhys Richards, who hated him, forever linked with his son! Was there a limit on how many godfathers you were allowed? He had hoped to ask Patrick; he thought it might make up for the hoops he had put him through. And did the godfather thing mean that Sally was planning to have the baby christened, or whatever Catholics did, or was it just a nominal thing for her friends? He hadn't thought that was her style, but perhaps impending motherhood was giving her an existential crisis. Would his son have to be a Catholic with a gay godfather (it was not that he was gay, per se, that was not the problem, the problem was that he was Rhys Richards)? What if she gave the boy a stupid name, one that he couldn't reasonably call across a football pitch without wincing? He couldn't think what he'd been doing, allowing her to make all these choices without him; the sooner he established his paternal rights, the less room there would be for mistakes.

Then he remembered Caroline.

Festival parties were all the same, Sally used to claim: same faces, same cheap fizz, same whining conversations about reviews and reviewers, about whose career could reasonably be described as on the skids, same fumbled efforts not to go home alone, regardless of quality, same fights and same dearth of taxis at the end of the night. This one, however, was radically different: this time she was sober. She was also confined to a sofa in the corner of the bar, with a nearly completed child re-enacting the Battle of the Boyne on her bladder.

'I don't think I told him where it was,' she said to Lola, who was perched on the armrest, periodically reaching down to feel the baby gyrating, a novelty that never seemed to wear off for her. Greg was already an hour later than he'd promised.

'Patrick's here. Patrick will have told him. Do you want another Coke?'

'No. I've already spent more time in the loo than I have in here.'

'Are you too hot?'

'Yes, but everyone's too hot. The party's too hot. Stop fussing.'

Freddie Zamora drifted past. He had a sort of other-worldly look to him these days, Freddie; like a teenage girl who's only just becoming aware of her own desirability. People who make things happen trailed in his slipstream; he simply let them.

'Hey, Sally, Lola,' he said, pausing by the sofa. 'How's your nipper?'

'My *nipple*?'

'Nipper, idiot. The baby. How is it?'

'Still in there, as far as I can tell.'

Actually, Sally's nipples had been causing her some trouble over the past days; they were beginning to leak. She had known that this would be part of the deal; nevertheless, the sight of it horrified her, as if she were mutating before her own eyes.

'Oh, and', Freddie said, preparing to move on, 'Patrick Williams is looking for you.'

'Well, I'm hard to miss. I'm right here, like a big hippo. I might just marry Patrick Williams, you know,' she said to Lola, when Freddie had gone. 'I see more of him than I do of Greg.'

'Then you'd only get 15 per cent of your child support.'

'I don't even know that I'm getting child support.'

'Oh, Sally. I thought that was one of the things you were supposed to be discussing yesterday.'

'Yes, but we were having a nice time. It would have spoiled the atmosphere.''For God's sake. You're not together any more, he's made that quite clear. And I don't know why you let him in last night, that's your business, but he's just messing you around – you've got to sit him down and make him put something in writing. Think of the baby.'

'I think of the baby all the time, Lo, I don't have a choice. And I wish everyone would drop it with the money, it's not about that. I'll get a bank loan if I have to.'

'Well, babies cost money, you haven't got any, and he's got a legal obligation. Rhys is right, you should get a solicitor.'

'Rhys isn't in this relationship.'

'Neither are you, any more.'

Patrick Williams appeared breathlessly in a gap between two groups of people dancing while eating canapés. He had the look of a battlefield messenger in *Macbeth*.

'Sally, Sally, thank God.'

'Patrick, Patrick, what?'

He knelt by the arm of the sofa.

'Caroline's here.'

Sally half rose in panic, or as near to either rising or panic as her bulk permitted.

'What? Where?'

'They're coming, any minute. She came up a day early, without Daisy, to surprise him.'

'That must have been a very surprising surprise.'

'Well, it nearly was, from her point of view. If she'd arrived an hour earlier he'd have still been with you. He told her there was a party. She wanted to come.'

'He didn't tell her I was here?'

'No, he did. That's why she wanted to come.'

'What, does she want to fight me, in here? Is this *Jerry Springer*?'

'I don't know, Sally – she's got some idea in her head. But it seems to me, you and Greg both know a lot of people at this party, important people, so do I, it's the last place you want to have a scene, I'd have thought. So maybe the best thing would be if you left before they get here.'

'Why do *I* have to leave? These are my people.' She gestured grandly.

Patrick stood up and held up his hands in submission.

'OK, Sally, no one's telling you what to do. I'm just trying to help.'

Sally smiled.

'Oh, Patrick, you're always trying to help, you're like the UN.'

'Too late,' said Lola, pointing with a straw.

Through the pretzled shapes of the dancing people's limbs, Sally glimpsed Greg and Caroline approaching the bar on the other side of the room. She was gripping his arm like a short minder, and Sally felt suddenly deflated, aware of her own tiredness. After the day before, the night before, she had really believed that he was on his way back to her; that all she needed was more time with him to persuade him that he was making the wrong choice. She had thought he was beginning to see it, too. Now she realized again what she already knew: that Greg lived in an eternal present, where only what was immediately in front of him had any kind of shape or substance. He wanted her and Caroline to coexist; he failed to understand that they automatically displaced each other, that where one was, the other could not be. It was a law of physics. Not even in this room, among all these bodies. She felt the brimming of tears. Patrick Williams wiped both hands up and down his face.

'Come on, Sal, let's go,' Lola said, touching her arm. 'I'll come with you. Before they see us.'

'No, you don't have to, you stay.'

'Don't be silly. It's a boring party, I've had enough.'

Sally knew this was not true, but she heaved herself to standing and allowed Lola to guide her around the edge of the room through the crowds, while Greg and Caroline still had their attention turned to the bar. They had almost made it to the door when Sally said, 'I'm going to have to go to the loo again.'

'Well, be quick.'

The Ladies was long and narrow, with seven or eight cubicles facing a mirror, into which girls peered at an angle, drawing unsteadily on their faces with lip glosses and eyeliners. The floor was strewn with paper. When Sally emerged from her cubicle she found Lola standing immediately behind the door; Lola grabbed her by both elbows and more or less carried her out.

'Wait, I haven't washed my hands.'

'You don't need to,' Lola said, urgently. 'Get the fuck out.'

She made the mistake of turning to look behind her; Sally followed the movement of her head and saw, at the far end of the mirror, Caroline, who turned at the same time. Their eyes docked; for an instant, Sally recognized murderous intent, the glitter of hatred.

'*Out!*' said Lola, and pushed her through the door, dragging her by the arm through another set of double doors that led out to a metal fire escape. They scrambled down it to find themselves in a concrete yard bordered with wheelie bins.

'The gate's locked,' Lola said, jiggling the catch frantically. 'We'll have to get over the fence.'

Sally opened her mouth to make a quip, but found she didn't have the energy. She also found that she was crying.

'I'm seven months pregnant, for fuck's sake, how am I supposed to get over a fence?'

'It's only little, look. Oh, baby, I'm so sorry. He deserves to be spayed.'

At the end of the yard was a low fence separating it from the car park. Lola turned a wheelie bin on its side and helped Sally climb up and over. On the other side, she sat down on the tarmac and covered her face. Lola paced in angry circles and held her cigarette like a weapon.

'Can you believe he did that?'

'Yes, I can.'

'After last night.'

'You should never have let him back into your bed.'

'He said he loved me.'

'Sally. Jesus Christ. You're as stupid as he is. Which is not to say that he isn't the lowest bag of shit for that performance.' She gestured up to the party room.

'Why would he bring her? What did he think that would achieve?'

'He probably didn't think at all. He doesn't, as far as I can see. And she probably thought she'd get to see him humiliate you in front of all your friends. Smug bitch. They deserve each other.'

Sally looked up. She wiped her face with the back of her hand, and tried to laugh.

'That has got to be the most absurd thing I've ever done in my life.'

'You'll write a play about it one day.'

'They'd say it was implausible.'

'They'd be right. Come on, let's go and get you some hot chocolate.'

Sally looked back at the dark wall of the building. The fire-escape door was still swinging, throwing flashes of light and sound into the empty night. Bass rhythms crashed, muffled, through the walls.

'If she'd been nearer she'd have killed me with her hairbrush. Did you see her face?'

Lola crouched down, took her by the shoulders and leaned into her face.

'Tell me something. Do you love Greg? Is he really worth any of this?'

'I thought I did. I don't know any more. I just know I don't want to do this on my own.'

Lola folded her arms around Sally's neck; her profuse hair smelled of tropical beaches. For the first time since she could remember, Sally allowed herself to be hugged by her friend.

'Well, you're not, you dolt. Just don't keep going back for more, Sal. See him for what he is and let him go. He's not strong enough. You've got to think of the baby.'

Sally thought of the baby; she thought of him as a little blond boy, waiting endlessly by a door for a dad who promised to come and never quite found the resolve to see his promises through. She thought of Caroline's face by the mirror, and knew that it was not the face of someone who would ever tolerate her existence, or the existence of her child. She thought about how much strength it would

291

take to be both mother and father, and then she thought that, just pos-sibly, she might dredge it up from somewhere.

'Lo?'

'Yes?'

'Can I have one of your cigarettes? Come on, it can't be any worse than jumping over fences.'

Lola hesitated, then appeared to acknowledge the extremity of the situation.

Sally lit the cigarette, then held it in front of her face and looked at it. From a corner of her brain, perhaps the part of her that passed for a conscience, she heard a small voice of protest. *You are not just you*, it said, or something to that effect.

Reluctantly, she handed it back to Lola.

'You know, I'm all right without this,' she said.

18

See this? This is your first home. Well, technically your second home, though you won't know anything about the first. It was above a café in a market. OK, it was noisy and it smelled of frying meat, it didn't have a washing-machine and in the summer you couldn't breathe or sleep, but it had this in its favour: it was in London. There was life. Look at this now: there's a proper kitchen, with a table; we could have people round. If we knew any people. There are doors that open on to a garden. A garden! And it has an upstairs, where you have your own room. We'll put pictures up. Do you know what it would cost to rent this house if it were in London? About four times more than we could afford. So we're very lucky; no, really, very lucky. The only downside is that it's in the Village of the Damned. This is where people come to die, and you've come here to be born. What does that augur for you? You'll be all right, anyway; you won't even notice. There are facilities for you and your people. It's me that's the problem. I'll just go slowly and quietly mad, alone.

September. With only five weeks to go until the birth, Sally had considered it time to start looking through the pile of books well-meaning people had delivered to her, most of which seemed to be full of advice that she should have taken months earlier. One insistent suggestion, though, was that it was important for the mother to talk constantly to the unborn child, to habituate it to the sound of her voice and massage it with the thrumming of positive energies. She had tried this, but the sound of her own voice had seemed to her ridiculous as it became lost in the corners of an empty flat, so she had developed her own variation: an internal one-sided dialogue with the baby which strove towards positive vibes but sounded mostly like a litany of complaint.

'Is that the last one?' said Jeff, her mother's husband, hoisting a crate of books on to the stairs.

'Where shall we put your computer?' Elizabeth said, too brightly.

Sally stood amid boxes in a room that smelled of carpet shampoo, flapping her arms uselessly. 'Just stick it down, I haven't figured out where to put anything yet.'

Jeff had rented a van to move her stuff to the new house in Crowbourne. Her mother, excited by the prospect of creating a new home for the baby, had spent most of the day recleaning the house, putting fresh sheets on the beds, flowers in the fireplace and on the kitchen table, while Sally had watched her stepfather huffing as he ferried the last vestiges of her life down the stairs of her old building. When the van was packed, they had stopped for a last cup of tea in the caff; the proprietor had embraced her with Mediterranean effusiveness, taken her face between his hands and made her promise to bring the baby back to visit just as soon as he was old enough to eat felafel.

From a doorway across the street, the fat tramp watched them checking the stability of the load. He had a new jacket; a kind of rugby-club blazer with brass buttons, which was too small for him. Sally took him a last sandwich.

'I'm moving to the country,' she said, as if he'd asked.

He nodded, sagely.

'And the world moves on,' he said.

'Yes. Well, good luck.'

'*The Tibetan Book of the Dead*,' – he stopped and took a mouthful of sandwich.

'Yes?'

'Says that souls choose the wombs they make their homes.'

'Is that right?'

'I'm sure you have been chosen by a very great soul, ma'am.'

'Thank you.'

He contemplated the remains of his sandwich.

'I'd shake your hand, but I don't know where I've been. God go with you.'

She had sat by the window in the van, watching the streets of London pass as if they were being snatched away from her for good. The feral traffic; the buses and taxis; the harried people shoving each other outside the Tube stations; the shops and bars; the noise, the collective anger and sex in the filthy air, that even the pigeons embodied; the sheer *life* of it all. She felt as if she were going to the gulag.

'It's not much of a garden,' Jeff was saying, as they passed Clapham Common, 'but I went round the other day and weeded your borders, and I think we can put some nice bulbs in there when the spring comes. And we could pop to the garden centre at some point and get you a table and some chairs so you can sit out when the weather's better – be nice for the little chap, eh?'

This is not my life, was all Sally could think. I didn't choose this. But there hadn't been a choice. She was on her own.

The kindness of people; it made her want to weep. Two weeks earlier, she had been disturbed by a delivery van; at the door of her building a man in a brown nylon uniform stood with a clipboard beside an impossibly large cardboard box.

'McGinley?'

'Yes. What's that?'

'No idea. You have to sign for it.'

Her first thought was that it had come from Greg; something for the baby, to show he was thinking of her. She had been obliged to produce a tip to get the man to carry it, with a great deal of swearing, up the stairs.

Inside, among the Styrofoam figure 8s she found a vast three-wheeled buggy, like a racing vehicle, cushioned as if for royalty, the kind she had looked at in magazines and known she would never be able to afford. She was overwhelmed, and reassured: a gesture like this surely proved that he was working on the situation. She continued to believe it was from Greg until the next day's post arrived, with a card which read:

My dear Miss McGinley –

I hope you will accept this small gift. You can keep it in the hall. There are those who call it the enemy of promise – I have every faith that you will not find it so.

With fond regards

Your friend

lars faldbakken@scx:

Disappointment knifed through her; she had sat down to write Lars a thank-you note with tears falling on to the page.

Crowbourne was less than an hour from London, but it struck her as several centuries removed. It was a moneyed town, its outskirts

295

decorated with the satin playing fields of expensive prep schools, its residential roads lined with SUVs and people carriers. The High Street was a jewel of Regency architecture and had been used in the filming of costume dramas, the ginger-brick façades offering rows of estate agents and antique shops, tea rooms and couture for the over-fifties.

'What am I going to *do* here?' she whispered as they drove through it, feeling herself already buried.

'You'll have a baby,' Jeff said, sensibly.

We could go back to London, you know, as soon as you're a bit more competent. Except that we can't; in London we'd live in a one-room flat and be equally depressed, and who would be there to tell me what to do with you? Not Lola, not Rhys – they have lives. I had a life. Now I've been prematurely ejected into middle-class suburbia. I'd always said I could never live in a place like this. But here we are. I'll put colourful stickers of farm animals around your room; if it glows, there's a chance you might not notice the silence. In the evenings, waiting for you, waiting for him; that's when I notice it. Just that: silence. The silence of all these other lives around us, contained between walls. The warmth of families, the arguments, the laughter, the private jokes and slamming of doors, all of it elsewhere. I have to fill that silence, for you. Fill it with songs and stories and games, I have to work on that, so that you don't realize the emptiness of – me. Your mother. So that you don't see the shape of what's missing. I'd put music on, but there is nothing that doesn't make the silence worse. It was never your fault; if you understand anything, let it be that. It's not that he doesn't love you, or me, it's just that – well, no, it is that. And you will break his heart one day. I hope you will.

Sally covered the baby's room with animal pictures and bright mobiles. Jeff spent an afternoon assembling a cot. Her mother washed all the tiny clothes that Lola had steadily been buying over the past weeks – all of them needlessly expensive, with the logos of New York designers emblazoned across the front – and the sight of these impossibly small bling-bling vests and shirts hanging on the drying rack shook her with emotion, predominantly fear. Whenever the phone rang she would trip over books and scattered debris in her haste to get to it, and always there would be the falling sensation, the shock of it not being him. It was not that she perversely refused to believe it was over, with Greg; simply that she *couldn't* believe it, she could not assimilate the information into any rational system of belief. He would be there when the baby was born, she was sure of it. She had nothing left to do but wait.

~·◆·~

'Right,' said Martin Parrish, from behind his desk, uncapping a Mont Blanc. 'Do you want to go over it again or is it all clear?'

'It's all clear,' said Caroline, leaning forwards, her hands clasped together over her knee, which was jigging with the impatience of the over-caffeined.

'Greg?'

Greg looked at Martin blankly. In front of him, on the desk, were arrayed a series of forms thick with fiscal hieroglyphs, swimming in front of his eyes. They required his signature, in black ink. Caroline and Martin were watching him, expectantly; it was his line, and he had dried. He felt as if he had swallowed a pint of black ink. What he was about to do was unforgivable by anyone's standards, even his own; unforgivable, but necessary, for the greater good. This must be how euthanasists feel, he thought, or the people who have to shoot the foot-and-mouth cows. Over the past few months he had had very little reason to find himself admirable, but *this* – this was second only to hiring a hit man, an option which Caroline, if she had believed there was even an outside chance of getting away with it, would surely have urged him to attempt.

'Effectively,' Martin was saying, in his sharp-edged accountancy voice saved exclusively for this office, 'you become a 49 per cent shareholder in yourself. With Caroline having 50 per cent, she nominally owns the company. For the purposes of any assessment, then, your income as a whole is no longer your own.'

Caroline flashed him a smile, all teeth.

Like everything else in my life, Greg thought. When she had explained to him about these conversations with Martin, he had understood: there would be no tolerance or compromise from her, not now, not in six months or six years, not until one of them was dead. He had thought that agreeing to make Sally and the baby take a DNA test would convince her of the extent of his loyalty, his willingness to inflict damage on the enemy; he now saw that this act of penance was not enough. More was being asked, and more would continue to be asked; he tried to look ahead and realized that, despite all his blithe assurances to Sally, he could not see an end to these demands for proof of their inseparability. It was another condition of his being allowed to continue to exist inside the structures of his life. But he had no more margin for error; the rest of his life would be cravenly lived stepping from plank to plank, not knowing which one might crumble beneath him. But look at the resolution on Caroline's face, the outline of her jaw; how hard she would have come after him with these shadowy figures in the garb of the law, these accountants and solicitors and social workers, if she had been the one he'd left. She'd have picked his carcass clean.

You can't *own* people, Sally had often said to him, and he'd liked the manifesto, at least; it would have given him room to manoeuvre with her. Now he was being asked to sign documents that would mean Caroline owned him, definitively and for good. Unless he one day bought out her shares in himself – he tried to picture this, a takeover bid for himself, and was left with the image of a boardroom farce. This was more binding than marriage. No wonder she wore such a look of quiet triumph. She had won twice over; against Sally, and against him. Most galling of all was that Martin Parrish was going to send him a bill for this whole performance.

'Won't they smell a rat?' he said, eventually. He wondered if Martin chose his own clothes.

'They can only operate on the basis of the information we provide. This is entirely legal, Greg, that's the whole point. That's why you pay me. We're not doing anything against the law, we're simply using the existing law to your advantage.'

'Sally will smell a rat.'

He saw Caroline wince at the intrusion of her name.

'You'll be covered by the Data Protection Act,' Martin said. 'And she may well try to appeal, but the onus will be on her to provide evidence that you earn more than we're going to say you do, and since what we're doing is a perfectly legitimate means for self-employed people to manage their money, there will be nothing she can do. As long as this company is up to date with its business tax, you're home and dry.'

Greg hesitated.

'She's pretty resourceful, you know. She'll get to the bottom of it.'

'Does she have the means to employ a tax lawyer?'

'I shouldn't think so.'

'Child Support Law moves at a snail's pace. Even if she could convince them that she had grounds for appeal, it would take years to come to a hearing. All that time you'll be saving money.'

'I still think it's –'

'Greg. We've already had this conversation.' Caroline's voice had taken on the timbre of warning, the vibrations of gathering force.

They had already had the conversation, many, many times; it swallowed its own tail. *If you want to give that slut your money, go and live with her. I don't want to live with her, but I have a legal – Every penny you give her and her bastard you're taking away from Daisy. She's not asking for much. How much is she asking? I don't know, she hasn't asked. She can get a job. She's got a job. Then she'll be fine. It's not for her, it's for the baby, she's not going to be spending it on cocktail dresses and yacht parties. HOW THE FUCK DO YOU KNOW?* And so on, and on.

Greg took the pen from Martin and, as he looked at the first form, had the sensation that he did not remember how to write his own name. Instead of his usual jagged signature, he printed each letter carefully, separately, as if only by taking them one at a time would he make it to the end without a mistake; each one depended on the prompting of the one before. He looked at the words Greg Burns and wondered how he might one day explain this to his son. If it could be delayed, until his son was a man, with a woman or women of his own, he might have a better hope of being understood.

'Congratulations, Greg Burns Limited!' Martin said, when all the forms were completed. But it was Caroline's hand that he shook.

'That's that, then,' she said.

Greg stood up, feeling more than ever that what he really wanted was to stand in a car park and be hosed down by a power spray, as if that might effectively cleanse his soul.

Later that afternoon, he phoned Patrick.

'Listen, there's some paperwork coming your way. I'm Limited now.'

'Is that right?'

He could hear the soft clacking of Patrick's keyboard.

'What are you doing?'

'I'm just sending an email.'

'Well, don't, I'm trying to talk to you.'

'Just let me . . . all right, it's gone. What were you saying?'

'I said, I'm Limited.'

'I wouldn't go that far, Greg. Anyway, you've built a career out of playing to your strengths, that's the main thing.'

Greg absorbed this for a moment.

'I mean, I'm a limited company. I'm now officially Greg Burns Limited, as of today. So you don't pay me any more, you pay my company.'

'I understand that.' Patrick's silence was fraught with disapproval. 'So you've set up a company.'

'That's right.'

'The better to what?'

'Manage my finances.'

'Would this have anything to do with the fact that you're about to get stung for child support?'

'It reduces your tax.'

'Is it going to get you out of child support?'

'Yes.'

'Isn't that fraud?'

'God, no. It's all legit.'

'*Legit*, is it, Del Boy. Sally will have you in court in a second.'

'She can't, apparently. The courts don't deal with child support.'

'Can't you just do the decent thing and settle it quietly, then you can get on with life.'

'I would if I made the rules. Caroline thinks Sally wants all my money to build a swimming pool in her grounds.'

'All right, look, it's not my business what you do with your money, spend it all on fast cars and hookers for all I care. I just write the cheques.'

'So now you write them to Greg Burns Limited.'

'You're a fool, Greg. This will explode in your face.'

'My face is immune to any more explosions.'

'If this gets out –'

'Gets *out*? Who's it going to get out to? Who would care? It's not as if I'm Minister for Child Welfare. I'm just the bloke who used to be in that vet thing.'

'You could be the bloke who's in the new Tony Czajkowski thing.'

'That's not very likely, under the circumstances.'

'If you want to strew your own path with landmines –'

'It's going to keep Caroline quiet. She's like a different person since we signed those forms.'

'You only ever think in the short term, Greg, that's your problem.'

Reading in bed that evening, as he waited for Caroline to finish her ministrations in the bathroom, he knew that he should have felt relieved. She seemed lighter, as if with the flourish of a Mont Blanc he had erased his own mistakes. Instead he felt sinister; this was the unspoken condition, the mutual pretence. This was not forgiveness, as he understood the concept, because how could forgiveness come into being without recognition of the act which demands it? Could you honestly say that you'd forgiven someone if the prerequisite was that you both pretended the transgression had never happened? From now on, he realized, his domestic happiness – no, not happiness, that was too remote a possibility at the moment – equilibrium was the word, status quo, depended on a whitewash. He had never been away. Sally did not exist. He did not have a son. These were the terms and conditions of his being.

Caroline came into the bedroom, smoothing moisturizer into her neck and wearing a nightdress he did not remember; it shimmered and clung. He put his book down and raised himself on one elbow, curious.

'I've been thinking, Greg.'

'Hm?'

'About all this. We can't just pretend it doesn't exist.'

'No. Right.'

'There are a couple of things that would put my mind at rest.'

Greg felt he had swallowed a cartoon anvil.

'What?'

'I think we should get married. Officially. I think that's been part of the problem. We've never made a public declaration of commitment.'

'We live together. How much more public could it – no, you're right. It's certainly – something to think about.'

Her expression was not one that invited negotiation.

'Good.'

She relaxed into a smile, and pulled back the duvet.

'What was the other thing?'

'What?'

'You said two things.'

'Oh, yes.' She leaned across and switched off the light. He felt her leg curl around his. 'I think we should try for another baby.'

~·~

Two weeks before the baby was due, Sally received a call from Greg informing her that he would be in London the following day, alone, for an appointment, and asking if she could meet him. He said, as if this would clinch it, that he had a present for the baby.

Elizabeth was doubtful.

'You can't be going to London at this stage. You can barely walk.'

'It's only an hour on the train. I'll get a taxi.'

'Why can't he come down here, if he wants to see you?'

'Because he won't.'

'Then he should be ashamed of himself. You're going to give birth any minute, and he still has you running around after him like a schoolgirl. What's the matter with you?'

'Mother.'

'What if you go into labour while you're in London? It could happen.'

'They have hospitals there.'

'You won't have any of your things. What about if it happens on the train?'

'It's not going to pop out in an hour, is it? We have phones.'

'I think you're an utter fool.'

'I know what you think, Mother. I want to see him.'

Greg had asked her to meet him at the Coach and Horses in Soho at two thirty. She was aware of the bizarre figure she cut, sitting alone at the tail end of the lunchtime rush, tented in a jumper of Jeff's, one of the few items that fitted her. She looked at her watch and tried to read the paper. Two men in their fifties, armed with pints of Guinness and with, evidently, no office awaiting, sat down at her table and attempted to engage her in conversation. She couldn't tell whether they were being avuncular or hitting on her. Now, she felt, there was no shape or form of male behaviour that could surprise her any more.

At three o'clock, she called Greg and was diverted to voicemail. She left a message, and tried again at five-minute intervals, fury flailing at her each time; not at Greg so much as at the limitations of a technology that promised round-the-clock communication and was failing so egregiously in its only task. At three twenty-five, he rounded the bar with a hazy grin.

'Oops. Hello. I had to have lunch with the BBC from the bloke – with this bloke from the CC – a bloke. From the BBC.'

'You're pissed, then.'

'Not in the strictest sense.'

'You're an hour late, and you couldn't call me?'

'Calm down, woman.'

'I've left you messages, could you not even have called me back once? I've been sitting here for a fucking hour.'

'Which number did you call?'

'The new one. The one you gave me in Edinburgh.'

'Ah, well, that's not the new one any more.'

'There's a *new* new one?'

'She found out in Edinburgh I'd given you the number I wasn't supposed to give you, so she made me get a new one. I know, don't look at me like that, *you* think it's confusing? It's, like, my fifth phone in the last six months, I've got no idea what my own number is any more and neither has anyone else. No wonder I've been getting no work.'

'So none of the numbers I have for you are any good?'

'I don't think so.'

'Did the last one go in the dishwasher too?'

'It went in the sea.'

'What am I going to do when I go into labour, Greg, how am I supposed to get in touch with you?'

'I thought you could phone Patrick.'

'*Patrick*? What if it's four in the morning?'

'Well –' Greg tilted his head and appeared to give this some thought for the first time. 'Probably don't phone him at four in the morning, obviously, he'll be asleep. Wait until it's a reasonable hour.'

'I'm having a baby! They just come when they come, and I want you to know when it's happening, because I want –'

'What?'

'I want you to be there.'

'I'll be there.'

'Do you mean that, Greg? You have to be there, I don't know how I'll get through if you're not.'

'If I can be, I will.'

'Well, that means nothing, that means you won't. If you're going to be there, you have to promise, and you have to do it, I need to know one way or the other, I don't want to be watching the door not knowing.'

'OK, I'll be there. I promise. You can call Patrick any time of day, I'll tell him.'

'I don't want to call Patrick. Why don't you just give me your number?'

'I really can't, Sally. She'll kill me. And I can't afford any more phones.'

'But, what, she'll be fine about you taking off in the middle of the night to come and watch me give birth?'

'I'll have to cross that bridge when we come to it.'

'We're going to be coming to it any day now, why can't you occasionally think about how you're going to deal with something and just do it, instead of waiting for someone else to deal with it for you?'

He slumped across the table and stretched his arms out to her.

'I'm not a bad person, Sally. Give me a break.'

She looked at him, and it occurred to her that lately he was looking his age. He had turned forty-five since she had last seen him, and the lines around his eyes and mouth appeared fixed. Next year, when their child was one, Greg would be nearer to fifty than forty, and she could already see in his face the outline of how he would look as an old man, more prominently than she could see the shadow of his younger self. Perhaps that had always been the case, and she had discounted it, part of her more general self-deception.

'No,' she said. 'You're a weak person. You want an easy life. You'd be the first one jumping up shouting "*He* is Spartacus!" if you thought it would save your own arse.'

'I wish I knew where we'd all be in ten years' time.'

'Yes, I used to think that. How much easier it would be if we had a map, because it would stop you having to make choices that you might get wrong. But that's horseshit, in the end.'

From behind the bar came the noises of a pub in its slump time; the churning of a dishwasher, the clink of glasses in plastic cages and indeterminate noises off. The lunchtime staff were unwrapping their aprons and laying them on the counter, preparing to leave.

'Where is it, then?'

Greg snapped his head up from a private thought.

'Where's what?'

'The present. For the baby.'

He looked at her, nonplussed, then his face ruffled with recollection.

'Oh. It's – I left it in the – thing.'

'The thing?'

'The BBC.'

'What was it?'

'What *was* it? You're asking me what it was.' He appeared to concentrate. 'It was a – dog.'

'A *dog*?'

'A furry dog.'

'Well, damn, I can't believe you forgot it. However will we manage without a furry dog?'

'Sorry. I can post it.'

'You can shove it up your arse if you want, Greg, because it doesn't exist, does it, and even if it did, why don't you buy the baby something useful? Something I actually need, since I've had to get everything myself.'

'Babies don't need that much stuff. OK,' – he caught sight of her expression – 'maybe they do, but people will always lend it you. You've got friends with kids, haven't you?'

'No, I haven't.'

'Well, didn't your mum keep stuff?'

'Did my mum keep baby stuff from thirty years ago? You know what – no, she didn't.'

'Oh. I'm sure your friends will buy you presents.'

'What about you, Greg? You're his father, what are you going to do about providing for him?'

'Ah. I didn't really want to go into that before you have him, you know, but apparently the best way to do it is for you to go through the Child Support Agency.'

'*What*? How can that be better than us just sorting something out? That's just crazy.'

'It's fairer, apparently.'

'Oh, OK. Because you wouldn't want to be giving your son a penny more than you absolutely had to in law, is that it? So months of bureaucracy, that's all worth it to make sure you get away with the minimum.'

'You can be a right sarky bitch sometimes, you know, Sally. It's not a very attractive trait.'

Sally gave a small shake of her head and lumbered to her feet.

'Goodbye, Greg.'

'Wait. Sorry. I'm sorry. I'm an arsehole. Let me take you out to dinner.'

'It's twenty to four.'

'Oh. Well, let me take you out for afternoon tea.'

'I should be getting home. I'm tired.'

'I'll take you to the station, then. We'll get a taxi.'

'So, I've been thinking that maybe I should get a solicitor,' she said, as they stood on the street, surveying the traffic, Greg keeping one arm firmly around her waist, such as it was.

'That's up to you. But I think the child-support people do all the stuff for you. It might be a waste of money.'

'I don't want to go through the Child Support Agency. Please, Greg, just do this one thing for me. It's so – demeaning.'

'It keeps it simple.'

'Who told you that?'

'My accountant.'

He stopped; Sally stared up at him.

'You've been consulting your accountant, and suddenly you want to introduce the Social Services, as if we're not capable of reaching a rational agreement. Why does that strike me as underhand?'

'Look, the CSA does all the maths for you, there's a set thing depending on your mortgage and your tax bracket and all that. And they organize the DNA thing, it's much easier.'

'Easier than just sorting it out like two reasonable adults?'

'If it were just you and me –' Greg held his hands out. 'Well, if it were just you and me everything would be different. But you've got to see it from Caroline's point of view. As far as she's concerned you've got a job, you earn your own money.'

'Not while I'm having a baby. Anyway, it's about the principle.'

Sally spotted a taxi with its light on and stepped off the kerb with her hand raised. There was no way to climb into a taxi with grace at nine months of pregnancy, she decided; still, she was mortified that Greg had to see her scrambling in on her hands and knees.

'Waterloo,' she said. 'Look, you don't need to come with me.'

'But I want to.'

He put his arm around her on the back of the seat and pulled her head down to his shoulder, so that she was sitting at an unbearably awkward angle. It struck her as a parody of how they were supposed to look.

'Caroline wants us to have a baby,' he said, absently rubbing her stomach.

'We are having a baby.'

'No. Me and her. She thinks – I don't know what she thinks. Anyway, she's decided she wants one.'

Sally sat upright. She thought at first that this was another of his ill-judged attempts at a joke, but realized, almost in the same moment, that of course it was not. It was a simple question of numerical supremacy. With one child each, they could make an equal claim on Greg's limited emotional resources. At two–one up, Caroline would be a clear winner. And this would be her insurance; it made perfect sense. Caroline, who indisputably had a firmer grip on reality than Greg, would be aware that this *coup de foudre*, when it had passed, would not have changed anything fundamental in their relationship, and in a couple of years' time, when his remorse had faded, there would almost certainly come another play, another girl who saw in him what Sally had seen at the beginning.

'She thinks, presumably, that you might not notice you've lost one if she can replace it.'

'Jesus, Sally. Don't talk like that. I haven't *lost* him. I'll be a good dad to him, it just needs time.'

'There isn't any time. He's nearly a person. And if you miss his birth, then what? You miss his first birthday, while you're still wait-ing for Caroline to calm down. And then you miss his second, and suddenly you find you can't just scrabble back all the time you lose. It doesn't come back. That's what my dad thought – that you could just skip a few years and no one would notice. Well, they do notice.'

'Not when they're one.'

'You're missing the point.'

'Front or back entrance, love?' said the driver, sliding the screen over his shoulder. Sally saw Greg poised to make a joke involving front or back entrances, then rein himself in. The clouds over Waterloo Bridge sagged with the weight of pent-up weather. Over the first floor of the National Theatre, a red LED display heralded in rapidly expanding and shrinking script a new play by Michael Frayn.

'My name will be up there one day,' she said, pointing. There had been a time when she had really thought this could be true.

'Course it will. I'm very proud of you, you know. And I can't regret this. Any of it.' He paused. 'Well, some of it, obviously. But you can't regret a life.'

Sally smiled.

'He might grow up to find a cure for cancer. He might be the Shakespeare of his generation. On the other hand,' she said, as they pulled up to the taxi rank, 'he might grow up to instigate the worst genocide in the history of the Western world. We can't know. His future is infinite possibilities.'

'The point is, he has a future. It's an awesome thing. And I'll be there, I promise, cheering him on. Not with the genocide, obviously, I'll give him a good hiding if he tries that. But anything else.'

Sally looked at him through the open window of the taxi, and knew then that he was not lying. Not consciously lying, in the sense of purposefully misleading her. At that moment, she thought, he believed himself. She knew, too, that he would not be there when the baby was born, nor afterwards. This meeting had a sense of finality.

She leaned forward and kissed him on the cheek. He touched her face.

'So you'll call Patrick when it happens?'

'I'll call Patrick. Maybe he can do 15 per cent of your stint in the delivery room.'

'It'll be easy. You're a strong girl. One cough and you'll be done.'

She took in his lopsided grin, and remembered the first time she had seen it, the photograph in the Avocet office, only a year earlier. The imperative of biology, she thought; the unpredictability, the force of our survival. That this relationship, which had endured less than a year, had given way to a relationship into which she was bound for the rest of her life. You could never stop being a mother. Anything else, you could choose to remove yourself from, just take off the badge. You could decide, if you wanted, to stop being a lover, a wife, a husband, a friend, just like that, and Sally realized how much of her life she had spent making sure she could easily get out of any relationship she might find herself in. But you were someone's parent, someone's child, for life, and beyond. These ties: they simply *were*. She was the only mother this child would ever have, and Greg was his only father; they would run through him like watermarks.

Greg leaned out of the window and sang, 'We'll meet again,' as the taxi pulled away. She turned away to the trains with a covert smile and took out her phone to text him a suitably withering retort. Then she realized that she didn't have his number. He had put himself beyond her reach.

Jeff knew everybody in Crowbourne, and so, naturally, he was in a position to recommend a reliable family firm of solicitors, who charged Sally two hundred pounds to explain to her what they were going to write in a letter, and a further twenty-five actually to write it; in spite of that, Sally noticed, they had twice used 'it's' wrongly. The letter, polite to the point of ingratiating, kindly invited Mr Greg Burns to participate in discussions about his financial contribution to the upkeep of his pending son, subject to a reasonable estimate of his former partner's outgoings.

'I could have written this myself,' Sally said, when she had shown it to her mother. 'Look, that's exactly what I've been saying to him all along, except that I get my apostrophes in the right place. That basically says stop arsing about and pay your dues, how did that require m'learned friends' years of expertise? So it's essentially two hundred and twenty-five quid –'

'Plus VAT,' said Jeff, from behind his *Telegraph*.

'– plus VAT, for a sheet of their headed notepaper. I could just photocopy it for next time.'

'They're awfully thorough,' Jeff said.

'Not that thorough if they don't know "it's" from "its". I might just send them two pounds twenty-five and claim I got my punctuation in the wrong place.'

Elizabeth said nothing. She was excessively careful with money, and Sally knew that she was converting the money wasted on solicitors because Sally was stupid enough to take up with someone so devoid of principle that he would father a child with someone who was not his wife and thereafter refuse even to discuss his obligations towards it into things that the same money might have bought for the baby. Sally was only just beginning to understand the ferocity of a mother's protective instinct, but already she understood why, if Greg had walked into the room at that moment, Elizabeth, the mildest of women, would have rushed to castrate him with the nearest kitchen implement.

Five days later, her new solicitors received a reply from a firm of solicitors with a King's Lynn address, informing them equally cordially that Mr Greg Burns was by no means certain that he was the father of their client's forthcoming child and that, while he was by no means attempting to shirk his financial responsibilities should the aforementioned child prove to be his, he was also by no means prepared to make any arrangements until such time as this could be conclusively and irrefutably proved.

There it was, on a page, in Times New Roman font. Third parties, men – and women, she supposed – in suits and, she imagined, judicial robes, both in King's Lynn and in Crowbourne, now thought on some level that she was the kind of person who wasn't quite sure who had fathered her child, and there was no way for her to vindicate herself without submitting to the deliberate insult of the test. Such was the injustice of biology. Sally did not show the letter to her mother; instead she sat on the floor of her new bedroom, still a wasteground of books and boxes, and cried for the rest of the day. Literally. She moved only once, to use the toilet. The rest of the time, she simply sat and wept. She had not known this was possible, and in the midst of it was aware that the weeping was entirely disproportionate to the contents of the letter, disproportionate, even, to the absolute nature of Greg's betrayal both of her, and of the baby; this unburdening was something elemental, as if she had been charged with articulating the sorrows of all hurting people, all the lonely, all the deceived, all the abandoned. She cried for herself, for her baby, for her father, her mother, the grandparents she had lost, for a university friend who had died in a car crash ten years earlier and whom she had barely thought of in recent years. It was primitive; her body's need to evacuate every possible residual emotion, as if to clear a space for – what? Perhaps for the new emotions that would be arriving, too copious to fit in the available space. All day, she sat on the floor holding the letter, without eating, until it grew dark, when she lay down on her bed feeling void, as if her soul had been shredded. Had it not been for the climbing thing inside her, she might have come to question her own capacity to endure this level of grief for much longer.

The following morning, she woke up with a sensation in her bowels akin to food poisoning, and noticed that her waters had broken. So this is it, she thought, in a state of acceptance that she had not imagined herself to possess. The raging had passed, and something as yet unnamed was taking its place.

END OF ACT II

ACT III

Thirteen months later. Surrey, London, King's Lynn and an unnamed town in the South-East.

19

Sally had come to understand that all along she had secretly viewed her pregnancy as a penance, a term that had to be served but which, in spite of its severity, was never the less finite. She realized that some part of her had truly believed that the great *They*, whoever was in charge, would arrive at the end of it to discharge her, to send her back to liberty. All right, *They* would say, we can see that you've learned your lesson. Now go back to your life and don't do it again.

A year later, she was aware that she was still waiting. In the world outside her house, four seasons had passed more or less according to expectation. The weather had changed, and changed back. After the first few months, the shocking mutation of days and nights into unrecognizable wastelands of unmarked hours had begun to recede; instead, as days regained something of their traditional shape, they became individual marathons. At the end of each one, there would be a momentary respite, when the baby finally went to sleep and Sally briefly congratulated herself on the achievement of having successfully kept him alive for another twenty-four hours, without dropping, scalding, freezing, starving, poisoning or inadvertently leaving him in the supermarket – Sally, who had never been able to nurture a pot plant successfully for more than a fortnight – before the realization dawned that she would have to get up the next morning, and very likely several times before that, and begin the whole thing again from scratch. Friends and relatives she hadn't seen in years would call to ask how she was enjoying motherhood and she would frown at the phone as if she didn't understand the question. These were words that, as far as she was concerned, had no place in the same sentence; it was like asking someone how they were enjoying the root canal surgery. The other mothers she encountered briefly at baby clinics gave the impression of enjoying motherhood, but what if they were all acting, Sally thought? What if it were like living under a dictatorship, with everyone afraid to say what they really thought, and saying instead what they thought they ought to be heard to say, because you never knew who was listening? Or – and this would be worse – what if it were not a conspiracy at all, and everybody else meant it, and there was something grievously wrong with her alone?

Her mother had assiduously documented the passing of weeks and months in photographs; these, gathered in an album, made up an edited version of her son's first year. Sally flipped through the pages with a face of puzzled estrangement, often finding that she had no recollection of her own of the occasion on which the picture had been taken. She would nod, mutely and politely, as details were pointed out to prompt her memory, feeling as if she had recently woken from a coma and was being shown the political and technological developments of all her lost years.

Her own memories tended to be of the significant landmarks in her journey back to herself. She remembered clearly the day when, after five months, she stopped breastfeeding, thus removing the baby's final claim on her physical being; the relief at being once again in sole possession of her body, however ravaged and unfamiliar it appeared to her, had been so great that she had cried (and had cried more from the guilt of such relief). She remembered when she first left him with her mother for a whole day and took the train to London for a meeting: the sudden awareness of her own fragility in a crowd, of how easily the train could spin off the rails, and all the other crouching mortal dangers of the city – the Tube, the traffic, the madmen on the streets, the terrorists in the public spaces – revealed to her that she truly existed now in relation to someone else, someone for whom her death would be an irredeemable tragedy. She had so much wanted to enjoy the freedom of a day in London without the baby's rigorous timetable of need, but she was constricted by the terrible stomach-dropping fear that she had lost something important, or perhaps missed a vital appointment; every few minutes she would rifle, panicked, through her bag to make sure she had not put down her wallet, phone or keys somewhere. It had been disconcerting, and almost hurtful, to arrive home in this state of fevered paranoia and find that the baby, for whom time had yet to solidify, did not appear even to have registered her absence.

Sometimes, as she went to soothe him in the night, saying, 'Mummy's here', she would find herself simultaneously looking around in desperate hope for the Mummy who was supposed to be there, making everything all right, and realize with a kind of dizziness that there wasn't one; at least not, in her perception, a proper, competent one, deserving of the name. Her situation had left her with all the responsibilities and constraints of family life, with none of the benefits of companionship or support, and in the evenings, when the baby was asleep upstairs and she found herself, flattened, with a few hours in which she might attempt to write, or at least read something, she experienced the silence as a physical symptom. It closed around her in her small sitting room. She was giving out all day, she felt – love, comfort, time, attention pouring out of her – and when the night came, there was no one there to put any of it back for her, no one to pick her up when she cried, and she had to attempt to fill her own dangerously low reserves of strength from some self-generated source. She read a lot more poetry now than she used to, but it was a limited substitute for someone to hold her.

Slowly, though, a functioning version of life began to cohere. When the baby was six months old, Sally placed him in a day nursery and started a job, of sorts. A recent restructuring of company finances based on the fortuitous involvement of a big investor had put Avocet Productions in the position of being able to afford a part-time administrative assistant; they had decided that, rather than advertise, they would offer the position to Sally. It was undeniably an act of charity; none of them bothered with the pretence that it could be anything other ('It'll get her out of the house,' she pictured Lola saying, to Rhys's intractable frown), since Sally's administrative skills were remarkable only for their absence. Nevertheless, they had invited her to make a vaguely competent show of answering telephones and reading scripts from the slushpile for three days a week, in return for a sum of money that matched almost exactly the cost of the childcare and her travel to London. Her mother considered this to be a senseless waste of both time and money, but, although she never made it explicit, Sally suspected that there was a deeper criticism at work beyond the merely budgetary, that had to do with Sally's apparent need to spend as much time as possible away from her child.

This was not something that Sally felt able to explain adequately to Elizabeth, and she concluded that the difference must be both generational and temperamental. There was no question that she loved her son; it was simply that she was at a loss as to how, for her, this love ought to show itself. Elizabeth would have told her unequivocally that a mother's love was about sublimation of the self, about surrendering to the many thankless hours of trailing in the child's wake, cleaning, feeding, picking up the jetsam it left behind; this unnoticed domestic round was the substance of a mother's devotion and (though Elizabeth would never say this outright) those mothers who didn't want to dirty their hands with the shop-floor work of caring were guilty of treating their children as mere accessories. Sally knew that she carried within her the potential to be one of these women, if only she had the resources. In Sally's adult experience, the notion of love contained within it, was synonymous with, the desire to be constantly in the presence of the loved one, and to yearn and hanker for them while separated, and she began to feel that Elizabeth must be right – what weight did her avowals carry, if she confidently claimed that she loved her son but did everything in her power not to have to spend a day actually caring for him? Was her motherly love purely abstract, then, a concept, meaningless both to her and her child? Was real mother love all about accepting the invisibility of the unexotic? Sally began to suspect, unhappily, that she was the last person in the world who should ever have been allowed to have a child.

> Be tender to your mother
> And treat her with great care
> For you'll only know her value
> When you see her empty chair.

Her maternal grandmother had often intoned this verse with a portentous sense of occasion, presumably for her father's benefit, but to Sally, as a child, the jouncing of its greetings-card rhythm was eclipsed by the naked horror of the final two words. She remembered the first time she had understood the impact of the poem's symbolism: the momentary time-lag before the chill of what the empty chair was supposed to mean had crept over her. She had understood properly one day that the emptiness referred to a permanent state, that it signified the non-being of her mother, and the knowledge that this emptiness was a future certainty had made her gulp and shiver. She must have been six or seven, and if she repeated the words softly to herself now, at the age of thirty, they had the same effect. A mother's presence was everything, the poem seemed to say, like air; noticed only in its absence. To her knowledge, there existed no such ditties on the nature of a father's love, but you rarely heard fathers criticized for choosing to spend their days on trains and in offices rather than wiping the noses of their small children. It occurred to Sally that she might have been better equipped to be a father than a mother, at least as far as traditional perceptions were concerned. Fathers, at least, seemed permitted time off now and again without being considered wanton or unnatural. Neither did any of this explain the moment when, in her second week of working in London, she had gone out at lunchtime for a sandwich and seen a woman pushing a baby of around the same age as her son, and exploded in a tearful chaos of pure instinct. It was the baby's hands that had done it; she had looked down at the baby, intending to smile indulgently, and seen its little fat hands, grasping expressively at the air, dimpled fingers curling around nothing, and the sight of them had caused a ricochet of fear in her throat at the thought of the sheer physical distance between her and her own child; she had jumped in the nearest taxi to Waterloo, found the next train to Crowbourne in a blur of panic and run all the way from the station to the nursery, only to find the baby asleep and oblivious. Even in Sally, it seemed, the need for separation had an equal and opposite counterforce, and she could not understand or control either.

Gradually, though, something changed. Around the ninth or tenth month of her son's life, a person began to emerge; a person who, to Sally's astonishment, had tastes and preferences, in food, music and toys, tastes that he was able, with surprising efficiency, to communicate. She found herself developing private jokes with him, games and responses which he clearly remembered and desired to repeat, and which produced bright and intoxicating cascades of laughter. There were days – coloured by the warmth of an English summer, soft days, of grass and the thrum of insects – when she would sit with the baby beside the local National Trust lake, watching him burbling at the ducks, and experience – not happiness, exactly, but intimations of pleasure, of the ability to feel something other than numbness seeping in. She had been fighting so hard to keep her own emotions battened down, far below the surface, but on these summer days she came to realize that she still had the capacity to smile spontaneously, now and again. As the baby approached his own significant landmark, the anniversary of his birth, she understood that they had achieved the beginnings of a relationship.

'I said, this might be the time for you to swallow your pride and ask your father for some advice.' Elizabeth was washing up at the sink in Sally's kitchen, but her shoulders were braced with a contained anger.

'I heard you,' said Sally, cross-legged on the floor of her sitting room, piecing together a jigsaw whose fat components revealed a fragmented orange digger.

'Dut,' said Manny, holding aloft a furry item.

Sally looked up.

'It's not a duck, it's a penguin.'

'Dut.'

Elizabeth came to stand in the doorway, a tea towel in one hand. 'Because he would know the ins and outs of this kind of thing, you know.'

'I know. But I'm not asking him to fight my battles.'

'He'd welcome any chance to help you out, especially since it's for Manny. And he is trained in family law.'

'Yes, but he's not a solicitor any more, is he, he's a beard-wearing pub musician. Will he cut much of a dash in court, I ask you?'

'At least he could point you in the right direction. Because, Sally, how else are you going to even begin to contest this' – Elizabeth fought to avoid an obscenity – 'this – *business*?'

Manny took three steps forward and toppled back on to his heavily wadded bottom.

'Uh oh,' he said, with resignation.

Manus Anthony Burns McGinley, convincingly and irrefutably the son of Greg Burns and Sally McGinley as demonstrated by a certificate from a government-approved diagnostic clinic, was, at thirteen months, a sturdy little boy, long-limbed and full-cheeked with (Sally privately thought) an exceptional grasp of language. He had working versions of the words Jeff, Grandma, that, there, duck and drink, and made passable attempts at more advanced concepts, such as moo and toast. He had no name, as yet, for Sally; 'mama', according to the manuals one of the elemental building blocks of the child's speech, had never passed his lips. Elizabeth reassured Sally that this was because Manny considered her to be merely an extension of himself, which gripped Sally with the urge to sit the child down and give him a good talking to. It reminded her of the moment in the delivery room when the midwife, in tones of jovial encouragement, had fluted, 'Look how nicely you're dilating! Ooh, you were just made to have babies, you were!', which had horrified Sally on several levels: not only could she plainly not look at her own cervix, nor would she have wanted to, but she felt this was perhaps the most inappropriate use she had ever heard of the word 'nicely'; most of all, she saw her destiny and *raison d'être* brutally reduced to the functions of certain of her internal organs, as if she had been congratulated on having a working spleen. She tried to persuade Manny to say 'mama', just to be sure that he did accord her some identity of her own, but he merely found this amusing. Now and again, he was heard to refer to her as 'that'.

Manus was for her paternal grandfather, Anthony a nod to Tony Czajkowski, both a not especially subtle slight to her own father, who was offered nothing but the continuation of his own surname. Burns was included on the birth certificate, as a gesture, but since it remained unreciprocated by any gesture on Greg's part, such as putting his own name against the line that said 'father', Sally had never written it again in the context of her son.

That morning, a thin grey day in November, Sally had received a letter in a brown envelope from the Department of Work and Pensions that had pitched her into monosyllabic shock. Her mother, arriving to take Manny to the park, had found her pacing the kitchen, waving the implausible paper in one hand while periodically banging it with the back of the other.

'Not that I know anything about accounting, but it must be fraud,' Elizabeth continued.

'Of course it's fraud. But they're adamant that it's all squeaky clean.'

Now that her mother was here to be angry on her behalf, Sally had subsided into a quiet bitterness.

'Well, they must be stupid.'

'Yep. That's a prerequisite of working there.'

'I mean, to accept that he's earning eighty pounds a week, it's ludicrous. No one earns that. People on the dole earn more than that.'

'And people on the dole have to pay child support. All the paperwork came through his accountant though. If I want them to investigate I have to prove that he's done some creative maths.'

'I don't understand why you have to prove it. Can't they look into it? A child could see it's not right. I've a good mind to call them.'

'Be my guest. Set aside a good three days just to get through to someone who was educated beyond the age of eight, and another week for them to find the wooden abacus they use for doing sums.'

After thirteen months of waiting for the Child Support Agency – which Sally had come to visualize as one fat bloke sitting in a small-ish shed surrounded by a thousand different-shaped phones, all ring-ing at once – to process an endless stream of forms which apparently had to be filled out in triplicate and countersigned by area managers in Tibet, she had been informed that morning, in writing, that Mr Greg Burns was exempt from paying child maintenance because his earnings came in below the minimum wage. Sally was uncompre-hending; dimly, through the mists of incomprehension, the knowl-edge that Greg had clearly gone to some lengths to hide his income was slowly assailing her as another, even greater, betrayal than those he had already inflicted.

She had not seen or heard from Greg since their meeting in London, two weeks before Manny was born. The Crowbourne recy-cling depot must, she imagined, be jammed with the sheer bulk of paper generated by her abandoned attempts at letters to him, but finally (it had taken several months) she had absorbed the informa-tion that he was not intending to get in touch. She had believed, against all evidence, that the result of the DNA test might occasion some kind of reconciliation – he could no longer pretend there was any room for doubt – but still he maintained his absolute silence. If he never saw the child, he could continue to pretend to himself, and to Caroline, that Manny was not real; this, she suspected, was his logic. It was part of Greg's perennial adolescence, and there was nothing she could do about it short of turning up on his doorstep with Manny in her arms, an option she had considered in her madder moments, but she did not possess the necessary will to self-abasement. This let-ter, though, signalled something far more sinister than an unreflect-ing urge to run away from responsibility, the result of a moment of cowardice and panic. It implied a coldness and a calculation that she had not imagined Greg to possess.

'And you've told them what he does for a living?'

'Yes, I told them. They said they couldn't confirm or deny if that was what he'd put down because of the Data Protection Act.'

'You told them he has another house and a child and two cars and goes on holidays?'

'Yes, Mother.'

'And they still believe he can manage all that on eighty pounds a week?'

'They said they can't discuss his lifestyle because of the Data Protection Act. I have to submit an application to appeal if I think his lifestyle is inconsistent.'

'What about his agent? He must have a record of all the work Greg's done in the past year, presumably they could requisition his accounts –'

'I don't think they do things like requisitioning,' Sally said. 'I don't think most of them could pronounce it. Anyway, they said they were satisfied with the information they had from the accountant and that for as long as that was the case, there was no reason for them to look into it any further. They said,' – she adopted the voice of a village idiot – '"You must appreciate, Miss McGinley, that most of our clients feel the payment calculated for them is insufficient. But we have rules."'

'Insufficient? I'd say no money at all is not insufficient, it's a bloody liberty.'

Sally looked up; she had not heard her mother swear since Mac had returned from his three-year jaunt.

'The bottom line, as far as I could understand from the Wurzels on the phone, is that I have to present them with incontrovertible proof that he earns more than he says he does before they'll even reopen it. As far as they're concerned, my case is rubber-stamped and in the out tray.'

'Well, we can and we will fight this.' Elizabeth knotted the tea towel around her fist. 'It can't be that hard, can it? He's an actor. When he works, people see him do it, it's not as if he's a handyman getting cash in hand. But Mac is the person to talk to, Sally, and he'd do it all for nothing.'

'I'd rather keep it professional.'

'How on earth are you going to afford a solicitor? You can barely afford your rent.'

'Dat!' Manny exclaimed in delight, pointing to the television, which was playing a music DVD.

'He really shouldn't be watching television all day,' Elizabeth said, with a hint of provocation.

'He doesn't watch it *all* day.' Sally disliked how defensive she always sounded when her mother made observations about Manny's upbringing. 'It's only on now so he doesn't put himself in the washing-machine while we're talking.'

'If you say so.' Elizabeth paused, watching her grandson. 'What work has Greg done this year? You need to start with that.'

Sally shrugged.

'There was the garden furniture ad, otherwise, I don't know. I haven't exactly sought out news of him, as you can imagine.'

'There must be some way of finding out. Would he have a website?'

'Patrick's got a website.'

'Patrick?'

'The agent.'

'That'll have a record, will it?'

Sally stood up, suddenly animated.

'You're right. I should have thought – it will have some kind of CV for all his clients.'

'Well, then. You know all about actors, you can extrapolate how much he will have earned when you see what he's done.'

Sally shook her head.

'Yes, but – there's got to be something bigger going on. He must have had to tell them about the work he's done, so if they're still taking it at face value – where's the money gone?'

'That's what you need to find out. Maybe he's transferring the money to someone else, the way people do in bankruptcy cases. You put your assets into someone else's name and they no longer count as yours.'

'Caroline, you mean?'

'I don't suppose they're allowed to look at her bank account, are they? So that's possible.'

'He let it slip that he'd talked to his accountant, you know. Before Manny was born. So he's obviously taken advice on how to do this legitimately. How low is that?'

'Well, I've never had very high expectations of his morals, Sally, I'm sorry. But look, the person who knows all about this is Mac. He'd be able to help you investigate. Let me give him a call. Whatever else you might think of him, he was a good lawyer.'

'Mum, it's been seventeen years. I can't get involved with Mac in the middle of all this, especially not to ask him a favour. There's too much past to get over.'

'He might be glad of the chance to do you a favour. He is your father, when all's said and done.'

'That didn't mean much to him.'

'And Manny's grandfather, if you prefer.'

'I suppose. If he could just point me in the right direction, that might be OK.'

'Good. Otherwise you'll have to get yourself a solicitor, and I haven't the money to lend you, I wish I had. I could ask Jeff, but –'

'I wouldn't take Jeff's money.'

'I know you wouldn't. But you might have to put your pride aside while you fight this out. Greg Burns needs to understand his responsibilities. I mean, he's not fifteen, he's quite old enough to know you don't just have a child and run away.'

'His problem is that he just gives in to her.'

'Don't continue to be such a fool, Sally.' Elizabeth had long since come to the conclusion that bluntness over Greg's true nature was the only approach with her daughter, who seemed, in spite of everything, to nurture a tiny hope that some day he would reappear with a clutch of plausible justifications. 'People like him always do what they want to do. If he really wanted anything to do with you or Manny he'd have made the effort long before this, and you wouldn't have that letter. He's not interested, he's not coming back, and the sooner you get that into your head, the better you'll be able to get on with your own life.'

Sally didn't reply. She had been as shaken by Greg's treachery over his finances as if he had raised a fist to her or the baby, but from the initial shock had grown a determination to face him down over this matter, born not of care for her own or her son's welfare, but of the mental picture that quickly asserted itself, of Greg and Caroline congratulating themselves at having the upper hand. She imagined them toasting their own cunning over dinner and, in this image, it was the smile of victory on Caroline's lips that she knew would torment her until she had fought this to its conclusion. Beneath the sense of injustice, however, she acknowledged another motive: the promise of renewed contact with Greg. Even in the context of hostilities, she thought – and the letter had been tantamount to a gauntlet thrown at her feet – she would remind him that she existed. War, after all, was a kind of communication. For most of her adult life, Sally had seen herself as the kind of person who makes an impact on those with whom she came into contact, particularly in her relationships with men. She had been told by others that she possessed a certain kind of force, and the implication that she – and, by extension, her child – could be so easily forgotten had been the biggest insult among all those that Greg had dealt her. She would rather fight him for ten years, she felt, than continue to be ignored. There was no legal process that could make him care about her or their son, but she could make him acknowledge them financially, if nothing else. He would learn that she could not be revised out of his history, even if it meant facing her own father again.

20

Cormac and Elizabeth McGinley had been an extravagantly hand-
some couple when they married, but if they had still been together,
Sally thought, her mother would have suffered from the inevitable
discrepancy of ageing between the sexes. Elizabeth wore her years
with grace but accurately, whereas Mac, at fifty-seven, could easily
have passed himself off as ten years younger, were it not for the
unforgivable beard which he insisted on, as a kind of hairy badge of
Celtic authenticity. It was not inconceivable, she thought, as they
walked side by side along Crowbourne High Street on a hard, frost-
edged November afternoon, Mac pushing Manny in the buggy, that
people would imagine them to be the child's parents.

After Manny was born, her father had written to her, not
wheedling but calmly asking if she could find it in herself to overlook
his past failings and give him the chance to make amends, at least as
far as his grandson was concerned. Finally she had relented, largely
thanks to Elizabeth's petitions on Mac's behalf, her quite reasonable
argument that, since Greg had chosen to deprive the boy both of a
father and a grandfather, it seemed excessively mean and perverse of
Sally to sever him from his other grandfather simply because she was
determined not to forgive Mac for an offence seventeen years old.
She had acknowledged the logic of this, and realized too that, if she
looked closely, she could no longer find good reason to hold Mac at
arm's length with such active rancour; it was as if she had long forgotten the cause of her grudge against him but had continued to act
out the symptoms of it because she had not known how to do otherwise. She was tired; there were already too many reasons to hate and
resent and she no longer had the energy to direct it towards her father
for something so long ago. Not forgiving Mac had fallen off her list of
priorities. She had written back to him, inviting him to see the baby,
although when the day had arrived, she had found that she couldn't

face the sheer mass of all the conversations it seemed they ought to have, so she had absented herself, and Elizabeth had officiated over Mac's only two encounters with his grandson; Elizabeth, who now seemed able to treat Mac with mild indulgence, as if he were an errant younger brother. Sally wondered if her mother were in some way still in love with him; if she compared him to her present husband and found Jeff disappointing, or whether she really had put the whole of that life behind her and reached a place where she was genuinely relieved that she was no longer responsible for the consequences of Mac's wild enthusiasms. Did the sight of him with her grandson awaken pangs of regret for everything that was lost, Sally thought, or did her mother now see Mac with clear eyes, as a separate being, unrelated to her life? These were not the kind of conversations she had with her mother, but she wanted to know because it seemed that the answer would have some bearing on how she might one day feel about Greg.

Now Mac was here, and the reality was oddly anti-climactic. She had spent more years not having a relationship with him than she had spent having one, and yet her unconscious mind and her body snapped awake with recognition: the shape of his fingers, a tilt of the head, the crease of a half-smile, a glance – all these gestures were written into the fabric of herself and her memories. In a sense she was relieved; she had been partly afraid that some undisciplined self from childhood might rear up at the sight of her father and attempt, quite independently of her self-control, to leap into his arms or climb into his lap. She felt no desire for any physical contact with him, and yet her body retained the memory of it; the only man whose body she had recklessly and uninhibitedly clambered all over with perfect innocence and unmixed delight. On the other hand, she thought, stealing a glance at him as he bent to pick up a toy Manny had casually jettisoned, he was no more than a man she had once known; the fact that he had begun her now seemed tangential and unimportant.

Sally wondered about the role of a father. Everything you did as an adult, all your motives and mistakes, were, according to contemporary wisdom, traceable to how you interacted with your father. If you didn't have one, it fucked you up; more often than not, if you did have one, that fucked you up just as comprehensively. But what did it *mean*? She had had a father and then lost him; her own son, to all intents and purposes, did not have a father at present but might, at some future date, find him. Which variation, if either, was preferable? Or did any of it really matter – was it all a question of semantics? You grew up with certain expectations of the person you knew as 'Dad', she thought, expectations that would almost certainly be disappointed, since it seemed there was no mechanism in place to ensure that the person attached to you by the biological label was necessarily the one best equipped to meet those expectations. Seeing Mac again had impressed upon her a kind of existential loneliness; these unbreakable bonds we rely on, she thought, are all of our own invention. In the end, it's just the random scattering of genes.

They drifted through an archway to the cobbled yard of the indoor market. Trestles piled with secondhand books sagged in front of one shop; from another, its window gleaming with crystals and occult statuary, floated scents of incense and snatches of whale song. Christmas lights already beaded the windows and gaudy stars and angels bedecked the lamp-posts. Manny's cheeks were pink with cold and his breath clouded in little smoky puffs as he fought to take off his mittens.

'Such a pretty town,' Mac said, after a while.

'It's smug, is what it is,' Sally said. 'It reeks of civic smugness. Look.' She indicated a poster on the bookshop door advertising the festive production of the local amateur dramatic society. 'All the Best Kept Village awards, and the twinning committee, all that shite. It keeps the rest of the world at a safe distance.'

'Or you might see that as people taking pride in their community.'

'You might, if you lived here and you were one of them.'

'You do live here.' Mac looked puzzled.

'It's the place where I sleep. In every other sense I still live in London.'

'Have you many friends here?'

'None at all,' Sally said. It was true.

'What about the other mothers?'

'What other mothers?'

'Did you not meet people at those, I don't know, mother and baby groups and so on?'

'I didn't go to them. I don't belong in that kind of thing. What would I have in common with them?'

'Well, you're a mother and you've a baby, would that not qualify you?'

'Only superficially.'

'Your mother's worried about you.'

'She worries too much.'

It was Elizabeth's favourite theme at the moment, the need for Sally to put some effort into making friends. For Sally, these conversations were a chillingly accurate repetition of the ones she had had with her mother as a fourteen-year-old, when they first moved to Crowbourne from London. They tended to run on rails, usually beginning with the truism that you couldn't sit around feeling sorry for yourself waiting for people to come to you.

'Perhaps you wouldn't be so lonely here, love, if you tried to make some friends,' Elizabeth would gently chide.

'I've got friends.'

'Yes, but they're in London, and they have a very different kind of life from yours now. Lola is single and she's very busy with her career, and Rhys is –'

There was always an awkward pause at this point.

'Gay. You can say gay, Mother. Anyway, *I'm* busy with my career.'

'Well, the point is, neither of them has a family.'

'I don't have a family.'

'You have a baby. But if you spend all your time with them, you just get resentful of the fact that your life isn't like theirs any more. You'd feel happier if you made some friends you could talk to about all the nitty-gritty of having a child.'

'I live with all the nitty-gritty, the last thing I want to do is talk about it as well. I need to spend time with people who remind me that I used to be someone else.'

She knew that Elizabeth viewed her own refusal to join any of the local mothers' groups as a kind of metropolitan snobbery, but in truth Sally was afraid of other mothers. There were some in her street; she would see them occasionally as she passed with Manny in the buggy as they loaded their children in and out of their Lexuses and Volvo SUVs. Sometimes she would smile shyly at them and say hello, half hoping they might take the initiative and prolong the conversation; the fact that they never did only confirmed what Sally feared about them: that they lived in self-contained units, with their husbands and children and, presumably, friends who also came in units of twos and fours, even numbers, because of the old tacit rule that couples were only really allowed to socialize with other couples, and therefore had no need of her. They were already validated in their lives; they had chosen their paths and seemed entirely on top of how to do it. Stronger even than her sense of her own irrelevance to the already complete lives of these capable wives and mothers was the fear that they would not like her. It had taken her eighteen years of life – until she reached university – to find other people who did not consider her unusual, who were even like her in many important ways, and she found it curious that her mother seemed to buy into this assumption that you would immediately and uncomplicatedly get on with everyone with whom you had the sole common interest of being in charge of people shorter than your knees.

'You must be going out of your mind here,' Mac said, gently.

Sally shrugged.

'I went out of my mind in this town for years. Then I got out. Now look at me. I'm right back where I started, and I still have to ask my mother for permission to go out at night.'

She said this in clipped, neutral tones, and was angry with herself immediately; she had determined not to worry at the old wound, and already she was making veiled criticisms of the way in which her father had disrupted her life.

'You're never right back where you started.'

Mac looked at her. He had done this almost incessantly since he arrived; scrutinizing her face, it seemed, and then Manny's, as if he could not divide his attention efficiently enough between his daughter and his grandson, as if he wanted to take them both in at once. She looked back at him. They were still in the process of reidentifying one another. There were traces of his face in Manny's, and they were the traces of her own face. People often said how much Manny looked like Sally, but they were usually the people who wanted to obliterate Greg from the child's history, to erase all trace of his involvement, and Sally was not blind to the fact that Manny actually looked like the result of someone with advanced computer skills having scanned her face on to a screen and then having superimposed Greg's over it. He was both of them and, through them, both their histories. Sally had no idea what Greg's father looked like, but she imagined that the ghost of him could be seen in Manny's features, too, if she had known what to look for.

Her father was here, at Elizabeth's request, to have one very specific conversation, but behind it were all the conversations they could have been having but were not, seventeen years' worth of conversations that it was now, Sally thought, too late to begin. And how were they to have this discussion? How could they sit and talk about Greg's dereliction of duty towards his son without ever mentioning Mac's own? Could he reasonably offer sympathy for Greg's behaviour without stinking of hypocrisy, or would he even attempt to see it from Greg's side? If he tried that, Sally thought, he would be straight out the door.

'Will we get a coffee, then?' he said, casting around for somewhere that might have tables.

Sally considered the multiple opportunities for disaster offered by the prospect of finding somewhere to have coffee. Assuming they could get the buggy through the doors without overturning something, Manny would not want to stay in it; he would want to be picked up and sat on her lap, and once he had been picked up, he would want to get down, and then he would career into tables and split his head open, or pull down boiling teapots on himself, or, in the very best-case scenario, would simply agitate for attention and disturb other people, making her acutely self-conscious and ensuring that whatever conversation she was to have with Mac would be conducted with about 3 per cent of her available brain. At least at home there was always the magic of the television fairy.

'Let's go back,' she said.

At home she made tea for her father, watching him from the corner of her eye as he played with Manny on his lap, unselfconsciously. The little boy was quietly fascinated by his grandfather; he stared at him from round blue eyes, occasionally reaching up to touch his beard. Sometimes, Sally saw in her son glimpses of the person he would become – his determination, his curiosity – and it filled her with hope, that one day they might be friends. Mac seemed easy in the child's company, reading him a book full of farmyard noises while Manny's head lolled comfortably against his shoulder, and Sally thought she remembered sitting in just such a posture, with just such a book. It jolted some kind of pain in her chest, and she turned back to the kettle.

'So, I think your mother would like to kill this fella with her own bare hands,' Mac said, eventually, still bouncing Manny on his knee.

'She's welcome to have a go.'

'Never seen Elizabeth so angry.'

'No, well you never saw her after –'

There was a troubled pause; Mac concentrated on a page of sheep jumping.

'You say he's an actor?'

'Yes.' Sally put a mug of tea down by her father's feet, feeling uncomfortable, and trying hard to think of Mac as free legal aid.

'So he'd come in as self-employed. Now, the way they calculate the self-employed income is a terrible minefield. But you know for a fact he earns more than he's telling them?'

'As far as they're concerned, he's earning about four grand a year after tax, which is impossible. But they say that's all come through his accountant and they don't find it suspicious. But that must mean that if he's hiding money, he must be cheating on his tax, too.'

'It's not as simple as that. I'll tell you what I think,' Mac said, as if he were about to begin a story to a bar-room audience. Sally forced herself to be patient. 'My betting would be, he's set himself up as a company there, and he's paying himself the minimum salary while the rest's in the company, like, you see? That's not illegal, you could do it yourself. So as long as the company taxes are up to date, there's no one going to be looking into it.'

'But why can't they see that that's what happened?'

'Because the system is lost in the dark ages. There's a wife, your mother says?'

Sally grimaced.

'Yes. Well, she's not technically his wife.'

'Whatever she is. So, I would guess he's got the wife on a salary there, and maybe if he's other children, them as well. But the child support can only legally be worked out from his own earnings, not the company's gross profits.'

'Even if they're the same thing?'

'They're not the same thing, under this arrangement.'

Sally was circling the small kitchen, her hands balled into fists. She felt queasy at the flagrant wrongness of it.

'You mean he's effectively turning his earnings into her earnings?'

'That could be one way. And she'd not be included in the calculation, you see.'

'How can that be allowed?'

'It just is.'

If there was one thing to be said in Mac's favour, it was that he had never been the kind of parent who fobbed off his daughter's enquiries with answers like 'it just is'; he had always provided patient and unnecessarily detailed explanations of why the sky was blue, or why birds could fly and Sally could not. Until the day he left home, when he had not been able to provide a convincing explanation. Strangely, Sally felt closer now to understanding her father's defection than she ever had in the intervening years; she thought she understood how family life might make you fear that you had irretrievably lost your self. And that was something you were not allowed to admit to thinking, never mind act upon.

'That's the trouble with the law, Sal, it just exists. It's not tailored to individuals. You have to fit to it, it doesn't fit around you. If you'd a company that was saving you on your taxes, you'd be glad of the system.'

'But they must know that people use it to fiddle their child support?'

'Most of the people going through this system are not people like you and your man, they don't have the wherewithal to consult lawyers and accountants. So I'd imagine it isn't brought to their attention all that often.'

'But he's done this deliberately! He even told me he'd been to see his accountant.'

'Well, they don't know that. They don't know he hasn't always had a company.'

'But he hasn't! He must have set it up right before Manny was born.'

'If you could show that, it might be a start. Your basic problem, Sal, assuming that this is what he's done, is that it's not illegal to put your earnings through a company. It means that, to all intents and purposes, he's not self-employed, he's an employee, and after that it doesn't matter if he's employed by – what's his name?'

'Greg Burns.'

'All right, Greg Burns Limited or Microsoft, he's still an employee with just his salary.'

'But that's horseshit, because he's demonstrably still an actor, he did an advert for garden furniture, so this company doesn't do anything. It's just him.'

'You should be able to argue that. I'd have to look into it.'

'How do we even find out if that's what he's done?'

'You look him up in Companies House. We could do it now on your computer.'

With Manny installed with a lump of biscuit amid an explosion of toys, Sally sat beside her father as he scrolled through search engines. She was oddly and disproportionately impressed, as if she had believed that his assumed folk persona would have retarded him in the world of modernity, gradually eroding his ability to use telephones or drive a car.

There was nothing listed under Greg Burns Limited.

'If he's done this, you know, he's a clever bastard,' said Mac. 'He hasn't put it under his own name. It means we'll have to do another search by the name of directors.'

'So do that.'

'You can't do it on this site, you need a particular level of access.'

Sally felt a rising anxiety.

'Well, how do we get that?'

'I've a friend who can do it for you. I'll call him when I get back to Dublin, then I'll send you the stuff in the post and we can think about what to do next. I'd say you can have a two-pronged attack. If you can get evidence of all the work he's done in the past year, and the date this company was incorporated, when we find it, then you might be able to persuade them that it's been set up as a deliberate front. The other thing you could do is give them some proof that his lifestyle is not commensurate with earning eighty pounds a week.'

'What, like take photos of him eating in expensive restaurants? Buying two pairs of shoes?'

'Well, I don't know. But, like, what kind of car does he drive? How many holidays does he take? What's his house like? That sort of thing.'

'I don't know that sort of thing. Not without following him around.'

'It's something to think about.'

'You mean, get a private detective?'

'No, that would be absurd. But you've mutual friends, acquaintances. There must be ways you can find out.'

Sally thought of Patrick Williams and a sudden cold settled in her stomach.

'His money comes through his agent,' she said. 'So, presumably, if he's got a company now, there must have been a day when his agent had to stop writing cheques to him and start writing them to Greg Burns Limited, or whatever he's calling it?'

'I'd say so.'

'So his agent's in on it?'

'Well, he'd just do what he's told by the client, right? Like I say, it's a well-known tax thing, he probably wouldn't ask any questions.'

'Oh no.' Sally's jaw clenched. 'He'd know.'

Mac stood up.

'The first thing to do is to have my friend make this search, see if we can find some company records. And you see what you can get on how he lives. Does she work, the wife?'

'Only part time.'

'They could argue, you know, that she's family money somewhere. That's always the trick with these things – if they're in it together, they can do all sorts because the child-support people have no legal right to look into her money. But we'll see what we can get.'

Sally felt braver, now that she had an ally; the fight did not seem so impossible. That it should have to be her father muddied the waters, but this first encounter with him had not been at all as she had dreaded.

Mac, too, had the sense not to outstay his welcome.

'I'd better be getting back to that train,' he said, and bent down to Manny. 'Come here to your grandad.'

'Moo,' said Manny, brandishing a wooden horse.

Mac picked him up and snuggled his neck.

'Manus is a fine choice,' he said. 'It would have made your grandfather very happy.'

Sally could not escape the implication that such a gift of happiness had been squandered, since her grandfather was no longer around to appreciate it, and that it might have been more thoughtfully bestowed by naming the boy after Mac himself, but she let it pass.

'He's a McGinley, no doubt about it,' Mac said, proudly, as if this were entirely his own doing. 'Did you love him? This Greg.'

Sally was ambushed without a ready answer, and had to tell the truth.

'I thought so. But you always think that at the time, don't you, then when it's all turned ugly, you think, no, that wasn't it, the thing I was looking for, I must have been mistaken all along.'

'Men can do terrible things at a certain age, Sal. It's the fear of

334

death comes on you. I don't say that excuses it.'

'No, it doesn't. Don't you think women would like to walk away sometimes? Don't you think I'd like to just walk out of here some days and not come back? Don't you think Mum ever fancied a different kind of life? But somehow we're not supposed to. We have to stay and deal with the mess you leave.'

Sally heard the pitch of her own voice; making a useless gesture with her hands, she returned to the kitchen to look for some distraction.

Mac didn't speak for a while.

'If he came back, if he said he was sorry and he wanted to make amends. What would you do?'

'I'd tell him to fuck off.'

Sally realized as she said this that it was not true.

Mac nodded.

'People do change, Sal. They act without thinking and when they've had a chance to look at themselves, they have a better notion of why. Though of course you're not obliged to give them a second chance, but it would be a hard world if everyone was as intractable as you.'

'You're not talking about him now, are you?'

'Ah, listen – I'm ashamed of what I did to you and your mother, I'll be ashamed of it for the rest of my life. For the way I did it. But I was living a false life, and I'd be ashamed to be doing that still. You understand that, I know you do, though you might pretend not to. I read your play.'

Sally came back into the room and stared at him.

'How did you do that?'

Mac laughed.

'I ordered it from the theatre bookshop. They have bookshops in Dublin, you know. I try to keep up with what you're doing. Didn't appreciate the irony at the time, of course. I wish I'd seen it. Was he any good, this Greg? As me?'

'It's not about you.'

'No, all right. There's a remarkable number of coincidences, though.'

Her father looked at her with a kind of tentative humour, as if the years had put him so far beyond the reach of reproach that he didn't mind what she said. She took in the shape of his face, which was also

335

her face, and her son's face, and found that there was nothing left to inspire resentment. He was just a man who had let her down and was trying to make amends. She found herself almost smiling.

'You weren't supposed to see it.'

'That play is the most you've said to me about that time in seventeen years.'

'I wasn't saying it to you. I never expected you to hear it.'

'Well, I'm glad I did.'

Suddenly Sally wanted him gone; they had reached capacity with one another for their first meeting, she felt, and she had seen quite enough of the past bubbling to the surface, when what they needed was to concentrate on the present. She reached Mac's coat down from the bannister; reluctantly, he lifted Manny down and accepted his cue to leave.

'So you'll speak to this guy in Dublin?'

'I'll do it tomorrow. He should have something for you in a couple of days. Don't let this grind you down, Sal, it may be slow but we'll nail the bastard.'

'Will you stop and see Mum on the way?'

Mac scratched his beard.

'Ah, I don't think so. Don't want to be interrupting her.'

'Jeff could fill you in on the Twinning Committee.'

She said it with a glint; they caught each other's eye and communicated, for the first time in seventeen years, what was almost a private joke.

'You'll not hear me say a word against Jeff, he's a grand fella altogether,' Mac said, but the corners of his mouth were twitching. Sally picked Manny up and settled him on her hip.

'Say goodbye to Granddad, sweetheart,' she said.

The child looked serious.

'Ad-dad,' he said.

Mac kissed the boy's head and opened the door.

'Mac?'

Her father turned.

'Listen – thanks for coming.'

'You're welcome.' He nodded, briskly, and left with an impressive lack of sentiment, but Sally could hear him whistling through his smile as he closed the gate.

21

Greg Burns was now a married man. *A married man.* He had tried repeating the phrase to himself, of himself, in the days leading up to the wedding, and could not avoid the conviction that it was only ever used in two very specific contexts. In farce, where Barbara Windsor-type characters would give it a glaze of sauce by using it of behaviour considered inappropriate to a married man (usually adulterous overtures), as in '*Ooh!* And you a married man!', or among men, when your friends would use it either to gloat or commiserate over what they saw as the effective termination of your life, as in 'You're a married man now, mate, there'll be no mor e . . . [whatever you might have once considered an enjoyable pastime]', or as an apology for their own slow descent into torpor and tedium, as in 'I would stay for one more, but I'm a married man.'

In the event, the reality had not been nearly as dire as he'd imagined it, and he wondered why exactly he had been so intransigent on this point for so many years. There had been a civil ceremony in a King's Lynn hotel, followed by a reception; the hotel was the kind that has function rooms converted out of medieval outbuildings, with naked timbers, and the tables were all set with white flowers and candles. The reception seemed to have been attended by more people than Greg could possibly have met in his life; during the months of preparation, he had once ventured that it might be nice to keep it small, since they had, after all, been living together for twelve years, but he might just as well have suggested that they get married in the back garden in their jeans. This was Caroline's event, and no one, least of all him, was going to have much success in scaling it down. She was spending far more than he had anticipated – every time she whisked a bill in front of his face just long enough for him to glimpse another accusing row of zeros, he felt he had the answer to the question of why he had put it off for so long – but he knew, with a slow clench of guilt, that this lavishness was not because Caroline was naturally flamboyant, or because she was making a point, having been denied this wedding for twelve years, but because she had decided she wanted to spend their savings now, while there was still time to enjoy them. That had been her phrase; the blaring subtext was that there should be nothing left for Sally to take, should she ever muster enough legal muscle to make anyone reassess Greg's obligation to the child. Caroline, who had always been so assiduous about savings, about having a cushion, about planning for the future, was now galloping through building-society accounts as if she had learned of a terminal illness; it would not have surprised Greg if she had suggested they sell the house and set off on an indefinite cruise.

She had worn a cream-coloured linen trouser suit, and had looked radiant, and not a little triumphant. He had worn – what? He found he couldn't remember what he had worn; very likely a linen suit, since Caroline had chosen it, and linen seemed to be to civil weddings what lace was to the traditional variety. Why such affiliation to a fabric that can't help but look sad and bedraggled and past its best after an hour of wearing it, Greg thought? There were photographs of him at the end of the evening, red-faced in his crumpled suit, looking like a corrupt Egyptian police official or an old colonial raconteur in an embassy bar. It had been towards the end of the reception that the doubts had set in. He had stood outside on the hotel's terrace for a smoke (only Caroline could have had the lack of foresight to arrange a party in a non-smoking venue, but apparently so few of their friends were smokers any more that he felt increasingly conspicuous every time he crept out), looking up at ghosts of clouds worrying at the rim of a June moon, and had realized that he was now mapped. He had done it; he had promised to continue along this course until he died, and there was nothing of him that was left uncharted. There would be no more surprises, no possibility of starting another life. Part of him felt relieved at the thought that all future choices had been taken out of his hands, and he was glad that it seemed to have made Caroline happy; he was pleased to have given her that much. But he also sensed that a kind of amputation had taken place, one that was still too numb fully to register, but which he would notice increasingly as the months and years wore by. He would grow old and die with Caroline; that had been his choice, and with it a part of himself had been shut down, decommissioned. If he were ever unfaithful to Caroline again, it would be strictly and legally defined as adultery, and she would have entitlements to his property and his daughter; this troubled him less than it might have done if he had not already made her the majority shareholder in everything he earned. He was bound to her on every level now, except the one that had begun to consume her, and for which everything else, including the extravagant wedding, had become a displacement activity: she was not yet pregnant again.

Greg had been standing out on the terrace, contemplating these things and smoking three cigarettes in succession, opportunistically getting them in before he was hauled mercilessly back to participate in a conga or something equally undignified, when he saw his father coming through the double doors. Tom was stooping more these days, Greg noticed, and each time he moved his right leg there was a slight bracing of the jaw and a frown, as if to anticipate and disguise pain. He looked thinner, too, and Greg wondered how he had failed to notice this. With a quantity of mid-range champagne inside him, he was rushed with a sudden tenderness for the old man, and approached him with his arms out.

'Get away, lad, I can still walk on me own, just about,' Tom said, easing himself down to a stone bench. 'Not a cripple yet.'

'Dad, do you cook for yourself when you're at home? I mean, do you eat all right?'

'I don't need fussing over.'

'You've lost weight.'

'I was a bit off colour a few weeks back. Nothing to worry about. Just old age.' Tom rubbed the small of his back for effect. 'Any road, you're a bloody fool, I'll say it again, anyone knows it'll kill you.'

For a chilling moment Greg thought his father was talking about marriage; that only now, far too late in the day, he was going to produce the patriarchal wisdom that might have saved Greg from a terrible fate. Then he realized that Tom meant the smoking.

'I know, I know. I'm going to stop. But it is a party.'

'Well, you'll have to give it up now, you're a married man.'

'To be fair, Dad, I have been living with Caroline for years, it's not as if anything's going to change.'

Tom shook his head. Greg took in the deep gulleys of his face, caught in shadow, and was struck by an image of himself and his own son (whose name was Manus, he knew, and what kind of a name was that to saddle a boy with, for Christ's sake?) at an equivalent time of life, and the image winded him. Perhaps it was already too late for them; perhaps his actions had already made such a scene impossible. He had turned his back on the boy when he was helpless and needy and if at some future time Greg should find himself old and helpless and needy, the boy would be quite justified (and quite likely, given that he was Sally's son) in returning the gesture. And the boy would be a man by then, and possibly a father himself, and what would he have learned from his own father to pass on? But it didn't work like that, Greg thought, watching Tom as he stared straight ahead; it was not so clean and simple. If you could just take qualities and hand them down the generations like a watch or a painting, he, Greg, might have made less of a mess of things.

'No, son,' Tom said, eventually. 'Marriage changes everything. You might not think so, the young generations, but it makes a man look at his life. Straighten himself out.'

Greg put his hands between his knees and looked down. The idea that Tom might die without ever seeing his grandson, or indeed knowing anything of his existence, had struck in him a terrible mute sadness, and he wondered if he could reasonably light another cigarette.

'A marriage, see,' Tom went on, 'it shows you've put some thought into where you're going with your life. It's not something you just drift into and then up and leave whenever you feel like it. However much you might sometimes feel like it.'

The heaviness of significance hung over this last sentence, but Greg could not tell whether it was supposed to suggest that he knew something of Greg's misdemeanours or whether it carried a note of personal confession.

'Did you ever want to up and leave?'

Tom turned slowly to face him.

'There's nothing more valuable in life than a home, Greg, that's what I've learned. A home, and a family that loves you, no matter what else life might seem to offer. And I'm very proud of you, that you've finally done this, son. That's what I wanted to say when I came out. And it would have meant the world to your mother.' He nodded meaningfully at the sky.

If they were in a musical, Greg thought, his mother's face would now appear, spangled together out of star formations, beaming

340

benignly. But it didn't, and the image of her and what she would have thought of him for what he had done, and the burden of his father's misplaced pride, and the bottle and a half of champagne misting up his thoughts, and all the fear and dread and guilt and regret of the past year conspired to make him collapse messily into tears.

Tom did not expect explanations; he merely rested a hand on his son's back and patted it absently from time to time while Greg covered his hands and suit with snot. When, finally, he stopped, Tom offered a pristine handkerchief (another emblem of manly dignity that had passed him by, Greg thought; he was never in possession of so much as a clean tissue).

'Dad, there's something I need to tell you,' he began, through hiccups, and at that moment, Martin Parrish, Greg's so-called best man, had popped his head around the doors and said, 'Ah, there you are! A heart to heart, I see, bit of fatherly advice for the wedding night, eh? *Eh?*' He produced a lascivious laugh. 'Good evening, Mr Burns. Greg, I think your good lady wife might be giving some thought to making your grand exit.'

'Go and wash your face, son,' Tom said, quietly. 'No need for folk to see you like that.'

Greg heard the words 'good lady wife' and remembered another reason why he had felt so viscerally opposed to marriage: because he was afraid it would turn him into someone like Martin Parrish. Someone who presided over his own Sunday barbecues like Henry VIII, and who had once been heard to stride into the kitchen at the beginning of one such evening and ask his wife, 'What's the nibbles situation?' Greg had whispered to Caroline that if he ever uttered a sentence along the lines of 'What's the nibbles situation?', she was to have him put down; she had laughed, but only a little, because she didn't like him making fun of Martin, since Martin was precisely the sort of friend she wanted him to have. He was unlikely to encounter any temptation to vice while in Martin's company.

It had been Caroline who had appointed Martin Greg's best man; he would have liked to have asked Patrick, but Patrick was very much *persona non grata* with Caroline at the moment, ever since she had stopped to calculate just how many times Patrick must have covered for him to facilitate his affair. It was as much as he could do to get her to agree that Patrick and Ashana should even be invited to the wedding. Once Martin was in place, Greg had decided that he didn't much fancy the idea of a stag night; that, and, in fact, all the other trappings of this wedding seemed to him too stagey and ridiculous, at his age, but Caroline had seemed affronted by the suggestion that he wouldn't want one, as if by implication he was not taking the wedding seriously. He wanted to explain that he was becoming infuriated by the way that everyone seemed determined to pretend that he and Caroline were twenty-one-year-olds who had never lived away from home before, much less had sex with anyone, rather than two people in their forties who had lived together for nearly thirteen years, had an eleven-year-old child and all the bath towels and dinner services their hearts could desire, and who were only getting married because the year before he had had a child with someone else and nearly left her, but naturally she knew that as well as he did, and all the arrangements and all the money being spent was an elaborate diversion from the truth of it, and so he had submitted to the dismal process of a stag night organized by Martin Parrish.

This had taken the form of a dinner at the golf club. Patrick was the only one of his friends from London who had been invited; Caroline's brother-in-law, Philip, was there, together with a handful of others, husbands of Caroline's friends and colleagues who had occasionally been to the house for dinner, people he would never have chosen of his own volition to be present at his funeral, never mind his stag do. Greg had hated every minute, and had drifted into a reverie about what kind of stag night he might have had if he'd been allowed any say in it; if he'd been in London and invited some of the boys from the theatre – Freddie, Gonzo, Dev, the tech crew; even Rhys Richards knew how to put away a drink, for God's sake – but such a night would have been entirely foreign to the whole spirit of the wedding project. Martin had made a speech about what a decent chap he was, and none of those present had made any kind of innuendo about the fact that he had just had a baby with another woman.

Neither had anyone made reference to it at the wedding, though many of them surely knew; the baby's unnamed presence had ghosted eerily about the timbered hall, threatening to erupt.

'She finally wore you down after all these years, eh?' relatives would smile, shaking him by the hand after the ceremony, and he would wonder if they knew, how they could *not* know, and why the idea of all this unspoken knowledge did not seem to have diminished the occasion for Caroline.

At his stag dinner, in the King's Lynn Golf Club, Greg had experienced a constricting headache, like some kind of primitive armour around his head, and he understood it to be born of the knowledge that he had already begun the process of his dying. He would be fixed, and grow old among people like these until he faded, and he couldn't shake loose the thoughts of the different life he might have had with Sally, if she hadn't got pregnant like a bloody fool. To combat the creeping inertia, he had suggest to Caroline that they go to New York for their honeymoon. She had looked at him as if he must have some ulterior motive, some mistress secreted away there, so out of character was the destination.

'Why would we want to go to New York?'

'Because we've never been.'

'Well, we've never been to a lot of places. But it's not the kind of place you go to for a honeymoon, is it?'

Greg didn't know. He didn't know what kind of places people went to for honeymoons because he had never taken the slightest interest; apparently, though, it was something that Caroline had studied extensively over the years, and she had fixed on one of the quieter Greek islands. It had been pleasant, and not overly hot; they had walked through whitewashed ports, taken boat trips and eaten fresh fish and drunk retsina in outdoor tavernas that smelled of warm pine and salt water; they had spent a lot of time lying on beaches and beside pools, which had driven Greg nearly out of his mind with boredom, but he had derived a kind of secondary enjoyment from witnessing Caroline's pleasure. Nothing had gone spectacularly wrong (he had lived in fear of bags going missing or the hotel being a disappointment, knowing that any deviation from the perfect honeymoon Caroline had promised herself would be indirectly his fault), they had not argued much, at least only over small things, such as what he had done with the room key; she held his hand as they strolled in the evenings in a way that suggested that she was genuinely happy, and he tried to get used to the idea of himself as someone who might never go to New York. But he had liked the fact that her happiness made him happy in turn; that there was still enough humanity in him to indulge someone else's pleasure, even when the activity would not have been his own first choice. Even so, following Caroline through the markets, listening to her small exclamations of delight over trays of alien sea-creatures and impossibly lush vegetables, he realized that his principal emotion on this honeymoon was relief at having apparently patched his life back together convincingly, and not the rekindling of erotic adventure that he had hoped for. It was as if the rubber stamp of marriage had anaesthetized his desire.

This was ironic, because over the past year he had been having more sex with Caroline than he remembered them having at any point in their relationship, even when they first met, and the most exquisite irony of all was that, in all of it, he was not the focus. Her desire, despite the volume and frequency of it, was not for him but for the putative child with which she might once and for all trump Sally, and therefore he could not help but see every occasion, her every watchful checking of calendar and thermometer, as her final and powerful insult to him. It was as if his wish had been packaged up and delivered back to him in a grotesque parody of itself. She wanted to have sex with him incessantly, these days, but she still didn't want *him*; he, Greg, was absent from the business except as a reliable supplier of active sperm. When, after five months of trying, he had suggested, thinking he was being encouraging, that they visit a doctor, and she had given him a look that had passed beyond words and then shut herself in the bathroom for an hour, to emerge bearing the ostentatious traces of a crying jag, he had realized his own unforgivable tactlessness; having so recently fathered upon his younger mistress a healthy boy, any mention of doctors only lit up the one thing she could not bear to think about nor hear voiced: the only possible conclusion that she was the one misfiring. He had realized, too, that if Caroline were not to have another baby, there would be no way back for him to his existing son. Although, even if she were to conceive, he found it hard to imagine that this would make her more amenable to the idea of Sally, or less territorial with regard to him and the amount of fathering he was able to parcel out among his children. It seemed that, in the short term, at least, he must learn to forget that, somewhere in the Home Counties, there lived a little boy with his genetic blueprint, as officially attested to by a letter which he kept in his desk in a foolscap wallet marked 'Solicitor'.

It had surprised him, the ease with which he had been able to shrug on the authorized version of his life, the version in which he had never been unfaithful and his son did not exist; surprised and occasionally horrified him. What did it say about him, he wondered, about the state of his soul and his capacity for love and loyalty and conscience, that he should find it so straightforward to resist any urge to see his child? He often wondered what the boy might look like, but with an abstract kind of curiosity, one he had no intention of submitting to empirical tests, in the way that he occasionally wondered what the inside of his lungs might look like, or what it would be like to have sex with a man. Caroline had been right, though, he was willing to admit; it was so much easier this way, this all-or-nothing choice, much easier than if he had been trying to maintain some kind of tenuous relationship, driving down to visit Sally and the baby every fortnight or once a month, quite possibly racked with residual affection for Sally and the pressure of spreading himself too thinly. At least this way, the boy would not be burdened with a tepid relationship with him; he would be a tabula rasa where fathers were concerned, and Sally would be free to meet someone else who would fill his place, both for her and for the boy. And the thought of this – of the son he had never met calling a stranger 'Daddy' – made his skin prickle, and at those moments he often found himself reaching for a drink. When he tried to picture his son's face, he found he only had the imagination to summon photographs of himself as a child. Already his memory of Sally's face was bleached and faded as if left in sunlight, and the one real photograph he had kept of her, the one in the theatre programme, had been found by Caroline and thrown out long ago ('thrown out' in the sense of doused in barbecue fuel and immolated in the back garden). The fact that Sally had never sent him a photograph of his son argued, he felt, that she didn't care about his involvement and wanted him actively excluded. So perhaps everything had worked out for the best. Perhaps everyone was happy now. Well, not *happy*, perhaps, but at least able to get on with a working version of their lives.

So why, a year after the baby was born, could he still not sleep? Why was he chased through fitful nights by terrifying pursuers, faceless glimpses in endless, Kubrick-style corridors, intent on murdering him? Why did he feel, permanently, as if he had built his house on a famous fault-line and were only waiting, now, for the inevitable day when some seismic horror would lash at its foundations and crash it down around him? His son's first birthday slid by, unfêted by anyone in King's Lynn, loudly ignored, with pursed lips and a brittle expression by Caroline, so that he felt obliged to present himself as extra-cheery and thrilled by his family on that day, and the knowledge that he had still not told his father chafed at him; he developed a tic of scratching at his neck as if in penance. 'You reap what you sow,' his mother had often said, usually with regard to schoolwork and application, but Greg had the distinct sense that he had not yet reaped in full, and that a grisly harvest was lying in wait for him. The worst of it was not knowing when.

At the end of October, a week after the son he had never seen had been in the world for one year, Greg's father telephoned him to say that he had been diagnosed with prostate cancer.

'Calm yourself, will you, lad, they say they've caught it early, it doesn't mean I'm going to die,' Tom had said, laughing, and Greg had heard the fear in that laugh. That was when he realized, properly, in his marrow, that his father would die – perhaps not immediately, but soon – and it seemed that something of elemental importance, something primitive to do with fathers and sons, life and family and continuity, was going to have to be faced and, in response, what he most wanted was to get another play so that he could go away and be someone else, as if none of it was happening.

22

Patrick Williams's offices in Fitzrovia were kitted out in a way that spoke to Sally of Patrick himself: tastefully understated, almost to the point of slight apology for being there in the first place. Two storeys up, above a boutique; Sally, aware that Patrick would probably require some preliminary statement of intent and then find several reasons not to see her, once the purpose of her visit was clear, had announced herself through the intercom at the front door as Lola. It was early in December, and London was festooned with tinsel, choking in creepers of lights and trails of aggressive gaudiness.

'He's just with a client at the moment,' shrilled a voice through the crackle of an ancient speaker, with the see-saw intonation common to personal assistants and receptionists that always came across as faintly patronizing, as if they were calming you down.

Sally pitched in the doorway: what if the client were Greg? It was not inconceivable; Greg must sometimes come here for meetings with his agent, and why not today, the day she had rumbled him entirely? Well, all the better if he was there; let them try to defend each other.

'It's OK, I'm early,' she said to the grille in the door jamb. 'I can just wait.'

She didn't wait, of course. Once she had been admitted, she ploughed through the waiting area, inhabited by a girl with peachy hair strung up with a collection of sparkly bobbles, who rose in some alarm at the pace and fury of Sally's trajectory and said, again, 'I'm afraid Mr Williams is just in with a client just at the moment', to which Sally had replied, 'Oh, don't worry, this *just* won't take a minute.' She noticed, to her right, a fawn-covered sofa by a round glass coffee table bearing a pristine *London Review of Books*, presumably where she was supposed to be waiting for the gift of Patrick's time. Of course the *London Review of Books*, she thought, how charmingly cultured and liberal, how very *Patrick*; Sally – stoked by the two vodkas and three coffees she had drunk on the train, and by the sheaf of papers that Mac's friend had duly unearthed regarding the incorporation of a private limited company by the name of CGB Ltd, which had arrived through her door that morning with an explanatory letter from her father, and which she was now brandishing like a writ as she crashed open the door at the far end of the room – was in a mood to be extremely sarcastic to Patrick Williams.

'Christ, *Sally* –' Patrick's face made a start on a number of expressions, but ended up with one that suggested she had walked in on him masturbating. It told Sally immediately that he knew exactly why she was there. He was seated behind his desk with his swivel chair pushed back, one ankle crossed over the other knee; opposite him, in a low armchair, was an Asian girl who seemed vaguely familiar.

'Tell me, Patrick,' Sally began, in full oratorical stance, 'do you take your 15 per cent from your clients' gross or net earnings? In other words, if one of your clients is earning eighty pounds a week after tax, does that mean you're getting twelve pounds a week out of it, or are you getting the full fifteen before tax? Either way, it hardly seems worth your while getting out of bed.'

'Sally, I'm just with a client at the moment.' Patrick gestured unnecessarily to the girl.

'Oh, hi!' Sally said, waving her papers. 'I'm Sally.' She extended a hand.

'Zoe,' said the girl, who looked wary of Sally's slightly manic and clearly insincere bonhomie. Sally thought she might once have been in a chewing-gum commercial.

'So you're one of Patrick's clients? Well, you might want to think about getting a new agent, because although Patrick's immensely charming, he's not very pushy. He can only get his clients less than the minimum wage, it seems, even for a garden furniture ad.'

'Sally, I think it would be good if we talked about this at another time,' Patrick said, rising from his chair.

'Do you?' Sally heard her own volume increasing, and realized just how mad she must look to everyone else in the room. '*I* think it would be good if we talked about it now. Let's talk, for example, about CGB Limited, the company formerly known as Greg Burns Limited, which is essentially a *money-laundering* operation, isn't it,

Patrick, as you very well know?'

The girl, Zoe, was staring at Patrick with bulging eyes and, Sally thought, a new kind of admiration, as if she had just learned that he worked for the CIA. Patrick's eyes tried urgently to communicate to her the unquantifiable degree of Sally's insanity and that none of this was therefore to be taken seriously; Sally caught the look. She seated herself jauntily on the edge of Patrick's desk, taking what pleasure she could from his acute and visible discomfort. She didn't actually dislike Patrick; in fact, he had always made an effort to be polite to her, but in more than a year this was the closest she had been to venting some of the things she wanted to say to Greg, and Patrick, as his imperfect representative, had never the less taken on something of Greg's shape and form.

'Sally –' Patrick held out a hand intended to lead her to the door, his face pleading for clemency.

'Sorry, Patrick, I'm waiting for you to show some recognition when I mention this company, because you must presumably write cheques out to it on a regular basis. So I'll remind you' – she pretended to consult her papers – 'Greg Burns Limited was incorporated on the twenty-seventh of September last year – ooh, *here's* a funny thing – there are forty-nine shares allocated to the director, Greg Burns, and fifty to the company secretary, Caroline Potts. That's clever, do you see, Patrick, you'd think it would be called Caroline Potts Limited, wouldn't you, because she effectively owns the company. That *is* clever.' She shook her head slowly, in heavily feigned admiration. Actually, Sally hated sarcasm and had a very low opinion of those who used it in arguments, but on this occasion it pleased her to see that Patrick was hating it even more. 'And then a month later, it officially changed its name to CGB Limited, and *that's* cleverly done too, because it means if you look for a company under the name Greg Burns you won't find one.'

'Zoe, I am really sorry about this, but is there any chance you could come back a bit later?'

Zoe looked from Patrick to Sally and appeared to understand that the drama was no longer for her benefit.

'I can come back at four?'

'Perfect.'

'Yes, I'm sure we'll be done by then,' Sally said, beaming at her like an air hostess.

Patrick closed the door behind Zoe and stood leaning against it. He seemed to be struggling not to put his hands on his hips, as if aware that the pose would rob him of some masculine authority.

'I'm pretty angry about that, actually, Sally.' He folded his arms across his chest. 'To do that in front of one of my clients.' His voice was controlled, but with an edge of disturbance.

'Why, don't you want her to know what kind of person you are? And – all right – let's talk about being pretty angry, Patrick, because how do you think I felt after a year of waiting for this child-support *horseshit* to get sorted out, all the time believing that he meant to do the decent thing, and then to find out that he's *paid – a – fucking – accountant'* – she found she was breathing awkwardly, too fast – 'to screw his own son, that made me pretty fucking angry, and *you!*' She pointed a shaking finger. 'You sent my son a *tiger!* What was that meant to be, some kind of compensation, an apology for the fact that you were assisting his father in cheating him? Here, have a fucking tiger and cheer up.'

'It was meant to be a gesture, Sally, I was trying to be sympathetic because I felt sorry for you.'

'Well, I didn't ask for your pity, I'd just like you not to be screwing my son. Or maybe do one or the other, Patrick, *either* screw my son and be honest about it *or* buy him a tiger, because if you try to do both that makes you look like a two-faced cunt.'

'I'm not responsible for what my clients do with their money. If Greg was spending everything he earned on crack and child porn that would still be up to him. I'm not his moral guardian.'

'But you might think again about whether you wanted to represent him. Let me ask you something else, then, Patrick – do you approve of child-support fraud? Just as a hypothesis.'

Patrick weighed his words.

'I think *fraud* is a rather serious accusation to be throwing around, Sally. There's absolutely nothing wrong with people in Greg's profession putting their earnings through a private company, it's well established.'

'Ah, but there is a thing in Child Support Law called Wilful Deprivation of Earnings,' Sally said, smug with her cribbed legalese. She had been delighted with the Dickensian overtones of the phrase when she first read it in Mac's letter. It was the *Wilful* that did it – it sounded like the kind of devious sleight of hand practised by a cadaverous smirking sort in a stovepipe hat. 'That's when – just in case it's not clear – you use a company to transfer your money to someone else so it can't be counted as yours.'

'He hasn't done a lot of work this year, you know – a few adverts, and there was a pilot that didn't get commissioned, but he hasn't done any long runs anywhere. It stands to reason that his earnings would be down.'

'To eighty pounds a *week*? Come on, Patrick, do you think I live on a fucking farm? Anyway, your accounts will show how much he's earned this year, won't they? They may have the power to subpoena.'

Patrick looked alarmed; Sally was not really sure what a subpoena involved, but she enjoyed the authority the word took on as she spoke it.

'Are you taking him to court, then?'

'Can't. The courts don't deal with it. I'm appealing the assessment, that's all. It goes to some kind of tribunal. Jesus, I'm not trying to get him sent down, Patrick, I only want to see this done fairly.'

'It's not my business what my clients do with their money,' Patrick said again.

'Can you look me in the eye and tell me you didn't know he set up this company specifically to dodge his child support?'

Patrick held her eyes for a moment and then moved to his desk.

'No, I thought not.'

With slightly more fumbling and less panache than she would have liked, Sally took out a cigarette and lit it.

'I'd prefer it if you didn't smoke in my office.'

'I'd prefer it if you didn't steal from my son.'

They looked at each other.

'Anyway,' Sally said, indicating, 'there's an ashtray beside that armchair.'

'That's for guests.'

'Consider me your guest.'

'I haven't done anything wrong.' He sounded tired.

'No, according to the letter of the law, Patrick, you're as pure as the driven snow. It's just how it might look, you know.'

'To whom?'

'Other people.'

'Which other people?'

'The ones that might hear about it.'

Patrick squinted at her.

'Are you talking about the press?'

'Not particularly. See, obviously I've only just unearthed all this, and I'm fairly stunned that anyone would behave to their own child with such a complete absence of conscience or humanity, and I imagine that if I were to tell my friends, they'd be outraged too, and they'd probably talk about it a lot among themselves, and the thing is, Patrick, that so many of my friends know you, and Greg. It might make them inclined to think less of you. And, now that you mention it, it occurs to me that quite a lot of them work in the media.'

'I'm sorry, Sally, is this some sort of threat?'

'Of course not.' Sally was wondering how long she would be able to sustain the bravado. 'I'm just trying to find out what you think. Just for my own peace of mind, and my opinion of you, which probably you don't give a shit about, but never the less, I'd like to know if you've known since last year that Greg never had any intention of contributing towards his son. If you knew that and went along with it.'

Patrick looked away.

'Sally, I've tried to explain. We all do whatever we can to reduce our tax bills, that's why accountants exist and drive better cars than us. All my clients are advised by their accountants on how to manage their money, mine does the same for me. It's not my job to start enquiring into their motives unless they're asking me to break the law.'

'You seem to be missing the point here, Patrick, which is that we're not talking about tax breaks, we're talking about child support. *Obviously*, everyone likes to get out of their taxes wherever they can, even if they have to smudge the lines a bit. But cheating your way out of child support – see, that would carry an emotive freight in print that tax dodging just doesn't have.'

'So you are threatening me – or Greg – with the tabloids?'

'God, no – I've got more class than that. I see it more as a social affairs investigation in the *Guardian* or something. After all, if this loophole is well known to accountants, who knows how many more children are being cheated by their own fathers as we speak? Might be good for Greg, anyway – the publicity. He never did escape the curse of Doctor Jeremy, really, did he? Such an infallibly *decent* bloke, Doctor Jeremy, and always typecast thereafter. Maybe if the public know what a shit he is, he'll be able to diversify.'

Patrick rubbed a hand across his chin, and moved some papers needlessly from one side of his desk to the other.

'You should be talking to Greg about this,' he said, eventually.

'No one wants that more than I do.'

'Yes, well, it's never going to happen. So get used to it. There's absolutely no flexibility on that point. Especially now that they're married.'

The instant deflation, the unlooked-for blow, so sudden; Sally felt herself cramp over slightly with the punch of it, the finality. So that was it. He had married her. She had got him and he – so craven, so invertebrate – had given in without thinking. One more ticked off on her list of demands, in return for which he was supposed to get, at the end, total absolution. But at the end of what? When she had eviscerated him entirely, when she had demanded Sally's – or baby Manny's – head on a silver tray and got them?

She dropped into the armchair.

'They got married?' she said, but it was not really a question. If Patrick had been a less decent person, he might have shown some pleasure in having just opened a trapdoor under Sally's swagger and threats. Instead he pinched his chin and said, 'In June. Do you want a drink?'

He took her to a bar at the end of the street, where she sunk herself into a large glass of wine.

'I didn't know if you knew,' Patrick said. He was drinking a peppermint tea.'Strangely, I wasn't invited.'

'I thought someone might have told you.'

'No, they generously didn't.'

'He was asked to make a choice, Sally. He had to think about his own child.'

Sally's head snapped up.

'Sorry – his *own* child? Do you need me to explain some basic biology to you, Patrick?'

'Sorry – that was a bad choice of words. But he had a life that came before you, and that was – all these things were part of the choice he made.'

'All what things?'

'The wedding. Not seeing you again, ever.'

'And the fake company? Was that one of the conditions?'

'I don't know anything about what went on between them in that regard.'

'What is that, anyway – CGB? What does it mean?'

Patrick made a small movement with his head.

'I would guess it stands for Caroline and Greg Burns.'

Sally felt again as if she had been slapped, and asked for it.

'Of course. Look.' Suddenly she reached for her bag under the table and took out a recent photograph of Manny, which she pushed across to Patrick. 'Just so you know what this is about. It's not about putting the frighteners on you, it's not about trying to get some kind of revenge on Greg, in case that's what you were thinking. It's just about him. What do I tell him, Patrick, when he's old enough to ask why his father's never seen him? He doesn't even have his name on the birth certificate. This is his *son*.' She heard herself sounding plaintive, and reined it in. She didn't want Patrick to see her as pathetic; when he told Greg about this meeting, she wanted him to say, 'Sally? Oh, she looked great, she seems completely together.' But it was costing her dearly, this overlay of competence that she had to maintain for everyone, including herself, a talisman to deflect their pity and ward off their concern.

'I know,' Patrick said, studying his tea. 'He isn't without feelings about all this, you know. It's an impossible situation.'

'No, it isn't, he could just *talk* to me. You've got kids – could you imagine ever doing this to one of your kids?'

'It's a completely different question,' Patrick said, diplomatically. 'I live with their mother.'

'And if you didn't? Would you pay someone to tell you how to get out of supporting them?'

'That's not a question I can answer. I can't put myself in that position.'

'What, you don't have the imagination? You can't even say to me, categorically, that no, that's not something you would ever do to your own child?'

'I'm not in Greg's situation.'

'This isn't a press conference.'

'If I say no, I'd never do that, you'll ask me how I can stand by while he does it, if indeed that's what he's doing, which is not to say that it is, and if I say yes, maybe I would in his position, you'll quote me on that, which is obviously not something I'd like attributed to me. So I can't win, can I?' Patrick considered the photograph. 'He looks like Greg, eh?'

'Yes, that's what the doctor said when we went for the DNA test.'

'That must have been very –'

'Yes, it was. Very.'

'You may not appreciate this, Sally, in fact you probably don't even realize, but I have had several conversations with him about this. I've told him to get the legal stuff sorted out so you can both get on with your lives with the minimum trouble. But – as you might imagine, my influence can't really compete. I'll speak to him again, though. He might be persuaded to make a settlement if he knows you're going to fight it.'

'Yes, I am going to fight it, you can tell him that. I'm going to take it to every level of appeal I can, and if that doesn't work, I'll get my MP on to it, I'll make them discuss it in Parliament – Tony Czajkowski knows politicians – and the point of it is that what he's done is unforgivable, and for my son's sake I won't just let him get away with it. And if you'd rather not have your name associated with any adverse publicity, maybe you should think about updating your client list.' She paused, and lit a cigarette. No wonder she had not been able to argue effectively with Greg while she was pregnant, she thought – how could anyone look convincing without these little props to jab at the air at moments of emphasis? 'There's a law, Patrick – there's a legal requirement about the percentage of income you owe your child, everyone else has to comply with it, and he's actually paid someone to get round that. Think of that – he's spent more money on an accountant's advice than he's ever given to his son. And if you're not even willing to tell me you think that's wrong, then you're as warped as he is.'

Sally finished her wine and stood up to shrug on her coat. Patrick reached inside his jacket for a wallet.

'You know,' he said, 'I knew as soon as I met you that you and Greg should never have been allowed near each other. You're like each other's evil twin. The real world is not enough for you. I tried to warn him.'

Sally drew her wallet too, in challenge.

'Maybe you should have warned me.'

'Well, I don't think you'd have listened either, you're too much like him.'

Sally acknowledged this with a small glance.

'Put your money away, I don't need any more of your charity.'

'Oh, for Christ's sake. It's not charity, I'm just buying you a drink.'

'If it's not charity, then it's some kind of amends, and I don't think one glass of wine is sufficient compensation. I'll pay for my own.'

Patrick pressed his lips together and flicked his head impatiently.

'I don't know how much success I'll have with Greg,' he said, as they were leaving. 'He's pretty preoccupied at the moment, with Christmas, and his dad's ill at the moment, so –'

'His dad?'

'Cancer. So he might have other things on his –'

'Serious cancer?'

'No, the funny kind,' Patrick said, holding the door open for her, and then pulled his cheeks in. 'I mean, they're treating it, but he's an old man.'

'Yes.' Sally found herself looking at the pavement in a blur of wine and unease. She had nothing to do with Greg's father, except that he was her son's grandfather and Greg had always spoken about him with an odd mixture of pride and resentment. She wondered if he even knew that he had a grandson. And Manny would only ever have two grandfathers – well, three, if you counted Jeff – but two real ones, and if one of them was dying then it seemed desperately wrong that Greg – no, Caroline – no, Caroline's malice and Greg's cowardice – should rob either Manny or Greg's father of the chance to meet before it was too late. He was, after all, a way for Manny to have some contact with Greg's family. 'Thanks, Patrick. Apologize to that girl for me. You can tell her I'm on day release from the hospital.'

She wasn't sure whether to shake Patrick's hand, but he leaned across and kissed her clumsily on the cheek, which she thought inappropriate. Watching him walk away in his neat suit, she felt that she was still unclear as to how much blame attached to him. He owed her no loyalty, after all, and yet if he knew, as he must have known, about the purpose of Greg's company, he had at best turned a blind eye. Yet he seemed sincerely distressed by her accusations. Sally wondered if her problem was too many years in the theatre; perhaps her perception of sincerity had been blunted. She had believed that Greg was sincere, once. But her more immediate concern was how she might introduce herself and Manny to Greg's father.

Waiting for her train on the platform at Waterloo, her eye was caught by one of the Metropolitan Police's Operation Crack Down on Drugs posters. Rat on a Rat, it said, with a helpful picture of a large rat looking as if it had just been caught red-handed smelting crack, above a free phoneline by means of which good citizens might nark on those who profited from the drug trade. As an afterthought, she went to the public payphone next to the chocolate machine, dialled the number, and informed the respondent, in her best South London accent, that the theatrical agent Patrick Williams was famous throughout the West End for dealing coke to allcomers out of his Charlotte Street offices. And the odd tab of E, she added. She felt a lot better after that.

~•~

Greg was wrestling his way in through the front door with his arms around a seven-foot Christmas tree which was equally intent on resisting him when he heard the phone ringing.

The tree was nominally wrapped in Cellophane, but enough of its upthrust branches remained at liberty to have snagged in his hair, gloves and coat and give the appearance of pushing him backwards as he attempted to guide them both into the hall. He swore vigorously into its malicious needles.

'It's Patrick,' Caroline called, from the kitchen.

'I'll have to call him back.'

'He says it's urgent. It might be work.'

He could just see her, the other side of the tree, holding the phone out hopefully.

'Caro, I'm dealing with this. Tell him I'll ring back, OK?'

'Hurry *up*, Dad. Tip it sideways.'

Daisy was jigging up and down on the balls of her feet in the porch behind him, desperate to assault the tree with flounces and glitter.

'I'm doing my best here. Why don't you go in the back door?'

Greg felt the tree give a sideways feint and disengage itself from his grasp; as he lunged to save it, a needle sheared off and speared right down under his fingernail.'Jesus!'

'I'll just tell him you'll ring him back then, shall I?'

'*Yes!*'

Greg glowered at the tree. Bloody Christmas had tramped round again and what had he achieved since the last one? A garden furniture advert and a piss-poor sitcom pilot about the pratfalls of a pair of daytime television presenters which, even in the unlikely event of a series having been commissioned, would still only have been available to insomniacs with NASA reception equipment, so remote and untraceable was the satellite station that had turned it down. That was the sum total of the career renaissance Patrick had promised him after his West End debut; of course, if he were allowed to take on stage roles, things might have been different, but a moratorium had been introduced on any work that would take him away from home for months at a time. Caroline wanted him to concentrate on television – a week or two filming at most, better money, higher profile – he could see the appeal from a layman's point of view, but after a year of unsuccessful auditions, he had given up trying to explain to her what he and Patrick knew very well: you don't suddenly decide you want television, it has to decide it wants you. And it seemed, for the moment at least, to have decided quite comprehensively that it had no use for Greg. There could be nothing Patrick had to tell him that could possibly require the word 'urgent'.

On the other hand, he thought, since he last did battle with a Christmas tree, he had managed to get married and have a child, and not with the same person, which some might consider an achievement of sorts. He wondered, briefly, what the little boy would be getting for Christmas, and felt a pang. Then he reminded himself that he was only one, he wouldn't even know it was Christmas, much less realize his father wasn't there.

'Did you call Patrick back?' Caroline asked him, ten minutes later, when he had persuaded the tree up to a jaunty angle of perpendicular, wedged in a bucket of sand that was clearly too small to support its weight convincingly, but was all he had without going back to the garden centre for a new one, which he was buggered if he was going to do on top of everything else. Her tone was chivvying, glazed in insouciance, and he wanted to point out to her that it was all very well, all this carefully disguised nagging about how little work he was getting, when she was the one who had effectively shut down his main source of income. She had even asked him, a couple of months earlier, why he didn't try to get more adverts – they paid well, and they only took a day to film. *Because I'm an ACTOR!* he had bellowed back, hearing himself sounding like a composite of everyone in the theatre that he hated. Advertisements stripped you of dignity; they flayed you open and exposed you to your peers. Besides, the kinds of adverts he got were barely worth the shame, in terms of remuneration. Barbara Bathurst had told him that she once turned down three hundred and fifty thousand for a two-minute airline commercial; to his incredulity, she had merely replied, apparently without self-consciousness, 'I feel about advertisements rather as those South American Indians do about having their photographs taken, you know – every time you do one, it robs you of a little bit of your soul.' Greg didn't tell her that they could cheerfully have had whatever was left of his soul for three hundred and fifty grand, but no world airlines had ever approached Greg. He had more of a wood-stain and lawn-conditioner type of face, apparently.

'Dad, can you get the ladder? Dad – get the ladder, Dad, I'm going to do the star. Dad, where's the ladder?'

'I can't do everything at once. The ladder's under the stairs.'

Daisy spun on her heel.

'No – I'll get it, it's stuck behind the – I'll call him when I've done this, OK? Wait for me, Daisy, you can't get it out by yourself.'

'I'm just thinking, it might be about work.'

'Yes, all *right*. He's not going to self-destruct if I don't get back to him within five minutes.'

'The star has to go on first, before the lights, otherwise they don't stay on the top branch.'

'All *right*, I'm doing it.'

The only thing to be said for Christmas, Greg thought, apart from the general licence to drink, was that it had the power to recall Daisy from the sullen murk of teen insolence that she seemed so prematurely to have entered, back to the bright field of childhood. It was the first time he had heard her voice register a tone other than disdain for months.

He and Daisy had just established the star on the top of the tree, and had braided the two strings of lights – both, miraculously, still working since the previous year – with careful weight around its branches, when Caroline opened the patio doors in the kitchen, admitting the dog, which came jackknifing through the hall, its big stupid tongue flapping around its ears like a windsock, caught its leg in a trailing flex and pulled the whole fragile enterprise down on top of it. Daisy cried, Greg swore with epiphanic fervour, the dog yowled and, in the midst of all this, the phone rang.

'It's Patrick again,' Caroline said, with the inexplicable calm of women, and held out the phone. Greg extricated himself with difficulty.

'Christ, Pat – *what?*'

'I had Sally here today. She's understandably not altogether happy with your scam. She's planning to take you to court and then drag both of us through the tabloids. I thought you'd like to know. Happy Christmas.'

Greg clamped a hand over the receiver superstitiously, as if Sally's name had the power to self-amplify around the hall.

'I'll just have to check those dates in my diary, hang on,' he said, loudly. 'I'll just go through to the office.' With the door shut, he said, in a voice of conspiracy and intrigue, 'Fuck. What else did she say?'

'She used the word fraud a lot. And – look Greg, what you do regarding her and the child is nothing to do with me, but she knows a lot of people, and I frankly don't want my business being mentioned in connection with child-support fraud. So get it sorted out.'

'How could she connect you?'

'You've told the Child Support Agency you earn eighty quid a week. She knows that's not true, and she also knows that my contracts will show how much you really earned. She said they might be able to subpoena my accounts.'

'I don't think they can do that.'

'Well, I don't really want to have to find out.'

'Martin says it's all within the law.' Greg was having trouble keeping his voice hushed. 'He assured me it was all legal.'

'Maybe you should get Martin to read the small print again. She seems convinced that what you've done comes under, what did she call it, Wilful Deprivation of Earnings. Anyway, Greg, it's about more than the letter of the law. If she goes around telling people you've hired an accountant to get out of your child support, which is basically the truth, then it will affect your reputation. And mine, if it looks like I've condoned it. So, for God's sake, talk to Caroline, just make some kind of settlement and get it over with. Don't let this drag through a court case and the bloody papers.'

'She can't prove it. She'd have to have my bank statements or something.'

There was a pause. He could hear the in-breath of Patrick's being-patient sigh.

'I think it would be a very big mistake for you to underestimate her any more than you have already.'

'It would be illegal for her to get access to my bank statements.'

'Yes, and it might well turn out to be illegal to dodge your child support with a bit of creative accounting, so just get this thing done and dusted, will you?'

'She really said she'd go to the papers?'

'Not as such. But she's very angry. If I were you I wouldn't push her. She suggested I might want to lose you as a client if I don't want guilt by association.'

Greg pushed a hand through his hair, creating half a mohican.

'That's blackmail, isn't it?'

'I wouldn't start trying to get litigious here, Greg. I don't think you could effectively argue that you're in the right. Just for God's sake get it buried before Christmas. I've got other clients, you know, and I'd like to remain on good terms with Avocet, for a start, and Tony Czajkowski. Don't make everyone's life difficult.'

'I'll talk to Caroline. But she won't want to be seen to back down.'

'Neither will Sally. So if you want a war, you'll get one. But if I were you –'

'Yes, if you were me, Pat, you'd never have needed to have this conversation.' There was a silence. 'How did she look?'

'Sally?'

'Of course Sally.'

Patrick hesitated.

'She looked thin.'

'She always was thin.'

'No, I mean – she looked sort of hollow. And tired. She looked ill, actually, Greg, though I'm not saying that to make you feel bad.'

'She's bound to be a bit tired, she's got a baby. Did she say she was ill?'

'No, but she was very – I don't know. Jittery. A bit manic. She looked like someone who's on the edge of something, although she was trying to cover it up.'

Greg felt suddenly alarmed, and at the same time could not make his brain move fast enough to swerve this thought: if Sally went mad and killed herself, that would solve all his problems in one move; she would no longer be a threat to Caroline, and they could adopt the child . . .

'On the edge of what?'

'I don't know, I'm not a doctor. But she had that look of – how can I explain it? Someone who doesn't much care what happens to them next. And you don't want to be provoking people in that state, because they might do anything.'

'I'll talk to Caroline. I'll make her listen.'

In his ear, he heard the silence of Patrick's lack of belief.

'How's your dad, anyway?'

'Oh, you know.' Greg began to pick at his thumbnail. 'It's hard to get anything out of the doctors. He's coming to us for Christmas, when he's finished the treatment.'

'Prostate's one of the easy ones, you know – they can blast it pretty efficiently.'

'So they keep saying.'

'Well, all the best to him, eh.'

When he emerged from the office, he found that Caroline had righted the tree (how? it was twice her size), rehung the lights and was hovering expectantly for him in the hall.

'What news from Patrick, then?'

Greg wished he could see what his own face was doing. He made an effort to pull it back to neutral.

'I didn't get that detective thing.'

'Oh.' Caroline did not bother to mask her disappointment. 'Well, I'm sure there'll be another one. You said it wasn't all that good, anyway. You said the plot was rubbish.'

'It was better than a wood-stain ad.'

This Christmas was supposed to be an especially parsimonious affair in the Burns household, on Caroline's instructions, given Greg's relatively thin year and the expense of the wedding; presents, entertaining and outings were to be conducted on a far more stringent scale than in the past, with clearly defined budgets, which Greg privately considered unfair on him and on Daisy in particular, since the wedding had been to a large degree Caroline's present to herself. He was having to fight very hard to keep such thoughts at the margins of his consciousness; his retrospective resentment at the unnecessary scale of her expenditure on the reception was growing daily in the shadow of his father's illness. Tom was now four weeks into his initial course of radiotherapy, bravely making his way to and from the hospital every day on the bus, until the side effects had begun to permeate – the day he told Greg that he had had to jump off the bus well before his own stop because he'd been afraid he was going to go to the toilet right there and then, with no warning, in his phrase, and had had to find a nearby pub, and to cover his embarrassment had felt obliged to stop and have a half, just to save face, and then in the confusion of the beer and the treatment had boarded the wrong bus, and it had taken him over an hour and a half to get home. Tom had told this story in the spirit of an anecdote on one of Greg's weekend visits to York, but Greg had felt the force of his father's sense of shame and indignity and the fear that had come with it, and was overcome with compassion. He had read the literature and knew that Tom had too; the inevitable tiredness he could make a show of covering, but the colonic response to the radiation was another matter, and the thought of what it would do to a man like Tom if he should ever soil himself in a public place pierced Greg so thoroughly that he wanted to cry. It would be crucifixion to his father, and he could see that this first near-brush with disaster had left the old man terrified of travelling alone. If he had been a better person, Greg thought, he would have offered to stay in York and take care of his father while he was having the treatment, and he despised himself for being instead the sort of person who thought that spending money could substitute for kindness or filial commitment; money for a local taxi firm to deliver Tom to appointments, money to the woman who cleaned for him to shop and prepare meals as well, the promise of more money for a private hospital next time, should more be needed. And it almost certainly would be, Greg reflected with considerable bitterness, and he was damned if he wasn't going to get the old man the best possible care he could find, which was why at least half of that money should have stayed in the building society and not been frittered away on table arrangements and a five-piece swing band who had sneeringly declined all his requests to play 'Rikki Don't Lose That Number', even though it had been his bloody wedding.

And now, on top of all this, he was supposed to tell Caroline that the child-support issue was back, with new teeth. Patrick was wrong; he had not underestimated Sally, but neither did he underestimate Caroline. This conflict, he suspected, had the potential to become Napoleonic in duration.

'Oh,' he said, as if it had nearly slipped his mind, 'and Patrick saw Sally today. She's going to take me to court over the child-support thing if I don't get it sorted out before Christmas.'

Caroline took whatever expression this had produced out to the kitchen; Greg could only see her back as she began emptying the dishwasher with purposefully explosive noises. When it became clear that she did not intend to engage with this subject, he followed her and stood in the doorway.

'Look – why don't we just get the solicitors to make a basic offer that'll keep her quiet and then we can all put it behind us and forget about it?'

Caroline turned, with a handful of cutlery; Greg stepped back.

'We can forget about it, can we? And since I'm the one who does the household accounts, do you think I'm going to be able to forget about it when I see money going out of our account to *her* every month? How much do you want to give her? I mean, more than you spend on your own child, or the same?'

It was funny, Greg thought, that when she said *your own child* with such emphasis, what she really meant was *her* own child. He thought it more sensible not to point this out.

'We didn't go through all that business of rearranging your accounts for you to just give up a year later and hand her money. Talk to Martin in the morning. He said she couldn't take you to court, anyway.'

'He said she wouldn't be able to get details about the company but she has. And Martin's an accountant, he doesn't know all the ins and outs of family law.'

'So we'll get someone who does.'

'That will cost money. There's Dad to think about.'

'Yes, and paying that bitch money will cost money too, for the next, what, eighteen years, presumably, so maybe you should have thought of that.'

'All right, I'll speak to Martin. But I just think it would be much quicker and easier to get something arranged without involving the courts.'

'Just give in to her, you mean?'

'There are laws.'

'I can't believe the law would really be on the side of a grasping little slapper who gets herself knocked up to try and trap you.' A hot stain of affront had appeared on Caroline's cheeks. 'You *will* fight her, Greg. Every penny you give her is being taken away from Daisy, look at it that way. And how do you think she would feel about that, when we've already told her she can't have what she really wants for Christmas because we can't afford it?'

'She's not getting an iPod for Christmas because I'm trying to stop my father dying and you spent ten grand on a wedding reception.'

The silence pulsed; Caroline's brow contorted briefly, and her eyes clouded. With a show of controlled grief, she took off her wedding ring and placed it on the kitchen table.

'I'm sorry you think our wedding was such a waste of money, Greg,' she said, in a voice thick with hurt.

'Caro!'

The click of the front door was loaded with accusation. Greg could not tell if she was acting.

'Where's Mum gone?' Daisy called, from the hall.

'She's just popped out for a minute.'

'Have you had another fight?'

'No, no. Everything's fine.'

'Why were you shouting?'

'I'm a bit uptight with your Grandad being poorly, that's all.'

For the first time in months, it seemed, Daisy quite spontaneously put her arms around his waist and laid her head against his solar plexus.

'It's going to be all right, Dad. Loads of people have cancer and get better.'

'Right.' Greg stroked her hair absently. Who had told her Tom had cancer – not him, he was sure. The same person who had given her such blithe assurance about the outcome? Caroline, or one of her teachers?

'I don't know *what* I'd do without Grandad,' Daisy said into his jumper, with a theatrical sigh. Greg was perplexed; Daisy only saw her grandfather every couple of months, at most, and over the past year had seemed only bored or inconvenienced by his visits. But perhaps grandparents had a special symbolism for children, he thought, beyond their individual reality; family is what anchors them. And he felt the pang again, the troubled sense that if his father was dying, he ought to have the chance to see the grandson he had always wanted.

But to bring the child to Tom – assuming that Sally would even countenance such a suggestion, which seemed increasingly unlikely now that she had rumbled his accounting strategy – would have to be done without Caroline's knowledge, and he was not sure that their relationship could sustain the weight of any more lies.

23

A week before Christmas, on a day of iron-brown hardness, a uniform colour of cloud and street and landscape, Sally sat in the driver's seat of a parked Nissan Micra in a residential street in King's Lynn, smoking her way through a pack of Camels and wondering, as if at a distance from herself, what she usefully expected to achieve from this endeavour.

On the passenger seat beside her were the cigarettes, the AA *Book of the Road* and her camera. Already the interior of the small car felt jaundiced with smoke, the staticky fabric of its seats kippered with Sally's filth, and it was her mother's car, she would object and quite probably ban Sally from borrowing it again, although Sally was hoping that a quick blast round the M25 with all the windows open on the way home might partially scour the traces of her wasted day. She had contemplated getting out of the car to smoke, but the air was cold as metal and she was already conspicuous enough, hunched there at the wheel for more than an hour, wearing a tweed cap of Jeff's pulled down around her ears.

She hadn't told her mother where she was going or why she needed the car; it had taken her nearly three hours to drive there, around the sour, wasted edges of London and further north, into scarred fields of East Anglia with its broad skies, pale with a queasy winter sun.

The houses in Greg's street were all detached, most of them whitewashed, some with ersatz half-timbering and leaded windows, although Sally was glad to see that his was not one of these. (Glad – why? Why should it still matter to her that he show himself to be above provincial tastelessness, when she was actively seeking reasons to think the worst of him? This she couldn't answer.) Ranges of conifers sequestered them from the street; in the gravelled driveways squatted upscale family cars, Audis, Jeeps and Discoverys, and all the street-facing windows, as well as some of the trees and hedges, were a riot of festive bulbs. Greg's drive was abandoned, but she could see a frieze of grinning reindeer Blu-Tacked to the inside of the front window, and a wreath of interwoven gilded twigs hung on the front door. Sally imagined that, over the years, these items and others like them would have acquired superstitious properties in Greg's family; she pictured the reindeer going missing one year, perhaps, and Daisy searching frantically through all the boxes of decorations, thinking that if the reindeer weren't in the window Christmas would somehow go wrong, would fail to be intact and itself. She had been the same herself as a child; a family Christmas was a thing of ritual, with its relics and fixtures, and any one element misplaced or forgotten was like a faulty bulb in a string of lights. Her mother's house was still full of such bric-a-brac; papier-mâché figures of Mary and Joseph that she had made at school; handmade German ornaments from a craft fair; glass spheres, delicate as bubbles, that prismed the lights back as they slowly turned.

With the gradual readmittance of her father into her life, other Christmas-related memories had regained contours, as if through fog; the shape of Mac on his haunches, lighting a fire, or the half-crouch before shouldering the tree, testing its weight; the sight of him laughing in his bright tissue-paper hat as he carved meat, or his back, solidly buttoned up in a donkey jacket, hands clenched in his pockets as he led them on the obligatory after-dinner walk in the prohibitive bluster of a December afternoon. During the years of Mac's absence, Elizabeth and Sally had fitted themselves into the gaps he left, and had continued with the repetition of the Christmas rituals, as if nothing had altered, a defiant little play of courage and denial. For three years, they had stepped round the gaping hole at the centre of their existence without ever mentioning that it was there at all. Sally remembered how they would sit over lunch, groaning over the cracker jokes, setting out the board and the pieces for Trivial Pursuit, and how she would know that they were separately wondering where Mac might be, and with whom he was spending his Christmas, and neither of them ever corralled these thoughts into a question, for fear of damaging the structure that kept them whole. That must have been when she learned to dissemble, she thought.

Then Jeff had arrived, trailing his own Christmas expectations: two married daughters and three grandchildren, whose rituals and relics were slowly incorporated into their own, and her childhood Christmas became diluted, or embellished, depending on how you looked at it. This – her own son's second Christmas – should have been the time to begin establishing a new store of traditions and memories, customized for her own new family. Except that she felt less and less like a family; she felt like an aberration in a world of secure family units, an appendix to other people's lives, and she pictured with a hiccup of dread a future in which she and her child spent their Christmases like the Virgin Mary, knocking mutely on the doors of friends and relatives, big-eyed with silent pleading, hoping to be invited in to share a corner of warmth and companionship. The thought of the effort that would be required to sustain good cheer in such circumstances left Sally feeling exhausted. Most thinking left her feeling exhausted at the moment.

Manny's nursery had organized a Christmas concert. Elizabeth had been beside herself, stationed at the front with her camera like a paparazzo, jostling companionably with all the other grandparents and parents. Sally had lurked awkwardly at the back of the hall, out of the audience's line of sight, looking more like a potential baby-snatcher than a proud mother, though her heart had been wrenched nearly out of her with love at the sight of her little boy, plumply dressed as a snowflake, his head whirling in bewilderment at the influx of people and noise as he tried manfully to clap his hands in the right places. Elizabeth had found her outside at the end, pacing the car park, tense and pale. 'What's the matter?' her mother had asked, as Manny struggled to remove himself from her arms to Sally's. 'Didn't you enjoy it?' She had cried then, because she had wanted so much to enjoy it, and had willed herself so hard to, and she couldn't explain to her mother that the problem was the dads. There had been so many of them, in their Ralph Lauren shirts and their pressed trousers, with their silver cases of video equipment and digital image-making; all the middle-class dads who took their parenting so seriously and read books about it on the train, who had taken the afternoon off work to cheer on the little parade of wonky costumes and distracted singing, whose mere existence lanced her with such a painful sense of her own incompleteness that she had been compelled to remove herself from their force field. It was not that she particularly wanted Greg any longer; not in himself, for his own qualities, but he had left her with a lack that had a specific outline and was visible to everyone, as if she were an amputee.

The twinkling lights in the window of Greg's house only underlined the chasm between his life and hers, and between the lives of his children. She had not really known why she had wanted to see any of this, the life he had chosen instead of her; the theory, attested to by the presence of the camera beside her, had been to gather some evidence that he was not living the life of a minimum-wage earner, but apart from the immediate realization that you couldn't simply stand in the middle of a street and take photographs of someone's house without arousing suspicion, especially not a street so emblazoned with Neighbourhood Watch stickers, Sally had found herself checked by something else. A reluctant comprehension, perhaps. This, like Crowbourne, was the kind of small town which bred the kind of small life that she and Greg both professed to fear; that he had wanted to get out, to a different kind of existence, she believed and understood. But she also understood better the impossibility of leaving. A home, with all its unique resonances and leitmotifs, was a powerful thing, it wound its tendrils around you invisibly, so that perhaps the only way to part from it was to do as Mac had done, to break every tie at once and not turn around. Greg had lacked either the steel or the cruelty to do that, and so home had slowly reeled him back. Sally realized that she had not had a home since leaving her mother's house; there were only ever places where she slept, and she never did much of that. The idea of creating a home had not interested her, but seeing Greg's house, the shine and pull of it, made her realize how much she must have craved it. Had that unarticulated need been at work somewhere in the decision to have the baby, she wondered, and it occurred to her that, on some profound level, she and Greg must have wanted to exchange lives, but failed to recognize that mirrored desire, each thinking that they would acquire the life they lacked in the person of the other. It was not Caroline who was unleavable, Sally thought; it had not been, as she had imagined, a straight choice between the two of them. He had contemplated unravelling an entire ecosystem with no certainty that he would survive in an environment outside it, and in the end he had not been prepared to gamble. Knowing this, she could see him with more compassion – though none of it excused the fact of the shell company, the foresight that had gone into that, she thought tightly, circling each shoulder in turn in an effort to ease the stiffness in her back.

What kind of mother was she, anyway – it was Christmas, and she was skulking in a car outside her ex-lover's house in a large hat instead of singing carols and making mince pies with her young child. She guessed that Caroline almost certainly made mince pies. Probably with an apron on.

Sally was considering starting the engine to drive home, or at least to a service station where she might make some pretence of pushing food over the surface of a plate between cigarettes – she seemed to have lost all her appetite lately – when she was disturbed by the guttural noise of a large vehicle and looked in the mirror to see a maroon Land Cruiser turning into the street behind her. She shunted herself down in the seat, pulled the peak of the cap down further over her face and opened the road map with it tilted towards the window. Now she just looked like an unskilled stalker – which was effectively what she was. A few other cars were parked along the street; most of the houses had double garages and drives. It would only take a glance for Greg to see her, and she could not analyse her own motives sufficiently to know whether she desperately wanted this to happen or desperately did not. In part she believed that Greg would simply look straight through her, such was her increasing sense that she was not really there, was not actually participating in her own life, but merely observing the husk of her physical self grind through the daily routines necessary to keep her child healthy and money coming in. If anyone had asked, she would have found it hard to name anything about which she felt excited, or was looking forward to, or was working on with enthusiasm, nor could she visualize a time in the immediate future when this would not be the case. She was sufficiently widely read to know these were symptoms of depression, and sufficiently self-deceiving to argue that if you were in a state of mind objectively to diagnose your own depression, you couldn't be all that depressed.

Greg rattled the Land Cruiser into his driveway without a glance at the small brown hatchback parked opposite, ratcheted the handbrake and sprang down into a crush of gravel. It ought to have been more of a shock, seeing him, Sally thought, but after more than a year he remained exactly as she remembered him: the long fringe, the lop-sided mouth, the eyes that she looked into every day in the face of her son. The shock was in the blankness she experienced on seeing him, as if the conflicting ferocity of fury and attachment that she had entertained over the past year had conspired to cancel one another out and leave her with only a flat line. This was the person with whom she had chosen to create a life, and yet, now, he was no more than a bloke she had once known. The life they had ignited was already entire and following its own course, regardless of either of them. Nevertheless, she could not deny an intense urge to rush across the street and kiss him, then slam his head in the car door.

Greg opened the passenger side and carefully reached in to help with the complicated descent of a fragile old man with patchy white hair, who leaned on Greg and walked at a painful incline. At the sight of him, Sally did sit up; this must be Greg's father, her son's grandfather, the one person she had come to believe could act as a convincing intercessor. He was still alive, then, she was pleased to see, but living with Greg and Caroline now, which pleased her less, but perhaps explained why he had not responded to her letter.

'You'd want to know, wouldn't you?' she had asked her own father, on the phone, while she was still working out how she might introduce herself and her son into Tom Burns's life as a means of reaching Greg. There were two subjects alone which had the power to animate Sally in her present state of mind; one was compiling her legal offensive against Greg and Caroline for the Child Support Appeal, the other was the idea of making contact with her son's grandfather before it was too late, and it was indicative of her sense of alienation that the one person she could talk to in any depth about either topic was Mac, who was involved with equal enthusiasm in the legal process, and whose old investigative instincts had been woken by the idea of crusading against an institutional injustice whose principal victim was his own small grandson.

'Imagine you were him. You'd want to know if you had a grandchild, wouldn't you?'

Mac had prevaricated; she could almost hear him plaiting and unplaiting his beard over the phone.

'It's a very difficult business.'

'But you were dying to see Manny, since he was born. And imagine if you had cancer and you didn't know how long you had – wouldn't you hate the thought that you'd a grandson you never met?'

'You know,' Mac had said, and she could picture him settling back, as if to begin a long story, 'you get older and you do spend a lot of time thinking about what you'll leave behind and who'll carry on your name, all that. I can't think that anyone would be unhappy to know they'd one more grandchild keeping the genes going. But your situation – you know, it could make a profound difference to the relationship he has with his son, do you see? And if he's sick and he has to depend on Greg to look after him. Would the discovery of a grandson be worth the discovery that his son is less than the man he believes him to be?'

'And what do you think?'

'Ah, now.' Mac was quiet for a moment. 'If I was dying, Sally, I don't know that I wouldn't rather go on believing the child I raised had grown into a decent fella rather than find out otherwise, you'd only blame yourself. If your man's very ill, you know, it might be a kindness to leave him in ignorance. The child's too young to remember, and it's a terrible thing, to overturn a man's faith in his own son. You don't want a revolution when you're old, if you can avoid it.'

'But if his faith in his son is misplaced? Doesn't he have the right to know what kind of person Greg is?'

'That he's not been a good father to Manny doesn't mean he hasn't been a good son. But you'll decide for yourself anyway.'

Sally had havered for a couple of days; so much seemed to depend on how ill Tom really was. If he was in any fit state to act as a willing conduit between her and Greg, then she owed it to Manny (she convinced herself) at least to make an overture. But she didn't know how she might go about ascertaining Tom's condition; the Internet had furnished her with the addresses of eight Thomas Burnses in York, two of whom had the correct middle initial; a phone call to the first had yielded an answerphone message in the voice of a young woman informing her that Tom and Sarah were not home at the moment, the second had merely rung unanswered, and she had taken this one to be Greg's father. She could, she presumed, make further calls to all the area hospitals asking in the guise of a relative if they had a Tom Burns, but was unsure of the protocol; even if she located him, would anyone tell her over the phone how serious his illness was, or would she be expected to produce some identifying shibboleth and by the want of it arouse suspicions, even alert Greg to the fact that she had been making enquiries?

She had not progressed with this dilemma when, three days after her visit to Patrick Williams, she had received a letter from Greg's solicitors advising her to stop threatening their client and his associates, which had so incensed her that she wanted to grab somebody – Greg, the lawyers, Patrick, or just the person who pushed in front of her at the cashpoint that morning – by the lapels and headbutt them until their face bled. She had had the utmost faith both in Patrick's diplomatic skills and in Greg's reason, though there had been scant sign of it in the past year; she had not believed for a moment that, even knowing she had uncovered his creative accounting, he would opt to go through a legal battle. That he had was a testament to either his irredeemable stupidity or Caroline's intransigence and his own craven submission to it. In that case, Sally had thought, he will get the fight of his life. She had few avenues left; there was the legal process, but that was time-consuming, orthodox and ordained to follow a set path. It would be a far better weapon, she felt, if she could get Tom Burns on her side. If Tom could come to love the little boy, perhaps he could persuade Greg to try. With the failure of Patrick as an ambassador, she had come to think of Tom as her last hope of communicating with Greg.

She had written him a letter, explaining herself as gently as she could, and taking care not to use any loaded words about Greg or the way he had behaved to her. She had enclosed a photograph of Manny, a portrait taken by the official photographer at the nursery in which, she thought, his expression was so purely Greg's in miniature that Tom could not for a moment have entertained doubts as to her veracity. She had not overtly suggested contact, but merely expressed a wish to let him know that his grandson existed, and written her details at the foot of the page in unmistakable black capitals, in case his eyesight was poor.

Now, watching Greg lead him to the front door, with its crown of golden twigs, she realized her own lack of foresight; of course he would be living with Greg and Caroline, if he was ill, so he would not have got the letter, and now she could not possibly contact him. And if he were to die, she reflected, and it fell to Greg to return to the old man's house in York and sort his possessions, he would find the letter, and recognize her writing, and what would he think? Would he despise her for deliberately upsetting a dying man and trying to conscript him to her cause, or would he be moved that she had tried, at least, to give Manny some sense of his paternal family? Might he even be moved enough to get in touch, even – or perhaps because of – having recently lost his own father?

The conjoined figures of Greg and his father were swallowed into the festive light and warmth of the big house, and the front door closed behind them. Sally remained behind the wheel, out in the freezing street, smoking another cigarette, under the stripped trees whose branches scratched at the unkind sky. In moments of pure rage, she had developed a fantasy of turning up on Greg's doorstep with a gun. It seemed absurd now, in the reality of daylight. If the unconscious purpose of her visit had been to inflict an even greater sense of loneliness and betrayal on herself, then it had not been an altogether wasted day, she thought. The Micra's engine coughed into life, and she dragged it into a three-point turn to face the journey home.

❧

Greg led his father into the sitting room and settled him in an armchair.

'Nippy in here,' Tom remarked, looking around; it was said matter-of-factly, but Greg took it as a criticism.

'Hang on, then, Dad, I'll put the fire on.'

'Could do with a cuppa.'

'Yes, I'll put the fire on, and then I'll make some tea.'

'We saw some nice things, didn't we?'

Tom said this with effortful cheeriness, as if to reassure him that he'd enjoyed the outing to town, the sight of irritable shoppers and their impatient children, Christmas consumer frenzy blaring out of them over the sounds of the Salvation Army band playing 'Hark the Herald Angels' outside the Town Hall, though Tom had not been strong enough to stand and listen for long. Greg wondered if he had enjoyed it, really, or if even giving the impression of pleasure these days was as much of a chore for him as the activities themselves.

'Yes, we did, Dad.'

He bent to switch on the electric fire, and the coppery-blue flame effect licked into life with a breath of gas over the artificial coals; he was caught, suddenly, by an image of his father on winter mornings, crouched as he was now in front of a grate, but patiently laying out newspaper, arranging kindling, setting logs he'd chopped himself and brought in from the shed: building a real fire, one of the ineradicable smells and sounds of his childhood. He, Greg, wouldn't have

375

known where to start. This is the kind of man I am, he thought; where he laboured, I press a button. He spent time, and got his hands dirty, and made something real. No wonder he never showed any interest in what I do. Everything about me is fake. Greg had been having many such thoughts since his father had finished his course of radio-therapy and come to live with them, visibly eroded. Tom was now having hormone therapy, which, as Greg understood it, was designed to reduce his testosterone to negligible levels, to take away what made him a man. Greg was more afraid of its import than his father seemed, though Tom was reluctant to discuss his condition in anything more than its essentials, even with the doctors; Greg found himself watching his father sidelong at unguarded moments for signs – absurdly – of Tom beginning to show womanish features, as if expecting his father gradually to start looking like his mother.

But Tom, who in recent years had made such artistry out of com-plaint, belligerence and fault-finding, with the world in general and the part of it filled by Greg in particular, now that his low-level grum-bling had been legitimized by circumstance, now that he had the best reason in the world to moan – pain, and the fear of death – was show-ing nothing but courage, gratitude and a desire to look on the bright side that at times verged on infuriating. And Greg flagellated himself inwardly at every demonstration of the old man's fortitude, for all the past occasions when he had guiltily resented Tom for having been the one who lived to old age instead of his mother; for the times when he had considered the old man a burden. The doctors were efficient-ly political in their inability to engage the words 'yes' or 'no' when presented with a question; they said things like 'promising' and 'monitor', and Greg still had no better idea of whether his father was going to die, but he understood very clearly, as Christmas approached that, for no one clear reason, he wanted to confess.

'I like to hear a brass band,' Tom said, frowning with the effort of keeping two hands steady around a mug of tea. 'Used to be you'd hear the Sally Army on every corner. I suppose folk don't join it so much these days, do they? Old-fashioned, now. Everyone's playing golf of a Saturday.'

Greg jolted at the word *Sally*; inside this house, it was a profanity. Let it slip inadvertently in front of Caroline, and you could almost hear her huge fury revving for take-off. If she had been within earshot even of Tom's innocently familiar reference, her eyes would have shot black fire at Greg, just to let him know that she'd heard it, that she was constantly alert to it, and would not forget. But she was not home; she and Daisy were Christmas shopping in Norwich for the day with Andrea and Molly, and he was alone with Tom.

'Dad?'

'Son.'

'There's something I need to tell you.'

'Fire away.'

'It's difficult.'

'Take your time.'

'This is – you mustn't say anything to Caroline. It's between you and me, you understand?'

'Right you are.'

Under his father's steady eyes, Greg felt his resolution wither. He looked away to the symmetrical choreography of the waltzing flames.

'The year before last – Caroline and I, we – had some problems.'

He glanced up to check that Tom was listening; his father nodded.

'I thought we might, you know. Split up. We weren't getting on, for lots of reasons.'

Already he was muffling it, he thought, spreading the blame, softening the impact. If he couldn't even be honest now –

'I did something very bad.'

He looked; again, Tom nodded.

'I – there was a girl. I had an affair.'

Tom, seeming to realize a response was expected, said, 'These things happen.'

'Yes. It lasted, I don't know, a few months. Then I realized that I didn't want to leave. I wanted to keep my home, my family. So – it was over.'

'So it was over.'

'Yes, but – this is the hard part.'

'Take your time, son.'

'She had a child. A boy. I've never seen him, but he's mine. He lives in Surrey. He was one in October. And I don't know why I wanted you to know, but I did. So there it is. You have a grandson. I'm sorry. I'm not proud of myself. I've made a mess of things, I know.'

Still the old man's face was as calm as before; he drank tea from his mug, and Greg watched its slow progress down his ragged throat.

The room ticked around them.

'Manus,' Tom said, eventually. 'Irish name. She calls him Manny.'

Silent shock tremored through Greg, and a concurrent sense of inevitability. His father knew; of course he did. His father had always known when he lied, perhaps that was why he never came to any of Greg's performances; he was unconvinced by his attempts to pretend.

'You know.'

'She wrote me a letter. Only recently – a few weeks ago. She sent a photograph.'

'You didn't say anything.'

'It was for you to tell me.'

'What did she say?' Sharp alarm squeezed him; Sally had the resources to find out his father's address, she had already found out about his accounting. She had this in common with Caroline: she would not lightly forgive his deceptions. What might she have told his father – and did Tom at this moment, had he already, for several weeks, begun to look at him with disgust in the light of it?

'You can read it yourself, if you'd like. It's in my suitcase, in the pocket with the zipper. Go on.'

The spare room was already heavy with the stale odour of old men, although Tom was scrupulously clean; a smell Greg associated with unwashed hair and dandruff on the shoulders of cardigans and those grim days in the room above the Cross Keys when Caroline had thrown him out. Tom's trousers were neatly folded over the back of the chair, his shoes paired squarely with the toes tucked under the wardrobe. In the front pocket of the suitcase at the foot of the bed, he found an envelope bearing his father's name in Sally's capitals, an arresting conjunction.

Cross-legged on the floor, he took with shaking hands a photograph; it was facing away from him, and he saw that Sally had written on the back 'Manus Anthony Burns McGinley (Manny), aged 1'. His heart, so insistent in its skidding and thudding only moments earlier, seemed to be silent, or to have disappeared. He was afraid to look at this, of what it might unleash in him.

Here was the face of a little boy. It might have been the little boy whose face had sat on his own mother's dresser for years; they had much in common: a certain lean to the smile, the same downward curve of the brows, the upturned nose, the quizzical eyes. But this face was modified: there was a length and fineness to its shape that came from Sally; the hair was blonder; there was a ferocity of expression that he recognized from her and not from himself. The child was a work of art; a thing of strong beauty. For a long time he looked into these eyes, blinking against his swarming thoughts. Then he picked up the letter.

Dear Mr Burns, It said.

Please forgive me for writing to you out of the blue. This little boy is your grandson. His name is Manus Anthony Burns McGinley and he was one on the 22nd October. We call him Manny. It was my grandfather's name. It has taken me a long time to write to you, and you may be wondering why. The truth is, I heard that you were ill, and I wanted you to know about your grandson, and have the chance to look at him.

How did she know Tom was ill? Everyone seemed to be communicating without him; somewhere there was a place where all the people in the carefully compartmentalized parts of his life were getting together to talk about him. What else might she know? What else might his father know, or Caroline, or Daisy, or his friends? Then he thought: Patrick.

I thought you should at least have the chance to make your own choice. That may be wrong or selfish of me, and I can only apologize, and assure you that I will understand if you would rather not know. I loved your son, but that is in the past. We have our own lives now. I don't know much about the future, but I can be sure that one day Manny will ask me about you, and I want to be able to tell him that I tried. If you would like to ask me anything about him, here is my address.

Yours
Sally McGinley

Between the clear-eyed stare of the child, and the phrase *I loved your son*, which seemed to be written in neon – why had she never said that to him, when it mattered? Might it have made a difference? – Greg was not sure how long he sat on the floor, nor at what point he started to cry, nor did he hear the usually unmissable noises that heralded Tom's slow progress up the stairs – the shuffle and wheeze and muted grunts to accompany each step – he only noticed that, after some time had apparently passed, his father was kneeling with difficulty beside him with a hand on his shoulder and a proffered handkerchief.

'He's a Burns, all right,' Tom commented, when Greg was less racked.

Greg crammed the heels of his hands into his eyes.

'I made her have a test.'

'To do what?'

'Prove he was mine.'

'Well. There's sense in that. But look at the lad. There's no question.'

'Caroline wouldn't let me see him. I had to choose. Do you see that, Dad? I didn't have a choice. I mean, I did have a choice, I had to choose between my children. I had to choose the one I knew over the one I didn't, and then I couldn't – I didn't want to see him, because –'

'You didn't want to be reminded.'

'My wife wants to behave as if he doesn't exist.'

'Well, of course she does. But he does exist, and you're both fools if you can only get along by pretending he doesn't. Because I tell you this, son, one day he will look you in the face and ask you why. And he could be five, or ten, or twenty-five years old, but you'll owe him that. It would be a dreadful thing to have a child of yours grow up to hate you. Children forgive. He won't forgive you so readily when he's a grown man.'

'What am I supposed to do?'

'What do you think your mother would say?'

'Christ, Dad.' Greg raised his knees and pressed his face into them; here was his father, depleted by weeks of hospital treatment, supposedly here to be looked after and instead having to crouch on a cold floor to look after a son who, far from being a capable middle-aged adult in command of himself, was behaving like a seven-year-old. 'She'd despise me.'

'Oh, no. No, no – not your mother. She'd be disappointed, but she had compassion, your mother, she understood how people can make mistakes.' Tom left a pause, and Greg wondered if his father might be about to unburden himself with a confession of his own. Instead, he said, 'You know as well as I do. She'd say, you don't walk away from a child. Whatever you do. You only get two people you can count on in this world, your mum and your dad, no bugger else is going to fight your corner. You mustn't take that away from the lad. That's what she'd be saying, if she was sat here.'

'You don't know Caroline.'

'I know you, though, Greg, and you're not a callous man. This'll do you some damage, in the long run.'

Greg wanted to tell his father how little he knew him; how callous he could be with minimal prompting. He wanted to confess that he was, even at that moment, being threatened with legal action because he had asked his accountant – or Caroline had asked, and he had agreed – how he might best avoid contributing to the welfare of this child Tom was urging him to acknowledge. He said none of this, because while his father might show unexpected compassion for human weakness, such a deliberate act could never be attributed to impetuosity and lack of forethought. Stupidity and selfishness were forgivable; cowardice and cruelty were simply inexplicable and, Greg suspected, outside Tom's range of comprehension.

He folded the letter and inserted it back in its envelope. The photograph he kept in his hand.

'Did you write back to her?'

'Not yet. I was waiting to see if you'd talk to me. I had a feeling you might, before too long.'

'Did you?'

'Because I'm dying. No, don't say anything. It does something to everyone's priorities. The letters I've had, folks I haven't spoken to in years. Everybody wants to tell you something before you're gone.'

'You're not dying, Dad. Doctor Katz said you'd responded very positively to the radiotherapy. And if the hormone treatment carries on working –'

'I might not be dying this minute, son, but I'm dying none the less. And I've had a good innings, as they say, but it never feels like long enough when you come to it. But the one thing I'll be thankful for when my time comes is that I don't have any regrets. Not real ones, not things it's too late to put right.'

'Do you want to see him?'

'I wouldn't mind.'

'Well, I won't stop you. But she couldn't bring him here, and you're in no shape to travel on your own. I don't see how it could be arranged.'

'You could drop me off somewhere in town. Or take me back to me own house, she could come there.'

'Maybe.' Greg levered himself up and rubbed his back. 'We can think about it when you're better, if you still want to.'

'I'd like to see him before I die.'

'You've got plenty of time.'

'None of us knows that. You're a stubborn bugger, Greg. Always had to learn the hard way.'

'Yes,' Greg said, because there didn't seem to be another response.

'But you're a good son,' said Tom, unexpectedly, moving in the direction of the bathroom. 'And one day, you might be in need of a good son yourself. It's summat to think about.'

'I do. I will.'

'Blood is blood,' Tom said, and nodded. It seemed to be his last word on the matter. What his father meant by it, he wasn't sure, but to Greg it summoned only images of theatre: prophetic, turbulent, final acts; the Greeks, Shakespeare, Lorca. Blood, family and revenge. Downstairs, he heard the click of the front door and Daisy's excited chirruping in the hall, and realized that he needed to wash the streaks of tears from his face before Caroline noticed him, with her eyes that could pierce lead. His life, he felt, had become not so much tragedy as low farce, ducking in and out of cupboards and trying to keep one room ahead. But even farce had the potential for catastrophe, he thought, as he heard his father calling for assistance from the bathroom, and braced himself to be a good son.

24

Sally was capable of extreme diligence and commitment when a project engaged her mind, and in this instance her mind was not so
much engaged as consumed; despite the growing anomie in every
other area of her life, she worked with obsessive energy on her legal
case because it was by this means, since all others had apparently
failed, that she would show Greg that she was not to be so easily dis-
missed. By the time the Christmas decorations were taken down and
the cards packed away to a recycling charity, she had assembled a
body of evidence sufficient, in Mac's view, to warrant an investigation into Greg Burns's finances. She had documents from Companies
House pertaining to the incorporation of Greg's company, its share
allocations and suspect change of name; she had printouts from
Patrick Williams's company website of Greg's recent CV, detailing
work undertaken in the past two years; there were, reluctantly
secured from Lola, wage slips from *Real* as an indication of what an
actor at Greg's level might expect to earn from a stage play; press
releases for television appearances, even a downloaded still from his
garden furniture advert and a recent page from the *Radio Times* showing him in a cast list as a murder victim in a minor detective drama to
demonstrate that, regardless of his professed status as a company
director, he was still doing what he had always done.

She sat up long into the night at her computer reading transcripts
from Hansard, searching for references to child-support legislation;
when she located relevant debates, she telephoned at their remote
constituency offices all the MPs whose questions indicated some
level of dissatisfaction with the present legislation and talked to them
knowledgeably about gross company profits and dividends and the
clauses in which Revenue Law diverged from Child Support Law.
These conversations she recorded, patiently transcribed and added
to her file. She pored over past White Papers on legislative reform,

dissecting their jargon even while her brain was beaten copper-thin by migraines; she continued to substitute smoking for eating (though only in the garden; nightly she stood tarpaulined in a huge coat under the rain, lighting one off another while squinting to read government statistics in the light from the kitchen window); she slept infrequently, and grew thinner and paler and more distracted until her mother urged her to see a doctor, who gave her the briefest of glances before prescribing anti-depressants. To keep her mother happy, Sally collected the small but unwanted packet from the chemist, but her mistrust only deepened as she took in the encyclopedia of potential side effects – suicidal tendencies, hallucinations, memory loss, libido loss, anxiety, mania and confusion ('I thought they were supposed to cheer you up?' she said, aloud, in the kitchen, to no one) – and when she reached the bold capitalled codicil at the end of the leaflet (@sc:**do not drink any alcohol while taking this medicine**@scx:), that was the clincher – how could anyone be expected even to fake happiness if they weren't allowed a drink? She quietly hid them in the back of a drawer and with what remained of her dwindling energies attempted to rouse herself to a semblance of cheerfulness whenever she was in her mother's company, though she suspected that her show of normality was itself indistinguishable from mania.

By the end of January, with Mac's approval, she sent off a brown envelope fat with accusation to the Appeals Unit of the Child Support Agency and waited for a response. After waiting for a month, she phoned one of the numbers on one of her many pieces of correspondence, provided her reference number, date of birth, post code and mother's maiden name and explained her query at length to someone who then passed her for almost an hour to five further people in different departments, two of whom were not there and one of whom appeared not to speak English, before she was connected to a woman with a thick West Country accent who demanded again all her identifying characteristics and a detailed biographical sketch before confirming that she was indeed through to the right section.

'I was just wondering if you could tell me how long an appeal takes to process?' Sally asked.

There followed an extended pause, during which it was conceivable that the woman had gone out for her lunch break and come back.

'Well,' the woman said, eventually, 'how long's a piece of string?'

Sally put the phone down and banged her head against the door.

After another month, she received a letter, gloriously if curtly informing her that her appeal was considered valid, that an investigation would follow and that she was now on a waiting list and would be contacted when a Tribunal date had been set. Lola took her out for lunch to celebrate and ordered champagne.

'This is a bit premature,' Sally said, drinking it anyway, 'we've still got to have the appeal. It'll take months, and I might lose.'

'Then you'll have another one. At least they've conceded that something dodgy's gone on and they're looking into it.'

'He'll get a good lawyer.'

'You've got a good lawyer.'

'I've got Mac. He hasn't been in court for nearly twenty years. He plays the piano in a Dublin pub band and has a beard down to his nipples. That's my crack legal team.'

'He knows what he's talking about. And you've done so much work.' Lola reached across and patted her hand. 'Everyone's really proud of you, you know. We really admire the way you've made a go of this.'

Sally withdrew her hand and reached for the bottle.

'There's nothing to admire here, ladies and gents. Please move along.'

'That's nonsense. You're bringing up a child on your own, you do an office job, you're fighting this legal stuff all on your own and you're writing a new play – I think you're fantastic.'

Sally waved a hand.

'If you wish.'

'How's it coming along, anyway?'

'What?'

'Your new play.'

'Ah.'

She couldn't help feeling that Lola's admiration was coloured in a large part by gratitude that she was not Sally, that her own life was so happily intact. In truth, Sally did not recognize Lola's version of herself; as she saw it, her mother and the nursery between them were effectively bringing up her son – she was the one who saw him for an hour in the mornings and often not at all when she came home, she was good for a few hours at weekends, which still seemed incalculably long, but even then Elizabeth and Jeff would often take him out in the afternoons so that she could have a couple of hours to herself, when she would feel so flummoxed by all that she wanted to cram into this free time – books, letters, writing, visits to the gym – that she usually ended up lying on her bed with the curtains drawn and failing to sleep. One night Manny had woken, crying, and she had gone in to find him standing like a desperate prisoner pressed to the bars of his cot, calling for his grandma; her appearance, she could tell, was considered a very poor alternative. That she did an office job was indisputable, but only the most generous employer, as Lola had proved to be, would claim that she did it with any degree of efficiency, and the idea that she was writing . . .

She had told Lola that she was writing a new drama because she wanted it to be true, because she thought that if she could make it true, it might save her. To create an alternative world; this had always been her solution. The stage was where she took her doubts and questions, and watched them from a distance, turned them into answers in the form of jokes, in words she gave to other people. If she could just find a subject that would take her out of herself, if she could create people whose lives became more real to her than her own at that point, she had a chance of freeing herself. But whenever she tried to make her scribbled thoughts cohere into some kind of plot, it always circled back to this: love and its negative.

Love, and its inadequacies; the illusions and expectations and projections and longings and all that we demand it to sustain, far more than its flimsy, fictional infrastructure can support. Is this how we get it so wrong, so often? Falling in love was, she suspected, about the vanity of recognition. She had thought she saw in Greg something of herself, but not the best part of herself, not the part she ought to have thought about nurturing. He corresponded to the weakest, most self-involved elements of her character; there had been nothing aspirational in what she had felt for him, and he had left this unappealing part of her exposed to her own critical contempt. Now she was only hollow: empty of love, empty of words. And the English stage, Sally felt, should probably be spared one more spurned lover railing in the dark about failure.

'Oh, it's going great,' she said, and poured herself another drink.

Three months passed. The skies grew higher and lighter as the clouds retreated northwards; in Sally's small garden the crocuses Jeff had planted poked their noses out of the beds and offered small nubs of colour. Faintly, hope began to show at the edges of life. New words clung to Manny every day like burrs, and Sally saw that he had grown into a sunny, laughing child whose mild nature defied every prediction in the books she had only half glanced at regarding toddler tantrums and villainous mood swings. She saw that she was exceptionally lucky. Released from the confines of the house, they undertook long walks at weekends, and trips to the coast; they talked, and laughed, and Sally noticed that her little boy was besotted with her. When she went into his room in the mornings, he greeted her with a face-splitting smile and the rapt eyes of the new lover, utterly gone; 'Mummy's here!' he would exclaim, or sometimes whisper in incredulous delight, and at times on their walks he would turn to her spontaneously, touch her face and say, with wonder wholly disproportionate to its object, '*Mummy.*' Motherhood began to seem less like a job for which she had applied on false promises and been ludicrously hired for want of anyone better, despite an alarming and obvious lack of qualifications, and more like a career which, with the right training and application, she had a chance of taking somewhere. She found herself looking forward to her son's company.

On a Saturday in early June, shortly after lunch, Sally drove her mother's car into the tidy parking lot of a block of warden-patrolled retirement flats outside King's Lynn. She glanced at the back seat where Manny lolled, asleep at an angle, clutching his penguin, and it occurred to her that she was spending another entire day driving to and from the north coast of East Anglia, this time for the sake of an hour in the company of an old man who had nothing at all to do with her, except that he was Greg's father and she hoped that this might prove to be a tangential step towards Greg himself, who was only a couple of miles away. It seemed absurdly circumlocutary. She gathered Manny into her arms and, as she rang the bell, suddenly wanted to run away.

Tom Burns, at his full height, would have filled the doorway, but he was hunched by age and illness, and his cardigan hung loosely from his shoulders. Never the less, he was an oddly imposing figure, and Sally realized that she was slightly afraid of him. She had expected to see more of Greg in him, but although there was an unmistakable identity around the eyes, he struck her as unconnected, entirely separate and himself. It seemed suddenly very presumptuous and foolish to have imagined that she could conscript him as a go-between. He looked at her, with neither affection nor criticism, and nodded.

'Best come in,' he said.

The flat was small, and inescapably clinical, with homogenous fittings and a pervasive smell of disinfectant. What did he think of her, Sally wondered, as she seated Manny, still warm and sleepy, on a narrow pink armchair? What had Greg told him? Did he think she was a terrible slut who was trying to ruin his son's life? Presumably Greg could not have told him the whole truth about his own actions, but he couldn't have painted such an appalling picture of her, surely, or Tom would not have invited her?

'Mulk,' said Manny, blearily.

Sally found a bottle in her bag.

'Do you mind if I just warm this up for him? Only it's been a long journey –'

Tom gestured.

'There's a microwave in the kitchen. I don't use it. They bring me all these meals in packets but I'm afraid of setting fire to meself. Here.'

He ushered her into the small kitchen and pointed.

'Put the kettle on, shall I?'

'Oh. Thanks.' Sally felt desperately awkward. 'I should just'- she glanced nervously towards the other room. 'I don't want him to touch any of your ornaments.'

'Nothing to break in there. Don't fret, I'll keep an eye on him.'

Tom shuffled back. Watching the bottle revolve, Sally heard him say, 'Now then. Let's have a look at you, young man', and hoped Manny wouldn't start to cry.

When she returned with the milk, she found Tom kneeling stiffly in front of the chair, studying the child's face intently. Manny seemed to be giving serious thought to the idea of smiling.

'Sweetheart, this is your –' She stopped and turned to Tom. 'What would you like to be called?'

'He can call me Granddad, that'll do.'

'It's just – He calls my dad Granddad. You could be Grandpa.'

'Whatever you like, love.' He reached out a finger and touched

Manny's plump hand. 'He looks like his father, no doubt about it.'

'There never was any doubt about it,' Sally said, with an edge.

Tom looked at her, with neither disapproval nor sympathy, and ratcheted himself to his feet.

'I'll make that tea now.'

'I'll make it, if you like.'

'All right, then. The teabags are in the – well, you can't miss them. Place is the size of a doll's house.'

'It's a nice flat,' Sally said brightly, from the kitchen.

'It is what it is. It doesn't leak and I can't fall down the stairs. Have to be grateful for small mercies. Nearly fifty years, I was in my house. But there – everything moves on. Could be worse. There's a volunteer woman comes on Thursdays to take us into town for a fish and chip dinner by the sea. I think she's from the church, but she doesn't go on about it.'

They sat opposite one another in unconsciously mirrored positions, both hands clasped around a mug of tea, while Manny toured the room in his balletic drunken totter. Sally could not think of anything to say. She wanted to ask him about Greg, but was hobbled by the fear censure; half a lifetime spent loudly avowing how little she cared about what anyone thought of her meant nothing in the face of this man's perceived opinion. Not only was Tom of a generation even more remote from her mother's in its morals, he was a man, and he was also Greg's father, and therefore, she imagined, predisposed to see Greg as the injured party and herself as the one brazenly taking advantage of a married man. Tom had said nothing to suggest he had a poor opinion of her, but already she felt chastened. Though he smiled indulgently at Manny, she could see that, with his curiosity satisfied, he had little interest in entertaining a small toddler, and she had no desire to make small talk about his soft furnishings for as long as a pot of tea might be made to last. After a while, she said,

'You must think' – and realized that she had no idea what Tom must think. Greg had always portrayed him as severe in his standards, but then, perhaps to Greg (she thought bitterly) possessing any moral standards at all could seem draconian. Tom waved a hand.

'What's done is done. No good talking about what's right and wrong now. The important thing is to do what's best for the little lad.'

'Does Greg talk about it?' Sally concluded that, whatever else Greg might have told his father, he couldn't have mentioned the court case. 'About Manny?' Or me, she wanted to add, but didn't.

'Greg's not much of a one for facing up to things. All the time I was ill, he's saying, "You'll be right as rain in a minute, Dad." Same when his mother was ill. Tends to wait and hope that things will sort themselves out, if you see what I mean.'

'Do you think he wants to get in touch, though? Does he ever say that he'd like to see Manny? I mean, isn't it all Caroline stopping him?'

Sally heard her own anxiety; Tom inclined his head and appeared to feel sorry for her.

'He's not the first bloke who's tried to have his cake and eat it, and you're not the first lass been left in this situation. But there – he's married Caroline and he's got to respect her wishes.'

'Then he'll never see his son.'

'You can never say never. We don't know what's round the corner.'

Sally suspected this might be the best she would get from Tom Burns. There was a silence. Sunlight threw gauzy shadows of branches on to the floor through the net curtains.

'Would you like to see the gardens?' Tom said, as if by sudden inspiration, as Manny careened into a dresser and howled in outrage.

At the edge of a striped lawn, neat as a cricket pitch, a robust elderly lady with a pair of shears was snipping aggressively at a bush.

'This is Ruth,' Tom said, authoritatively. 'She's always busy in the garden, is Ruth. Ruth, this is my grandson, Manny. And this is Sally, my – er – friend.'

'Well, aren't you just a little pudding?' said the old lady, struggling to her feet. Manny beamed and held out his penguin. Tom ruffled the boy's hair and, Sally thought, appeared to display a certain pride of ownership.

They walked, at a pace of painful slowness dictated by both Tom and Manny, along a path between beds of phloxes. Sally felt again an acute sense of loneliness, of having somehow failed to make a vital contact. She had thought that this meeting might bring her a step closer to breaking Greg's silence, but all she could think of was the wrongness of the present moment; how it should have been Greg introducing them, presenting Manny proudly to his father. She felt entirely alienated from both Greg and this gruff old man who was, to all intents and purposes, a stranger; she was also bored. With an acknowledgement of her own selfishness, she recognized that, whatever she had pretended, she had no interest in Tom for his own sake or as Manny's grandfather; she had thought of him, and introduced herself into his life, purely in the hope of finding a counter-influence to Caroline with Greg; she wasn't sure if she could be bothered to repeat the visit if it was not likely to achieve this end.

'How long were you and Greg – ?'

Sally looked down.

'A few months. Not even a year.'

'Not long to have a baby.'

'No. We probably made the wrong decision.'

'You must never say that. My wife used to say all children are a blessing. You wouldn't be without him.'

'No, of course not.'

People often said this to Sally, as if they were asserting it on her behalf.

'Greg says you write for the stage,' Tom continued.

'Oh. Yes. Well, I haven't done much lately, but I'm trying to work on a new thing.'

'He said it's very well paid.'

Tom looked sideways at her.

'Oh. He said that.' Sally stopped walking. 'Well, it sort of depends.'

'But you do well out of it, do you? You get by, at least?'

Sally hesitated. Was he inviting a discussion of Greg's financial contribution, or lack of it?

'I'm getting by at the moment. But it's not easy.'

'No.' Tom coughed and looked away, and made a big show of foraging in a pocket to distract from whatever she might have been going to add. 'Well, I'd like you to have this, for the lad.' He brought out a folded cheque.

'I can't,' Sally said, taking a step back.

'Don't be silly. Here.' He pushed it into her hand. 'You can put it in his savings or buy him something, they always need things, don't they?'

Sally opened it and saw that it was for a hundred pounds; a sum at the same time so significant, coming as it did (she assumed) from an old man's savings, and so meaningless in terms of the vast bills piling up for childcare, that she felt choked.

'It's too much, really. I couldn't –'

'What am I going to spend it on? Fish and chips? Take it. He's my grandson, at the end of the day. Only wish I could do more.'

'Thank you,' said Sally, humbled, and thinking that she would have liked to have hugged him, if she'd been a hugging sort of person. Instead she shook his hand, which Tom seemed to appreciate.

'I hope you'll come and visit again,' he said, as she strapped Manny into the car.

'That would be lovely,' she said, though neither of them suggested an actual date. She wasn't sure if Tom meant it; Manny, after all, was family, in a sense, but she was nothing. There was not even a word for her relation to Tom Burns, as they had discovered when he tried to introduce her in the garden. Their connection had no name, because it had no substance. Perhaps they would, in time, come to be friends. But as she drove home, she found herself growing increasingly angry with Greg, for having led his father to believe that she was financially successful, so that any subsequent discussion of the court case would look as if she were simply vindictive, and trying to bleed him dry, and wished that she had been less afraid of Tom, and told him the truth. She wondered what Tom would tell Greg about his son, and about her.

In September, at Lola's insistence, Sally agreed to a meeting with Lars Faldbakken who, according to Lola, was still keen on facilitating a film drama about Afghan women.

'Like I'm going to go to Afghanistan now,' Sally said.

'You don't have to,' Lola said. 'He's in touch with a psychologist who works with asylum seekers here and can arrange interviews with Afghan women and girls waiting to have their cases reviewed. It could be a piece about trying to get to Britain after everything they've endured at home. It could be great. Just go and talk to him.'

'There are any number of people better equipped than me to write something like that.'

'Don't be so defeatist! You're a perfectly capable dramatist, you just need to do the research and you'll be as well equipped as anyone. He really thinks you should do it. If you can come up with a decent script, I'm confident we can find the money. Besides, you need a project other than this court case. It's eating you.'

'It's quite a big deal to me, actually.'

'I know that, but you can't let it be the only thing in your life. Do you think Greg's losing sleep over it? Do you think he sits up half the night reading White Papers off the Internet?'

'I think he pays a team of experts to do that for him. Which is why I have to work doubly hard.'

'Why don't you just talk to Lars and go and meet some of these women? I guarantee when you hear their stories you'll want to write something. Take your mind off yourself.'

'Off myself?' Sally bristled. 'I'm sorry I'm so self-involved. I should have volunteered to go to Iraq with the Red Cross as soon as I stopped breastfeeding, I see that now. No wonder you despise me.'

'Oh, for God's sake, Sally. It's just that your whole life is about either getting back with Greg or getting even with him. You've got to forget about him and think about something else. You're a writer, write something.'

So she had met Lars, and the psychologist, who made her feel, as such people always did, that her own life had been utterly squandered on selfish pursuits and the forgettable spillage of useless words. The woman told her stories of hardship and pain and defiant, uncrushable determination, and so it was that Sally began to meet and interview a number of Afghan refugees, collating their narratives into notes out of which, gradually, the possible outline of a plot was beginning to emerge. More than the mere fact of having a subject at last, she found, as she hurried back to her computer in the evenings to shape these disparate accounts into snatches of draft dialogue, that she began to care about what she was writing, and that, slowly, it came to assume a greater importance than Greg, or the court case, or the need to sit in the garden with a bottle of wine fuming and cursing and regretting.

But it was at night that they came for her, the lancing shadows that company and work and a renewed engagement with a larger world had helped to banish to the edges of her daylight hours. At night, in an empty bed (which, they reminded her, she had not shared with anyone for over two years), they gathered – grief, loneliness, abandonment, silence, betrayal, fear, despair, self-pity – they searched her, circling, they undid the self she tried to build during the day, which was why she rarely went to bed before three in the morning. To divert them, she stayed awake, drinking, reading, watching films, listening to music (in that order, as progressive stages of drinking eroded her concentration); anything to keep the demons in a holding pattern, where she could keep an eye on them, anything to divert the violent thoughts, whether self-focused or turned outwards to Greg. But she didn't talk about any of this, fearing that, in her case, the fine membrane between reason and madness had worn altogether threadbare in places and she was no longer sure of what would be considered normal; when people assumed she looked so tired because her child was a bad sleeper, she didn't speak up in his defence. It was easier to let them wield their certainties. She had had enough of pity – though the universal admiration for her superwoman powers was becoming almost as wearing.

25

On a drably damp November morning, almost a year to the day since she had first been notified by the Child Support Agency about Greg's meagre earnings, and under the kind of weather best suited to attending tribunals, or waiting at empty stations for delayed trains, Mac appeared at Sally's front door, clean-shaven and in a suit. She was almost jolted out of the hovering anxiety of the day; for the first time since they had re-established a connection, he looked like the father she remembered. A plump sheaf of papers was bunched under his arm, and he wore the smile of someone for whom victory is assumed, and the battle itself a minor inconvenience to be tediously managed before the celebrations can begin.

'You look like a lawyer,' she said.

'I thought we might fool them with that.'

'You look like *you*.'

Mac glanced down at his suit.

'I feel like one of those Beerbohm cartoons of the Old Self meeting the Young Self,' he said, grinning. 'I'm telling you, it's disconcerting.'

'Will you get kicked out of the band without the beard?'

'Could be I will. Now will you get yourself ready?'

The thick envelope containing these papers had arrived at Sally's house four days earlier, delayed by the vagaries of the postal service and the leaden bureaucracy of the appeals unit; she had sent them by overnight courier to Mac in Dublin so that he could read them before the Tribunal date. The envelope contained three years' worth of Greg Burns's bank statements, demanded by the officiating experts and made available to Sally and her representatives prior to the Tribunal, but with all personal information blacked out, so that she was left with almost three hundred pages showing only columns of figures that smeared in front of her eyes like a runaway computer error. With these papers was a letter detailing how to locate the dismal municipal dungeon in which the hearing was to take place, and assuring her that she and Mr Burns would be placed in separate waiting rooms to avoid potential unpleasantness.

'To avoid *unpleasantness*?' she had said to her mother. 'They've got to be kidding. Why do they think we're going there, a cocktail party?'

'Perhaps they think you might attack him before you go in,' Elizabeth had said mildly, unwittingly adding another fantasy image to Sally's psychopathic video library.

Mac understood the figures. He had called her the morning after receiving the papers, and before he even spoke she could hear the phone humming with a quiet certainty.

'We've nailed him,' he said, and his smile was audible.

'You can tell that just from those numbers?'

'If you know what to look at. There's at least fifty grand unaccounted for in his official earnings coming out in regular payments from those accounts. What we don't have is any kind of joint account there – I'm guessing she refused to give up the papers, which is her right, but there's a regular transfer going out of that company to what I'm willing to bet is a household account or an account in her name.'

'But we haven't got any of the transaction details. He might have reasonable explanations for all that.'

'In my arse does he have explanations,' Mac said, with conviction, and Sally decided that she could only trust him.

Now he said, as they climbed into the car, 'You're looking very dressed up. Are you expecting him to be there?'

Sally halted. The question of whether Greg would attend the Tribunal had preoccupied her since the day they wrote informing her of the date; it was this, rather than the outcome of the proceedings, that provoked the panic attacks and sleepless nights, more notably sleepless than usual, which was some achievement. And she had dressed carefully; this would be the first time he had seen her since she was pregnant, and she wanted him to get a shock, to be mortified by the realization of what he had cast aside. She had even had her hair cut, though she knew it might be in vain; he was not obliged to attend, and might very well have been banned by Caroline from seeing her in person.

'Is it too much?' She looked down at her jeans and tailored jacket.

Mac paused, leaning on the open door of the car, and screwed up his mouth.

'It's maybe a bit glamorous, you know?'

'I should look more like an impoverished single mother? I thought it was about his accounts, not what I look like.'

'Well, but you want their sympathies from the off. You don't want to go in there like some hard-faced ball-breaker because that's how he's going to paint you. If you just gently give the impression you've been hard done by, they're likely to be well disposed towards you. It's not about beating him, remember, you've struggled and you just want a fair deal for your child. That's the image we're looking for.'

Sally went inside and changed the jacket for a jumper with holes in the elbows and wiped off her lip gloss. Mac nodded. They drove through autumn-gilded countryside to a town twenty miles away; a weary, down-on-its-luck town that seemed to have been purpose-built to house the administrative centres of unwanted government departments, processing the sparse handouts to the lame, the dispossessed, the forgotten. It was the kind of town that didn't even have a Starbucks, Sally thought, as they crawled the length of its high street in search of a car park; instead it had discount carpet warehouses, and shops whose windows offered plastic kitchenware and beige support stockings together, advertising permanent closing-down sales. There seemed to be a higher than average number of teenage girls with scraped hair pushing prams in the street; higher than in Crowbourne, certainly. She had always known it would look like this, and still, when they located the buildings of the appeals unit, tucked into the corner of a tiled precinct, and were shown into a waiting room of expressionless office furnishings, acrylic and formica, she felt a terrible disappointment at the inappropriate setting; she had pictured this denouement as the classy kind of legal drama, in rooms of teak panelling, where Mac would orate majestically in a wig and gown and a benignly patrician judge would eventually eye Greg from his perch and pronounce a verdict of 'Guilty'.

Instead, the walls were a flaking pistachio green and they might easily have been in the smoking room of a small anonymous company on an industrial estate somewhere. There was a smell of urine that seemed to originate with the only other occupants of the room, an old man with one leg stretched out in a brace, a silver sheen of grizzle on his chin, and a younger, very fat woman with a hand on his arm, wearing a nylon smock that might have come from any one of the shops in the precinct below them. Catching Sally's sociological curiosity, he leaned forward and said, in a voice cracked with grief, or possibly just tobacco, 'They cut them, just like that. It's criminal, is what it is.'

Sally nodded. The fat woman rubbed the old man's arm in sympathy, but reflexively, as if she had heard this already, more times than she cared to remember.

'I mean, if they gave you some explanation. But three months it's taken just to get here, and I rely on that money, I've only got me pension otherwise, but you try asking them on the phone, you're there all bleeding day, no one gives a monkey's, and when I think of all them people fiddling the dole – I mean, I been a working man all me life and I paid me taxes fair and square – and then they go and cut me disability benefit for no good reason, I mean, I'm still bleedin disabled, in I?' – he turned to the woman, lifting the leg a fraction; she nodded confirmation – 'And you have to go through all this malarkey' – he gestured to the walls of the room – 'just to get them to put it back where it was. I mean, I'm seventy-seven, it's not like they'll have to pay it out for much longer, is it, but you want a decent life while you've still got your facilities, I mean, isn't it?'

A trembling finger was pointed at Sally; the silvered chin jutted at her as if challenging her to just try giving him a politician's answer in the face of such incontrovertible evidence, and she felt for a moment as if she were his MP, as if it were solely her responsibility to ease his distress in the face of unmoving clauses and by-laws and paperwork; she experienced a sudden welling of pity for this poor old man, together with a thought of such awful snobbery that she instantly hated herself, and the thought was, *at least this is not my real life.* Followed by the even more disgusting thought that these people would never go to a party at Dame Barbara Bathurst's house.

'What they done to you, then?' said the old man, conversationally.

'Child support,' Sally said, flatly. Mac glanced up from his stack of papers; a warning not to talk about it.

Sally stood up and stretched. Just then, the door opened to admit a young man with well-cut hair and a well-cut suit, holding a leather folder. He took in the room, closed the door behind him, smiled at her and said, *sotto voce*, 'Ms McGinley?'

She nodded, thinking him to be one of the Tribunal officials.

He extended a hand.

'Peter Kelman. I'm Mr Burns's barrister. I wondered if we might have a quiet word?'

Immediately Mac was on his feet like a boxer, cutting in front of her.

'You can speak to me, I'm Ms McGinley's representative.'

'Ah.' He looked wrong-footed for a minute, but resumed his poise. 'Mr –?'

'McGinley.'

'Oh. Any relation?'

'I'm her father.'

The barrister seemed relieved.

'Oh. You brought your dad.'

Condescending shit, Sally thought. 'He's my solicitor.'

'So you are a qualified solicitor as well?'

'Yes, I am. Lucky, eh?'

'Well – good. May I sit?'

'Be our guest,' said Mac.

'Well, now.' Peter Kelman tapped the folder on his knee. 'This may seem rather unorthodox, given that we're about to go in, but it occurs to me that we might all make this simpler for ourselves if you were interested in discussing a private settlement for maintenance.'

Mac moved to touch the space where his beard should have been, and the smile at the corners of his mouth was wolfish.

'It occurs to you, now, does it?'

'Er – simply that, as you know, it can be a very lengthy process, dealing with this kind of bureaucracy, and often it's not beneficial to anyone in the long run.'

'It's been extremely beneficial to your client for two years.'

'I'm merely hoping to test the waters, as it were. If you were inter-ested in reaching an agreement outside the rulings of the Child Support Agency –'

'I was interested in doing that two years ago,' Sally said. 'Greg asked me to do it this way. It was his choice. Now we know why.'

'Well – *well*,' said Kelman, looking at his folder as if for inspiration. 'I'm just looking for a solution that would allow everyone to avoid any more unpleasantness.'

Unpleasantness again, Sally thought, as if we were all talking about drinking wine that was slightly corked. She looked up at Mac, expecting a dart of disabling sarcasm. He put a hand lightly under Kelman's elbow and prompted him to his feet.

'I suggest you go back to your client and remind him that he's had plenty of chances to talk in the past two years,' he said, quietly, 'and we'll see you in that room where you can present your case as you're being paid to do, and I have to tell you, I'm looking forward to hearing it.'

Kelman coloured to his ears.

'Just doing my job,' he said.

'Wait,' said Sally, as he reached for the door, 'is he here?'

'Mr Burns? Yes, he's just across the corridor. We'll see you in there.' His smile was as barbed as Mac's.

'Was that legal, what he just did?' Sally asked, when the door closed, but she was thinking only of the imminence of seeing Greg.

'It was unprofessional. Ah, he's trying to save face. He knows he's going to have his little arse kicked. He's seen the figures too, you know? He probably thinks they might get away with less than they'll be obliged to pay once this is all through. Your man's the bigger fool for paying a barrister to defend the indefensible. He must know that.'

'Cheeky bleeder,' remarked the old man in the corner, with an echoing sniff.

Greg sat beside Peter Kelman at one end of the table and tried not to look at Sally. He also tried not to look at the elderly gentleman in the blazer peering over his half-moon glasses at the printouts of his bank statements and occasionally shaking his head in a mournful fashion, the Chair of the Tribunal who, from the outset, had addressed Sally as if she were a four-year-old who had fallen off her bicycle and scraped her knee, and himself as if he were the pervert who had stolen her ice-cream while she fell. Instead he looked down at his hands and thought about how much he disliked Peter Kelman. He disliked him personally, of course – the air of London smugness that suggested this job was very far beneath his talents, that he would much rather be unmasking corporate fraud or international drug rings in the High Court, and the nebula of aftershave in which he floated, and the fine but noticeable drift of dandruff on the shoulders of his Savile Row suit – but he also disliked him in principle, because Kelman's presence was just the latest manifestation of his capitulation to Caroline even when he could see that she was clearly in the wrong. He disliked the fact that Kelman was costing him three hundred pounds an hour, which would include the hour it had taken him to drive from London and the hour it would take him to drive back, and he disliked intensely the fact that Kelman was so defeatist about the likely outcome, that he was going to be humiliated in front of Sally and, worse, in front of her father, and, worse *still*, that he was going to be seen to be paying to be thus humiliated. He disliked the fact that he had ever allowed himself to be talked into any of this horseshit, to use Sally's word.

God, how that man must hate him, he thought, sneaking a glance at Mac's shrewd face across the table. He tried to imagine himself sitting beside Daisy in similar circumstances and hoped that, if such a day ever came, he might have some small degree of empathy with the poor bastard in his chair. But he knew Mac McGinley's story; he had hardly been the ideal husband and father in his time, had he? All very fine for him to turn up now as the great crusader for justice, but he was in no position to take the moral high ground . . .

She was still beautiful, he thought; his father had said as much after she'd been to visit him with the child and it had been difficult to discern in his father's tone whether he thought that Sally's attractiveness made Greg's behaviour more understandable or less forgivable. Tom seemed to have liked Sally, to have approved of her in some way, and Greg had experienced a pinch of jealousy at his father's uncomplicated freedom to see Sally and her son without compromising himself. He wondered, watching her, why he should have felt surprised at her appearance; as if he had expected childbirth and the rigours of single motherhood to have destroyed her youth and looks, or to have turned her into one of those fat women in cheap coats and trainers you saw with toddlers in supermarkets. She seemed quieter, more subdued, but then she would hardly be dancing and shouting with a glass in each hand, which was how he remembered her best. So she was still beautiful, but he found himself curiously unmoved by it; he registered barely a flicker of desire when he snatched a brief look at her (she was looking at him constantly, her eyes never swerving), and when he conjured some of the things they'd done, he was troubled by a kind of detached disgust, as if he were being asked to pass moral judgement on someone else's confession. It all seemed so long ago, so buffered by the vagueness of drink. He had to remind himself of why they were there at all, in the airless room with the old gent and his silent assistant, who seemed to be all forehead; this was the mother of his *son*, he told himself, but since he had never seen his son, even this statement took on a necessary objectivity, like something he might have read off a cue card.

'I'm really rather intrigued, Mr Burns – you seem to have your *daughter* on the payroll of this company?' the elderly man was saying, as he turned over another incriminating sheet. Greg snapped back to the moment. 'And how old is she?'

Greg sat forward.

'She's eleven,' said Kelman.

'And what exactly does she *do*, work-wise?'

'She –'

'She contributes in various ways, Chair,' said Kelman.

'Mr Burns?'

'She – ah – helps with the filing,' Greg said, his mouth dry. 'Sometimes she helps me learn my lines. And sometimes –'

Kelman laid a restraining hand on his arm.

'She helps with the *filing*,' repeated the Chair, as if he were writing it down. Mac McGinley was smiling into his hands.

The man with the forehead leaned across to the Chair and muttered something at length.

'Ah, yes. Thank you, Mr Dyer. Mr Dyer here has suggested that we address the question of the regular standing order from your company account.'

Greg swallowed. He watched Mac's smile widen. Kelman wiped the palms of his hands on his trousers.

'Now then, Mr Burns,' said the Chair, adjusting his glasses and not looking at Greg. He's good, Greg thought. He should be on the stage. Law is just another kind of theatre. 'You signed a legal declaration, did you not, confirming that you receive no income from CGB Limited other than your stated salary as a company director?'

Greg nodded.

'And your wife is not, according to your statement, in receipt of a salary as company secretary?'

'No, that's right.'

'Though she would naturally received the same dividends from the company as yourself – slightly more, in fact, given that she is a majority shareholder?'

Greg looked at Kelman.

'She will receive dividends as a shareholder, yes, Chair, that's entirely within –'

'Does that constitute transferral of income, Mr Dyer? To me it looks very much like it, but perhaps you'd just check to be sure. Now, I'm perplexed, Mr Burns,' said the Chair, in a voice that heralded the opposite of perplexity, 'by the monthly standing order of eighteen hundred pounds from this company bank account to another bank account which doesn't tally with any of the personal accounts you've provided us with here. I put it to you that this might be the joint account that we don't have statements for here?'

Greg opened his mouth. Kelman glared at him.

'It is possible that that is my client's joint household account, yes,' he said, his body language one embarrassed apology.

The Chair took off his glasses.

'I'm aware that it's *possible*, Mr Kelman, it's theoretically *possible* that it's the account of a Columbian drug cartel who provide your client with a kilo of uncut cocaine every month, but since your client is sitting right next to you, why not ask him if it is in *fact* being paid to his joint household account?'

Kelman raised an eyebrow at him, as if holding Greg personally responsible for this professional abasement. Greg nodded and looked at the table. He had recollections of being sent to the headmaster for various unspecified misdemeanours and encountering the same withering sarcasm designed to bring you to your knees, but this was worse.

'I'm rather *baffled*, then, Mr Burns,' said the Chair, in the same voice.

Greg felt suddenly very tired; no, you're not, he wanted to say, you're not baffled at all, you've got me bang to rights, just give her the money, give the bastard lawyer the money, take all my money and just let me go home. I give up.

'I'm rather baffled that you should have made a statement declaring that neither you nor your wife are in receipt of any income from CGB Limited other than the stated director's salary and dividends when your household account clearly receives regular transfers of money from your company account. I put it to you that you have deliberately misled the Tribunal?'

Greg looked helplessly at Kelman.

'I think, at this point,' Kelman said, with an amphibious swipe of

403

his tongue around his lower lip, 'we might request an adjournment so that I might just discuss this question with my client.'

'My client would object to that very strongly,' Mac McGinley said, with quiet authority, fixing Greg with his terrifying eyes.

The Chair stared at Kelman as if he had suggested they all take a break to enjoy group sex. He replaced his glasses and removed them immediately with the other hand.

'Don't you know your job, man? Did you read these papers before you came into this room?'

'Yes, of course, Chair, but –'

'Was it not the first thing that struck you about these accounts? An adjournment – I've never heard anything so ridiculous. These are matters you should have cleared with your client long before you got here. You're wasting my time, and Mr Dyer's time, and indeed Miss McGinley's time. Let's move on. Mr Dyer has pinpointed – what was it, Mr Dyer?'

The man with the forehead leaned in and said something inaudible.

'Twenty seven thousand four hundred and thirty-three pounds, give or take, of undeclared income received by Mr Burns directly to his personal bank account during the same accounting period which has not passed through CGB Limited. Let's begin with the fourteenth of April last year, a deposit of three thousand pounds. Would you like to clarify that for us, Mr Burns?'

And so it went on, for another hour. They tweezered his transactions to pieces. One by one, they held eighteen months' worth of Martin's ingenious deceptions up to the grey light of morning and mocked them for their crudeness, their lack of subtlety. Greg drifted, his attention boomeranging back at odd moments when he sensed that Kelman had asked him a question, otherwise only vaguely aware of Kelman flapping and beaching himself horribly at his side. The battle's lost, Kelman, he wanted to say, give it up.

He raised his eyes to Sally, and found her still looking at him. He might have expected to see some kind of spiteful triumph in her face, and God knew he would have deserved it, but he could divine nothing except the blankness of disillusion. He wondered if she really had loved him, and if she had, whether she still might, and whether, this being the case, she might dredge some buried reserves of forgiveness and give him a chance with the boy – one day, when Caroline was –

when Caroline could – some day, when they could all put it behind them and forgive each other. Well, forgive *him*, specifically. And it would be the day they cancelled Third World debt and found a cure for cancer, he thought, gritting his teeth. He looked away first; the unspoken sadness and accusation in her eyes would stay with him in the night for months to come.

After an hour of what had begun to seem like professionally orchestrated contempt directed at him and his comically inept barrister, they were asked to withdraw to their separate waiting rooms while the Chair made his decision, egged on, no doubt, by the enigmatic Mr Dyer, who had emerged as the financial brains of the operation. Greg and Kelman waited for Sally and her father to leave first; as he opened the door, Mac put a hand on her shoulder and Greg heard him whisper, 'You're laughing.' Except that she wasn't. It had been Caroline who had encouraged him to think of Sally as the enemy, to consider this whole accounting business as a means of thwarting her plot to steal money from Daisy, as if that had been her malicious intention all along, and it had been so much easier to participate in that picture, and to forget that she, too, was a mother, and that she had not chosen any of this with the express purpose of making his life difficult. No – he had not treated her fairly, and she was not laughing. She looked only as drained as he felt. Greg wondered how he would explain any of this to Caroline. Caroline, whose response to losing this battle he could gloomily only guess at.

When they trooped back in, the Chair had already gathered his papers into neat piles and was looking at his watch, as if checking how near lunch might be.

'The Tribunal has decided', he intoned, as if a whole jury had convened in their absence, 'that Mr Burns and his accountants have created deliberately misleading statements as to the true nature of Mr Burns's income, and that therefore, since the company CGB Limited has obscured his gross income over the past financial year, a new maintenance assessment should be made based on his self-employed earnings from the previous tax year.'

Which was the year of his West End run, Greg thought, and more than he usually expected to earn. So this was really going to sting.

'My client does of course have the right to appeal this decision?' Kelman was asking, while he gathered his papers.

The Chair looked at Kelman sadly, as if he were a schoolboy who had still not learned his lesson.

'It could go to an independent assessor, yes. But your client would be advised to bear in mind that an independent assessor might pick up on aspects of this case that would not be helpful to him in the long run.'

'What did that mean?' Greg asked, when he and Kelman had filed back into the waiting room.

'Means that if you push it, they might choose to remind you that giving false information is technically a criminal offence,' Kelman said. He reached to shake Greg's hand, in the cheery professional way that he had shaken Mac McGinley's as they left the Tribunal, like Wimbledon players. 'Listen, I'm sorry, and all that.'

'Oh, don't apologize. At least you get paid for being here. That's your skiing holiday taken care of.' He heard his own bitterness.

'Well, to be honest, there wasn't much for me to work with. I did my best. You didn't have a leg to stand on. You could have had the O.J. lawyers and you'd still have been screwed.'

'Cheers.'

'My advice – get a smarter accountant next time.'

'*Next* time?' said Greg, his expression wasted on Kelman's retreating powdered shoulders.

In the car park, as he threw his jacket into the Land Cruiser, he happened to glance across two rows and saw, with a jolt, Sally, beside a brown Nissan Micra, smoking a cigarette in hungry, aggressive gulps, as if she had just come off a long-haul flight. Instinctively, he took a step towards her before realizing that there was nothing he could possibly say that would be of any use, but she turned and saw him, and for a moment they looked at each other. She began to walk towards him.

They reached each other halfway across a wet strip of tarmac. Her face was as sharp and inscrutable as it had been the first day he had seen her, in the Avocet office, when he had tried to gauge whether she thought he was right for the part. The difference was that he no longer felt the need to impress her; only the sad recognition that he was too far beyond that ever to claw his way back.

'Do you have a cigarette?' he said, eventually, to break the silence of her terrible stare.

'Buy your own.'

He looked at the floor.

'Are you proud of yourself?' she said, suddenly.

'No.' He didn't feel it was worth attempting any kind of apology or excuse; it could only sound empty.

For a moment he thought she was going to walk away, but, looking away to the other side of the car park, she said, with a kind of urgency, 'The first couple of days, in the hospital – he wouldn't feed.'

'Feed?'

'Yeah. You know. He couldn't suck properly. They hooked me up to this machine and they had to give it to him in a little cup, you know, a medical cup, because he was crying all the time, he was starving.'

Greg waited.

'And all I could think was – what if he dies? What if he dies now, without you ever seeing him?' She turned suddenly and looked him straight in the eye, and he remembered how completely her eyes could unbalance him.

'Christ.'

'Yeah, well.' She lit another cigarette without offering him the packet. 'That was when I thought it still mattered. When it mattered that he should have a father. But you might as well be dead to him. It would be better if you were, then at least I could make up something good to tell him about you.'

'It was impossible for us.'

'You've made it so much worse than it ever needed to be.'

'I never wanted it to end up here.' Greg gestured towards the miserable building they had just left.

'Fucking right you didn't! You didn't want me to get it this far, you thought I wouldn't be able to find out.'

'I meant –'

'There's running away, and then there's *this*.' She moved a hand briefly over her mouth, as if she might physically retch at the thought of it. 'You're unspeakable. There are no words for what you are.'

Greg glanced across the car park and noticed Mac advancing towards them; seeing them together, he halted with his hands in his pockets and affected an interest in the tariffs on the ticket machine.

'I kept hoping that –' Greg stopped and tried again. 'I had to try and –'

'Don't bother. It's all too late. The irony – don't you see this – the irony is that if you hadn't tried these fucking tricks I'd have been out of your life long ago, we could both have moved on, and you wouldn't have a child who will grow up to hate you.'

'It was all too –'

'No, stop there – I don't ever want to hear any of your reasons. There is nothing you can say. I just hope –' She paused, and sucked in an almighty lungful of smoke. 'You know what I hope? I hope that one day someone will do this to Daisy. I hope she falls in love with some cunt like you, who puts her through the same thing and you have to pick up the pieces, because then just maybe you'll realize what you are.'

She stamped on her cigarette as if it was his face, and walked to her car without looking back. He saw her father hurry towards her, and thought – her *father*. I brought them back together. I gave her a son *and* a father – one day she might even be grateful.

He climbed shakily into the Land Cruiser and sat for a long time with his head on the steering wheel, waiting for the telltale tremble in his voice to subside so that he could call Caroline and tell her that it had all been a wasted effort.

~·◆·~

'So that's over, then,' Mac said, as they sat in the car.

'Yes,' said Sally, staring out of the windscreen at the blighted car park. 'It's over.' She felt as if she had been drinking during the day and suddenly, horribly, sobered up with a crashing ache behind the eyes, at around teatime.

'And we won.'

'We didn't *win*. We just didn't let them win. It's not what I call a triumph.'

'Well, no, I'm not saying we should be high-fiving round the courtroom, but I still say it deserves a pint. I'll take that by way of legal fees.'

In a dismal pub on the edge of the town, Mac thumped down two pints of Guinness with a shamrock twirled in the top, and Sally remembered the night in Dublin when she had thought she was losing Manny, before she even knew he was Manny. Whatever else had happened, she thought, he was here, and he would grow and thrive without Greg, and the world was a richer place because of him.

'I don't drink stout.'

'You do today. Come on, it'll put some colour in your cheeks.

Here's to us.' Mac raised his glass. Sally didn't respond. 'Ah, come on, Sal, you should be celebrating. You got what you wanted.'

'You think this was what I *wanted*?'

'Well, not in an ideal world, but it isn't. It's the best result in the circumstances.'

'I said a terrible thing to him. In the car park.'

'I think today of all days you're entitled to say terrible things to Greg Burns.'

'I said I hope someone does the same to his daughter.'

'He probably knows you didn't mean it.'

'I did mean it. That's why it's terrible.'

'I don't expect you'll be struck down. Anyway – it's time for you to start being positive. What about a toast to your film? We can celebrate that.'

'OK.' She lifted her pint without enthusiasm.

'Channel 4? Come on, it's great news. Didn't you say you always wanted to write for television? Who knows where it might lead?'

'They liked the treatment. That doesn't mean it'll get made. I've got to finish the script first anyway.'

'But they like it, that's a good start, isn't it? You'll finish it, and it'll be wonderful, I have every faith in you and so do the people whose judgement matters more than mine. And you won't have to worry about money for a little while. Especially if Greg pays up now.'

'I don't expect him to pay up. But at least I've made my point. I showed him he couldn't just write me off.'

'Yes, you did. You showed them all. You can move on now, Sally, that's the point. Life can go back to normal.'

But the point, Sally felt, was that it couldn't, and that she had to learn this in order to move on. Life would never return to what she had come to think of as normal. Her life was irretrievably changed and the key to moving on, she understood, was to accept the new version of normality instead of waiting for an impossible restoration of the kind of life she had before Greg, before Manny. She had not quite achieved this with tranquillity yet, but the recognition that she had to evolve and adapt and could never go back was the beginning.

So it was over. Her last thread of contact with Greg had been snipped. There was no longer any reason to fight him, to think about him, to sustain any shadow of his presence in her life. She could forget him, as everyone was constantly urging her.

It was possible, she thought, as she looked at her father's eager smile across the table, that fighting Greg had only been a substitute for loving him, and that ceasing to do either might leave her with an unimaginable absence. But Nature abhors a vacuum; she would find another focus. Manny, and her writing, or – though it seemed remote – someone else to love, someone with a clearer eye and a firmer notion of what could be offered, someone for whom she was more than a diversion from reality.

'It's the first day of the rest of your life,' Mac said, slapping his hands on his knees. 'Say that to yourself in the mirror.'

'Would you ever shut up.'

But she smiled back. It was at least the first day of a life that didn't include Greg Burns in any capacity, and the thought left her curiously sad, but hopeful.

END OF ACT III

CURTAIN

REAL

STEPHANIE MERRITT

REAL

faber and faber

First published in 2005
by Faber and Faber Limited

3 Queen Square London WC1N 3AU

Printed in England by Mackays of Chatham, plc

A CIP record for this book
is available from the British Library

ISBN 0–571–22263–3

2 4 6 8 10 9 7 5 3 1